THE
BEAR KING

www.penguin.co.uk

THE
BEAR KING

JAMES WILDE

BANTAM PRESS

TRANSWORLD PUBLISHERS
61–63 Uxbridge Road, London W5 5SA
www.penguin.co.uk

Transworld is part of the Penguin Random House group of companies
whose addresses can be found at global.penguinrandomhouse.com

Penguin
Random House
UK

First published in Great Britain in 2020 by Bantam Press
an imprint of Transworld Publishers

A CIP catalogue record for this book
is available from the British Library.

ISBN 9781787632165

Typeset in 11/14.25pt Plantin MT Std by Jouve (UK), Milton Keynes
Printed and bound in Great Britain by Clays Ltd, Elcograf S.p.A.

Penguin Random House is committed to a sustainable
future for our business, our readers and our planet. This book
is made from Forest Stewardship Council® certified paper.

MIX
Paper from
responsible sources
FSC
www.fsc.org   FSC® C018179

1 3 5 7 9 10 8 6 4 2

For Elizabeth, Betsy, Joe and Eve

And fate? No one alive has ever escaped it,
Neither brave man nor coward, I tell you –
It's born with us the day that we are born.

Homer

Sometimes even to live is an act of courage.

Lucius Annaeus Seneca

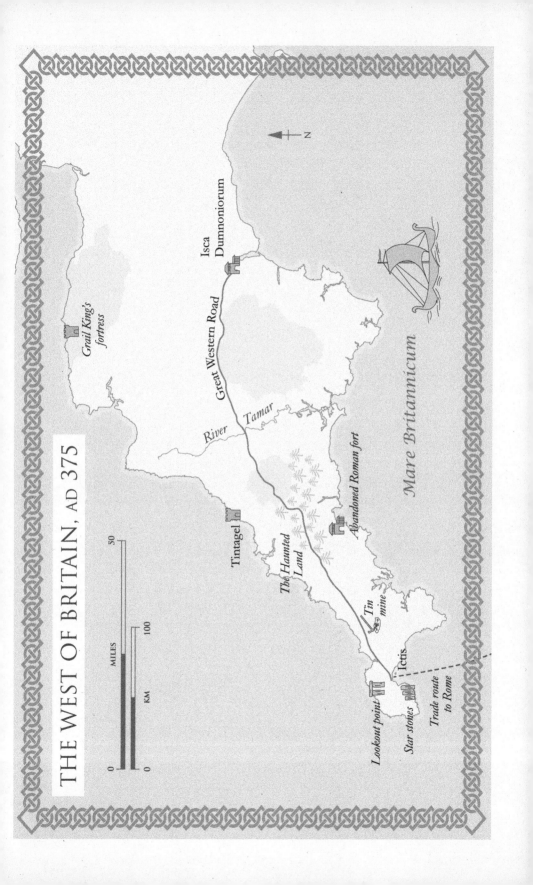

PART ONE

The Island

Each of us bears his own hell.

Virgil

CHAPTER ONE

Red Sails

AD 375, Tintagel, in the far west of Britannia

THE YEARS OF PEACE SEEMED A DISTANT MEMORY NOW. Each turning season was punctuated by death, and though the red-rimmed tide ebbed and flowed there would be no respite from battle, they all knew that.

Catia stood among the huddled women on the stony beach and peered out to sea. Though the salty wind whipped strands of blonde hair across her face, her stare never wavered. She was queen of this land, for what it was worth. All that meant in truth was more swords pointed at her heart, hard decisions, sleepless nights.

The ships bobbed closer under the pink-streaked sky. Scarlet sails glowed along the horizon like blood-roses on a shroud.

Catia glanced above the bowed heads of the keening women to where Amarina stood, bundled in her emerald cloak against the dawn chill. Her auburn hair had streaks of silver now. Faint lines marred her pale skin. In the years since they'd travelled into the west, she seemed to have aged a notch faster than others, as if she bore some hidden burden.

She looked back at Catia, her cold green eyes giving nothing away. That was Amarina, a stone chest of secrets.

The ships swept towards the cove, six of them. Catia imagined she could see the Hibernian raiders on board, braced against the heaving swell. All red beards and wild hair and eyes like nail-heads. The steady thunder of the drums rolled out, and when the wind dropped she could hear their full-throated song.

They'd known this day was coming. It had only been a matter of time.

The legend of Niall of the Nine Hostages had surged around the coastline of southern Britannia like the tide. Soon to be the High King of all Hibernia, some said. A warrior gifted with the powers of the gods, others countered. One thing was certain. He and his fierce raiders smote the coastal settlements like a smith's hammer striking the anvil, and they had done so for long months now. Treasure plundered, stores snatched, men cut down like stalks of barley before the scythe. The Dumnonii who occupied those wind-blasted south-western lands lived in daily fear that Niall would descend upon them again.

'Oh, they come,' Amarina cried, her voice dripping with acid. 'What chance do we stand?'

The keening of the women echoed louder. Soon those raiders would hear it.

'Courage,' Catia called.

Niall was cunning. He'd saved the best until he was certain what feeble defences existed along that coastline. Catia craned her neck back to look at the towering fortress perched on the cliff-top that had been their home for seven years now. Raised up into new life from the ruins once occupied by the great kings in the west. Creamy stone shaped by the finest masons among the Dumnonii. And inside, treasure beyond reckoning: gold and silver, coin and ingot and plate, lapis lazuli jewellery from the hot lands in the south, the finest pottery and statuary, oil and wine, all of it tribute or trade sent to this place by those who knew the standing of the new occupants.

How Niall had resisted until now, she didn't know.

But then, just before dawn, one of the beacons had been lit further along the coast. The Hibernian pirate must have heard the stories of their army's foray into the east, and that they were now defenceless.

'Perhaps they'll sail by when they see what a miserable force awaits them,' Amarina said. 'Hardly worth shaking an axe at.'

Catia pushed her chin up. Even in that moment, their enemies should know they faced a queen.

The cries of the women soared up to the heavens, drowning out the shrieks of the gulls.

The ships came on towards the narrow horseshoe-shaped cove. It was surrounded on two sides by granite cliffs, and on the third by a steep wooded valley. Currents and swell tossed the vessels and the helmsmen fought to guide them to their destination. The cove wasn't broad enough to allow entry to the entire fleet, so four held back while the remaining two skimmed towards the shallows. If they'd ventured just around the headland on which the fortress stood, they would have been able to land all six ships.

But the queen stood there, and so the raiders had come to her.

The anchor-stones splashed into the brine. The rowboats pulled towards shore.

The Hibernians were wrapped in furs smeared with lamb fat to keep out the ocean's cold. Catia's nostrils wrinkled at the reek. Underneath the furs, she glimpsed creaking leather armour. They carried short-hafted single-bladed axes and round wooden shields brightly painted with reds and yellows and blues, each carrying a design that was a token of good fortune to the bearer.

Catia nodded when she saw the one she knew instantly to be Niall of the Nine Hostages. He was taller than the others, broad-shouldered, his white teeth gleaming in his bristles. But it was the eyes that identified him, the confident look of a man used to ruling. All fellow leaders knew that look. His shield was red, with a curled black dragon at the centre.

She had to smile at that.

'Hold your tongues,' she called.

The women choked back their cries, but kept their heads bowed.

Niall splashed into the shallows and squelched up the wet sand to stand on the stones in front of her. He looked her up and down.

From the corner of her eye, she saw one of the other raiders approach Amarina, the only other woman standing. 'Take care,' she said. 'That one bites.'

Niall laughed. 'We've heard tell of you, even in Hibernia. The Queen of Fury. Where is your rage now, eh? Where is your defiance?'

Catia forced a cold smile.

'It takes wit to be a leader, and strategy, and cunning,' continued Niall. 'We lured your army away. We left you defenceless so we could sail in and take what we want with impunity.' He screwed up his mouth, feigning disappointment. 'From the tales, I expected more.'

'We are never defenceless,' Catia said.

He must have seen something in her face, for his eyes widened. He opened his mouth to bark an order, but he wasn't quick enough.

A flash of silver on the edge of Catia's vision. Amarina's blade, whipped from the depths of her cloak. Slashing across the throat of the raider who stood in front of her, so fast it blurred. The pirate was still gaping, not aware that he was dead. The blood gushed over Amarina from his severed artery. She stood there in the torrent, smiling.

And then the whirlwind.

As one, the women surged to their feet. Short blades gleamed in hands that had been hidden, stabbing and slashing.

Catia and Niall backed away from each other.

'You think we won't slaughter you because you're women?' the pirate-king bellowed.

Catia snatched up her bow from where it had been hidden, nocked an arrow and loosed. She cursed as it whined a finger's width from Niall's head and smacked into the eye socket of the man standing behind him.

Drenched in blood, the women scrambled back up the beach to the valley's mouth before the bewildered men could fight back.

Amarina lurched up, eyes white in her gore-streaked face. She seemed breathless with exhilaration. 'It takes wit to be a leader, and strategy, and cunning,' she said. 'Never forget.'

And then she was gone with the women, into the shade beneath the trees. Catia stood alone on the edge of the beach, watching the raiders surge in confusion. Rage crackled between them. Five bodies littered the stones; three more men clasped deep wounds.

Niall cupped his hands around his mouth and bellowed to the ships out on the swell. He waved an arm, urging them to draw in. Then he spun back and fixed a murderous gaze on Catia. She nocked another arrow and waited.

The men pounded up the beach. This time she ignored Niall, showing him he wasn't worthy of her attention. She thumped her shaft into the chest of another pirate. Then she slipped away into the trees and found a hiding place from which she watched the cove through a web of branches.

The four ships swept towards their sisters heaving on anchor in the shallows. As they reached the edge of the headland, the deluge began. Shafts rained down, ripping through the pirates who had nowhere to hide. She could hear the howls of agony, see the bodies plunge over the sides.

A helmsman fell with an arrow bursting from his neck. His ship rolled into the one nearest to it. The groan of timbers merged into a terrible rending that echoed even above the crashing of the waves.

And then came the fire.

Catia breathed in the stink of pitch on the breeze. A moment later, a sheet of scarlet and gold rushed down the rock face. The burning pitch swamped the third ship as it tried to find space in the lee of the cliffs. Throat-rending screams rang out, and the sail erupted in flames. Shimmering sparks whipped up on the sea breeze. A thick black pall rolled across the rosy sky.

The sea was on fire.

Catia watched Niall and the first group plunge into the trees. Though they were little more than shadows, she could sense their confusion, and perhaps smell their fear too. They'd never encountered resistance like this before. They'd grown too complacent in their many victories.

Catia huddled in a twisted net of roots, her bow clutched to her breast. Through the half-light, she glimpsed the silhouettes of the raiders lumbering like wounded beasts, roaring their fury as they roamed. Screams echoed above the pounding of the surf and the crackle of the conflagration.

Disaster has struck you down, she thought. *You are doomed, but you don't yet know it.*

And the howl of a wolf moaned, low and long.

Smiling, she cocked her head, but heard nothing more. As it should be.

The first pirate thumped to his knees. The blade was withdrawn and the attacker moved on in a blur. From nowhere, the trees throbbed with life.

Her army flooded from its hiding place. Not in the east as Niall of the Nine Hostages had believed, but creeping back under cover of darkness to lay this trap. Why wait for an attack you knew was inevitable?

Wit. Strategy. Cunning.

Catia thrust herself to her feet, nocking another arrow as she ran. One of the raiders backed away from the treeline, his face twisted with shock. Her arrow crunched into his breastbone and he spun back.

She glimpsed Niall, his furs now soaked with blood. He wrenched his axe free from one of her men and dashed out into the thin light. Fleeing? No. To his credit he merely stood on the shore, furiously waving his arms to urge his remaining men to retreat.

Raiders on the one intact ship were plucking survivors from the swell. Others raced past the pirate-king and dived into the sea, striking out for safety. Once he was sure as many of his men as possible had escaped, he lurched forward to follow. Too late. Catia's guards had emerged from the wooded valley to surround him and the few stragglers. Blades whipped up to his throat.

Niall of the Nine Hostages pushed his head up just as Catia had done earlier. His eyes were half closed. She could see no fear there, no desperate plea for his life. He was their bitter enemy, but she admired him for that.

Crunching over the pebbles, she felt the eyes of her guards flicker towards her. These were loyal men who had been by her side since the first moments of the great struggle that had upended Britannia. She looked around their faces and felt her heart swell that she was so blessed. Once they'd been the Grim Wolves, a rag-tag band of spies for the army of Rome, known as the *arcani*, who wandered the wilderness beyond the great wall to watch for the empire's enemies.

Bellicus was the oldest and wisest there, his once-red hair and wild beard now almost the colour of snow. He was as big as a bear, still strong despite his years. Some said he could cleave a man in two with his sword. He held her gaze, waiting for her order.

Beside him stood Mato, tall and slender and as fast as the wind. His heart was huge and he had the soul of a poet; a priest by any other name. Even in the thick of battle he refused to kill a man, and carried no weapon beyond a gnarled staff.

Solinus was the sour one, his tongue always dripping acid. Perhaps that bitterness was a result of the old scar that quartered his face. He found his sport in bickering with Comitinus, a worrier, a doubter, at times a whiner, but whose caution had saved Solinus' life on more than one occasion. Yet those who didn't know would think them the worst of enemies.

Four brothers, bound by the spirit of the wolf, and a life of hardship. Her anchors in this turbulent ocean of strife.

Once there had been another. But if she thought of him her heart would break.

Catia stepped in front of Niall of the Nine Hostages.

At first she thought he wouldn't deign to look at her. But then he lowered his head and she nodded when she saw the gleam of respect in his opening eyes.

'You shouldn't have come here,' she said.

Niall nodded thoughtfully. 'I should not have underestimated you. True, I heard the stories of the great Queen in the West, but—'

'You thought a woman couldn't match you in battle,' Comitinus chipped in.

'I thought you were weak Romans.' Niall cracked a cold grin. 'You all rolled over and bared your throats when the tribes attacked. Scoti, Picts, Alemanni . . .' He turned up his nose. 'None of them are as fierce as us. And yet they swept across your great wall with impunity, and flooded across Britannia. If they had had more wits they could have carried on to the walls of Rome itself.'

'They were beaten back,' Bellicus growled. 'Where are they now?'

'Aye, beaten back, finally, when Rome sent its fabled army to save you. And even then it was not an easy task. And now those self-same saviours are leaving you. Garrison after garrison is being abandoned, in the west and in the south. They return to Rome to shore up your flagging emperor, you know that.'

'He's not my emperor,' Catia said.

Now she could see mirth in the pirate-king's grin. 'The empire is abandoning Britannia. If not this day, then soon. And that leaves you poor lambs at the mercy of wolves like me.'

The Grim Wolves chuckled at that. Niall eyed them uneasily.

'And yet you're the one looking down the length of a blade,' Catia said. She nodded to her guard before heading off. 'Bring him to the fortress.'

Solinus shoved Niall between his shoulder blades. 'Step lively, you pirate bastard. Your better has spoken.'

'What now?' the raider said as he strode after Catia towards the winding path to the fortress looming over them. 'Take my head so your men can piss on my body? You've shown some wisdom so far. Let me see some more. A good queen would find some gain in this situation beyond cheap vengeance.'

'What can you offer me?' Catia said, without looking back at him. 'Gold? Jewels? We have plenty of those as it is. We have riches here greater than anywhere in this isle.'

'I have something greater than riches, to you certainly. Information.'

Catia kept walking, giving nothing away. But now she was intrigued.

The fortress sprawled from the headland to a near-island across a narrow land bridge. Anyone approaching could see its impregnability. The path to the gate was barely wide enough for a cart, and so steep a man would be left breathless before he'd climbed half its length.

Catia craned her neck to survey the great walls towering above them and felt pride. They'd worked hard over the years since they'd arrived at this place. Those walls had been shaped and strengthened and raised high. There was no safer place anywhere for her son Weylyn, or for the royal bloodline he represented, the House of Pendragon. The bloodline of the great war-leader of Britannia, one chosen by the druids since the oldest times, and given form once more by her husband Lucanus, and by herself. She had been selected by the wood-priests to be the chalice that would carry that regal blood, a legacy which made them vast and powerful enemies. Here they could hold those threats at bay.

The gates of Tintagel creaked open and Catia strode into her home. The courtyard was broad and flagged with granite, and beyond it was the keep. Her husband's banner, now hers, fluttered above it, a gold dragon on a red background.

Pausing as she always did, she bowed her head once towards the object that dominated the scene before her: a sword, the tip of the blade rammed in a crack between the flagstones. It was ancient, made of bronze, and when the light caught it at the right angle, the blade revealed black tracings of runes that no one could decipher.

'Is that it?'

Catia glanced back to see Niall staring at the weapon. His face shone with deference. She was puzzled. 'The blade?'

'The shining sword of the god Nuadu, one of the four great treasures of the Tuatha de Danann—'

'Who are?'

'Gods, by any other name.'

Catia turned at the rich voice rolling out across the courtyard. The wood-priest Myrrdin strode up, leaning on his staff. Though he now slept on a bed in a warm room, he still carried the air of the Wilds with him. His raven-black hair fell in ringlets, tied at the ends with leather thongs. A tattoo of a snake twisted down his cheekbone, past those fierce eyes and hooked nose to his jawline.

'They are the children of the goddess Danu, and they travelled to this world from four magical cities, bringing with them four treasures of the gods.'

Niall looked Myrrdin up and down. 'One of the wise men. I thought your kind had long since faded into the mists of history.'

'A few of us still remain.' Myrrdin's face darkened for an instant, but then he hid his true thoughts with another honeyed smile. 'You are right: the sword that stands in the stones is one of those great treasures.'

Catia heard Solinus snort behind her. The wood-priest weaved stories until none of them knew what was truth and what was a lie, all of it to advance his own aims.

She looked at the figure who stood beside the druid. Her son Weylyn was tall now. Soon he would be as tall as his father had been when he vanished from their lives. He was still bleary-eyed from sleep, but at his tutor's words he grinned and strode over to the blade. Almost as if it might burn him, he rested the palm of his right hand on the hilt.

'Its name is Caledfwlch,' he said. 'My father the Wolf wielded it when he led the people to the great victory over the barbarian horde. And one day it will be mine.'

Catia turned back to Niall of the Nine Hostages. 'How do you know of this?'

'Tales travel far, and faster than men,' he replied. 'And the tales of heroes and gods more so. The story of the great Pendragon, the war-leader, the Head of the Dragon, was brought to Hibernia by the warriors of the tribes who fled the devastation he wrought.'

'A great hero he was,' Myrrdin said. 'Chosen by the gods themselves. The guardian of the royal bloodline of the King Who Will Not Die, the saviour of this land, who will lead the people out of the long dark into a new golden age.'

'I've heard that tale too. That story was old even in my father's father's father's time.'

One of the 'eternal stories', Catia remembered Myrrdin saying. All religions had a version, and all believed their own to be true. But only this one *was* true. Or so he said.

'His name was Lucanus,' Weylyn said, and pulled his hand back from the sword.

Catia winced. She could hear the hero-worship in her son's voice and she felt a pang that Weylyn had never truly known his father, but only the stories that all there told.

'Lucanus, yes,' Niall repeated, rolling the name around his tongue. He looked up to the gulls wheeling through the wisps of smoke floating against the rosy sky.

'Lucanus is dead now and we mourn him still,' Catia said, her voice cold.

'Not dead!' Weylyn blurted, his eyes blazing. 'One day he'll walk back into our lives, once his great work is done.'

'No.' Many a time Catia had warned her son not to accept those dangerous fantasies. He would never grieve until he learned to accept the truth. But this was not the time to press.

Weylyn bowed his head, his eyes sullen. 'My father isn't dead,' he muttered.

'No,' Niall said. 'The stories tell us he sleeps in a cave with the fiercest warriors this world has known, waiting for the moment when he's summoned to fight again.'

Another snort from Solinus. Catia eyed Myrrdin. He held her gaze for a long moment and she felt her heart harden. Lucanus was a man, who had loved and hoped and sacrificed for those who were close to him. That was forgotten these days, it seemed.

'A story,' she said, her voice defiant.

'Some stories are true,' Niall continued. 'This is the information I would offer you for my freedom. I know where he sleeps, this great hero, this Lucanus of the House of Pendragon. I know where he sleeps, and I know how to bring him home to you.'

CHAPTER TWO

The Two Kings

CATIA PERCHED ON HER THRONE AND WATCHED THE DUST
motes dance in the shaft of sunlight breaking through the
window. Only Myrrdin stood before her in that chamber. Everyone else had been dismissed for fear she wouldn't be able to
contain her emotions.

'See what you've done with your *stories*,' she said, unable to
hide the contempt in her voice.

'You don't have to heed him. Lucanus is dead, we both know
that.'

'Thanks to you and the deal you made with the Eaters of the
Dead. They aided us in our hour of need, and in return you
promised them the flesh of a king to feast . . .' The words choked
in her throat.

'Whatever I did, I did for the sake of your son.'

'You did it for your grand scheme! This lie you wood-priests
conjured up about a king who will not die, a lie you made truth
by force of will alone.' Catia pushed herself to her feet and strode
to the window. The western lands glowed in the sunlight, as
beautiful as when she had first ventured here. But they were also
harsh, and could steal the lives of anyone who didn't treat them
with respect.

For long years, the Attacotti had been horrors conjured up to
frighten folk gathered round the hearth on a stormy winter's
night. Beasts of hell more than mortals, who crept from the

14

darkness to consume human flesh. But when the barbarians had swarmed across the great wall in the north, the Attacotti had come with them, skin crusted white with clay, eyes circled with charcoal so that each face resembled a death's head.

And they had all learned then that the real world held horrors the equal of any imaginings.

'For a while, I considered having you killed.' She barely recognized her own voice, so quiet and devoid of emotion it was.

'I thought that may have been the case.'

'You stole my husband from me—'

'He chose to go. To save you and Weylyn from the Attacotti. If the deal had not been completed, they would have taken you in his stead, all of you here.'

'You stole my husband from me,' she snapped, harsher. 'At the moment when we'd finally found happiness after a lifetime of hardship.'

She let her thoughts fly back across the years, across the green land of Britannia to the cold moors of the north. Lucanus had been beside her almost all her life. Playing as children in the fields beyond the fort of Vercovicium. And when they were grown, and there seemed for a moment a chance that they'd come together in the love that they each recognized within the other.

But then her father had been cheated out of his fortune by her treacherous mother, Gaia, who had since proved more treacherous and murderous than Catia could ever have believed. She'd been forced to marry into a rich family to save her father from ruin. And then had come her new husband's fists and the broken bones and the misery, day after day, night after night, until the barbarian horde had invaded. How bitter she felt that they'd slaughtered almost all the folk she knew while saving her from a life barely worth living.

And Lucanus, brave, flawed Lucanus, had been at her side through the long flight south. They'd saved each other time and again, and survived through sacrifice, and then the barbarians had been defeated. For a while there had seemed hope. A chance for joy. For peace.

Until the Attacotti came to collect their dues.

'I should have had you killed,' she concluded.

'Then Weylyn would not have had a teacher.'

'And you've been like a father to him. That is another reason to keep you alive,' she added begrudgingly. She breathed in a deep draught of the warm, salty air and turned to scrutinize the wood-priest. He almost seemed to flinch under her stare. 'But what's done is done. There's no gain in letting the past corrupt the present.'

Myrrdin nodded, as if thankful that she'd spared him, and said, 'We're moving into a dark age, you know that. Whatever you think of me, the King Who Will Not Die is the only one who will be able to unite the people and lead them back into the light. If not, the long night will close in for ever and there will only be years of savagery.'

'I've heard your argument a thousand times. I know our responsibility to those yet unborn.' She pushed past him and plucked up one of the honey cakes from the cloth on the stool by the hearth. Breaking off a knob, she popped it into her mouth and thought as she chewed.

'Lucanus is dead,' Myrrdin said, as if he could read what rolled through her head.

'You *want* him dead.'

'That is harsh.'

'You need him dead so your tale has life.' She smiled at her play on words. 'Lucanus disappeared so his story has no end. Tellers can fill that emptiness with all sorts of magic. A great hero, taken by the gods to the Otherworld. Ready to return in our hour of greatest need. Hope. Wonder. If Lucanus returns, he is just a man again, and your tale dies on the lips.'

'And that magical tale has spun its web around Niall of the Nine Hostages. He repeats it back to you, and you fall under its spell too. That's how this magic works.'

'The pirate-king believes he has evidence that Lucanus is alive.'

'"Believes". Garbled words from a terrified shipwrecked sailor.' Myrrdin paced the chamber. 'There's no easy way to say this. But if the Attacotti took Lucanus, he will not be alive.'

Catia couldn't allow herself to consider the fate her husband might have endured, not if she wanted to stay sane. 'And if there's even the slightest chance he yet lives, I would walk through the gates of hell to bring him home.'

Flames flickered in the depths of the wood-priest's coal eyes. 'Carry on along this road and that may well be your fate.'

'I am queen,' she said. 'And you . . . are nothing.'

Bellicus leaned on the ramparts and peered down into the cove. Anyone watching would think a giant wolf hunched there, waiting for its prey. The pelt of the beast he'd slain when he first became one of the *arcani* stretched across his back, and he'd pulled the snout down low over his eyes, as he always did when he was thinking.

The blackened bones of the burned ship bobbed on the swell. His men had retrieved all the bodies of their enemies, dragging the remains up into the mouth of the valley for a good send-off. Now they could return to their lost loved ones in the Summerlands under the eyes of whatever gods those pirates worshipped.

'Brother!'

Mato was striding along the path from the gates, twirling his staff as if it were a part of him. Bellicus silently cursed when he saw his fellow Grim Wolf's dark face.

Trouble.

Behind Mato, Apullius was hurrying to keep up. Could this really be the boy they'd rescued mere moments from death at the hands of the advancing barbarian horde that had slaughtered his parents? When had he grown as tall as Mato, broad-shouldered and strong, with the kind of looks that sent hearts pounding among the women of the Dumnonii?

'It's true, then,' Bellicus grunted.

'Our worst fears.' Apullius hardened his voice, as if Bellicus wouldn't otherwise understand the seriousness of what he was about to say.

'Apullius returned only moments ago. We came straight to you,' Mato said. 'We need to reach a decision. I say it's now time to tell Catia, and Myrrdin. We can't keep this to ourselves any longer.'

'The bastard wood-priest can go and boil his head for all I care.

I'm sick of his schemes and his lies and his Great Plan, which seems to be little more than making everyone else's lives miserable.' Bellicus sighed. Mato was right, as always. 'We tell Catia.'

They found their queen wandering through the herb garden at the end of the headland, overlooking the great, shining ocean. She liked to go there to be alone with her thoughts before the business of the day began. Bellicus felt a pang of guilt at disturbing her with such news.

She frowned as they neared. 'What's amiss?' she asked. 'Have Niall's ships returned?'

Bellicus thrust Apullius forward. The younger man bowed his head to his queen. 'I've been away . . .' he began.

Catia nodded. 'Agreeing new trade routes with the Dumnonii settlements along the south coast.'

'Ah . . . that was not exactly the truth.'

'It was a lie,' Mato said, 'but a lie with good intent. We wanted to say nothing until we were certain.'

'He's become a good scout, and a good Grim Wolf,' Bellicus added. 'Lucanus would have been proud of him. We sent him out, alone, across some of the most dangerous territory we know, to discover if the rumours we'd heard from travellers were true.'

'Speak.' Catia's face darkened. 'I'm not some little girl to be spared bad news, or have it sweetened with honey.'

Bellicus felt a deep sadness. He'd hoped Catia could long enjoy the peace she'd earned after all she'd endured. 'Tell her.'

'I travelled east through the lands of the Dumnonii, and across the Tamar, almost to the Isle of Apples,' Apullius said. 'I was following a trail of words . . . of stories . . . of a new force that had arisen in Britannia. A massing army, far from Londinium and the last of Roman rule. An enemy.'

'Our enemy?' Catia asked.

Apullius nodded. 'I came across a band of warriors on horseback. But they weren't plundering the villages, like the barbarians we knew of old. They were stopping in those settlements, and . . . talking.'

'The wood-priest has many faults, but he's always told us words can be more dangerous than a blade,' Bellicus said. 'And this time he was right.'

'They told of the coming of a king, the True King, who was of the royal bloodline. He'd bring forth the saviour who would lead the people of Britannia out of the darkness they all could see descending. Those warriors moved from village to village, spreading this story. I ventured into one of the settlements, pretending to beg for bread, and I saw what spell had been woven. Hope is thin on the ground for these folk. They hunger. The sickness is rife. They feel that Rome has abandoned them—'

'Rome *has* abandoned them,' Mato interrupted. 'Forts have already been deserted, you know that. The army is pulling back and leaving Britannia to fend for itself.'

'And into this dark hole of despair, these warriors shone a little light,' Apullius continued. 'The folk are turning towards this True King . . . this false king . . . in the hope that he can protect them, from men like Niall of the Nine Hostages, from the barbarian horde returning.'

Bellicus had watched Catia's lips growing thin and bloodless. She was clever. She was already many steps ahead of Apullius' tale.

'My mother,' she spat. 'Gaia.'

'This false king is called Arthur,' Apullius replied. 'The name—'

'The name of the bastard your mother bore from the seed of her own son, that mad soldier, Corvus,' Bellicus said. 'We always knew she would return to stake her claim to power.'

'She's no fool,' Mato said. 'She's winning the hearts of the people. Once they turn on us, all is lost. This fortress here in the far west will become the place where we're trapped until the army of the false king decides to pick us off.'

'The days of peace are already done,' Bellicus said. 'We have no choice but to fight.'

'War, then.' Catia's voice was so flat he winced. It was the sound of someone who saw the inevitability of death.

CHAPTER THREE

The War Council

NIGHT HAD FALLEN. THE ROARING FIRE IN THE HEARTH threw swooping shadows around the chamber. For the first time in many a year, the war council had been called.

Bellicus looked around the faces in the circle, at Catia, and the wisest advisers any queen could wish for, Mato, and Amarina. Only Lucanus was missing from the original circle that had formed in Londinium at Myrrdin's bidding all those years ago. Bellicus felt an ache for his long-lost friend. Now they needed him more than ever.

Myrrdin stood in one corner, out of the light. Apullius was there too and had just finished retelling his story.

'We thought we could hide away here and let history pass us by.' Mato's voice creaked with weariness. 'Thought we could wait out the years until the world finally comes to believe in the legacy that Weylyn represents. Now we know that was a foolish hope.'

'We can shout as much as we like. True king. False king. Our voice will never be as loud as theirs, not now they've already begun spinning their web of lies.' Amarina walked around the chamber, the gold thread in her emerald dress glinting in the firelight.

Bellicus cracked his knuckles. 'You know the size of their army?'

Apullius shook his head. 'I saw only three war-bands.'

'That already suggests a good number,' Mato interjected.

'Any word on where they have camped?' asked Bellicus.

20

Apullius shook his head again. 'Some shining fortress in the north. That's what they told the village folk.'

'Of course they did,' Bellicus rumbled. 'Not some tent city reeking of shit and piss with dogs barking night and day.' He glanced at Catia and thought how distracted she looked, how drawn her face appeared. Was she thinking of Lucanus too?

'I'm sick of fighting; sick of running,' Amarina said.

'We all are.' Bellicus softened his voice. 'If we try to ignore them, sooner or later they'll sweep into the west and drive us into the ocean. They can't afford to have a rival claim to the power they desire.'

Myrrdin stepped into the light. His face was like a storm at sea, the dragon tattoo twisted so that it seemed its mouth was ripping wide. 'We should have killed the boy Arthur when we had the chance.' His glowering eyes fixed on Catia.

Bellicus cast his mind back to their journey into the west and the hour when all had seemed lost. When they'd been confronted by Catia's mother, Gaia, and by her murderous renegade son, Corvus. The boy Arthur had not long been born. Then, Catia had had the opportunity to slay the false heir. But she'd chosen mercy, as Catia always would. And she had sent her mother and the child away.

'Killed the *baby*, you mean.' Catia's eyes flashed. 'Stabbed it with a sword? Cut out its heart? Like one of the barbarians we'd been fighting? If we dishonour ourselves the prize isn't worth winning.'

The wood-priest shook his staff. 'The prize is too great – saving all, saving knowledge, lifting the people out of the darkness.'

'With a crime like that, we would always be in darkness.' Catia looked away, dismissing him.

'We have a fight on our hands, sooner or later.' Mato lowered himself on to a stool. 'Better we fight sooner, then, before they have the time to fully prepare.'

Bellicus wandered to the window and looked out into the night. In the distance, he could see the lights flickering in the Dumnonii settlement further along the headland.

'We have a small army here,' he said. 'We don't know if that's going to be enough. One wrong calculation could lose us every-thing.'

'We can raise new recruits from the Dumnonii,' Mato mused.

'You think they will follow us so easily?' Amarina's lips curled into a cold smile. 'They're farmers and merchants, not warriors. Men will fight if they think their families and livelihoods are threatened. These followers of the false king promise them a golden age, rather than the endless night they all feel they are facing. How do we fight that?'

Bellicus felt his heart sink. Amarina was right. He was good with a sword or an axe, but winning the hearts of plain folk was not something for which he had any talent.

A deep silence fell across the chamber, broken only by the crackle of the logs in the hearth.

'We need Lucanus,' Catia said.

'Lucanus is dead.' The wood-priest stepped back into the shadows.

'We need the Head of the Dragon, the war-leader of old. Folk will rally to him. And if it's not the Lucanus we know, then another Lucanus. Who will know the difference? That is how your stories work, is it not?' She spat the final words.

'Wait.' Apullius jumped to his feet. 'You think Lucanus might be alive?'

'The pirate-king believes so,' Bellicus told him.

'Then why are we sitting here? Why aren't we already riding out to bring him home?' Apullius shook his head with incredulity.

Why, indeed? Bellicus looked down. Were they afraid of the answer, now they were clinging on to a little hope?

'You must!' Apullius blinked away hot tears.

The others shifted. They all knew Lucanus had been like a father to Apullius after his parents were killed. When Lucanus vanished that night, the lad had been so heartbroken many thought he'd never smile again. Bellicus looked around at those present. The shock still lingered among all of them, and the hor-ror, that their leader had turned his back on his family and his friends, seemingly voluntarily giving himself up to the flesh-eating Attacotti.

'I beg you!' The youngest Grim Wolf reached out a trembling hand.

'Listen to him,' Bellicus grunted to the wood-priest.

'If anyone can save us, it's Lucanus, you all know that.' Apullius had begun to babble, but his eyes gleamed in the firelight. 'He was a hero . . . a great hero . . .'

'This is the hour of greatest need,' Mato pressed, taking up the call. 'This is how your legend works.'

For a while, there was no reply. A log cracked, the flames shot up, and in the wavering light Bellicus saw that the wood-priest was lost to deep thought. Myrrdin was wrestling with himself.

'Release Niall of the Nine Hostages from his imprisonment,' he said at last, breaking the spell. He hadn't been convinced, that was clear. 'Bring him to the courtyard and let's hear what he has to say.'

The torches guttered in the sea breeze as Bellicus watched two guards lead the pirate-king out into the courtyard. He held his head high, no doubt certain that he was about to be executed. But no fear twisted his face, not even a flicker. He was a brave man. Bellicus admired that.

Myrrdin tapped his staff on the flagstones to the beat of the Hibernian's steps; a funeral march. Amarina pulled her cloak tighter around her against the chill and rolled her eyes in weariness at the pretence.

'Niall of the Nine Hostages,' Catia intoned. 'You committed a crime against us. You would have slaughtered us where we stood. We owe you nothing.'

'Get on with it,' the pirate-king said.

'But we are not raiders and pillagers like you. We have honour. And we have the strength to show mercy to our enemies.'

Through narrowed eyes, Niall looked around the gathered group. A grin spread in the bristles of his red beard. 'You like the sound of my deal.'

Mato grasped the raider's arm and dragged him to where the sword Caledfwlch was rammed into the crack between the flagstones. He waved the tip of his staff at it.

'Show your respect for the sword of Nuada,' Mato said.

Niall stared at the blade, his face tightening. Trembling, he dropped to his knees and bowed his head. Reaching out one hand, his fingers fluttered close to the sword hilt, but he didn't touch it; almost as if he didn't dare, Bellicus thought.

'What do you know of it?' Mato asked. He glanced at Myrrdin, looking for reassurance that he was following the druid's plan correctly.

'My people tell of an ancient race, the Tuatha de Danann, the children of the goddess Danu, who walked this earth as men walk.' Niall's strained voice was almost plucked away by the whine of the wind. 'They came from the Northern Islands – Falias, Gorias, Finias and Murias – and from each one they brought a great treasure, an object of power. This sword was one, and it was said that no enemy ever escaped from it, once it was drawn from its sheath.'

'And the others?' Myrrdin demanded.

'The stone of Fal, which would cry out when touched by the true king of the land. The spear of Lugh. Whoever held it could never be defeated in battle. The cauldron of the Dagda, which provided for all who sought sustenance from it.'

'Do you see?' Myrrdin asked of those gathered around.

Bellicus did.

'I know where the cauldron of the Dagda is hidden,' the druid said.

Niall's eyes widened. 'This cannot be.'

'It is one of many secrets kept by the wood-priests.' A lie? The truth? Who knew with Myrrdin? The druid wagged the top of his staff. 'You saw how folk followed the golden crown of the Pendragon. Imagine where their loyalties would lie if they knew we carried two most magical gifts of the gods. With the cauldron, and this sword, we could raise an army capable of defeating any enemy.'

'And this priceless treasure is lying around in some hovel, with a gap-toothed old wood-priest hovering over it, waiting for us to scoop it up?' Amarina mocked.

Myrrdin eyed her. Bellicus saw the glimpse of steel in his gaze, as did Amarina, no doubt, but it would never be enough to make her back down. 'The cup of the gods is protected in ways that mean no unworthy soul can lay hands upon it. Only the most courageous, the most honourable, the truest of seekers will be able to overcome the perils that defend it.'

'A trial, then,' Mato said.

The wood-priest nodded. 'As with all of the gods' gifts, men must prove they are great enough to receive it.' He looked around the group. 'Choose wisely who must embark on this quest. The tests are so great, not all may return.'

'Lucanus.' Catia stepped forward and rested a hand on Caled-fwlch's hilt. Niall of the Nine Hostages recoiled as if he had been burned. When he'd recovered, he looked up at Catia with wide eyes and a face glowing with new-found respect.

'Lucanus is dead,' Myrrdin snapped.

'The most courageous, the most honourable. You were describing Lucanus.' Catia locked eyes with Myrrdin, almost daring him to defy her. 'If this quest is so dangerous that all but the best must fail, would you not give anything to try one final time to see if my husband is still alive?'

Myrrdin's jaw tightened. Bellicus choked back a chuckle. The wood-priest, the arch-manipulator, had been twisted round Catia's little finger.

'You are the queen,' the druid said. 'We will bow to whatever you command.'

Catia smiled. 'Then I command that we offer Niall of the Nine Hostages mercy, and in exchange that he leads us to wherever he believes Lucanus to be held. And then we will know the truth once and for all.'

Amarina laughed. 'To the home of the Attacotti? I will bid you good fortune at the quay, and then make plans for the rest of my days.'

For a moment, Bellicus felt his vision cloud, and before him one of the Eaters of the Dead loomed up, ghastly white, with black-rimmed eyes and teeth stained with blood.

'The daughter of the moon is right,' he heard Myrrdin say. 'There is no hope of return.'

CHAPTER FOUR

At Sunset

'**I**S IT TRUE THAT THE DEAD LIVE IN THE WEST?'
Mato sat cross-legged on the headland, the salty breeze stirring his long hair. His hands lay on the staff across his lap. Lost to his thoughts, he hadn't moved for long moments as he watched the red sun sink to the horizon. Now he turned to the boy who stood beside him. Lucanus lived on inside those eyes, in the strong line of jaw, in the poise and the confidence.

'So some say,' he replied.

'But is it true?' Weylyn asked again.

'That is a good question.' Mato smiled. He always enjoyed his back and forth with the lad. Weylyn had his mother's wits, there was no doubt of that. 'There are many truths, that is one thing you will learn as you grow. And there are some who believe that a man creates his own truths.'

Weylyn snorted. 'You play with words as much as the wood-priest. How can there be more than one truth?'

'There is the truth of the world, and the truth that men believe in their hearts. And sometimes wise folk imagine stories of won-der, and if others believe hard enough, those imaginings become real. They become true. And they can change the destinies of men as much as the commands of any emperors.'

'Words are more powerful than swords, that's what the wood-priest said.' The lad eyed him, still testing to see if he was being tricked.

'And on that occasion he was correct.'

'Why don't you use a sword?'

'Because I choose not to.'

'You could die in battle for want of a blade.'

'That would be my choice.'

Weylyn snorted again. 'What man chooses to die?'

Mato didn't answer.

The boy flopped down on the grass, irritation crackling in his exaggerated movement. After a moment, he calmed and watched the ruddy waters. 'Niall of the Nine Hostages says my father is alive. Do you believe him?'

'We will do all in our power to find out the truth.'

'And Myrrdin claims you will lose your fool lives chasing after a ghost.' He paused. 'One of the Dumnonii girls says my father is dead, yet still living, in the west. Waiting to be summoned home in the hour of our greatest need.'

Mato winced. The face of his sister floated in front of his eyes, killed all those years ago. How many times had he wished he could summon her home? Death shaped a man: in this too the druids were correct. The cold stone that transformed a man of lead into a man of gold. He was who he was because of his sister's passing. And Weylyn would for ever be shaped by the loss of his father.

He moistened his lips, selecting his words. 'Wiser folk than I say the gods make special dispensation for great heroes – and no hero was greater than your father, the Pendragon – and they are allowed to pass between the Summerlands and the world of men with impunity.'

Weylyn sat in silence for a long moment. 'I'll do all I can to be the man my father was.'

And would the boy have said that if Lucanus hadn't been lost? Mato wasn't sure. 'Keep that light in your heart,' he said. 'It will guide you in the darkest of nights.'

'Ho!'

Mato looked round at the hail. Apullius and his brother Morirex, five years his junior, were striding through the banks of tangled bramble along the trail from the valley. Weylyn jumped to his feet and threw himself at the younger brother. They spun back, rolling and wrestling on the path. Apullius sighed and raised his eyes to the heavens. Morirex was the elder by a few years, but Weylyn almost got the better of him. Apullius snarled a fist in Weylyn's tunic and yanked him up, tossing him to one side.

'I'll beat you. One day,' Weylyn said, jabbing a finger at his friend. Morirex laughed.

Apullius squatted in front of Mato. 'The ship sails at dawn. Bellicus has put out a call for volunteers. I'm going. I owe Lucanus everything. You?'

Mato nodded.

'Who else, I wonder?'

Mato eyed Weylyn and Morirex, wrestling again in the long grass. There would be no shortage of volunteers, he knew that. If anything, the fealty to Lucanus had only increased since the night of his disappearance. No one could ignore the peace and security he had bought them through his sacrifice.

'Niall spins a tale about an island of daemons and ghosts, half-way between Britannia and Hibernia,' Apullius continued. 'His people won't venture near it. Magic, he talks about, and spells that bewitch sailors. Any who are washed up ashore are never seen again.'

'If that is the home of the Attacotti, then we know the fate of those sailors.' Mato looked out to the setting sun. 'Who should go? The fewer the better, I say.' He locked eyes with Apullius and the other man understood the silent communication: a number they could afford to lose.

'We'll return if the gods are willing,' Apullius said.

'And if not, we will have done our duty to our old friend.'

CHAPTER FIVE

Dark Horizon

U NDER A STEEL SKY, A STORM ROILED IN THE WEST. IT WAS NOT an auspicious day for setting sail on a voyage of such magnitude, but no one could bear to delay departure any longer. They needed to know the truth.

On the quayside, Bellicus wiped the salt spray from his forehead. Sinking deep on the soles of his feet, he made the most of feeling dry land beneath him. He hated sailing as much as he hated riding.

'You'll be back here soon enough.' Mato watched the ship straining at its mooring on the high swell.

'Say you. Going out on to the whale road on a few bits of wood and nail and pitch. Madness. Little wonder that sailors are all jolt-heads.'

'You've said your prayers to the gods?'

'Aye. All of them. Myrrdin's old gods. Roman gods. The Christ. Mithras. Better safe than sorry.' At dawn, he'd also laid a beef bone on the grave of his dog Catulus. He missed his old friend.

Amarina drifted along the quay, her cloak billowing behind her. She wore that taunting smile, and only made it stronger when she saw him looking. Easy for her to be pleased with herself; she was staying on solid ground.

'I once stood on the Wall with Lucanus, looking out into the Wilds, and told him we were on the boundary between two worlds,' she said when she arrived at their side. 'And here we are again, brother wolves. The western sea separates the world of men from the world of the dead, from daemons and ghosts and magic. From the land of the gods. Once you sail into it, all things change and you will not return the same men. If you return.'

Mato laughed. 'We can always count on you for words of comfort, Amarina.'

'If you need comfort from me, you are already in a dire place. What say you, Bellicus?'

He fixed his gaze on the horizon, not meeting her eyes. But he had heard a serious note behind her sardonic humour. 'We owe it to Lucanus.'

'You do. Afraid?'

'I'm always afraid these days. Age does that to a man.'

'Wisdom. Finally.'

A bolt of lightning crashed in the distance. The wind whipped up, the swell heaving.

Their vessel was a sturdy, ocean-going craft, an Etruscan design that Catia had paid good gold for, and one of five that they kept in the harbour. *Waveskimmer* was its name. The prow and stern curled up into columns a good spear's length above a man's head. A single mast held a sail the colour of the sun that would be unfurled once they were out of the cove and into the currents. Benches spanned the deck for the oarsmen, and painted shields with dragon designs lined the sides. A small hold would store enough supplies for the voyage.

A crowd was gathering along the quay to see the voyagers off. Only the Grim Wolves and a handful of the most seasoned men would be leaving that morning. The bulk of the army would remain to guard the fortress should the false king attack in their absence.

Bellicus looked over the heads of the gathered throng and saw bodies parting. After a moment Catia and Myrrdin pushed their way through. Their faces were drawn, their eyes fixed ahead, Bellicus could see, and he could sense the tension crackling between them. Catia had never forgiven Myrrdin for what had happened to Lucanus. Who of them could?

The queen strode up to him and reached out a hand. A blue

ribbon fluttered from her fingers. 'For Lucanus,' she said. 'My token. When . . . if . . . you find him.'

Bellicus nodded. He took the ribbon and pushed it into the pouch at his waist. Catia showed a cold face, as she always did, so no one could see her emotions. She'd learned her queenly ways well. But he knew her and he could see the desperate hope in her eyes.

'Any advice for the valiant travellers, wood-priest?' Amarina asked, as if she didn't care.

'Valiant? Aye, you are,' Myrrdin said. 'I think you're all fools for going on this voyage. You know as well as I what the Attacotti are capable of, and what the fate of Lucanus will have been . . .'

Bellicus glanced at Catia. She kept her head high, and if the druid's words had pained her, she didn't show it.

'. . . but I wish no ill upon you,' Myrrdin continued. 'The waters surrounding that place are turbulent, and many a ship has been sent to the bottom. But Niall of the Nine Hostages knows the whale road. If the gods are with you, he will get you there in one piece, if only to save his own neck. But once in that land, I warn you: do not sleep. Do not rest. You are fine scouts, but the Attacotti are better than all of you. They can smell a man's sweat on the wind from miles away. In their home, they will be upon you in a multitude. Do not sleep,' he repeated. 'Move fast. Go in at dawn, and be away from there by nightfall. And if you haven't found Lucanus by then, do not venture back. The gods' patience is thin and they'll only look after fools once. Do you hear my words?'

'We do,' Bellicus replied.

Myrrdin nodded. 'I'll petition the gods here on your behalf.'

Catia looked around, her gaze eventually falling on Morirex. The Mouse was sitting alone on the quayside, swinging his legs. 'Where's Weylyn? I would have thought he'd want to see you depart.'

'He's still angry that we refused to take him along,' Mato said. 'He's his father's son.'

A commotion erupted in the crowd, and the sea of bodies parted once more. Niall of the Nine Hostages strode out, a defiant look sweeping across all who were gathered there. His wrists were bound behind his back. Solinus glowered at his right arm, the scar that quartered his face crinkling. Comitinus guarded the left, his own gaze skittering as if he expected an attack at any moment. Behind them, soldiers herded out the small group of Niall's pirates who had been taken prisoner.

'I can't see the wisdom of having so many of our enemies on board,' Bellicus grunted. 'They could slit all our throats under cover of night and heave us over the side.'

'You need their help to navigate the currents,' Catia replied. 'Only seasoned sailors will be able to chart a path through those waters. Besides, you'll have more than enough men to keep watch.'

'Even so.' Bellicus looked from Niall's cold stare to the furtive gaze of the cut-throats who followed him. His neck prickled with unease.

Solinus shoved Niall between the shoulder blades so that he almost fell at Catia's feet. The raider glared at the Grim Wolf from under heavy brows.

'Stare all you want, you Hibernian bastard,' Solinus said with a grin. 'One of us is a snivelling captive and it's not me.' At his side Comitinus fluttered a hand to urge quiet, and Solinus screwed up his nose at him. 'Stop whining. He's never going to be friends with us.'

'He's an honourable man,' Catia interjected. 'A king,' she corrected.

Niall held her gaze. 'I stand by my word.'

'A pirate,' Bellicus sneered.

'A warrior,' Niall retorted, eyeing the pelt hanging on the other man's back. 'A wolf of the sea. Do you blame the wolf for filling its belly with the lamb?'

'But we are not lambs,' Catia said. 'And now you know the truth. We are the same, wolves together, and in this pack you must go shoulder to shoulder, as you vowed. And in return you'll get your freedom, as I promised.'

'I stand by my word, and my men stand by me. You have nothing to fear.'

Catia nodded. With a grunt of reluctance, Solinus sawed through the bonds at the pirate-king's wrists.

Niall of the Nine Hostages rubbed the blood back into his hands, then turned to the remnants of his raiding party. 'Make ready,' he boomed. 'We'll be away to the north before that storm hits.'

The pirate nodded to Catia, only once but with respect, then clambered down on to the heaving deck. His men leapt in, and with practised ease took up their posts at the helm, along the oars and with the bailing tools.

Bellicus raised one hand and their own carefully selected crew stepped out of the crowd and dropped on to the deck. These were men who had had some experience on the waves – although not as much as the pirates – but also could be counted on to be courageous in battle. And for what lay ahead, they needed strong hearts more than anything.

The leader of the Grim Wolves turned back to Amarina. 'Your witch-sisters can call up storms and kill them with their spells. Can't they do something about that one?'

'I have no witch-sisters,' Amarina said, her face blank. 'But the Hecatae will no doubt have more important things to do than worry about rats clinging to timber in the vast ocean.'

Bellicus snorted and jumped down into the ship. Once he'd made his way to the prow, he looked back and watched Mato, Solinus and Comitinus drop on to the deck. After a moment, Apullius joined them. The Grim Wolves were bred to run in the Wilds under the moon; here they were out of their element and heading into the unknown.

The gods were testing them indeed.

The ship heaved out on to the swell. The lines cracked and the oars splashed as they cut white lines into the grey waters. Bracing himself in the prow, Bellicus forced his gaze away from the dark horizon where the storm roiled to the cheering crowd lining the quay. His early life had been a lonely existence spent roaming the Wilds, but he'd come to know these folk well over recent years. He was surprised to feel a pang in his heart to be leaving them. Perhaps he really was getting old.

'Ho!' someone shouted.

He looked down the ship to where a man crouched over the

dark hole that was the entrance to the cramped hold. The sailor seemed to be calling to someone inside. After a moment, he leaned in and dragged up a writhing figure. Bellicus muttered a curse into his beard.

Standing on the end of one of the benches, Solinus threw back his head and laughed. 'That's the biggest rat I've ever seen!'

With a growl, Bellicus threw himself along the deck, tossing men this way and that, until he stood next to the pair by the hold. Weylyn looked up at him with flickering eyes.

'Cower you might,' Bellicus roared. 'What possessed you?'

Weylyn pushed himself up to his full height. 'It's my right to accompany you.'

'It's not your right to end the bloodline with a miserable death.'

'I deserve to stand at your side when you find my father. When he was young, he would have done the same.' Bellicus couldn't argue with that. 'So I'm coming whether you like it or not.'

Bellicus nodded. 'Well said.' Weylyn grinned, and Bellicus grabbed him by the scruff of his tunic and tossed him over the side.

A cheer rang out from the oarsmen, and laughter from others. Weylyn had no time to cry out before the splash.

Looking to the quayside, Bellicus saw Catia's hands fly to her mouth, but he knew the lad was a good swimmer. Beside him, Solinus leaned on the side and roared, 'Swim back to your mother, little rat!' Bellicus glimpsed a face twisted with a mix of anger and embarrassment before the lad struck out for the quay.

'He'll hate you for ever for that,' Mato said at his side. 'But you've probably saved his life.'

'For all the thanks I'll get,' Bellicus grumbled, marching back to the prow.

'The cry of fathers everywhere.'

Bellicus felt his cheeks burn, but he put his head down and kept walking. He'd never admit it to anyone, but he'd promised himself he would be a father to the boy after the night Lucanus disappeared. He'd been a father to Lucanus too after the Wolf's own father vanished, and it seemed it was for ever to be his lot in life. Besides, the boy needed someone other than Myrrdin whispering in his ear to teach him the miserable ways of men.

Waveskimmer rolled with the churning currents as it moved out of the cove. In the prow, Bellicus gripped the rail and fought the urge to look back. Soon, the sounds from the quay vanished beneath the whine of the wind and the splash of the oars. When open water lay ahead, Niall of the Nine Hostages barked an order and the sail unfurled. It billowed with a boom and Bellicus felt the vessel leap forward. His chest tightened as he watched bolts of lightning lance down along the black horizon.

'Have no fear. We'll skirt this storm.' The pirate-king rode the bucking deck with the ease of a man on solid ground. 'But there'll be more.'

'I've seen worse.'

If Niall recognized his bravado, he was kind enough not to mention it. 'Your queen has some fire in her breast.'

'She's a match for any man.' His thoughts flew back to a blood-drenched Catia saving him, and Solinus and Comitinus, from death at the hands of the barbarians.

'That she stands with Lucanus tells me as much about him as the legends I hear.' Niall held out a hand, and one of his raiders stepped up and handed him a loaf of dry bread. The pirate-king braced himself against the side and leaned over the grey water. Bellicus frowned as the Hibernian broke off knobs of bread and dropped them into the wake. The raider seemed to sense Bellicus staring for he said, 'An offering to Manannan mac Lir, the Son of the Sea, in the hope that he will protect us while we are far from land.'

Bellicus leaned on the rail and looked down into the churning brine.

'Sometimes, if you're fortunate, you can see him rising from the deep, on his chariot drawn by his horse Enbarr,' Niall murmured, his words almost a prayer.

'Have you seen him?'

'He whispered to me one night as I sat astern, drifting on the edge of sleep under the northern stars. It was bitter cold. I was wrapped in my furs, fresh smeared with lamb fat, and my breath was white clouds. We were becalmed, and thought we would never see land again. I remember . . .' He closed his eyes. 'I remember the fire-pot swinging in the dark. A beacon. And then, as my eye-lids fluttered, on the edge of being claimed by the warm sleep, I heard his words float up from the waves.'

'What did he say?'

'All will be well. All will be well. You will be king one day. You have work to do.' Niall opened his eyes. 'And the wind came at dawn, and since then I have held no fear of death. The gods have shown me a path to walk, and my life will not be over until I have walked it.'

Bellicus nodded. He liked the sound of a life lived without fear. These days it seemed that fear was all there was.

'Perhaps Manannan will bring your king back to you. He is the Ferryman, who transports the dead into the Otherworld, into the west.' He paused. 'The island we visit is named for him. It is a sacred place, a doorway between this world and the next.'

'This island you speak of . . . you've visited it?'

'Only one man I know has set foot upon it and lived. And he died from terror not long after he was rescued from the waves. He'd been shipwrecked. Was taken in by these strange folk who spoke no tongue that he recognized. But then he stumbled across the mountain of bones, and he ran, with the Eaters of the Dead nipping at his heels. He threw himself off a cliff into the ocean rather than submit to their hunger.'

'I've heard this tale too.' He had, in the House of Wishes in Vercovicium, what seemed like an age and a different life ago. He watched the lowering grey skies to the north, the storm now for-gotten. 'Then the Attacotti have the protection of Manannan mac Lir?'

The helmsman urged the ship into a fast current.

'It was not their original home, so the stories tell us,' the pirate-king replied. 'But they travelled there and made it a place of horrors. Some say they were born of the Land of the Dead itself, and now they have made it a part of this world too.'

CHAPTER SIX

The Queen in Exile

'S TOKE THE BRAZIERS. IT IS DAMNABLY COLD IN HERE.'
Gaia sat upon her throne of oak and bone, her hair now grey, her face as hard as granite, carved with deep faultlines. No mirrors existed in the High Fortress. She had ordered them all to be smashed. Her white gown glowed in the ruddy light. The jewels and gold thread stitched into the Syrian silk flashed. A queen must always look like a queen, even when she is far from the land she calls home.

Stripped to the waist, her loyal men toiled at the eight braziers positioned around the walls, their dripping sweat sizzling in the hot coals. She wondered why none of them seemed to feel the chill.

The door creaked open and the Hanged Man crept in. Sometimes Severus looked like an insect, she thought, tall and spindly and dressed in black, his head hanging at that twisted angle from the injury he had suffered so long ago. He'd been loyal enough since he'd accompanied her from Rome, guiding first her beautiful son Corvus and then her as she assumed the mantle of power. But increasingly she felt convinced that he was sucking the life out of her, sucking her blood, this disgusting human insect, sucking her soul . . . She caught herself as her thoughts skittered.

'What news of my daughter?' she demanded.

Severus clasped his hands in front of his chest and bowed his head in deference. Was he scared of her? He should be.

'Our scouts tell us that Queen Catia—'

'Do not call her queen!'

'That . . . your daughter repelled an attack by Irish raiders. She tricked them, hiding her army in the woods until the attackers were drawn on to dry land.'

'Tricked. She is a cunning bitch. Trickery is all she has. Are we strong enough to attack?'

'Not yet. But soon. Our army is powerful. Well armed. Seasoned soldiers, the followers of Mithras who were loyal to your son . . . and a war-band of Pictish mercenaries. We are winning the hearts of the Dumnonii. But we do not yet have the numbers. We have called for more reinforcements, and when . . .'

Gaia fluttered a hand to silence his wittering. Gripping the arms of her grand chair, she levered herself up. Her joints cracked. She was not old, she told herself; it was just this chill sapping the life from her.

Hunching over the nearest brazier, she rubbed the warmth back into her hands. Her eyes watered from the acrid smoke.

This was not what she had dreamed for herself years ago. By now the fight should have been done. Instead of a cold, draughty fortress, she should be sweeping through an opulent palace, the riches piled high in every chamber. Instead of an army of scarred brutes with broken teeth, and breath reeking of raw meat, she should be presiding over elegant courtiers.

Her daughter, her loveless, sly, bitter daughter, had done this to her.

Gaia watched her twisted shadow on the grey stones of the wall, and pushed her chin out until it showed a regal profile. The road had been long, but she survived because she kept walking it, over every obstacle, and soon that long-held dream would emerge from the mists.

How long it seemed since she'd first dreamed it. In the bitter cold of that hard, snow-streaked northern land along the great wall, in Vercovicium in the shadow of the Roman fort guarding the edge of empire. Her life had changed for ever, and she had changed, become golden, when she had been chosen to be the chalice, the mother of the bloodline that would eventually give the world the King Who Will Not Die.

She had been chosen by the powers who shepherded this ideal, by the wood-priests, by the gods themselves. Only her, of all the women who could have been selected. The dragon eating its own tail had been branded into her shoulder. The Ouroboros was the symbol of the bloodline, endless, always resurrected. It was a sign of the life she deserved.

She'd tried to give the powers the heir they needed. Time and again, she'd strangled her daughters at birth. She needed a son, who would grow to be a strong and powerful man. Not a weak woman. And then Catia had been born, and she'd taken this new babe out into the hard winter of the Wilds beyond the Wall, and left her to freeze to death. Days had passed, and the pretence of her grief was hard to maintain.

But then a search party discovered Catia. Still alive, even in that harshest of winters. Nurtured by a she-wolf, and living amongst the pack. Blessed by the gods, everyone said; Catia was the true chosen one, for how could nature have rebelled against itself, if not by the influence of the gods?

And in that moment, the powers that had raised her up turned upon her. She had no choice but to run, with a new protector, her husband's brother, as far from Britannia as she could: to Rome, where she could be safe, and plot to regain what was rightly hers.

Two sons came to her in rapid succession, and one of them had the strength and courage and wisdom to follow the path of the dragon.

Corvus; beautiful Corvus.

Gaia choked back a sob when her son's face floated in the smoke rising from the brazier. How her heart ached for him. Dead and lost, somewhere on the great high moorland. Catia may not have wielded the blade that ended his life, but she might as well have done.

Her daughter had robbed her of the only thing she ever valued: her son.

The days after that loss had been as hard as the winters of her youth. But somehow the Hanged Man had guided her away and navigated a path through her grief. The remnants of the force that had been loyal to Corvus came with her, and they had bided their time once more, plotting, scheming, waiting for the stars to align so that she could reclaim her legacy. She would never leave it in the hands of Catia and her vile offspring!

For now she had another focus for her dreams. A new son, born only days before Corvus was killed.

Her child. Her son's child.

'. . . open the trade routes to the east,' Severus was saying. She hadn't heard a word of it, hadn't even known he was still speaking.

'Arthur!' she cried, like gulls shrieking in a winter sky. 'Arthur!'

A steady step echoed through the silence and the great door of the throne room creaked open.

There he was. Her beautiful son. Corvus reborn in all but name.

Arthur was tall for his age, hair the colour of a raven's wing, eyes like deep wells. When she looked into them, she could never know what he was thinking. He was a mystery to her. The jaw was strong, the cheekbones sharp lines in his pale skin.

'Corvus,' she murmured. 'Corvus.'

She threw her arms wide, and Arthur strode up and buried his face in her breast. His arms clasped each other round her back, as Corvus' had once done, and she folded into him. After a moment of peace, she cupped his face and showered it with kisses. He didn't like it, she was sure, but he never resisted her. She loved him all the more for that.

'You have completed your studies?' she asked.

He nodded. 'Severus is a good teacher.'

'You know why you must learn so much of the world, to become wise, and strong, and just?'

'So I can be king one day.'

Gaia kissed him again on the forehead, long and hard. 'Our destiny rests on your shoulders.'

'Arthur is a good student,' Severus said, 'and he will make a good king, with the blessing of Sol Invictus.'

The boy's lips twitched into a smile.

'You are too serious by far,' she breathed in his ear. 'And your swordplay? Are you growing more skilled?'

'I practise every day, Mother.'

'If only we had that sword of the gods . . . Excalibur . . . the one the Pendragon wielded. Corvus believed it was vital to encourage the people to follow Arthur. No sword . . . no crown. What are we to do?' She heard her voice spiral into a shriek.

Severus flinched, as he always did when her emotions escaped her. 'Come.' He beckoned. 'Come.'

One of the servants hurried to throw a fur cloak over her shoulders as Severus crept through the door and across the hall, still beckoning.

Out on the steps leading down from the grand entrance to her quarters, she winced. The wind cut like knives, even through the fur, and her lungs burned every time she breathed in. Arthur took her hand and gave it a squeeze, as if he could sense her discomfort.

The Hanged Man swept out one hand. Across the terraces down to the walls, her army was in motion. Tossing hay for the horses, warming themselves by stamping their feet by the fires, slaughtering deer on the trestles outside the butchers' shacks, painting their shields. The main gates rumbled open and another war-band rode in, past the bitter smoke belching from the blacksmith's shop where their weapons were forged.

'You have a force here to be reckoned with,' Severus said. 'The people of Britannia recognize power, more now that the army of Rome is leaving these shores by degrees. They will turn to you for protection, crown or sword notwithstanding.'

Gaia looked over the shaven-headed Picts to the loyal, leather-faced legionaries. 'I need more men,' she said. 'So many men that the ground shakes as they march, and people fall to their knees in awe at the terrible sight of them.'

'I have sent word out for more mercenaries.' Severus formed each word with care. 'There are still barbarian war-bands roaming the land, and the Scoti are once more raiding the north and west. But . . . we will need to pay for them.'

Gaia stamped her foot. Their treasure room had once been filled with gold looted in the devastation wreaked by the barbarian horde. But she knew it must be depleting by the day. 'We need more.'

'If we loot the settlements, the people will turn away from you.'

'Mother.' Arthur was tugging at her sleeve. She looked into those dark eyes. 'If we act quickly, all will be well. Don't wait for months or years to build the army. Use all the gold we have now to buy more men and strike before the year is out. Once the false king has been defeated, we will control the trade routes. The people will have no one to turn to but us. Gold will flow into our coffers. In victory, we will have more than we need.'

'See!' Gaia said, shaking her small fist at the Hanged Man. 'This is why Arthur will be king. Already he has more wits than you. But of course, he is Corvus' son. Send out word now. Promise the world. Let the mercenaries flood through our gates—'

'I would urge caution,' Severus interjected. 'It is a risky strategy—'

'Still your tongue! My son has spoken, and his will shall be made real. We will build our army. We will attack the false king before the year is out, and put them all to the sword. My daughter's head will sit upon a spike outside the gates of their western stronghold, while Arthur will snatch up Excalibur, and hold it proudly above his head, and be proclaimed the one true king. And then our bloodline will rule for all time.'

CHAPTER SEVEN

The Storm

LIGHTNING SLASHED THE SKY. A WALL OF BLACK WATER SOARED up to the height of three men. In the white flash, Mato glimpsed faces the colour of bone twisted with terror.

Niall of the Nine Hostages was bellowing some order or other, but the howling gale swallowed his words as it ripped across the deck, threatening to tear those seasoned sailors from their benches and fling them to their deaths.

Mato gripped on for dear life.

The ship reared up, smashed down, spun from prow to stern in a dizzying current. Every man on board must be thinking the same thing: they would be dead long before they even set foot on the island that had haunted all their dreams. Mato muttered a prayer. His stomach surged up into his throat and then fell away. Seawater sluiced around his ankles. The men who were bailing couldn't keep up with the deluge.

The storm had hit on the very last leg of the voyage. The pirate-king had used all his vast skill to steer a course between the gales that blasted the ocean between Britannia and Hibernia, and to navigate the turbulent currents that had dragged many a vessel to the bottom. But in the approach to the island, there was no place to hide.

Mato felt the ship heave almost on to its side. Desperate to see his friends one last time, he scanned the cowering crew. Bellicus' head was pressed almost to his knees. Apullius and Comitinus were huddled together. But Solinus had his head back and was laughing like a madman into the storm.

When Mato saw that, he felt his spirits surge. This was the life he remembered with the Grim Wolves in the Wilds, with death always at their elbow, and them laughing in its face.

Though they could not possibly have heard it, Solinus' laughter seemed to stir the others too. Bellicus pushed his head up and roared. Comitinus and Apullius sat up straight and stared around.

And then the ship crashed back down.

In another white flash, Mato glimpsed Niall standing in the prow. He was drenched, his red hair blasted to his head, his mouth open, bellowing. His finger jabbed aft and Mato swivelled on his bench.

An arc of flame swept back and forth as the fire-pot swung. In the ruddy light he could see the helmsman slumped across the tiller, dazed. Whatever had happened to him, the ship was now at the mercy of the currents.

The vessel tossed and heaved like an unbroken stallion. Without a second thought, Mato threw himself into the seawater swamping the deck. Hand by hand, he clawed his way forward. A gush of brine flooded his mouth. The stern swung up and he scrambled to clutch a bench so he wasn't sent spinning towards the prow. But then he was at the tiller and he heaved himself on to the bench. The helmsman had slumped to the deck, and the bar smashed against Mato's ribs, swung away and smashed back again. The Grim Wolf folded across it and tried to hold it fast, though it fought him like a wild drunk.

He felt a calm settle on him, and for a moment he was sure he could hear his sister whispering in his ear, telling him that he would finally find peace in the Summerlands. In that instant, he looked up. In the glare of another lightning flash, he made out Niall sweeping his arm to one side, and heaved the tiller in that direction. It took all his strength. He braced himself to hold it there, his feet sliding on the slick wood. But hold it he did.

For what seemed like an age, he fought with that wooden bar. His muscles ached; his wits drained away with exhaustion. A world of lashing rain and buffeting wind and constant, sickening movement engulfed him.

And just at the moment when he wondered if he had any strength left to endure it further, he realized his violent battle was almost over. The wind dropped, the crashing thunder rolled away, and the walls of water became little more than ridges. As voices started to rise up out of the departing storm, he slumped across the tiller and smiled at the jubilation of men who had marched past death.

Niall splashed along the deck, barking orders at the bailers to work faster.

'You saved our necks,' he said, reaching Mato. 'That current would have taken us into the heart of the storm. We would now be food for the fish.'

'I thank you for the opportunity to prove myself as a sailor,' Mato croaked. 'Take no offence, but I'd rather crawl through ditches for the rest of my days.'

Niall laughed, but only for a moment. He looked towards the northern horizon, and Mato saw his face darken.

'The storm has pushed us off course,' he said. 'We will not now reach the island by dawn.'

'How much longer till we get there?' Mato asked.

Niall of the Nine Hostages shook his head. 'We won't make landfall before the sun has set.' He hesitated, then added, 'I wouldn't wish to move through that place in the dark, not for all the gold in the world. But we have no choice.'

The low sun carved a ruddy path across the black ocean. *Waveskimmer* ploughed through it, skirting the distant silhouette to an area where Niall of the Nine Hostages hoped they would have a better chance of remaining unseen.

Bellicus stood in the prow, watching the darkening landmass. His stomach still twisted from the torment of the storm, and acid burned his throat. How they'd survived he didn't know. Perhaps the gods really were smiling on them.

Or, as was sometimes the way with gods who liked their sport, they were being saved for a far worse fate.

The setting sun lit enough of the sky to give shape to the island of the Attacotti. Bellicus squinted, making out thick forest and a range of hills close to the southern approach.

'We've sailed round it many times. One day, when we are brave enough, we'll conquer it,' Niall said at his shoulder. 'You want to know the lie of the land?'

Bellicus nodded.

'More than a day's march from end to end, about half a day from west to east. There's another range of hills in the north, and a valley separating the two ranges. One mountain, on a good day high enough to see Hibernia and Britannia from the top, I'd say. In the far north, there's a flat plain. We don't want to get caught there. No cover.'

'And the home of the Attacotti?'

'That's where the danger lies. They could be anywhere in that forest.'

'The valley would be best.'

'I think so. But we can't be sure.'

'We tread with care from here on,' Bellicus muttered. 'I've seen too much of those bastards. Myrrdin was right – you don't want to face them in the dark.' He paused, then added, 'You don't want to face them in the light, either.'

CHAPTER EIGHT

Island of the Dead

THICK CLOUD SWALLOWED THE MOON. BELLICUS SCANNED THE dark bulk before them, but he couldn't see light glimmering anywhere, and when he sniffed the wind all he could smell was brine. Perhaps he'd have more luck once they were on dry land.

As the Grim Wolves lined up to lower themselves over the side of the ship into the rowboat, Comitinus muttered, 'Why does the pirate-king have to come with us?'

'You want that raiding bastard to stay on board so he can sail off and leave us with nothing but the Eaters of the Dead for company?' Solinus rapped the other man's head.

'He's an honourable man.'

'They all are. Until they're not.'

When Bellicus thumped down into the rowboat, it rocked so wildly that Mato had to grip the sides for fear it would tip over.

'Eaters of the Dead ready to make us their dinner, and I'd rather be standing on that island than sitting here,' Bellicus grumbled.

'If there comes a time when you regret saying that, I won't be waiting for you to catch up.' Solinus planted himself on a bench aft.

Apullius lowered himself on to the boards with the elegance that had turned him into the best swordsman in their band. He eased himself next to Mato, and Bellicus thought in that moment how much he reminded him of Lucanus. They could well have been father and son. He'd be a leader one day.

Niall of the Nine Hostages dropped down, finding his balance in an instant like the seasoned sailor he was. He stared into the gloom.

'What do you see?' Comitinus asked.

'Nothing,' Niall replied. 'It's night.'

Solinus sniggered as the raider settled on to a bench and grasped an oar.

'I bought my freedom by agreeing to bring you here,' Niall continued, 'but if things go as badly as I fear, don't think I'll wait to die with you. I've already met my side of the bargain.'

'We'd expect no less,' Bellicus grunted. 'You've been true to your word.'

As they rowed towards the island, Bellicus felt his neck prickle as if there were eyes on him. The Attacotti seemed not of this world, but surely even they couldn't see through the dark. The others, too, held their backs rigid and their heads low, and he sensed the same suffocating apprehension in each.

The oars dipped in rhythm. Not even the slightest splash, nothing to reveal their approach. The night swallowed *Waveskimmer*.

Bellicus found himself yearning for a lamp to keep the dark at bay. He breathed in to still his thumping heart, trying not to recall any of the horrors he had seen the Attacotti inflict.

The pirate steered them around the coast of the island to where he promised a sheltered shingle beach, and soon the swash of the surf rolled out through the night. Niall eased his oar out of the water, and the others followed his lead. Bellicus felt the tide take them in.

Once they were close enough, Niall hissed a soft whistle between his teeth and Bellicus splashed into the shallows beside him. Together, they heaved the rowboat up on to the pebbles.

On the edge of the beach, silhouettes of trees darkened the lighter gloom.

'I'll go first,' Bellicus breathed, his words only just rising above the tinkling of the surf. 'Keep close.'

'And you keep close,' Solinus muttered to Niall. 'You're in our world now. All that dancing across the deck won't serve you here. If you're not careful, you'll be crashing around like a wounded bear.'

Once they'd prowled over slick stones to the edge of the woods, they dug their hands into loam and smeared it all over the exposed parts of their bodies to mask their natural musk among the scents carried far and wide by the strengthening breeze. Bellicus looked round at the pale eyes staring from blackened faces and nodded. They were ready.

One step into the trees and all light fled away. He breathed in the scent of cool, damp vegetation. Droplets of rain pattered on the ground as the breeze brushed the leaves.

'Do we have a plan yet? I'd like a plan,' Solinus muttered, babbling with unease. 'If Lucanus is still alive, where will he be? In the heart of them? How do we get him back? Walk right in and demand they let him come with us?'

'When we find him, we'll see a way.' Bellicus thrust ahead. Things had seemed so much simpler back on the mainland. Here, in the endless dark with death a whisper away, he felt the rising hopelessness. 'We're not going to give up now,' he said, as much to himself as the others.

The ground rose steadily along a twisting rift between dizzying cliffs. The Grim Wolves picked their way over tangled roots as thick as their arms, hauling themselves onward with the aid of low-hanging branches. Niall followed silently. Slick with sweat, Bellicus pulled himself out of the climb and looked across a rolling landscape of wind-blasted grass. In the distance the black bulk of mountains loomed up. The breeze whined in his ears. Still no lights glimmered. They could have been alone in all the world.

Balancing on his haunches, Apullius pointed to the black slash where the valley cut through the island. 'If they're hiding in there, we may find it easier to slip in under cover of the night. Surely they wouldn't place guards on an island in the middle of the vast ocean? Who would dare venture here?'

'I'll tell you who'd venture here,' Solinus said. 'Fools.'

'We shouldn't take any risks,' Comitinus said. 'Skirt the valley. Sniff the air. Take our time until we're sure, then go in and be ready to get out as fast as we can.'

'At least we have the dark to hide us,' Bellicus said.

And at that moment he heard the gods laughing. The clouds

parted and the full moon peeped out, carving their shadows across the silvered grass.

'Do you think we were seen?' Comitinus stuttered.

'Still your tongue and keep running.' Bellicus threw himself through the trees. The branches lashed at his face.

Dropping low, they'd loped across the grassland as fast as they could, hoping that if anyone had seen them under the lamp of the moon they'd have resembled nothing more than fleeting shadows, a trick of the light and the night.

They'd found a copse where they could gather their breath, but they'd been loath to wait in one spot for too long. A sea of bracken gave them some cover until they could reach the trees that edged the valley. Bellicus spied paths there, some worn flat by many feet, and he herded the others away from them. And then they were running again.

A low whistle echoed. Bellicus ground to a halt and looked round. Mato was holding up a hand, the other cupped to his ear, while the moon punched shafts of white light through the canopy among the impenetrable pools of darkness. Then he heard it. A snort, like that of a bull, then another. Something large crashing around in the undergrowth. The crack of branches, the splintering of trunks.

Comitinus' eyes were wide and white.

And then Bellicus' neck prickled and he realized he'd heard something of the kind before. When a low, rumbling roar rolled out, almost lost beneath the moan of the wind in the trees, he felt his heart pound. *Cernunnos, who stands in the forest and howls.* Could it be that great god, part man, part animal, part vegetation, with antlers curving from its head? Why would it be there? What moment of import was it witnessing?

'An ox,' Apullius whispered, 'loose from its pen.'

'Aye,' Bellicus murmured back. 'An ox.'

Time slipped away in that black-and-white world, and for what seemed like an age his head echoed with the pounding of his feet and the pounding of his heart. Every time they came across a well-trodden path, they darted across it as fast as they could, praying that they were moving further away from any Attacotti settlement so that they could find a place to get their bearings.

He sensed the other Grim Wolves fanning out through the trees, keeping low. The hour before dawn, he thought – he prayed – would be a good time to creep closer in search of Lucanus.

And if he is not here? He had no answer for that.

He leapt over a fallen tree, then dropped to his knees, his heart like thunder once again. Something had flickered on the edge of his vision. The others fell too, following his lead.

Framed in a shaft of moonlight among the trees, a figure waited.

Bellicus' fingers hovered halfway to the hilt of his sword. Now he could see it wasn't moving, and that its shoulders twisted at an unnatural angle. Creeping forward, he hunched on the edge of that circle of light and looked up at his predecessor: another stranger, no doubt, who had dared to trespass on the land of the Eaters of the Dead.

The remains hung on a spike, the rotting remnants of a tunic shifting on the night breeze. Dead for a long time, the flesh mostly stripped down to yellowing bones.

'A warning,' Niall of the Nine Hostages muttered at his shoulder.

'Or a marker for the edge of the Attacotti land,' Comitinus said in a low voice, looking over his shoulder.

'A sacrifice to whatever gods they worship,' Mato added.

'More like a warning to us not to be lead-footed bastards,' Solinus grunted.

Bellicus couldn't be sure of the truth. Nor did it matter. He looked round at those seasoned scouts, men who'd stared into the shadowed cowl of death many a time. Despite their impassive faces, he recognized the glimmer of fear in their eyes.

'This place,' Apullius whispered as they moved away, even more cautiously now. 'I'm no longer certain it is of this earth. Perhaps we've already crossed over to the land beyond. A land of daemons and gods—'

'Enough of that talk,' Bellicus snapped. They'd scare themselves into fleeing back to the ship. Only the thought that his friend Lucanus may still be alive in this island of horrors kept him moving forward. And as he crept through the trees, breath burning in his chest, he glimpsed more and more patches of starlight twinkling overhead. The woods were thinning. Eventually they stepped out on to another expanse of high land blasted by the elements.

'Look,' Apullius said, pointing.

Bellicus squinted and thought he could see a blue light shimmering not far away. Perhaps his eyes were playing a trick on him. He couldn't be sure about anything any more. Nevertheless, at a wave of his hand, they marched towards it. Black bulks loomed up on the moon-washed grassland. As he neared, Bellicus realized he was looking at a circle of standing stones.

In the starlight, Mato's face brightened. Bellicus wasn't sure why, but his friend strode on ahead until he was in the circle. He rested a hand on the nearest menhir, almost caressing it. 'Can you feel it?' he said. 'There's peace here.'

The sapphire light was limning the edges of the stones, no doubt a trick of the moonlight playing on some element in the rock surface.

'When I was a boy, I was told these circles were built by the gods themselves.' Apullius' eyes had widened with wonder.

'Or those damned druids,' Solinus said.

'No. The wood-priests became the custodians of these places after the ones who originally raised these stones up,' Mato interjected. 'Myrrdin told me.'

Comitinus trailed his fingers across one of the stones. 'Then those folk were here, on this island. Before the Attacotti? Or are the Attacotti the last of them?'

'I don't like it,' Bellicus said. 'These places smack too much of magic and witchcraft and daemons. As a lad I was told that if you ventured to the one outside Vercovicium on Samhain, you could see the faces of your loved ones who'd gone over to the Summerlands.'

He craned his neck up and peered at the moon, now dropping on its arc. Not long until dawn. 'It's time,' he said. 'We go down into the valley and get ready to make our move.'

He stepped away from the stones.

'Here.' It was Solinus. Bellicus looked back and saw him kicking up mud beyond the edge of the circle.

They gathered around to look down at what he'd unearthed. A skull. The Grim Wolf continued to kick here and there. A thigh bone jabbed up. Shattered ribs. More skulls, eye sockets staring, all of them browned with age. And still Solinus moved on, further from the circle. A spine, another skull, this one unbearably small.

'A pit of bones,' Solinus breathed.

Apullius gaped. 'How many have died?'

'And why bury them here?' asked Comitinus.

'So they pass more easily to the Summerlands.' Mato looked around at the stone circle.

'Or they were sacrifices.' Niall wiped his mouth with the back of his hand. 'To buy the good fortune of the gods for themselves.'

'With this number, the gods must be well and truly on their side by now,' Solinus said.

'I don't like it here,' Comitinus said. 'Let's be away.'

The valley's sides plunged down into the deep dark at a dizzying angle. Bellicus clutched on to a branch to stop himself skidding to the bottom in a heap. Though they all risked breaking their necks, it was the best route. They were unlikely to cross any more well-used paths.

The trees were crushed together here, a jumble of trunks and low branches and twisting roots. Only intermittent shafts of moonlight broke through the cover. The Grim Wolves eased silently down, used as they were to creeping through the Wilds. But every now and then Niall of the Nine Hostages would crunch a dry branch underfoot and they would all freeze, hearts pounding. Each time, Bellicus cocked his head, desperately trying to pick the slightest sound from the whistle of the wind in the high branches. Sweat soaked his tunic.

Finally the valley side began to level off. He rested one arm against a tree and breathed in. There it was. The first sign, the merest hint of smoke from a hearth-fire. They were getting close.

He made the faintest exhalation as a warning, knowing the

others would hear it, and then, dropping low, he crept past a tangle of bramble to the valley floor. Sure enough, he saw the compacted mud of a track there, the ruts shadow-streams in a strip of moonlight.

A hand fell on his shoulder and he jerked. Mato crouched beside him, eyes darting. 'Something is out there, brother,' he whispered.

Bellicus searched the dark. 'That ox? Or whatever it was?'

'I saw movement, but heard nothing.'

Bellicus' breath burned in his chest. He knew what that meant. For a moment, he peered into the gloom. Mato's eyes had always been better than his, though. He crept to the edge of the track.

'Go down there and we'll be in clear sight,' Solinus muttered.

'Stay in the trees and we won't be able to move fast,' Apullius countered.

Mato scanned the shadows. After a moment, he whispered, 'Make your choice. We should move.'

Bellicus threw himself along the edge of the track, praying there was just enough dark to keep them hidden. The others loped behind him. As he ran, his senses tingled. Movement on both sides now. Fleeting shapes, darker than the shrouding gloom. His eyes darted this way and that. At first only a few flashed past. A moment later, he shuddered. The whole valley seemed to be seething with silent activity, as fluid and fast as a hunting wolf pack.

'Faster,' Solinus urged. 'Faster.'

Bellicus hurled himself on. But then he glimpsed one of the predators caught in a shaft of moonlight, and the rush of horrific memories threatened to dash his wits away. In the ash-smeared torso, he saw only the dead flesh of something that had clawed its way out of the grave. The face was turned towards him, the black-ringed eyes and hollow cheeks a death's head.

And in that look, he saw only his doom.

The Eaters of the Dead were upon them.

CHAPTER NINE

The Wild Hunt

'STAND AND FIGHT!' SOLINUS BELLOWED. 'THAT'S OUR ONLY hope!'

'Are you mad?' Comitinus exclaimed. 'They'll swamp us in the blink of an eye!'

Mato raced on along the muddy track. The other Grim Wolves and Niall tried to keep up, but they didn't have his legs and they were flagging. The Attacotti were herding them, he realized, presumably driving them towards their settlement or trying to exhaust them so they'd offer no resistance when the time came. But his eyes were better than the others' too, and now he could make out faint movement ahead. They were being forced into a trap.

'Bellicus, draw your sword and follow my lead,' he yelled.

He threw himself away from the track, plunging into the tangled mass of holly and oak and ash. He heard the others crash into the vegetation behind him. At least in that deep dark under the canopy, they were equals.

A ghastly figure loomed in front of him. The Attacotti hunter lunged, but Bellicus was there. He rammed his sword into Mato's attacker and ripped up. As the enemy convulsed, Bellicus slammed his shoulder into the dying man and flung him back into the ones racing close behind.

'Confusion is our friend,' Mato shouted.

The others seemed to understand. He glimpsed blades glinting in the moonlight, slashing and stabbing. He heard the cries of the wounded and dying and prayed none of them were his friends as he smashed his way through the undergrowth with his staff, trusting in the others to protect his back.

Keep going, he thought. *Cut through their lines. It's the only hope.*

Ducking under a low branch, he rolled across a fallen tree, throwing himself on, and then up the valley side with no regard for what lay ahead. Gradually, the cries died away, and soon he was surrounded only by the gasps of men fighting to climb on weary legs. He sank his fingers into loam and clawed his way up a near-sheer face. The silence behind was terrifying. He couldn't tell if the Attacotti were breathing on his neck or if they'd left the Eaters of the Dead behind.

It was the silence of death, always at their heels.

How he clambered over the lip of the valley side still in one piece, he didn't know. But then he felt the cool sea breeze on his face and he was racing with the others across grassland punctured here and there by slabs of brown rock.

'Back to the boat,' Niall insisted. 'If we can row away, we live to return another day.'

'You think I'll be coming back?' Solinus said.

'Still your tongue,' Apullius snapped. 'We are here for Lucanus. Never forget that.'

'He's dead, you mad fucker. You saw them. You know there's no chance of him surviving that. We're just doing this out of duty, and now our duty is done.'

'No!' Apullius shouted. His voice cracked. 'We're not going to give up on him!'

Mato bounded across the grassland, trying to get his bearings. They'd been turned around so much he wasn't sure where the cove was. The dark was beginning to grey. Soon the sun would be up, and however much he had hated the night on that island, he knew the day wouldn't be any better.

'Don't look back,' Comitinus cried.

They all looked back.

The Attacotti were swarming out of the trees at the top of the grassland. Mato felt queasy. So many, as if an ant hill had been disturbed. Feet whisked across the ground. So fast, so relentless, seemingly tireless. He heard a grunt and a crash. He glanced back and saw that Niall had stumbled. Without missing a step, Comitinus and Apullius hooked hands under his arms and wrenched him onward.

Behind them, the row of silent, white hunters formed a crescent, the two horns growing.

The dark began to fade. Mato picked out a track through the grass, perhaps a cliff edge in the distance. Behind, the horde's left flank was sweeping in.

Bellicus cursed and plunged off the track. The others followed.

A seam of silver gleamed on the horizon.

Mato squinted, looking along the edge of the land. A line of cliffs. If he remembered the chart Niall had shown him, the drop ended on rocks. Little chance of surviving a plunge, not like that shipwrecked sailor who had escaped the Attacotti's feast.

'They're driving us towards those cliffs,' Bellicus shouted. He'd seen it too. 'Death above or death below.'

'Wait,' Mato called. He squinted again, trying to pick detail out of the grey smudge. The sun clipped the eastern horizon and the shadows lengthened. 'There.' A line in the grass ran into a cleft between two rocky outcroppings, perhaps a path that led down to the shore.

Mato pushed his head down and sprinted towards it. Now he thought he could feel the ground shake with the rumble of the feet at their backs. Darting between the rocks, he skidded to the edge and peered down. He'd been right. A narrow path wound to the crashing surf where the cliff had crumbled into an easier descent.

Solinus whooped. 'Pale-skinned bastards thought they had us.'

'We can swim round the coast from here,' Niall panted.

Mato clambered over the fallen rocks and picked his way along the winding path. All around, the gulls were screeching and the air tasted of salt.

'Faster,' Comitinus called from the back. 'They're nearly here.'

'I don't want to die from a broken neck.' Bellicus heaved his bulk over the treacherous rocks.

Across the cliff face and back they went, creeping steadily downwards.

Mato felt his neck prickling and looked up. Along the edge of the cliffs, white faces peered down at them.

'Why aren't they following?' Apullius asked.

Mato stiffened. Leaning out over a rock, he looked down to the surf smashing across the shore, where figures were gradually appearing out of the receding gloom. A band of Attacotti warriors formed at the foot of the path, axes hanging at their sides.

Mato felt his stomach knot. The Grim Wolves and Niall juddered to a halt.

'They herded us into a trap,' Bellicus muttered.

They'd been too naive, that was clear now. The Attacotti were cunning, used to driving prey to its doom.

'What do we do?' Comitinus asked fearfully.

'Can't go up, can't go down,' Solinus said. 'Can't stay here.' He crawled to the edge of a rock and sat, looking along the shore. Mato knew that he was thinking of throwing himself off. Better to be dashed on the rocks than torn apart and consumed while still alive by the Eaters of the Dead.

'Here.' The voice rang out, weak and somehow muffled.

Mato looked across the jumble of rocks and saw that Apullius had crawled to one side and had pushed his head down low. Examining something. While the others looked up and down, down and up, trying to make an impossible choice, Mato pulled his way over to the youngest Grim Wolf.

A spring gushed out from beneath an overhanging rock. Apullius had his head pressed in beside the stream of glittering water. 'There's a space behind,' he said, his voice echoing back. 'A channel, just big enough for a man. It could lead nowhere . . .' he pulled his head out and looked at Mato, 'but it's all we have.'

Mato had to agree.

The others clambered over and hovered by the opening.

'Might as well crawl into our own grave,' Solinus said. His voice was low, edged with fear.

'You'd rather die at the hands of the Attacotti?' Comitinus asked.

After a long moment, Solinus replied. 'Crawling in there . . . getting stuck . . . not being able to move forward or back . . .' He choked back whatever he was going to say next, then wiped the back of his hand across his mouth.

'You'll get in there if I have to ram you in myself,' Bellicus snarled. He looked up and Mato followed his gaze. The Attacotti were moving on to the cliff path.

'No time to stand here talking,' Niall said. 'Who goes first?'

'You're mad,' Solinus insisted. 'It might go in for a man's length and then we're done.'

'It's all we have,' Apullius repeated.

Solinus glared at him, and then closed his eyes in weary acceptance. 'You're bastards and I hate you all.'

'I'll go first,' Mato said.

'You're only saying that because you're afraid Bellicus and the pirate will block the way with their big shoulders,' Solinus grumbled.

Mato pushed his way past him. He felt the freezing spring water splashing on his back, and then he was dragging himself into the reek of earth and the deep dark.

CHAPTER TEN

The Underworld

E CHOES RANG AROUND HIM, LOW MOANS AND CHOKED GRUM-
bles as the other Grim Wolves clawed their way into the
narrow channel behind him. Mato thought he could almost smell
the dread. For men who lived their lives under open skies, this
was the greatest fear.

His nose flooded with the stink of earth and wet rock. Endless
gloom lay ahead. He couldn't tell if the tunnel would close up,
trapping him there, or if he would suddenly find himself plunging into a dizzying drop.

What if there was no way out?

What if they became jammed there, unable to move forward
or back, as Solinus had feared, choking on thin air and dying
slowly amid their screams? What if the storm came back and the
channel flooded and their lungs filled with water and they
drowned? What if they kept descending deeper and deeper into
the earth, down to the underworld where Arawn ruled over the
dead with his pack of red-and-white wish-hounds?

Mato swallowed, calming himself by force of will. The others
were relying on him. 'All is well,' he called back, pushing the
tremor out of his voice. 'There is a way here.'

The moans ebbed. That was good. Flat on his belly, Mato
dragged himself along. The tunnel roof scraped the top of his
head. Barely a hand's width lay on either side. Solinus had been
right – Bellicus and Niall would struggle to force themselves

through. The channel dipped down. He swallowed again. *Don't think about having to back up.* Slow and steady would do it.

A strangled cry echoed from behind him. 'What's wrong?' he called, and heard his words fly from lips to lips along the chain of desperate men. The cry bounced back, mounting in intensity.

'The Attacotti are coming,' Comitinus cried at his heels. 'They're crawling into the tunnel. Faster! Faster!'

Mato imagined the terror whoever was at the rear must now be feeling, waiting for hands to clasp his ankles, dragging him back towards his doom. Throwing caution to the wind, he pulled himself down the incline as fast as he could go. If he pitched into a dizzying drop, so be it. His life meant nothing.

His knees and elbows burned. His fingertips felt slick. Blood. Still he hauled himself on, one hand after the other in rapid succession. The ceiling of the channel pressed down, scraping his back. It was growing narrower. As was his throat. He heard his breath wheeze. His lungs cried out for air.

His forehead bumped into rock, and for a moment he thought with a wash of terror that the channel had reached its end. But then he felt a hollow. Reaching under, his fingers groped around until he realized the tunnel dipped beneath a tooth of stone protruding from the ceiling. His back would not bend enough to get under it.

'Stay calm, brothers,' he called back, swallowing hard. 'I must go slowly here.'

There was only one way to proceed. Squeezing his shoulders tight, he forced himself to turn on to his back. Blood rushed to his head as he lowered it into the hollow and pushed himself down. Driving his feet into the rock, he wriggled under the fang. He pressed, and he pressed, bent almost double, and somehow he felt himself slide up until the ground beneath him flattened out once more.

His eyes stung with tears of relief and he rolled on to his belly again. Once he'd called back instructions to the others, he closed his ears to their anguished cries and dragged himself on.

What else could he do? There was no going back now.

★

His thoughts floated in the dark. He couldn't tell if his eyes were shut or open, but faces of those long gone floated in front of him. Were they warning him? Welcoming him to the Otherworld?

His sister was there, smiling, and he felt his heart leap. Once again he was cradling her bloody body, tears burning his cheeks in that moment when his life changed for ever. She seemed to be saying something to him, but then she was gone and there was only the dark again.

Mato jolted to his senses and realized he could no longer feel the rock against his back, and when he rocked from side to side he couldn't feel the walls of the channel. He called back to the others and he felt his heart sing at their jubilation.

The tunnel was now big enough for him to crawl on his hands and knees. Fire raged through his joints, but still it felt good. On he went, faster now. A beacon of hope glowed. Yet barely had he crawled on a spear's length when his hands plunged into icy water. He could not feel the bottom.

'What is it?' Comitinus whispered. The echoes rustled all around.

'The tunnel ahead is flooded.' The other Grim Wolf began to whimper. 'It may only be for a short way,' Mato urged him.

'But how can you know? You could dive down and your breath be gone before you reach the end of it. And if you reach the far side, how will we know?'

Mato heard the panic crack in his friend's voice and he reached back a comforting hand to grasp Comitinus' arm. 'I'll come back to tell you.'

'And if you don't return? What then for us?'

'You don't have to worry about that.' Solinus' voice rang through the dark. 'Because I'll have choked you to death to end your fucking whining.'

'All we can do is put our faith in the gods, brother. We are in their hands now. And if they decide this is the time we pass through the gate into the Land of Endless Summer, so be it.'

Mato couldn't tell if his words soothed the other man or not. It didn't matter. Steeling himself, he sucked in a huge breath of air and dived down before his fears prevented him.

The water thrust daggers of ice into his head. Fumbling along the walls of the tunnel, he pulled himself onward. He felt his back grind against the roof, but on he went, kicking out, knowing the channel was too narrow to swim.

And on.

And on.

He felt his lungs begin to burn. His mouth wanted to open in a desperate need for breath, but that would be the end of him. *You are a dead man*, a voice in his head whispered.

Darkness and cold.

And then he realized there was no stone above him and he thrust up, bursting out into the air with such a gasp it burned his throat raw.

He pulled himself out on to the tunnel floor and lay there, shuddering and gulping air as if he could never get enough of it. His wits seeped back and he looked up. His skin prickled: a current of warmer air was washing over him.

Mato grinned the grin of a man who'd been saved the moment before the executioner's axe came down.

How he made the hellish journey back to the others he didn't know, but soon they were all slumped in the warm tunnel, calming themselves.

'I'd rather face a thousand barbarian swords than suffer that again.' Bellicus' words floated in the dark. Mato imagined him with his head hanging, his sodden hair dripping between his legs.

'How close were the Attacotti behind?' Comitinus asked.

'Close.' One word, but Apullius, who had brought up the rear, sounded haunted, Mato thought. 'They fell back when we crawled under that tooth of rock.'

'Feel that warm air, brothers. Let it soothe you. If that can get in, we may follow it to find a way out.'

'And then what?' Niall asked. 'You've lost the element of surprise. If we do get out of here in one piece, we shouldn't tempt the Fates any more. Sail away. Flee. Never return.'

'And disappoint Catia, and Weylyn?' Bellicus' voice was low. 'I wouldn't be able to look them in the eye.'

'You're mad, all of you,' Niall said, his voice crackling with anger. 'I vowed to bring you here, but—'

'Let's get out of here first,' Mato interjected to suck out the poison. 'Then we can turn to tearing each other's throats out.' Before anyone could respond, he crawled away.

The tunnel dipped and rose, but Mato felt sure that overall it was moving up. Towards the light, he prayed. And sure enough after a while the dark seeped into grey, the walls and floor and ceiling taking shape.

When the roof soared high enough over his head, Mato pushed himself upright and stepped into a cave illuminated by a shaft of light. The opening, at the end of a short walk over jumbled rocks, was edged with grass and dangling ivy, and beyond it was the blue sky he'd thought he would never see again.

A few minutes later, in the centre of the cave, Bellicus reached his arms out wide and threw his head back. Niall laughed, and Apullius and Comitinus clapped each other on the shoulder. Solinus, though, was prowling into the depths of the cavern.

'Have you not had enough of the dark, brother?' Mato asked with a laugh.

Solinus glanced back and there was no humour in his face. 'Look here.'

Mounds of rocks lay side by side in rows. Some of them were decorated with flowers that had become arid husks, and trinkets, and goblets. Two more had bronze swords lying on them.

'Graves,' Solinus muttered.

'And well cared for,' Apullius added.

During the early days of their arrival in the west, Mato had heard Lucanus talk about the day he had spent as a prisoner of the Attacotti. The experience had left his friend baffled. These were monsters that consumed human flesh, yet they loved and sang and prayed to their gods. What was their true nature? Lucanus had never been sure.

'Can they be all bad if they grieve for their dead?' Apullius asked.

'Ask them that when they're chewing on your foot,' Solinus snapped. He spun back to the light. 'Let's be away. I'm sick of thinking about those bastards.' He clambered over the rocks and disappeared into the light.

Close behind him, Mato felt his eyes ache from the glare. Stumbling into the fresh air, he smiled and breathed deep.

'Bollocks.'

Mato blinked, letting his eyes focus. Solinus was standing in front of him, staring.

A band of Attacotti warriors waited in a crescent in front of the cave entrance. They stared back, coal eyes unblinking, swords already in their hands.

'The bastards knew where the tunnel opened out,' Solinus said, his voice flat.

They'd only delayed the inevitable.

The sky and the grass and the trees blurred by. Mato spun this way and that, rough hands grasping his arms as he was propelled in the churning centre of the Attacotti. His brothers were caught up in that mad confusion too, still alive for now. Their curses and oaths rang in his ears.

Those white faces whirled all around him, holding him in the grip of their black, staring eyes. He could see no compassion in their depths, no emotion at all. Their features told no tales, nor hinted at any feelings. Not anger, not contempt, not jubilation. Nothing. As flat and unstirred as a millpond. Somehow that was worse. His nostrils flared at their meaty musk and the reek of the loam that caked them. It smelled like graves.

Someone fought to break free; Bellicus, he thought. Sword hilts cracked down on his skull and then rained down on all of them. His wits flew, and the rest of the journey seemed like a rush through the approach to hell: those faces looming in and out of relief, that oppressive stink, the constant motion, and what sounded like the keening cry of lost souls.

After a while, he realized it was the sound of the Attacotti singing. Inhuman, rising and falling, mere noise that somehow still managed to pluck a wave of dank fear from the depths of him.

Once the pace slowed, rough hands hurled him to the muddy track. When he looked up, he saw they were on the edge of a settlement. Wooden huts tumbled away from him along the floor of the valley and up both sides. A pall of smoke from the hearth-fires

hung over the roofs. More Attacotti were flooding out of the door-
ways. Old men, women with babes, children. Unlike the silent
warriors, they erupted in a wild clamour. Baying for blood, Mato
thought. Another blow from a hilt cracked against his temple and
his wits flew away.

When he came round a moment later, he tasted soil in his
mouth. His thoughts fluttered, his vision fractured. Faces flashed
by. Those unearthly cries swallowed him. He felt himself lifted
up, dragged along, as if he were caught in a storm at sea. Except
that the wind was dragging him along a street now lined with the
Eaters of the Dead.

That was how it would end: ripped apart and consumed while
still alive.

But then he crashed to the ground once again. Silence fell,
eerie after the tumult. He sensed the Attacotti had come to a halt
in a half-circle at his back.

When he pushed himself up from the trampled mud, he stared
into the dark maw of a hall. He marvelled at its size, grander than
the surrounding shacks, timbers soaring up to support a roof
covered with turf, and walls of wattle and daub. They'd thought
these barbarians little more than wild beasts. But to construct
this hall took skill, and care.

His fellow Grim Wolves sprawled beside him, rubbing their
knocks and bruises. Mato looked at their faces. Features were
drawn, stares hanging in the middle distance as they watched the
horrors parading across their minds. He wanted to tell them that
this would all pass, but he knew it would do no good.

'They want us to go inside,' Apullius breathed.

Comitinus bowed his head. 'Is this their feasting hall?'

Niall was craning his neck up, scanning the towering struc-
ture. 'This is the hall of a king, mark my words.'

Mato followed the pirate's stare and had to agree, given the
way the Attacotti hung back, too, and bowed their heads as if in
deference.

Bellicus stood up, closed his eyes and raised his face to the sun.
For a moment, he drank in what might be his last taste of that
warmth, and then he said, 'If they want us to meet their king, so

be it. But I won't grovel.' The leader of the Grim Wolves strode to the entrance and waited for the others to join him.

As they gathered before the door, Mato glanced back at the Attacotti. They were watching in silence. None of the warriors were venturing forward. He frowned. 'They are sending us in to meet their king. Five of us. Yet they don't fear we'll attack him?'

'There're probably guards aplenty waiting inside,' Solinus grumbled.

But a light glowed in Comitinus' eyes. 'This king . . . could it be . . . ?'

Mato barely dared consider it. 'That would explain why there was no need for guards.'

'What are you two fools talking about?' Solinus said. But then Mato watched realization fall on him too, and his eyes suddenly brightened.

'We'll know soon enough.' Mato even heard hope in Bellicus' low rumble. The leader of the Grim Wolves stepped into the dark. The others followed.

Two torches guttered inside the door, the only light in the place. Mato blinked, letting his eyes adjust to the gloom after the glare of the sun. The ruddy glow wavered towards the centre of the vast space. It seemed empty, as far as he could tell, and as silent as a temple.

Was that a low moan? A whisper? He cocked his head, but only quiet followed. Bellicus stepped into the half-light.

As they moved across the packed mud of the floor, Mato's nostrils wrinkled. He smelled the pitch of the torches, and something like rotting vegetation. Behind that, though, he caught a hint of sweat. 'We're not alone,' he said, squinting into the gloom. Now he could make out a wooden throne at the far end of the hall. As he watched, he thought he could see a figure hunched in it.

'Fetch a torch,' Bellicus ordered.

Apullius raced back to the door and pulled one of the torches off the wall. The dark swooped away as he stalked back to the tight cluster of Grim Wolves. The red light picked out the throne, ornately carved with dragons along the back and the arm rests. The seated figure huddled inside a cloak, and as the glow of the torch played out Mato gasped. This was no cloak for a barbarian king. Gold thread glowed in an intricate spiral design along the edge, a fine piece of workmanship. But there was more to it than that.

'That is Lucanus' cloak,' Apullius gasped. 'The one Myrrdin gave to him, the one the wood-priests wore for their rituals.'

Mato swallowed. Still he couldn't bring himself to believe that his old friend survived.

The figure shifted underneath the cloak, as if the occupant of the throne had been sleeping and the new arrivals had disturbed him.

'If one man could beat the odds and end up ruling this bunch of misbegotten bastards, it would be Lucanus,' Solinus said.

'Lucanus!' Comitinus called out, unable to restrain himself any longer. They all ran forward.

The king jumped from his throne and whirled towards them, the cloak billowing out. 'Wyyvvvgggaaahh!' he cried.

Mato didn't know what he was seeing. His mind had prepared him for Lucanus, but this . . .

The king leapt forward and then scurried away, spinning and crying out as he whirled around the hall. The Grim Wolves pressed back in horror. 'Abbbthhhhbbbb!' cried the king.

Beneath the flowing cloak, he was short and twisted, a hunchback. The face too was distorted, one eye large and wide and higher than the other, swollen lips dripping drool from a mouth that seemed to hold only one misshapen tooth.

'An idiot,' Solinus said, gaping. 'A mad idiot. This is their king?'

The malformed barbarian scurried behind the throne and peered out at them, whimpering. Mato felt his blood run cold. 'He wears Lucanus' cloak.' The meaning behind those words drove them all to silence.

'All of it for nothing,' Bellicus growled after a moment. Mato felt a pang in his heart at the desolation he heard in those words. Surely they had been in hell from the moment they'd set foot on this island.

CHAPTER ELEVEN

Three

Tintagel

L IGHTS BOBBED IN THE VAST OCEAN OF NIGHT. THE TORCHES winked as the search party weaved among the trees along the valley running up from the cove. Every now and then a cry soared above the crashing of the surf on the shingle. Catia would lean out over the ramparts, stiffening with desperate hope, only to sag back when another disconsolate call came a moment later.

Amarina breathed in the scents of the sea and for a moment thought of sailing away into the west without a backward glance.

'Why does he torment me so?' Catia gripped the ramparts until her knuckles were white in the amber glow of the torch.

'He's a boy. It's his job to torment his mother,' Amarina replied. Weylyn had been missing since first light, when his bed had been found empty.

Catia glared at her. 'How can your heart be so cold? All these years, you've never softened.'

'There's no gain in being soft. Survival, that's what this life is about.'

The steady click of wood on stone rolled nearer, and Amarina watched Myrrdin ease out of the shadows, leaning on his staff. He locked eyes with her, a greeting of a kind, she supposed. But they were like competing species. They would never find common ground.

'You're his teacher and guide,' Catia spat at the wood-priest. 'Where is he?'

Amarina studied the worry etched into the queen's face and wondered what it was like to care so much about someone.

'You know he's not forgiven you for stopping him joining the search for his father.'

'My fault, then?'

'His hurt burns. He feels powerless. And like all young men, he wants to claw back some of that power.'

'*All* men,' Amarina stressed.

'Besides,' Myrrdin continued, 'we have other concerns. Soldiers are deserting our army. We're losing support among the Dumnonii. The myth told by the false king is growing more powerful—'

'There's no fairness in that,' Amarina interjected, turning up her nose. 'We've proved time and again that the true bloodline lies here.'

'Fairness means nothing,' Myrrdin said. 'Whoever tells the strongest story wins.'

Catia jabbed a finger at the druid. 'Why so relaxed, wood-priest? You've twisted lives and brought misery to plenty with your plot to bring the King Who Will Not Die into this world. You would have killed us all in our sleep if it meant Weylyn could survive and the royal bloodline flourish. And now you care not a jot if he's eaten by wolves . . . or . . . or taken by the false king's army and put to the sword.'

She choked back her feelings. She'd already lost one son – Marcus, murdered by his own father – and a husband she loved. That had loaded all her desperation on to Weylyn's shoulders, Amarina knew. Bad for the boy, bad for Catia. It would sour things between them if left to flourish.

'I have my spies out there too.' Myrrdin's low voice rumbled. 'The false king's army is far from these walls. They wouldn't risk a conflict, not yet, not until they've decided the time is right. And as to wolves . . . I know a woman who was taken in by a wolf-pack as a babe and survived that experience. Indeed, she prospered.'

Catia narrowed her eyes, but before she could respond Myrrdin continued, 'That is different? I think not. The great Wolf

Spirit has always protected you and your kin – that's why he brought Lucanus into your life. And he will protect Weylyn too.' He leaned in, his eyes pools of shadow. 'Have more faith in your son. I've been at his elbow as he's grown. He has the heart of his father, and the courage, and the determination. He carries the destiny of the King Who Will Not Die for a reason.'

'And you'd simply let him run away into the night in the hope that one day he comes to his senses and returns before misfortune can strike?'

'If he doesn't want to be found, your lumbering, lead-footed soldiers will not uncover him.' Myrrdin eyed Amarina. 'There are others out there who move like ghosts through the trees, see all, hear all, but leave no trace in their passing.'

'The forest folk?' Catia asked.

The wood-priest didn't respond, but Amarina knew what he meant.

Unable to contain her frustration, Catia marched away from them into the dark of the fortress.

'It must turn a blade in your gut that you don't have the power you so desperately want, wood-priest.'

Myrrdin smiled. 'The battle for power is sometimes subtle, moon maid. Often it's the one who whispers in the ear or guides with only a gentle touch who wields true influence. But then you know that.'

'I have no desire for influence.' Amarina turned away to follow in the footsteps of the queen. 'I have said it a thousand times and everyone refuses to believe me. All I want is survival.'

As she walked down the steep, winding path from the gates, Amarina could hear the call and response of the guards still echoing in the valley. Myrrdin was right. They'd get nowhere. Weylyn would be listening to the cacophony and laughing as he skipped in the opposite direction.

And Myrrdin had been right on one other matter – oh, how she hated thinking that. There were others who would know better where the lad had gone.

The moon hung high over the treetops, casting deep shadows

across the bright landscape. She picked her way along the track leading up from the cove to the high headland. In the woods beyond, she found one of the secret paths marked by the way-stones carved with the head of Cernunnos. The face made of leaves and ivy stared at her out of the granite. Most would have thought it a track beaten by the woodland animals. She knew better. She trudged along it, deeper into the dark heart of the forest, where the vegetation was so thick as to be almost impassable, and the trees clustered hard together. Most were wise enough not to venture here, not even hunters pursuing a stag.

When she heard a gentle clacking carried by the breeze moaning through the branches, she knew she'd reached the right place. Overhead, a shaft of moonlight picked out the gently turning charm, twigs bound together in an intersecting square and circle with the skulls of birds hanging beneath on leather thongs. They rattled together in the swaying motion.

'Sisters,' she called. She would have lit the torch that was planted on the edge of the moonlit clearing, but she didn't want to draw the attention of the searching guards. After a moment, she called again, louder this time. 'Sisters.'

Her neck prickled long before she glimpsed movement deep in the trees. Shadows shifted, darker than their surroundings, drawing closer. Three approached. Three, the number that symbolized all there was.

Heaven, earth and the waters.

Body, soul and spirit.

The beginning, the middle and the end.

Darkness fell away like a cloak being shucked off and the women stepped into the circle of moonlight. The Hecatae had arrived and Amarina felt her skin turn to gooseflesh as it had the very first night she'd encountered them, that time when she thought her life was over.

One was young, one matronly, one like a wind-blasted tree clinging to a moor. All were naked, their bodies caked with mud and swirls of charcoal that masked them in the woods. Where that covering cracked, Amarina could see spiral tattoos. Their hair was wild and clotted with ivy and leaves, so that when they turned their gaze on her it was as though she were looking into the face of Cernunnos.

The youngest one crouched like a wolf ready to pounce. 'Sister,' she said. A smile spread across her lips, somehow both seductive and threatening. 'You have news for us.'

Amarina winced. Yes, she would do all she needed to to survive, but she still felt guilt at betraying Catia and the others. For years now, she'd travelled to this place to pass on all the information she gleaned in the chambers of the fortress, the comings and goings, the movements of the army, the latest trade arrangements, and most of all how Weylyn was growing into the king he was intended to be under the tutelage of the wood-priest.

Quite what the Hecatae did with the news she passed on to them she wasn't sure. Perhaps she simply didn't want to consider it. But that was the bargain she'd reached with them long ago. That was the lot she had chosen for her life. Traitor, queen of deceit, who could never have friends, could never forge bonds. Who would live alone until the end of her days. But they would never have survived the journey into the west, through this daemon-haunted land, if she had not made that choice.

'No news this time, sisters,' she said.

'No news of a ship sailing into the western sea to try to bring a man back from the dead?' That smile.

Amarina shuddered. 'That is no secret. All know of what transpired. I would not waste your time with idle gossip about things that are on every tongue.'

The crone cackled. 'Then if you are not here to tell us things, you are here to ask.'

She nodded. 'But I have nothing left to give you in return.'

'Every mortal has something to give,' the mother said.

Amarina shuddered again.

'I've given you years of service. I ask for only one thing—'

'The whereabouts of the young king. The True King.' The youngest shook with a silent laugh.

'You know?'

'We know all, we see all, we hear all, sister. The wind that whines through the great forest brings all to us.'

'Is he—'

'He is well.'

'The boy is curious, as all boys are.' The mother walked to the edge of the clearing. 'He has learned there is a world beyond the fields in which he once played. And he has learned he can bend that world to his will, should he try. He does not have to dance to his mother's tune any longer. All boys, all girls, learn this, and this is his time.'

Amarina licked her dry lips. 'In the fortress, everyone is afraid he'll walk into danger. As boys exploring this new world are often wont to do.'

'Aye, danger.' The oldest cackled again. 'Danger lies everywhere. The world is full of traps for the unwary.'

'Three, there are.' The youngest prowled around the moonlit circle, flashing feral glances at Amarina. 'Three who would lay claim to the bloodline of the King Who Will Not Die, where all power lies in days yet to come.'

'The queen's boy Weylyn is one, born of the union of the wolf-sister and the Pendragon,' the mother added.

'Arthur is one, the false king, son of a madman and a mad woman, one who betrayed all for her own gain.'

Amarina watched thunder roil across the features of the youngest as she spoke of Arthur's parents. But then she softened, and smiled, and this time her smile had all the light of the moon. 'And the third is a girl, for why should not the King Who Will Not Die be instead the Queen Who Will Not Die? We weave these stories out of the threads of fate. Nothing is fixed. Everything is fluid. And words are silver magic that can change all destinies.'

'The girl is your daughter,' Amarina said to the mother.

'Sprung from my loins and the seed of the Pendragon, stolen from him while he flew with the owls to the edge of the Land of Endless Summer.'

Amarina looked around the three women, her thoughts racing. Had Lucanus ever mentioned to Catia that Weylyn had a half-sister?

'Her name is Hecate. But her name is also Morgen, for she is sea-born, and she sails between this world and the Other, where the source of all stories and all magic lies. And her daughter will be called Morgen, and her daughter's daughter, for this is the way the threads bind the years. The crows guide her, and the Morrigan is with her always, as she is with her father.'

The Morrigan, Amarina thought. *The Phantom Queen, the goddess of war, and death, the red and the black.*

Her racing thoughts fell into relief and a wave of cold washed over her. 'You would kill Weylyn to seize power?'

'Murder? Sometimes a gentle touch is all it takes. Sometimes a whisper.'

Amarina stiffened. These were almost the same words that Myrrdin had uttered to her. Perhaps the Hecatae truly did hear all.

'The men of Rome will leave these shores soon enough,' the youngest continued. 'They are already drifting away in their ships, seeing their empire crumble around their ears. And what will be left here in Britannia? Why, an age of darkness, and an emptiness to be filled. Three powers face each other to decide the course of Britannia into days yet to come. Three. Yet the one who sits upon the throne may not be the winner.'

The Hecatae were talking in riddles again, as they often did. Amarina shook her head. This meant nothing to her life. 'All I want is to find the boy and take him safely home.'

'Why do you care about him?' The crone leaned forward, her eyes wide and white.

'Catia has already lost one son. I would not see her lose another.'

'Why do you care?'

Amarina showed a cold face. This was not a question she was prepared to answer, perhaps not even to herself. 'Where is he?'

For a moment, she thought she'd offended them. Silence hung hard over the clearing. Then the youngest of the witches pointed away into the dark. 'Follow the *ignis fatuus*, sister. See the strands that are being drawn.'

Among the trees, a blue flame danced. It was moving slowly away.

The Hecatae were already retreating into the night. Amarina flashed one last look at the three women who cupped her life in their hands, and then she stepped away from the moonlight and into the dark.

Before the flickering flame came to a halt, she heard voices caught on the breeze. One was Weylyn, the musical notes captured from Myrrdin underpinned by the harder tones of his father and mother.

The other was a girl.

Amarina slowed her step. The light too had come to a halt, and as she passed it she saw one of the forest folk hunched by an ash tree, his hair and beard so wild, his skin so mud-stained and his tattered clothes so filthy that he was one with the trees and the vegetation. From his raised right claw hung an ornate brass lantern of a kind Amarina had never seen before. A dragon appeared to be curling round the top, and the blue flame flickered within it.

The light glimmered in the man's eyes as he stared at her, hard and unwavering, and then he nodded into the dark ahead.

Amarina pushed past a towering holly bush and saw another moonlit clearing ahead. Weylyn sat cross-legged in the centre, his mouth hanging slightly open, his eyes dreamy, almost hypnotized.

He was watching a girl dance with slow, assured steps around him. Her precise movements were almost a ritual, Amarina thought. The girl was naked, the same age as Weylyn, her long blonde hair flying with each movement of her head. But she was caked in the same mud and charcoal as the Hecatae, the same tattoos swirling across any skin that was visible.

'Will you tell me your name?' Weylyn breathed, entranced. 'I beg you.'

'One day my name will be Hecate,' the girl replied with her mother's smile.

'You speak in riddles, always.'

The girl bowed deeply before him, her hair sweeping the ground. When she raised her head, she whispered, 'For now you can call me Morgen. I am sea-born.'

'Morgen,' the lad repeated as if it were a spell.

'We are tied together for all time.' The girl spun into another dance, throwing her hands towards the moon.

'How? I've never met you before this night.'

'I will teach you things of which you never dared dream,' she continued, ignoring his question.

Amarina thought the girl sounded much older than her years. And when she caught sight of the fire in those dark eyes, she thought the young witch seemed far, far older still, as old as the crone.

'I have a teacher, but . . . I would listen to you,' Weylyn said with a nod. 'I like to learn new things.'

Morgen smiled. 'New things. Aye, new things there will be aplenty.'

'Where do you come from?'

'I live under the moon, in a world beyond the edge of what you see. In my world there are daemons, and spirits, and the gods speak to us. In my world there is—'

'Magic,' Weylyn exclaimed.

'Aye. Magic,' the girl replied with a shrug, as if this were the most normal thing ever. 'Magic shapes all worlds. No swords are needed. No bloodshed. Only whispers and nudges. Prayers and spells.' Morgen cupped a hand to her ear as if she could hear someone speaking to her. 'Those who live in the Otherworld will have their say in what happens in this one in days yet to come.'

Amarina sucked in a deep breath to steel herself and stepped forward. This was only a girl, not the Hecatae, and yet she felt wary none the less.

When she saw the new arrival, Morgen glared and crouched like a wolf ready to pounce, her fingers clawed and her teeth bared.

'Your mother waits for you,' Amarina said, standing her ground.

The child cast a glance at Weylyn, one that seemed to hunger, Amarina thought, and then she slunk away into the dark.

'Your mother waits for you too,' Amarina told the boy. 'Enough of these games. Be the man your father would have wished you to be.'

This seemed to sting him as Amarina had intended and he jerked to his feet. But as they walked back towards the fortress, he glanced back and said in a voice that was still edged with dreaminess, 'I've found a new friend.'

CHAPTER TWELVE

The King of the Dead

RED SKY BURNED BEHIND THE STARK SILHOUETTES OF THE branches. Though jubilant birdsong soared over the home of the Attacotti, Bellicus found himself only able to think of the stink of rot that choked him every time he breathed in.

His head rang with the echoes of the last beating. Barbs of fire seared his joints where his arms had been bound too tightly behind his back. With his head pressed against the mud of the floor, he stared out of the gaping doorway at the tranquil scene. In the Wilds, he loved morns like this. He'd taken all of them for granted, he knew that now, for he'd believed there would always be another bright dawn.

This was to be his last. Now he wanted to drink in every sight and sound.

But that reek! The charnel house was next to their prison hut. He'd seen the piles of bones as the Grim Wolves had been herded past, heard the *whick-whick-whick* of small knives cleaning off the last of the flesh.

The Eaters of the Dead lived every day with one foot in the grave.

'Are you awake?' Niall's lilting voice rolled out through the shadows at his back.

'I am now, you bastard,' Solinus grumbled.

'Aye,' Bellicus replied. 'I slept as soundly as if I was in my bed at home.'

'You'll be sleeping soundly for the rest of eternity soon enough,' Solinus said.

Bellicus rolled over and heaved himself into a sitting position. The truth was, his night had been filled with terrors. He could feel the sweat trickling down his back and the clamminess of his tunic. But he would never tell the others that. He looked round at the other five shapes, slowly taking on form and detail as the ruddy light of their last dawn leaked through the doorway. At least he would die with his brothers. He couldn't ask for more.

It was warm enough already. The rest of the day would be a furnace – what part of it he would see.

'We knew it would come sooner or later,' he said.

'But this way!' Comitinus' voice cracked. 'All the battles we've fought. All the enemies we've had at our heels, to go this way! There's no justice.'

'Or the gods have seen fit to punish us.' Apullius sat up and leaned back against the wattle wall.

'We were mad to come here,' Comitinus went on. Solinus kicked out at him.

'Mad, aye, but honourable,' Niall of the Nine Hostages said. 'Lesser men would have found some excuse not to travel to this foul place. But you did it for the love of your friend Lucanus, and the love of your queen. Men like you, you had no choice.'

They fell silent for a long moment. Too much honesty stung.

'Though I can't say I'll ever forgive you for bringing me with you,' Niall added after a while. 'When we get to the Land of End-less Summer, I'll kick your arse every morning and twice at night.'

'Will they bleed us?' Comitinus asked. 'Will they roast us alive? Will they feed on us as we lie in their hall?'

Mysteries. That's all there was in this place. Bellicus watched the sky grow rosy, trying to force from his mind the image of the mewling idiot-king gambolling around his hall. What did it mean, to be led by someone like that? Was he the twisted product of some poisoned bloodline? Did they choose him? He was not fit to guide anyone, that was certain.

What gods did they worship? Why did they consume the dead, when there was food aplenty? Those strange, soaring songs that sounded like birds at feast. The silence that hung over them like a shroud when they fought. No oaths, no battle-cries. And yet they loved their families and honoured their dead. There was no sense in the world.

Apullius shuffled beside him. 'What are you thinking about?'

'Catulus.'

'Your dog?'

'Do dogs run through fields in the Summerlands?'

'All that you want you'll find there, so Myrrdin says, and he knows these things. You'll see Catulus again.'

For a moment, Bellicus felt a pang of regret for all the mistakes he'd made, and a desperate yearning for peace. He pushed it aside. Life was good as long as you didn't weaken.

Voices echoed through the stillness of the dawn. Whatever peace there was in the world outside was already gone. Bellicus cocked his head, picking out the cries of children, the greetings of women emerging into the first light. The grunts of men came next, the whole merging into a hubbub of excitement.

It began to draw their way.

'This is it,' Mato said. He'd been sitting to one side, his head bowed as if in prayer.

'Keep the fire in your hearts, brothers,' Bellicus said, his voice rising to thunder, 'and we will meet again in the Summerlands and we will drink wine and ale until we drown in our cups.'

The clamour crashed around their hut, and then a band of white-crusted Attacotti warriors surged in, grabbing them and hauling them out into the light. Bellicus thrashed with his shoulders and kicked out, roaring a curse on all their hides. A hilt cracked against his temple and he crashed to his knees. As he fought to hold on to his wits, those rough hands grabbed him again and he was flying away.

Buffeted by the surging crowd, he glimpsed the lines of shacks blur by, and then they were in the woods once more. Oak and ash and holly flashed by, branches criss-crossing a sky turning blue. On to a narrow track plunging away from the settlement, into the dense, dark heart of the woods. Over a glinting stream, past a rock hunched like a sleeping bear, the din never subsiding even for a moment. It seemed as though everyone in that settlement had come to witness his final moment.

And then the pace slowed. Bellicus glimpsed two towering yew trees ahead, knotted with age. The narrow track passed between them. His whirling thoughts half remembered something Myrrdin had said about a gate formed by twin yews, but it was whisked away before he could catch it.

All the excited tumult vanished in an instant as the branches of the yews swept by overhead, and then there was only birdsong. Bellicus felt his skin prickle at the eeriness of the quiet after the deafening clamour of the excited crowd.

They came to a halt. The hands pulled away from him and he pushed himself up. Mato stepped to his right elbow and Apullius to his left. He sensed the others breathing heavily at his back.

'What is that place?' Apullius breathed.

Ahead of them, in the deep shade of the greenwood, was a building that looked as if it had been thrust from the earth itself, as ancient as those mighty yews. Rocks had been piled up around the base, green with lichen and sprouting fern. Branches and turf formed the roof. The entrance was a jagged slash like the mouth of a cave.

Bellicus' gaze flickered towards what lay all around. Skulls, a mountain of them, piled up by the walls, tumbling away into the undergrowth, some brown and shattered with age, others gleaming as white as if they had been picked clean only the previous day. Two spikes guarded the path to the entrance, and on the top of them were heads, the eyes mere black holes that still seemed to peer into his soul, the cheekbones protruding through the fraying remnants of leathery skin.

No one spoke.

For a moment, the crowd waited soundlessly. One of the Attacotti stepped forward. He was festooned with necklaces of bones – perhaps a priest, Bellicus thought. He stared into the dark maw of the building and uttered five words in that strange, rolling tongue. A spell, it sounded like, or a prayer.

The echoes died away. Bellicus stared, feeling his chest tighten, unsure what was to happen next. And then he glimpsed movement in the darkness of the entrance, and a figure lurched out into the light.

Bellicus squinted into a dazzling ray of light that carved through the canopy of the woods over the figure's head, almost as if the gods had blinded him so he would not lay eyes upon this Attacotti recluse. But then he shifted to one side, and as his vision came into focus he felt his heart begin to pound.

'Could it be?' he heard Mato breathe beside him.

The man was tall and slender, his hair and beard as wild as those of the forest folk, though the cheeks beneath were gaunt and the eyes hollow. His tunic and leggings were little more than filthy rags, and a cloak hung from his thin shoulders that seemed to have been patched together from the remnants of many other cloaks. Yet even through the grimy trappings, Bellicus could see the man he had known since he was a boy.

'Lucanus?' he whispered, a question becoming realization that ended with a jubilant 'Lucanus!'

As his long-lost brother turned that gaze upon him, he felt his joy wash away in an icy deluge. The eyes were like deep pits in a frozen land, and in them Bellicus could glimpse no recognition. Indeed, he thought, they looked like the eyes of that idiot-king in the great hall, devoid of wits, tinged with the madness of the Wilds.

'What's wrong with him?' Apullius cried, the words filled with a terrible chill. His joy at seeing the man who had been like a father to him was cracking by the moment.

The Attacotti priest swept one hand out towards the captives. His display ended with a strange cacophony of shrieking sounds.

Lucanus stepped between the two severed heads and peered down at the men he once knew better than any other. Bellicus watched that cold gaze sweep across them, focusing on each in turn, and then Lucanus seemed to reach some conclusion. He turned to the warrior-priest and flicked back the patchwork cloak.

Comitinus gasped. Bellicus reeled.

Lucanus' left arm was missing. The stump at the shoulder was tied in a filthy rag.

In that moment, Bellicus understood the source of the madness, perhaps the reason for those lost wits. Was this how Lucanus had survived among the Eaters of the Dead for so long? He was not consumed in one great feast, an old king giving up his powers to these hellish people in a ritual that was as old as time. No, they would draw on those powers for as long as they could, take small sips from the cup.

Bellicus felt sickened. What magic did they use to keep his friend alive? What agonies must he have suffered? And then he looked into his brother's eyes, and all thought fled.

Lucanus levelled that terrifying stare at them one more time and said, 'They are worthless. The secrets of this place must be kept close. Kill them all.'

CHAPTER THIRTEEN

The Labyrinth

BELLICUS FLUNG HIMSELF FORWARD AND STARED DEEP INTO his friend's eyes. 'Wake yourself from this madness,' he commanded. 'Remember Catia, your wife. She's waiting for you. Remember your son, Weylyn.'

A tumult exploded at his back. When Bellicus heard the cries of the other Grim Wolves, he realized they were trying to block their captors from reaching him. He had only a moment.

'This pouch, at my hip,' he urged. 'Take it.'

Lucanus' eyes flickered down.

'In there . . . a token from your wife. A token that shows all Catia's love for you. Don't abandon her, brother. She needs you more than ever.'

Hands gripped his arms and wrenched him back. He spun to the ground, blows raining down. Those ashen faces blocked out the sky, black-ringed eyes staring down, unblinking, until darkness swallowed him.

When he awoke, he breathed in the familiar reek of rot. He was in the hut again, the *whick-whick-whick* of tiny blades echoing from the charnel house.

Solinus' voice rolled out. 'Thought you were dead.'

Bellicus eased himself up, blinking away the lances of pain in his skull. The others sat around, heads hung low.

'Nothing can kill him,' Apullius said after a while.

'Not even the Attacotti,' Comitinus added. 'Lucanus is the King Who Will Not Die.'

'He fucking killed us, though, didn't he?' Solinus grumbled. 'Could have said no, no, set them free. I remember having a drink with them in the tavern in Vercovicium, but no. Die, you bastards. That's all the thanks we get for being loyal.'

'What happened to him?' Apullius asked.

Mato heaved himself to his feet. 'What man could survive among the Attacotti and keep both hands on their sanity?'

Niall of the Nine Hostages grunted. 'Well, I was right. You have to give me that.'

'Little good it does us,' Solinus said. 'We were lured here on a promise, only for all that hope to turn to shit. As usual.'

'Lucanus is pretending,' Apullius said, forcing desperate hope into his voice. 'The only way he could live among the Attacotti was to act as if he was an ally. A great leader from a different tribe who could counsel them. That was the bargain he made. When he saw us, he couldn't do anything to save us then and there. He'll be cunning – that's the Lucanus we all know. He'll find a way to save us.'

Bellicus stared at the young Grim Wolf. 'I looked into his eyes. The Lucanus we once knew is long gone.' He turned away as he saw the despair rise in Apullius' face; it was too painful to watch. 'False hope won't help us.'

A grim silence fell across the hut, broken only by the endless *whick-whick-whick* from the charnel house that whispered of their coming doom.

And yet for all his words, he still felt a spark of hope deep inside him. A wish. A prayer. At this point, nothing more. But it was all he had.

The pouch that he had carried at his hip was missing.

There is a labyrinth, and at the end, in the dark, awaits a monster.

Lucanus closed his eyes and stepped into the maze. He'd been venturing into the winding tunnels ever since he was a boy and his father had first told him the tale. He'd never dared reach the end. The terror had always gripped him when he'd heard the low rumble of breath and the snorts in the gloom, and he'd fled back into waking.

Lucanus. That was his name. It felt odd when he turned it over. The name of a stranger. The name of a man who once had a life, and a love, and friends, and had walked a hard road but found peace. There was no monster waiting for that man.

Lucanus, the Wolf.

His stomach knotted when he remembered it.

A step into the dark. Then another. Acid rose in his throat as the dread wrapped its arms around him.

His fingertips crumpled the soft blue ribbon, and he raised it to his nose, breathing in the faintest scent of perfume. A rush of sensations followed, of a kiss in the dark, and a hand in his, warm breath upon his ear and words that gave him the strength to keep going when his legs wanted to fall away beneath him. The delirium of a soaring heart.

Too much.

He yanked the ribbon away. The dark was better. On he went, blindly, a turn here, another there. Lost in the labyrinth.

A soft padding whispered ahead. He flinched, but this was not the monster. Out of the dark prowled an old wolf, silver-backed with age. It came to a halt, staring at him with luminous eyes, and he recognized it instantly. This was the majestic beast he had killed in the bitter cold of the Wilds beyond the wall near Vercovicium, that night of ritual when he had moved from being a boy to becoming one of the Grim Wolves. It had sacrificed itself for him, and he had drawn its spirit inside, so he could gain its powers. Just as the Attacotti did.

The old king must die so the new king can rise. That was always the way. And a good king always offered himself willingly to the great, never-ending cycle of existence.

'Your time is not yet done, Lucanus,' the wolf said. 'The Pendragon, the great war-leader of the Britons, is needed.'

'Lucanus is dead,' Lucanus said.

He turned away, down another path, to avoid the judgement he saw in those eyes.

As he walked, memories surfaced, and he realized he had been here not long ago, that night in Goibniu's Smithy, when Myrrdin had fed him the ritual mushrooms and invited him to meet the gods. And he had. Cernunnos, and the Morrigan, her beauty and ferocity driving him to the edge of madness. The Morrigan had warned him how his end would come. But there was honour in it, and sacrifice for his loved ones, and he was not to be afraid.

More footsteps, tiny ones, running. Braided blonde hair flying, a laughing girl raced out of the dark from a side tunnel, pausing briefly to stare at him before continuing on her way. It was Catia, he remembered now. From that time when they first ran together in the fields of the north, when they were truly happy and he realized he loved her and would love her for all time. The simple views of a child. And yet there was truth in it.

In the dark ahead, the monster rumbled and paced, snorting hot breath. He felt dread knot his chest and he wanted to flee back.

Around the next corner, Myrrdin waited, leaning on his staff. On his open hand, a mushroom. Such a small thing, but it allowed a man to speak to the gods. Used by the followers of the Christ, and Mithras, and Jupiter, and Cernunnos, by all priests since the earliest days, so the wood-priest had said. This was one of the secrets the druids kept.

Myrrdin snapped his fingers shut, and when he opened them again, the mushroom was gone. Of course. He must have eaten it, as he had eaten one of the ritual fungi every day since he had walked out of Tintagel and into the long night with the Attacotti. They had fed it to him as part of their ritual, as they fed.

Without the mushroom, he would have gone mad, he was sure of it.

His nostrils flared at the sense-memory of the bitter unguents they had smeared on his vanishing arm, that had somehow kept the rot at bay, and the foul potions they had forced across his cracked lips to keep him alive when other men would have long since given up the spark.

He could not remember this. He could not.

Other figures came and went in the dark, some he barely recognized. Old friends, old enemies, many who had long since sailed across the western sea to the Summerlands.

Lucanus sensed the next visitor long before he saw him. Perhaps it was a familiar musk, though how he could remember it after so many years he didn't know. But when he rounded a corner his father was waiting for him, as he had known he would be.

'Are you really here?' Lucanus asked.

'Aye,' Lucanus the Elder lied. He had died long, long ago when he had vanished into the Wilds, Lucanus knew that. And yet he felt troubled by one thing. His father's tunic and leggings were smeared green from a life in the forest, and he rested one hand on the hilt of a broadsword, the tip touching the stone of the floor. Under his arm was tucked a familiar helmet, twin eyelets and a slit down to the chin with sides that reached to the jawline. The last time he had seen it, it was being worn by the Lord of the Greenwood, the servant of Cernunnos, who moved among the forest folk, far from the eyes of civilized men.

'I've missed you, Father.'

'We'll be together soon enough, as we once were. For now, I have a message for you. Your work is not yet done.'

Lucanus' shoulders sagged and he felt a bone-weariness flood him.

'You've walked the edge of the great black ocean, and you've stood at the gates of the Land of Endless Summer,' his father continued in the rough tones of the north, 'but a light has been lit in your home, calling you back. The work is not yet done, my son. The dragon has not yet risen. And all that you've fought for stands to be lost if you don't return.'

'What use is a one-armed man?'

'Are you man or are you Wolf?' His father's voice crackled, and Lucanus felt a pang of fear as he had when he was a boy and heard that tone. But then the older man softened, and Lucanus saw a sad affection gleam in his eyes. 'Your sacrifice will not go unnoticed. For Catia. For Weylyn. For Britannia.'

He stepped to one side and swung out a huge arm. When

Lucanus eased past him, his father disappeared as if into a dream, and then there was only the dark ahead summoning him.

The snorting and snuffling echoed louder, the thump of hooves upon stone beating like a war-drum. His heart pounded to the same rhythm.

And then he came to the chamber at the end of the labyrinth, and he paused at the doorway for only an instant. At first he thought the room was empty. But then he blinked and realized a figure hunched in one corner.

This was no monster. It was only a withered husk of a man, muttering and drooling in his madness, his hair and beard wild, his eyes like nail-heads.

He only had one arm.

Soon after, Lucanus heaved himself up from the dank floor of the place that had been his home for so long and lurched to the doorway. Blinking, he peered out into the day.

The sun was bright and the sky was blue and his friends were dying.

With each step through the forest, memories burst like bubbles in a marsh. They hadn't yet fed him the mushrooms that day, and the seductive grasp of the ritual fungi was loose. His stump drove fiery spikes into his shoulder. That, too, helped clear his head. The birdsong swirled around him, heard and felt for the first time in an age, and he blinked away tears.

The work is not yet done.

When he reached the settlement of the Attacotti, the folk stared at him, but none attempted to block his way. Why would they? He was elevated above all others in that tribe. More than a man. A source of power, a connection to the endless, crackling blue fire of the dragon eating its own tail, the Ouroboros, which was gifted by the gods.

'Where are they?' he muttered. Then, raging, 'Where are they?' and as if through a fog he realized he sounded like a ranting madman.

Eventually, he stumbled towards the Sacrifice Hall next to the charnel house. When he saw the Attacotti gathered at the door in their ritual bone necklaces, their tiny knives in hand, he felt his stomach tighten. Praying he wasn't too late, he thrust his way through the knot of ashen men.

In a shaft of sunlight, the Grim Wolves and one tall, red-headed stranger sat cross-legged as if they were resting after a hard day. He searched those faces and felt his heart rise. Not a trace of fear was etched there, although they must know what terrible fate awaited them. Lesser men would have been crawling and gibbering and begging for mercy they knew could never be.

Shock twisted their blank features when they saw him.

'Come to join the feast?' Solinus said.

'Leave us,' Lucanus mumbled to the clustering Attacotti priests. Black, unblinking eyes weighed on him. 'Leave us,' he insisted. 'My judgement was wrong.'

After a moment, the priests ebbed away, but not before he had snatched one of those small blades.

'Fuck me,' Solinus said, incredulous. 'Are you their king now?'

Lucanus lurched into the hut and moved around his friends, sawing through their bonds. 'When you were brought to my . . . to me,' he began, 'my wits were gone. I didn't recognize you. I'm still not the man I was . . . I may never be again . . . but I won't let you suffer here as—' He swallowed his words.

'Your arm . . .' Bellicus began. Lucanus shook his head, too hard, and his friend clamped his mouth shut.

Once he was free, Apullius hugged the man he considered a father. Lucanus felt hot tears soaking through his tunic. He stood there for a moment, his good arm clasped to his side, trying to comprehend his feelings as though he were a countryman watching a ship from a clifftop. It had been so long since he'd felt anything.

The mist of the mushrooms drifted further and Lucanus felt as if sunlight were shafting not only in that hut, but through the greyness of his mind. Memories formed like fields and trees emerging from the dark into a dawn landscape. Memories that he hadn't examined for longer than he could remember, because the pain of staring at them directly would have been too great. All his life was there, all but forgotten for so long. Feelings surged with such strength that he feared they might dash his wits away. All that had been lost, all the love and the dreams and the worries, all the scents of spring flowers and damp groves and sweet wine, all of it rushing back to him.

And then he looked around him and he jolted. His friends, whom he knew and loved as much as any kin. He gaped at lines in faces he couldn't recall, and silver in hair. But they were there! Not a dream. Not some mushroom-induced vision. His brothers.

Lucanus stared at the Grim Wolves, and they stared back, no doubt wondering if he was mad, from the intensity of his attention, or his wild-eyed, giddy-with-feeling expression. And as that rush of euphoria passed, he felt stab after stab of pain. That his friends could all die here, in this isle of horrors. That he had lost so much in the years since he'd been spirited away. He'd felt nothing for so long, and now he thought he might die from all the agonies being inflicted on him at once.

Eventually Apullius fell away, looking up at him. 'You're alive,' he croaked.

After a fashion. But he approximated a smile and nodded.

When he came to the red-headed man, he frowned.

'My name is Niall of the Nine Hostages,' the broad-shouldered man said. 'Soon, if the gods are willing and we can ever leave this foul place, I'll be king of Hibernia. From one king to another, I give my greetings.' He paused and gave a lopsided grin. 'Your wife is a fine woman, and a frightening one. I wouldn't be here if not for her, and if not for me your friends wouldn't be here, and you'd still be dying slowly in a hut in the woods.'

Catia. Lucanus staggered back and Apullius lunged to save him from falling. *Catia.*

Once again he was swept up by that turbulent ocean. Tears burned his eyes and his heart felt as cold as ice. From the moment he agreed to this hellish situation to protect the people he loved from an unimaginable end, he'd forced down all thoughts of the life he'd had before, did his best to forget he even had a wife, or a son. It was the only way he could cope with the pain of never seeing them again.

But now their familiar faces were rising out of the dark cave of his head, old memories of their time together, old feelings, rich with meaning. Catia was there, as if they'd never been separated, and his son, Weylyn. He swallowed, sickened by how much he'd been forced to sacrifice to save them. He turned away before the others could see his emotion.

'Why have you jolt-heads risked your necks to come here?' he asked.

'A fine way to talk to friends,' Mato said.

'You owe me money,' Solinus added. 'You bastard.'

Comitinus sniffed. 'We were sick of doing your daily chores for you.'

Despite their words, Lucanus could hear their stifled feelings in their strained voices. He turned to Bellicus. 'You're the only one I'll get any sense out of.'

Bellicus cracked his knuckles, but Lucanus could feel his gaze upon him as if he, Lucanus, were a stranger to this friend who'd been as close as a brother. 'There is a false king challenging Catia and Weylyn's right to the royal bloodline.'

'Corvus' bastard?'

Bellicus nodded. 'He's drawn an army to him. The Dumnonii are already drifting to his side. That means other folk across Britannia will be doing the same. The battle hasn't been won, much as we hoped it had. War is coming. As it now stands, we're going to lose, and badly. We need a leader, someone who can rally what few men we have and draw others to our standard.'

'And no one else can do this?'

'You're the Pendragon. That means something. You think you're just a man, but to people back there in Britannia you came from the gods, with your magic sword. You can never die, that's what they say in all the villages. You'll return in the darkest hour to save them all.'

Just as Myrrdin intended, Lucanus thought. The wood-priest had told him that a good story was more powerful than any truth. 'If I abandon the Attacotti, they'll come for all of you. That's the deal Myrrdin made with them.'

He watched the shock rise in their faces, shading to fury. Only Mato hung his head. He had known, or suspected.

'The bastard,' Solinus said.

'Don't blame him,' Lucanus continued. 'We were fighting for our very lives—'

'For his plot,' Apullius spat. 'He'd sacrifice all of us to win this great game the druids have been playing for so long.'

'Nevertheless,' Lucanus said, 'the wood-priest did what he had to do in that moment.'

'Then we're trapped with no way to turn,' Bellicus said. 'If we can't take you back with us, the false king wins. And if he wins, they won't let Catia and Weylyn live, you know that.'

Lucanus sagged down to his haunches. But he was not broken. He refused to be. The others fell silent, watching him, waiting for his response, as they had so many times in the past.

'I want to see my wife and son again.' And he did. He felt that more powerfully than he had felt anything in a long time, a deep yearning that reached far into his soul.

'Your monstrous brethren won't let us go, or you,' Niall said.

Lucanus stared ahead, through the wall, across the great ocean, to Britannia. Now other memories were surfacing, this time of the man he used to be. The fire flickered back to life in his belly. He would find a way to save his brothers from the horrors of this island. He would scheme, he would bargain with the Attacotti, he would find a way to get them all home. And then . . . ? That was for another time.

'I am Lucanus Pendragon,' he said, his voice hardening with each syllable. 'The great war-leader of Britannia. And I will not be defeated.'

CHAPTER FOURTEEN

The Cauldron

A T NIGHT, THE FORTRESS AT TINTAGEL WAS A PLACE OF GHOSTS. The constant pounding of the waves thrummed through the thick stone walls like a heartbeat, and the scent of candle-smoke drifted through the still chambers. For Catia, that aroma ignited memories of the past. From the corner of her eye, she caught sight of those who were long gone: her father, broken by her mother's cruel machinations; her son, Marcus, his neck snapped by her weak, unmourned first husband. Others, who had brought so much light and life to Vercovicium before the barbarians had invaded.

Would they ever return to those glorious days of peace and plenty? Now life was a constant battle against the fading of the light, and the relentless drawing in of this dark age. She'd received word that morning of more ships sailing from Britannia's south coast, taking with them Roman soldiers to be deployed elsewhere.

Some said the empire was crumbling fast. And when Rome was finally gone from these shores, what then? Was it the long night that the wood-priests had prophesied? Starvation? Sickness? Murder? The breakdown of all the civilization that had thrived in Britannia for so long?

Who could stand against that?

Catia breathed in deeply, feeling the weight of responsibility on her shoulders. Who would ever have thought the wolf-sister who ran through the fields of the north was one of the few who was prepared to stand and fight. The Fates were strange and cruel.

Now she understood why the druids had crafted their plan for the King Who Will Not Die. The folk of Britannia needed hope, even if it was a fantasy for children. And she would do all in her power to keep that story alive.

Her feet whispered on the flagstones. She might have been alone in all the world. Her court slept. Her army slept. A few men walked the walls, peering into the night, but that was all. And her closest friends were far, far away and might never return.

Catia hovered at the door of her son's chamber. Taking care to ensure the wavering lamplight washed only to the foot of his bed, she was relieved to hear his steady breathing. Since he'd run off into the woods, they'd fought time and again. He had a fire in him that would serve him well in the hard years that lay ahead. At least he'd stayed close enough to keep the fears of a frightened mother at bay.

As she pulled back, she heard an echo deep in the fortress. The merest sound, gone in an instant. The clink of iron on stone, she thought.

Others might have dismissed it. A night watchman doing his rounds. Myrrdin casting bones in his cauldron. But she'd slept under the stars, her chest tight as enemies crept closer, trying to slit her throat. She'd long since learned that nothing could be ignored. And others might have called for one of their guards. She never entertained the thought.

Holding the lantern high, she strode through the ringing silence of the fortress towards where she thought the sound had originated. The dark swirled around that circle of light. Though she held her breath, she couldn't hear any other noise.

Just as she started to convince herself she'd been mistaken, her nostrils flared. A new aroma floated through the familiar smells of dust and wood, and stone and candlewax. She breathed in the scent of the forest, of leaf mould and lichen and loam. The heavy reek hung in the chamber, so strong that whoever had brought it with them could only have departed a moment earlier.

Her neck prickled. She had no bow, no sword.

Slowing her step, she moved into the throne room. The moment she crossed the threshold, Catia smelled sweat, just the faintest hint beneath the woodland odour.

'Who's there?' she called.

Her words rang out in the silence. Though no response came, she felt the odd sensation that someone was watching her, that that person was grinning, though how she might know that she had no idea.

She stepped further into the chamber. The moon hung in one of the windows. Catia looked into the stark shadows beyond the path of white light.

Empty.

'Catia.'

She jerked at the voice, her heart thundering. Only then did she realize that a figure waited in the dark in one corner, so still it could have been a statue.

Catia swung her lantern and the sweep of light revealed a war-rior who at first glance seemed to be surrounded by an emerald glow. A helmet obscured most of the face, what was visible through the slit mere shadow. A cloak and tunic were smeared with green from life in the Wilds. One hand rested on the hilt of a short sword in the sheath at his belt.

'You,' she said, but the moment the word left her lips she realized this was not the Lord of the Greenwood that she remem-bered. His shoulders were not as broad, and his body was slender, not a muscular form hardened by a brutal existence. And then he shifted his stance, and his cloak fell open, and she saw his with-ered right arm hanging limply at his side.

'Aelius?' she gasped.

'Greetings, sister.'

Catia stiffened at the voice, which a part of her felt had come from beyond the grave. Her words were swallowed by a rush of emotions, shock giving way to an overwhelming relief that her brother was alive, then anger that he had deceived her.

'How could you be so cruel? I thought you were dead. One day you were here in the fortress, the next you had vanished. We searched for weeks. I thought you'd been eaten by wolves. All that grief, for naught.'

'I had no choice. There are deeper currents dragging us along here. You know that. At times we're little more than flotsam.'

She heard the regret in his voice, and softened. Tears streamed from where they'd been locked away for so long and she dashed forward and flung her arms around him, burying her head in his shoulder. But as she breathed in his scent, she couldn't discern any of the Aelius she knew, only that heavy, dank smell of vegetation and clay.

He wrapped his arms around her too, but awkwardly, the embrace of someone who had had little human contact for a long time.

Catia felt her thoughts rushing back across the years. They'd been so close as children in Vercovicium, driven together by their harsh family environment. Gaia had had no time and little love for the boy from the moment she saw his deformed arm. In their mother's eyes, he would always be less than a man, not worthy of any care. But Catia had leapt in to fill that void with love, and she'd defended Aelius from the bullies who tormented him in the settlement. In turn, her brother had always fought ferociously for her too. He'd read widely and become more learned than almost anyone she knew. A scholar and a wit. A good man with a big heart. And now?

Shortly after their arrival in Tintagel, Aelius had vanished and her heart had broken. The mystery of his disappearance had haunted her ever since. Now she could see the first glimmers of the truth.

She stepped back and held up the lamp so she could see the light reflected in his eyes. 'You're no warrior.'

'The Lord of the Greenwood you met is dead. Who he really was, I'll never know. But there was a champion of Cernunnos before him, and there will be another after me. It is one of those strands that bind what is long gone to days yet to come. A responsibility that cannot be refused.'

Catia narrowed her eyes. Some note in his voice told her that if he had refused that responsibility he wouldn't be here now. More of the same, then. Lives that meant nothing beyond their parts in a greater plot.

Aelius held out his good arm, and when he spoke, his words were laced with the humour she remembered and loved. 'Sadly, I'm only half a man and couldn't wield the traditional blade handed down to those who take up this role.' The long sword, she remembered, so large she would have had trouble lifting it, and she was no weak woman. 'But one makes do.'

She heard no bitterness in his voice. That was a good thing. For too long Aelius had found solace in the bottom of a goblet to avoid the harsh treatment that had always been inflicted on him because of his withered arm.

'Why here?' she said. 'Why now, after so long?'

The concealing helmet dropped a little, and though she could no longer see her brother's eyes, Catia felt his change of mood.

'The season is turning again,' he said. 'And this time there will be a final battle to end all battles.' He paused, choosing his words. 'The gods have stepped aside, for now, as should I. Whoever wins this war – the followers of Weylyn, or those of Arthur – will have earned the right to lay claim to all the glorious hopes of days yet to come. The losers will be crushed down into the mud, forgotten. Only strength, and a cold, relentless desire for victory, will see us through the dark days to come. That is the thinking as I hear it, deep in the forest. But I couldn't stand by, Catia. I couldn't. You, Weylyn, you're my blood, my heart. You're all that matters to me, and I would freely give up my own life if I could save you from what's to come.'

'We know of the false king's threat.'

'You're not aware how quickly time is running out for you.' An edge appeared in his voice. 'The army of Arthur is growing by the day. The whispers I hear as I move about the land tell me how fast you are losing the support of the folk you'll need if your line is to usher in the golden age that we all pray for. Everything rides on your shoulders. I hate the fact that once again you're carrying this burden, but it can't be denied.'

For the second time, she wondered if she should have killed Gaia and Arthur that terrible, blood-soaked night on the high moor. But she was who she was, and she couldn't sacrifice that identity, not when she'd nurtured its flame through so many years of hardship.

'The Grim Wolves are searching for Lucanus. If he is still alive—'

'You can't wait for them to return.'

'With the crown missing, and the druids – or most of them – dead, Myrrdin insists we need to find the cauldron of the Dagda if we're to convince the people to follow us.' She paced the throne room, the lamp swinging at her side. 'He told me who guards it and where it might be found, but the road to it is filled with peril, so he says. Who can I trust to seek it out, if I'm not to wait for the Grim Wolves to return?' After a moment, she answered her own question. 'Me. There is no other.'

'You're the queen. You're needed here.'

'Whatever duties I have here are meaningless if we're to be crushed by our enemy.' She watched the Lord of the Greenwood nod slowly. He understood duty as well as she did.

'You'll go alone?' he asked.

'It's for the best. I'll need as many good men as possible to stay here to protect Weylyn.'

'Then I'll come with you.'

'What will the powers who forced you to take up this role think of your taking sides?'

'We share the same blood, sister. I am my own man, regardless of consequence.'

She felt a wave of deep affection rise up in her, and she hugged Aelius again, tighter this time.

'One other thing,' he murmured. 'There's a third child, a girl, Morgen, who is Weylyn's . . .' He paused, again selecting his words carefully. 'What part she has to play, I'm not yet certain. But the Hecatae will not let power slip away from them, and they believe this Morgen is crucial to their plans.'

'So many plots.' How hard her voice sounded, how distant from the joyful tone she once had. 'So much energy expended for the dream of a few old men yearning for power. What if it's all for nothing? A story told to children that can never be made real, however much blood is shed.'

Aelius had no words to answer her.

The tolling bell rang out deep in the night and she jerked back from her brother's embrace. The alarm, raised by her guards on the walls.

'Can it be?' she gasped. 'Our enemy is attacking? So soon?'

She raced away through the empty chambers, hearing the shouts of her army as they roused themselves. Only when she was out in the night did she realize Aelius hadn't followed her.

Between the barracks and the offices of her rule, golden light flitted like fireflies. Catia lifted her skirts and darted after one swinging lamp to the gate. Amarina was there, the hood of her cloak pulled low. She turned her shadowed face towards Catia, but said nothing.

'This way!' someone bellowed. Soldiers were streaming down the steep path from the fortress, lamplights flying alongside them.

'So much excitement,' Amarina sighed.

Catia hurried after them, winding down into the mouth of the valley where the moonlit stream tinkled down to the sea.

In the cove, the slick pebbles gleamed. A white path ran across the waves to where the moon hung in the starry sky. The soldiers huddled together, holding their lamps up so that the wavering light twisted their faces into grotesqueries.

'What's wrong?' Catia shouted through the hubbub.

The men turned to her, and now she could see the dark lines of concern carved into their features. One of them pointed along the stony beach to the black slash of a cave that ran right through the headland to the ocean on the other side. Her men had christened it Myrrdin's Cave, for it was somewhere usually hidden from prying eyes where the wood-priest vanished to divine entrails or speak to the gods, casting runes and mixing potions, whenever the urge took him. Within the black depths the embers of a fire glowed, like the eye of a resting beast.

'Show me,' she said.

The man who had pointed edged towards the cave, glancing back at his comrades, who remained rooted.

'What are they scared of?' Catia asked.

'They're a fearful lot,' Amarina replied, appearing at her side. 'Men.'

Catia picked her way over seaweed-slick rocks, skirting the pools that had been left at high tide. She breathed in the gassy reek of bladderwrack. The lamplight flared up the dank walls of the cave, and a wisp of blue smoke from the dying fire swirled in the breeze. Scattered around the ashes and charred sticks were three wooden bowls and a goblet, bundles of herbs, and pots containing the foul-smelling unguent Myrrdin smeared on his skin. Catia looked round, but the wood-priest was nowhere to be seen.

'Here.' Amarina pushed past her and pointed at a long broken stick lying half submerged in a rock pool. It was Myrrdin's staff, shattered.

'What happened?' Catia asked.

The man who had led them there said in a tremulous voice, 'The guards heard a scream, a terrible, throat-rending scream. And when they rushed down here, they saw—' He choked on his words. 'The wood-priest summoned daemons, and they carried him away to hell.'

Catia turned up her nose.

'Don't dismiss him so easily,' Amarina said. She was staring down at another rock pool, but the seawater there was black.

Catia edged closer, and as the lamplight gleamed off the surface she saw the crimson tint.

'Blood,' Amarina said. 'More than a man can stand to lose.'

'We saw a body drifting out on the waves,' the soldier muttered. 'The wood-priest commands magic, everyone knows that. If even he can be killed, what hope is there for the rest of us? What has he summoned? What's out there?'

'This is just the blood of a lamb whose throat Myrrdin slit for his ritual,' Catia said. She could feel Amarina's eyes on her, but she didn't meet them. 'No more superstition. Leave the lamp, and go back to the fortress with the others. The wood-priest will be back soon enough, and then you'll all feel like fools.'

Once the soldier had trudged away, Amarina said, 'A lamb?'

Catia crouched beside the ruddy pool. There was more blood there than any lamb could hold.

'The Dumnonii know of the wood-priest and are afraid of his power. They would not have attacked him,' she said.

'Warriors from the army of the false king, you must know that,' Amarina said. 'Only they would dare kill a wood-priest. They've set out to weaken us by degrees.'

'And they've succeeded. Once word gets out that the druid has been murdered a spear's throw from his home, everyone . . . our own army . . . will know how powerless we are.'

Catia listened to the relentless pounding of the waves and felt alone in all the world.

CHAPTER FIFTEEN

Strange Allies

THE BLASTING SEA WIND WHIPPED THE FOUNTAIN OF SPARKS up into the funnel of smoke. The fire roared, all but drowning the crashing of the waves on the stones. Howling like lost souls, the warriors danced around it, their pale figures little more than spectres in the thin light of dawn.

Lucanus watched the ritual, breathing in the acrid aroma of woodsmoke and the strange herbs the Attacotti tossed into the flames every now and then. That strange yowling set his teeth on edge. What were they saying in that rolling, unfamiliar tongue? What dark gods were they petitioning?

'Do you know what this means?' Bellicus rumbled at his side.

He shook his head. 'I've lived among them all these years, and they're as strange to me as the first time we encountered them. There are days when I wonder if they are mortals at all.'

One of the priests walked up to the edge of the bonfire, his bone necklace clattering. He thrust both hands into the air, and the dancing ended and the howling faded away. The warriors became statues, not even blinking.

'I tried to understand them at the start,' Lucanus continued. 'Though I could never grasp their words, that priest would scratch things in the dry mud with a sharp stick. Drawings of the sun and the stars, of men and women in ships with strange curved prows, the stories they tell themselves. This island is not their true home, so it seems. They travelled here from somewhere in the east long, long ago. That is my understanding, at least. Beyond that . . .' He shrugged.

'Then how did you persuade the bastards to let us live?' Solinus stamped his feet against the early-morning chill. 'More than that, how did you do this deal with them?'

Lucanus shuddered. The ache in his stump was deep this day, and he could feel spikes lancing into the heart of him. 'With patience, and more scratchings in the mud.'

He thought back to those long hours squatting outside the great hall of the idiot-king, not knowing if his friends would live to see the dawn. The guilt had gnawed away at him. The Grim Wolves would not be there if not for him. He should have guessed his loyal brothers would never let him sacrifice himself without risking everything to bring him home.

One by one, the Attacotti shook off their rigid pose and knelt in front of the priest. He moved among them, tapping each one on the forehead with an old bone taken from the pouch at his waist, then pressing the yellowing fragment into their palms. Each one snapped his fingers around it, and held it next to his heart.

'They haunt my dreams,' Comitinus said, hugging his arms around himself. 'They eat the flesh of the dead, and now we're to call them allies?'

'We have no choice.' Lucanus turned away from the knot of Grim Wolves and Niall of the Nine Hostages and looked out across the waves to where his brothers' ship strained at its anchor. Home lay beyond that horizon. He had not thought he would ever see it again.

Catia was so clear in his mind's eye, it was as if he could throw his arms around her and embrace her. His heart ached for the feel of her against him, for the smell of her skin and her hair, for a glimpse of that bright light in her eyes. One more time. Just one more time. And Weylyn – how he would have grown. He had so many things to pass on to his son, to teach him how to be a good man.

A hand clapped across his shoulder and he jerked from his reverie. Niall of the Nine Hostages looked down at him, grinning. 'Who wouldn't be lost to the relief of escaping this hellish place?'

'This hell can never be escaped. I carry it with me.'

Niall leaned in and whispered, 'No more sour talk. We are kings, you and I, and the men who follow us want to see the sun shining on the waters ahead, not be told there is always another storm coming over the horizon.'

Lucanus nodded. 'Good advice.' Niall was right. This burden was his to carry, and he shouldn't let it fall on the shoulders of his friends. 'Come,' he said. 'Once the Attacotti are done here, let's set a course for the south, and home.'

The ritual continued until the sun was midway in its climb up the sky. The Grim Wolves paced and kicked stones, cursing under their breath. They could not be away from the place too soon.

The Attacotti warriors who were to accompany them lined up along the shore. There must have been thirty of them, a goodly number, and Lucanus felt surprised to see so many. Though for this strange people he was the greatest prize of all, and the Attacotti wouldn't let him slip through their fingers. They would be allies and captors in equal measure.

As they watched the gulls wheeling across the blue sky, he caught sight of the ship sailing around the eastern edge of the island. It was as strange as he'd been led to believe, resembling none of the vessels he'd watched put into port near the fortress, and they had come from all corners of the earth.

The deck was shaped like an eye staring up at the sky, with a long arched tiller aft. The single mast sported a sapphire sail with a yellow eye in the centre. The prow curled into a horse's head so the ship would look as though it were cantering through the white wake, and a streak of gold ran along the rails on both sides. What warship could this be? That gold would catch the sunlight and it would be seen long before it neared, allowing any enemy to prepare their defence. Perhaps the Attacotti had no need to care about things like that.

It was a sturdy, ocean-going vessel, though, and he was certain it could cover long distances with ease. A rowboat cut across the swell soon after to collect the Attacotti. While they moved away towards their vessel, Lucanus heard Niall hail him as he splashed through the shallows to *Waveskimmer.*

'Are we to be friends now, us and those Eaters of the Dead?' Comitinus was still grumbling.

'Oh, aye, it'll be all laughing and drinking until you find yourself face down in their pot,' Solinus replied.

Lucanus felt Bellicus' eyes on him. His old friend knew the truth. The Attacotti recognized Lucanus' power and tried to accommodate his wishes, but they would never be friends. They wanted to protect their interests. They would be his shadow to the end of his days. No chance of escape.

'You need an army,' Bellicus said, 'a powerful one. There are no fiercer fighters than the Attacotti, you know that. When the warriors of the false king see them coming, they'll throw down their weapons and turn tail.'

'It's true,' Solinus said. 'I'd rather have them at my side than looking into my eyes.'

'And when the war is done,' Mato asked, 'will they sail away and leave us alone?'

CHAPTER SIXTEEN

Homecoming

LUCANUS CLOSED HIS EYES AND LET THE SEA WIND LASH HIS face. When he opened them again, Tintagel was still there. Not a dream.

The honey-coloured stone of the fortress all but glowed in the afternoon sun, and he could see his banner, the gold dragon on the red background, flapping above the quarters where Catia and Weylyn would be waiting for him. His heart swelled at the vision of his loved ones. He felt himself begin to tremble from the rush of feelings. In this moment, the reunion was all that mattered, not war, not the great destiny in store for his son, nor the plots of the druids. Just to see his wife and son again: that was a prize greater than any other. Yet he still felt pangs of pain over the time that had been lost. He would make it up to them both, do anything to try to recapture those missing days.

He rested his one hand on the prow, feeling *Waveskimmer* skip across the water, urging it on.

'Never thought you'd see it again, I'd wager,' Niall of the Nine Hostages said. 'Nor that wife of yours. I've never met a woman with more fire in her. You've chosen well, Pendragon.'

'She chose me.'

'I wish you success in the fight to come. It'll not be an easy war, but then what wars are? Tales will be told about it for years to come. You're not fighting for the easy things – for gold, for land. You're fighting for a hope of better times. That's a noble pursuit, and if truth be told, I can't think of a king or emperor who ever fought for it before. You'll earn your place on the tongues of storytellers for that alone.'

Lucanus licked the salt off his lips. 'Give me my wife and son and a full belly, and days free of fighting, and I'll be happy enough. I don't need to be remembered.'

Niall clapped him on the shoulder and laughed. 'No statues for you, then, Pendragon? You'll sail off into the mists and be forgotten for all time!'

To be forgotten. That sounded perfect.

'For my part, I'll be happy to return to the life I had,' Niall continued. 'There are places still to plunder, and I have expensive tastes. I plan to sit on a throne of gold when that crown finally gets dropped on my head.' He glanced back at the Attacotti ship streaming along in their wake, and Lucanus heard his voice grow cold. 'And if I never return to the Island of the Dead it will be too soon. This world was not meant for those things. I cannot even imagine the horrors you must have seen.'

Aye, horrors.

Lucanus pushed them out of his mind, as he would be doing until his dying day.

Lucanus stood in the rowboat as it drifted the final lengths to the quay. The side throbbed with people, cheering and yelling and waving long streams of coloured silk that fluttered in the breeze. He shook his head, marvelling at the din. But the Grim Wolves were well liked among the court and the Dumnonii so he wasn't surprised. But then he heard his own name repeated time and again until it became a full-throated cry, and he realized the welcome was for him. He felt bewildered.

'You don't know how they feel about you,' Mato murmured. 'You're their saviour.'

'I'm no saviour.'

'You are. You will be. You've conquered death. We told you. You've sailed back to them in their hour of greatest need. You're not a man any longer, Lucanus. You'd better get used to that.'

Too true. Nor had he been a man to the Attacotti. To them he was a symbol, a captive king who would reinforce their supremacy. Only two people would see him as the man he truly was: his wife and son. How much he needed to be with them again.

Playing his part, Lucanus raised his good arm high to the waiting crowd, and the cheers whipped up into a frenzy. He scanned the faces for the only ones who mattered to him, but eventually gave up. Too many had gathered there. And if he knew Catia, she would be waiting in the fortress to greet him. Their joy would be private, and richer for it.

Once the boat had been moored, he clambered up the stone steps into the throng. Hands clapped him on the back here and there, but as he moved through the crowd he saw faces turn away from him, eyes lower; a deference, almost a fear, that he had never experienced before. He was not one of them. He was loved, but removed.

The Grim Wolves melted into the heart of the churning crowd, revelling in the adulation and telling tales of their great adventure. But Lucanus pushed on through the last of the well-wishers and hurried up the steep path to the fortress. His army lined the road from the gate. More cheering. He endured their greetings for as long as he could, and then thrust his way past them. His measured step broke and he ran, his heart pounding, until he burst into the palace.

'Catia!' His shout echoed through the empty chambers.

'She's not here.'

Amarina was waiting for him in a beam of sunlight breaking through one of the great windows.

'Not here?' He felt a rush of ice-water.

'She's alive, don't worry. But she has done as queens do and has ridden off to save her people.'

Lucanus winced as if he'd been stabbed. Bitter disappointment burned in his chest. 'When will she be back?'

'There's much to tell . . .'

Amarina said more, but he heard none of it, lost as he was to a wave of dismay that his longing to hold Catia in his arms that day had been dashed.

When he shook off his sorrow, he realized Amarina was

walking round him, looking him up and down. She tugged his cloak to one side, revealing the space where his left arm should have been. Her nose wrinkled, but she only said, 'Whatever they say, you look the same old Lucanus to me.'

As he drew breath to ask all the questions that had backed up in him, she shook her head and snapped her fingers. A moment later he heard footsteps and a boy appeared from one of the inner chambers; tall, strong, his eyes clear, his features too serious.

At first he wondered who this stranger was, and then he realized it must be his son and felt another rush of regret for all the time lost. He held out his arm, and the lad stepped forward.

Lucanus didn't know what to say. He could see Weylyn didn't know either. The boy bit his lips, and his eyes gleamed; he seemed to be on the brink of crying, then anger, then some emotion Lucanus couldn't read.

'You've kept up with your studies?'

The lad nodded. 'I'm good with a sword now. You'd be proud.'

'You must show me later.' He paused, searching for words that seemed to come from the bottom of a deep well. 'It's good to see you again, Weylyn.'

The boy nodded, blinked too many times, and then walked away.

Though once again he forced his face to remain impassive, Lucanus felt hollowed out. This was far from the reunion that had filled his dreams on the voyage back to Tintagel. Weylyn was so shy and distant. Perhaps the bonds that tied father to son had been shattered by his absence. Perhaps all the warmth he had hoped to reclaim with his family was nothing more than a dream. Was this it, then? The ultimate torture? To be back in their orbit, only to be for ever distant from them?

Once Weylyn's footsteps had vanished, Amarina said, 'When the sails were seen on the horizon, he was like a drunk, spinning between worry and hope. You have work to do there, you know that. You have to teach him you're not a stranger.'

Lucanus swallowed. Would it have been best if he'd stayed dead? 'Now we need to speak.'

Amarina led him to the throne room. He could smell Catia's

scent in the air, and that made his heart ache all the more, but he pushed the feelings aside. Over bread and cheese and wine, he watched Amarina's face as she told him of the false king, this Arthur, the bastard son of a son and a mother, and the threat he posed to Weylyn and Catia and all of them; of the slowly ebbing faith of the Dumnonii and their support which was the root of their power in the west, and of the desperate need to find some way to fight back in the war that was coming.

He felt a weight on his shoulders when she told him of the murder of Myrrdin. The wood-priest could never have been a friend – indeed, much of the misery they'd suffered had been set in motion by him – but his wisdom had at times been all that kept them from disaster.

Only then did she speak of Catia. He knew she'd saved it till last because had she not done so he wouldn't have been able to give attention to the rest of her worries.

'She left at dawn, riding into the east,' she said.

'Alone?'

Amarina nodded. 'Something woke me. A dream. One of those daemons that seems to whisper in my ear in the dark hours these days. At the window, I saw her on her white horse, moving into the trees.'

'She's queen. Why would she abandon her responsibilities?'

'Because what she seeks is greater than her responsibilities, of course.'

'What can be greater than keeping her people safe? Keeping Weylyn safe?'

'I can think of only one thing.' Amarina slopped more wine into his goblet. 'When we fled south from Vercovicium, you saw how folk rallied around the golden dragon crown and the old title Pendragon. Myrrdin told her he believed we needed more of that magic, his old magic, if we're to find an army to follow us and folk to cheer us on.'

Lucanus sipped the wine, fearing the worst. 'What magic?'

'One of the old treasures, brought to Britannia by the gods themselves, so the wood-priest said. But who can believe any words that tumble out of his mouth? Is it another of his tales that have all the substance of an autumn mist? Are these treasures real? He says your sword is one.'

'It's just a sword.'

'But is it? You're just a ditch-crawling mudlark, Lucanus, yet somehow you've become the saviour who can survive death. If that's not the work of the gods, what is?' She smiled in that familiar way that had always taunted him.

'And this treasure?'

'The cup of the Dagda, or cauldron, or some such. I confess, my ears went deaf whenever the wood-priest spoke.' She laughed silently to herself. 'An object of great power. Of course it is. Only the purest heart and truest warrior can seize it from its keeper. And when all hear that we possess this pot that holds the power of the gods, they will fall in line. Though in that the wood-priest is probably right. There are none more gullible than those who put their faith in pots and cups and cauldrons and swords and spears and magic stones.'

'Why would Catia venture out alone to find this cauldron?'

He watched Amarina's face tighten. 'Our army grows weaker by the day. She didn't want to risk the safety of those here . . . Weylyn's safety . . . by taking a war-band with her.'

'So she risked herself?' Lucanus felt a burning pride, but also fear.

Amarina nodded. 'A woman travelling alone, in Britannia, now that Rome is loosening its hold, and the rule of law is fading? These are dark times, and getting darker by the day. Worse than that, this cauldron is supposed to be in the possession of someone calling himself the Fisher King, who lives in a place so perilous that all who travel there die before they reach their destination.' Amarina cocked an eyebrow. 'I can't decide if your wife is brave or the greatest fool I've ever known. If I was one who wagered, I'd say she won't be coming home. Too harsh? You know I'm right.'

The Wolf swilled the last of his wine and wiped his mouth with the back of his hand. It was trembling, and Amarina saw. But he could no longer hide the agony burning inside him. The Fates were cruel. He'd escaped the Attacotti – for a while – in the expectation of being reunited with his wife. But here they were, still separated, and now Catia was in danger of losing her life in that dangerous countryside.

'I'm going after her.'

'Of course you are.'

'I'm taking the Grim Wolves with me.'

'Of course.' She smiled. 'Well, we got there in the end, exactly where I expected we'd be.'

Lucanus leaned back in the throne, letting his fingers fold around the smoothed wood of the armrest. He'd sat here so many times before he'd walked away from Tintagel that he could no longer distinguish one occasion from any other. Listening to foreign dignitaries telling him of life beyond Britannia, and debating arrangements with merchants offering trade from distant ports. Discussing the defence of their lands with the Grim Wolves and hearing the troubles of local folk who wanted him to solve their disputes.

The chair felt solid underneath him, an anchor that had held him fast in Tintagel. For a while he let the silence of the throne room wash over him, and then he heaved himself up and trailed through the chambers of the palace that had once been his home. His fingers scraped across tapestries rich with colour. He lifted gold plate, weighing it, and rested his palm on the cool alabaster of a bust of some ancient hero whose name he had forgotten. He sipped sweet wine from Rome itself, swilling it around his mouth, marvelling at the taste and the aroma. Refamiliarizing himself with a life that he had taken for granted before he agreed to become the Attacotti's prize.

At the end of his tour, he leaned his head back and closed his eyes and breathed in the aromas of the place: warm stone and sea air, lavender from the bunches the servants hung in the corners of the chambers, bread baking in the kitchens, the musk of the men and women who moved through the passages. Life in all its glory, life so valuable to him now. How could he ever let this go again?

Storm clouds rolled in from the west, draining the light into a thin grey haze. Lucanus watched Bellicus pace around the horses that had been brought out for them, checking their strength, ensuring they were fed and watered. Not far away, Solinus and Comitinus bickered over how much hard biscuit they needed to take with them. Mato waved away the gaggle of boys who had come to see them off. Apullius knelt beside his brother Morirex, brushing away his tears with a thumb. The younger boy had prayed every night for their return from the sea, and now he couldn't believe they were departing on another journey into danger so soon.

None of them could.

'Take me with you, I beg you.' Weylyn marched up, holding out both hands.

Lucanus shook his head. 'There is too much danger.'

His son's cheeks burned. 'I am grown now. I can wield a sword. I can—'

'No,' Lucanus insisted, with perhaps too much sharpness. 'You must stay here.'

'With Amarina and the women?' Weylyn sneered. 'Is that what you think of me?'

The Wolf felt a barb of sorrow. But he was not prepared to see his son put at risk, as well as his wife. If Weylyn hated him, he would carry that burden. 'Go now,' he said. 'You'll be king in my absence, a beacon for our army and the Dumnonii. That's an important role.'

Weylyn showed a cold face. He was unmoved by his father's attempts to soften the blow, no doubt feeling both insulted and annoyed. 'Very well. There are other things for me here. Other folk.' He spun on his heel and marched away before Lucanus could ask what he meant.

Niall of the Nine Hostages was standing near by, watching the activity. If he'd heard the exchange, he didn't show it.

'I'll say this for you: you don't wallow in comforts,' the pirate-king said. 'After an adventure like the one we had on that foul island, my men would have demanded six solid days of drinking. At least.'

'Catia has several hours' start on us,' Lucanus replied. 'Only if we leave now is there a chance we can catch her before she ventures too far into danger.'

'Those bastard Eaters of the Dead?'

'They're camped in the woods so they don't frighten those who remain in the fortress.'

'They'll let you out of their sight?'

Lucanus thought back to that ritual on the beach the other dawn. When he had looked into the eyes of the priest, there'd been an understanding between them, perhaps even trust. Their agreement was sealed in blood. His. But even so he couldn't begin to comprehend their intentions. Would they let him leave in search of Catia? Would they send out scouts to track his journey? 'We'll see,' he said.

'Of course, you realize I'll be the first to pillage your villages and arrange a trade deal with the false king if I decide he has the upper hand?'

'I'd expect no less.'

Niall nodded. 'A wise king, what's left of you.' He held out a hand, and Lucanus shook it.

'I know you didn't accompany my brothers out of the good in your heart, but you have my thanks anyway.'

'And I wish you well in your quest. I wouldn't like to be walking your road, that is certain. In my calculation, the forces arrayed against you are overwhelming. You'll need the gods on your side if you're to survive.' Niall glanced back to where his crew was being led out of captivity. Lucanus had already arranged for a ship to be filled with supplies for their journey back to Hibernia.

'Don't think of attacking while we're away,' Lucanus said. 'Amarina will watch over the fortress in our absence, and she's more cunning than anyone you know. If you dare challenge her, your balls will be hanging from your mast by the next dawn.'

Niall shifted his attention to where Amarina stood beside Weylyn, watching the proceedings, a dark cloud in a green cloak. 'A woman after my own heart. I might ask her to my bed before I depart.'

'I wouldn't if I were you.'

When Niall looked back at him, the Wolf saw an odd light burning in the pirate-king's eyes. Was that respect?

'What I saw on that island of horrors will haunt my nights for ever more,' the Hibernian said, his voice barely above a whisper. 'How you endured it, I will never know.'

'We do what we have to do to survive.'

Niall nodded. 'That is true.'

Lucanus studied the towering man, and as he did so he felt a notion begin to settle on him. 'We have much in common, you and I,' he ventured.

Niall narrowed his eyes, seeming to sense what lay beneath those words. 'I could imagine standing alongside you. From time to time.'

'An alliance, say?'

The pirate-king nodded. 'If we could reach an agreement.'

'Then we should talk.'

The Hibernian slapped him on the shoulder. 'I like you, Pendragon! But I drive a hard bargain!'

Lucanus strode over to where the Grim Wolves were now huddled in the dying light. 'I can make this journey alone,' he said.

'Aye, but what happens if you want to pick your teeth and scratch your arse at the same time?' Solinus asked.

'Who needs to rest?' Comitinus said. 'It only makes you soft.'

'We've known worse,' Bellicus added.

'Besides,' Mato said, 'if all goes well, we'll be with Catia by noon tomorrow.'

Lucanus looked to Apullius. He still seemed too young to be running with the Grim Wolves, though he was no younger than Lucanus had been when he joined the *arcani*. 'You've said your goodbyes?'

Apullius nodded.

Lucanus pulled down the snout of the wolf-pelt on his head, letting the shadows pool into his eyes. There was only one more thing to do.

As he strode across the flagstones, he glanced at Weylyn. His son showed a cold face, hiding the hurt he felt that his father was abandoning him again, so soon. But he was strong, he had Catia's blood, and he already understood the meaning of duty.

The soldiers who had come to watch pushed back to the walls, allowing him a path to his goal, almost as if they knew what he intended. Silence fell across the throng.

Lucanus stared at the sword embedded in the crack between the flagstones. He thought how poor it looked, with its scratched bronze blade and the nicks in the edge. In the grey light, he couldn't see the runes that had been etched into it. He'd left it there the night he'd walked out to sacrifice himself to the Attacotti. His intention had been that Weylyn would claim it when he was of an age to ascend to the throne. He never expected to hold it in his hand again.

At that moment, he could only think of Myrrdin. The wood-priest had successfully wormed into his mind, so that even now he was dead he was still whispering. Lucanus recalled his telling him the tale of this sword of the gods on the day he'd pulled it from the bony hand in the cold waters of the lake in the far north. He knew what the wood-priest would expect of him here.

One gesture could fill a heart with fire. One brief spectacle could spin a tale that would rush out across the land.

He watched the lightning dance along the horizon and tried to count the moments between the peals of thunder. When he was ready, he grasped the hilt of Caledfwlch and wrenched it out of the stone. He thrust the blade over his head and pointed it to the heavens, to the gods themselves.

Thunder boomed. Lightning flashed.

'Let the false king be afraid,' he roared. 'The Dragon has risen.'

CHAPTER SEVENTEEN

The Lights are Going Out

S NOW CAPPED THE MOUNTAIN RANGE IN THE HAZY DISTANCE TO the south. Sometimes, when the wind changed, it brought a bitter cold from those summits, even in the warmest part of the year. Gaia stood on the walls of the fortress she had rebuilt from the ancient ruins and shuddered as she imagined that chill. This entire land was too cold, too damp. She dreamed of Rome and its opulence and its warmth, where civilized men had yearned for her.

Not this place of barbarians, of grunts and oaths, where greasy meat was torn from the bone and the men fornicated like rutting beasts.

Despite the sun on her face, she tugged her cloak around her and scowled. The fortress towered over the road that led to the mountain pass, atop a wooded, rocky hill, both guarding the route and allowing her to tax the merchants who travelled between north and south in Cambria. The grey stone had been heaped up on the foundations of a much older fort. The inhabitants had long since vanished. Ramparts marched up the hillside.

She was safe there. Arthur was safe there. Enemies lurked everywhere.

Gaia winced as she heard the familiar *click-click-click* of the Hanged Man's staff as Severus guided his insect-like frame over the flagstones. He would be wearing his black robes, which only made him seem more saturnine. How she wished he would die. But then who would teach Arthur in the ways of being a king?

She turned and felt a burst of surprise when she saw that twisted frame was not alone. A tall, broad-shouldered man with fiery red hair and beard strode beside him. He looked strong, powerful, and his grin showed the confidence that she admired so much. She smiled back, opening her eyes wider, lifting her head and pushing her breasts out.

'This is Niall of the Nine Hostages. He is a . . .' Severus paused to choose his words, 'a king, from Hibernia.'

'And I am the queen here,' Gaia pronounced, throwing her arms wide. 'Welcome to Dinas Ffaraon Dandde.'

Niall bowed. Respect; she liked that. But she knew he lusted after her too, as all men did. Perhaps she would take him to her bed. It had been too long since she'd enjoyed careful attention.

'We have a band of the king's men captive, here in the fortress,' the Hanged Man droned. 'Our army took them when they were raiding one of the ports to the west.'

'I would not have sent them to attack this land if I'd known it was ruled over by such a wise and beautiful queen.' Niall leaned forward and kissed her hand.

She shivered.

'He would like his men returned to him,' Severus said.

'Very—'

'I have told the king you would consent to his request,' her adviser continued. 'However, a queen would of course require something in return. In this case we have agreed on a payment of information. Nothing too onerous. Is this what you wish?'

Gaia felt her smile tighten. She hated the way Severus emphasized the words to draw from her the response he required. 'And what information do you have, Niall of the Nine Hostages?'

'I have sailed from the south-west corner of Britannia where, I believe, you have enemies—'

'I have no enemies. No rivals. I rule justly and I am loved by all.' She heard the sing-song lilt in her voice and hoped the flint in her eyes didn't mute it.

'Of course. However, they would consider themselves enemies and they are prepared to threaten your . . . just rule.' Niall glanced at Severus, his eyes twinkling. The Hanged Man nodded in response. 'You would have some interest in their comings and goings?'

'Perhaps. Walk with me, and I will hear what you have to say.'

She led the way down the stone steps to the courtyard. Her nostrils flared at the apple-reek of horse dung and the sour smoke wafting from the smith's shop. The throom of hammer on anvil would drown out all words, so she tilted back her head further still, half closing her eyes, and walked in silence, pretending the stinking men who lumbered around were not there.

Inside the steamy warmth of her quarters, she relaxed her shoulders and said, 'Now, speak.'

'The Queen in the West fears your power,' Niall said. 'Her army is crumbling and the local tribe turn away from her.'

'This we know.'

'The queen has a fire in her—'

'My daughter is a cold witch,' Gaia snapped.

Niall gaped for a moment. The relationship was news to him. 'Apologies,' he said. 'Our paths crossed only briefly and you will know her better than I do. What is of import here is that she will not let this decline continue. She believes she can draw new swords to her army, and win the hearts of the local folk, by securing a great treasure, a magical cauldron, or cup of some kind.'

Gaia looked to the Hanged Man, who shook his head slowly. 'The followers of the Christ have some tale of a cup which caught the blood of their saviour when he died upon the cross,' he said. 'Perhaps it is that.'

'If my venomous offspring succeeds in finding this cup, will she achieve what she desires?'

Severus shrugged. 'Simple folk are easily swayed by talk of magic and gods.'

'Then we must make sure she does not succeed. See to it.' She heard the granite in her voice and flashed a smile at Niall. 'Come. I will show you my wonderful palace.'

As Severus scurried away to make the arrangements, Arthur emerged from the throne room, his pale face like the moon in the half-light. She felt a twist of irritation. She had hoped to be alone with this potent visitor.

'This is Arthur,' she said.

The lad walked forward and bowed his head slightly.

'I've heard of you,' Niall said. 'The . . . ah . . . the True King, yes?'

'I am the True King.'

Gaia watched the Hibernian scrutinizing her son. No doubt he saw in Arthur all the courage and wit and hope that moved her to tears every day.

After a moment, Niall nodded. 'Aye . . . well . . .'

'Come,' Gaia said, a little too hastily, 'let me show you the rest of my home. You will see why it was chosen as a fit place to house the bloodline of the King Who Will Not Die.' She walked away before he could resist.

'The simple folk who live around here tell stories of the wonders . . . of the magic . . . of Dinas Ffaraon Dandde,' she went on as she led the way through the fortress. 'Of blue flames flickering among the trees . . . the light of the gods. Though I must say, none have been seen since we arrived. Voices booming from deep within the hill. Long-dead family members encountered on the road to the mountains. Frogs raining from a clear sky. Gold rings in the streams.' Gaia chuckled. 'And it is true that when the masons were building the towers they would rise at dawn to find the previous day's work torn down, the stones scattered far and wide. The superstitious said we were building on sacred ground. More likely the locals were sneaking in to cause trouble for the strangers. When my guards kept watch, with sharpened swords at the ready, the disruption quickly stopped.'

'In my experience, I wouldn't laugh too much at simple folk,' Niall muttered. 'There is usually good reason for such tales being attached to a place.'

'We all like a good story. I have another one. You will judge for yourself whether it is true or not.'

Gaia swung open a door and they stepped into deep gloom before she led him down stone steps. 'Arthur,' she prompted at the foot.

Her son plucked a torch from the wall and stepped ahead of her. The flames twisted in a blast of dank air.

'Cold as hell in here,' Niall muttered.

Gaia kept the smile on her lips, but she always felt uneasy in this place, and it troubled her how even a strong torch failed to push the shadows back far. Their footsteps echoed off the walls, and after a moment Arthur stepped on to a wide stone platform. The orange glow of the torch gleamed off a deep black pool.

Coming to a halt, Niall stroked his beard as he peered into the depths. Gaia edged closer to him, so close she was almost brushing his arm.

'Water?' the Hibernian rumbled.

'Keep your voice low,' she breathed. 'You wouldn't want to disturb what is sleeping in down there.'

She sensed Niall glancing at her to see if she was joking.

'This pool is why the fortress is here. Why we are here. Of all the tales told of this place by the local folk, this is the only one that fills their voices with awe. Perhaps with dread. Some of them say the pool goes down for ever, others that it is a gateway to the world where their gods live. Any who dare dive in are never seen again. Be that as it may, the belief is that whosoever has ownership of this pool will become the rightful king . . . or queen . . . of all Britannia.'

Niall leaned forward, watching the amber glints dancing across the oily surface. 'And what sleeps in the depths?'

'Dragons.' Gaia let the echoes disappear before continuing. 'Two of them. One red, one white.'

'You've seen them?'

Gaia shuddered, recalling the first time she came down here alone, not long after the fortress was built. 'I've heard their screams, and seen their dark shapes rolling beneath the surface. When they are awake, they fight, but so far there has not been a victor.'

She closed her eyes. This Hibernian barbarian could never know what this pool meant to her, to her son. This was more than the home of fabulous beasts. The dragon was the symbol of everything they fought for: the never-ending bloodline, the eternal cycle of the fall and the saviour rising to lead the world into a new golden age. The Ouroboros, the dragon eating its own tail, was branded into her shoulder, as it had been into the shoulder of her son, Corvus, and as it soon would be made real in the flesh of her other son, Arthur.

'Dinas Ffaraon Dandde is a very old name,' she breathed. 'In the local tongue, I am told, it means the Fortress of the Fiery Pharaoh. These dragons have existed here for a long time.'

Niall grunted. 'I would like a pair of pet dragons myself. Their fiery breath could warm us all up during a cold night at sea.'

Gaia winced at the disrespect in his voice. Did he think this was some kind of joke? 'Come,' she said, marching back in the direction of the door. 'Let us reunite you with your men and send you on your way. I have important business to attend to.'

'If he comes within an arrow-shot of the fortress again, make sure he is cut down and hung out for the ravens,' Gaia told the captain of the guard as she watched Niall of the Nine Hostages march away from the gates with his band of cut-throats and thieves. They were clapping each other on the shoulder and laughing like drunks making their way home from the tavern. Gaia simmered. Niall did not even glance back once.

Before the captain could respond, hoofbeats thundered and she saw a band of her men riding hard for the fortress. They swept past the ragged group of pirates, paying them no attention. What could be the reason for such haste, she wondered? Though she was keen to return to the heat of her throne room, her curiosity got the better of her and she walked down the stone steps to the reeking courtyard.

The gates swung open and the riders rumbled in. Severus emerged from whatever hole he inhabited and hurried across the dusty square to greet them. For a moment, excited words rang back and forth and then he turned to her with a look of excitement.

Intrigued, Catia stepped closer. What she had taken to be a bale thrown over a horse at the rear began to squirm and she realized her men had taken a captive, perhaps some assassin sent by the false king and her vile daughter to kill her, or Arthur. She felt her blood grow cold. She'd order him gutted and spiked on a pole outside the gates so he could ruminate on his failings while the birds feasted on his entrails.

One of the men wrenched the captive off the horse and hurled him to the ground at her feet. He was filthy, his ragged clothes sodden from the rain. His hands were bound behind his back and he had a rotting sack pulled over his head.

The Hanged Man lurched forward so fast in his eagerness, his rolling gait almost upended him. 'A prize,' he exclaimed. 'The greatest prize!'

Gaia looked down at the squalid captive and turned up her nose. 'This?'

Severus leaned down and ripped the sack off the man's head.

'Oh.' She took a step back in surprise.

The captive flicked his braided hair aside and looked up at her, his eyes burning. She saw the unmistakable tattoo of the druids curling down the left side of his face to his jaw.

'This is Myrrdin, one of the last of the wood-priests,' the Hanged Man said. 'The false king no longer has his guide. He is lost in the wilderness. And we now have all the secrets we could ever want to know.'

In the seething heat of the throne room, Gaia threw her hands to the heavens. There were times when she was certain the gods were punishing her, though for what she had no idea. But this . . . this was a gift beyond value.

If the wood-priest could be broken and brought to their side, any lingering doubts about Arthur's claim to the royal bloodline would be crushed. As would any opposition from her hated daughter, when all of Britannia flocked to her own banner. Wait. Had she said that out loud?

She spun round. But Severus was still waiting patiently, his hands clasped in front of him. Myrrdin hunched on the flagstones where the guards had thrown him. She forced a pleasant smile. 'Here you will have any comfort you ever wanted,' she said in her sing-song voice.

Myrrdin eyed her. 'I live in the woods in winter and sleep in

ditches and eat the lights of game birds raw. You think I am someone who cares about comfort?'

Gaia winced. Anyone else would have been slaughtered in the
blink of an eye for such disrespect. But she needed him, and she
felt sick when she looked in his face and saw that he knew it too.

'Capturing this wood-priest was not a simple matter,' Severus
began in his dull drone. 'My men hid in the forest for long days,
waiting for the right moment to take him. And even though he
was surprised in his cave by the sea, where the pounding of the
waves hid the sound of the approach, he still succeeded in killing
one of ours. My men had to beat him unconscious with his own
staff to bring him out.'

Myrrdin looked round at the Hanged Man. Sizing him up,
Gaia thought. The two men locked eyes, neither giving an inch.
Gaia smiled. She liked it when men competed for her attention.

The wood-priest seemed to be weighing his predicament. After
a moment, he nodded, almost to himself. Acceptance. When he
glanced up at her, she saw an odd light in his eyes, and a hint of a
smile, one she couldn't quite read. 'How beautiful you are, if you
will forgive me for saying so.'

Severus grunted behind him, no doubt jealous and irritated
that this wood-priest was filled with such admiration. Gaia glared
at the Hanged Man to silence him. He sniffed and bowed his
head, chastened.

'More beautiful than your daughter by far,' Myrrdin continued. 'And wiser too.'

'That is true,' Gaia said. She decided she quite liked this
wood-priest.

'And your son,' he went on, once again almost to himself.
'The royal bloodline coursing through his veins.'

'The one true king,' she replied.

Myrrdin bowed his head, humbled, she was sure. He seemed
to be reflecting deeply on what lay ahead for him, for all of them.
That was a good thing.

Gaia looked down at the druid. 'I was there when Lucanus
Pendragon slaughtered your fellow wood-priests. Cut down the

wisest of the wise. Destroyed, in the blink of an eye, the knowledge of aeons. Your kind have shepherded mankind since the
first days. And now that light has been all but extinguished, by a
man you have stood by ever since. And his son who lays claim to
the royal bloodline. How do you justify that to yourself? Does the
guilt and the shame not crush you by degrees? Do you not feel
like a traitor to your own kind?'

Myrrdin looked up at her. She expected to see defiance in his
eyes, perhaps loathing for the way she had challenged him. But
there seemed only more acceptance.

'We will grow again. A few of us have survived. Many are
hiding among the followers of the Christ, and they mark their
presence by the sign of Cernunnos in the churches.'

Gaia let her voice fall to barely a whisper. 'That is not what I
asked.'

Myrrdin hung his head, his braided hair falling across his face.

'There is a way to make amends,' she breathed.

Only the wind in the eaves echoed, and she realized the silence
was his way of prompting her to continue.

'Join me. Recognize my son Arthur as the one true bearer of
the royal bloodline. The voice of one of the last druids will give
such weight to our claim that all who oppose it will be crushed.'
Gaia felt her hands trembling and she pushed them behind her
back. 'Tutor Arthur. Give him the benefit of all your wisdom so
that when he is grown he can be that great leader, the King Who
Will Not Die, and guide Britannia into the new golden age. What
say you?'

For a long moment, the wood-priest kept his head down. So still
was he that he seemed to be asleep. Gaia felt her heart hammer.

And then Myrrdin looked up and his eyes were all afire. 'I
say aye.'

PART TWO

The Quest

Life is one long struggle in the dark.

Lucretius

CHAPTER EIGHTEEN

Tempest-Tossed

T HE WIND HOWLED THROUGH THE BRANCHES AND THE RAIN drummed. With a shiver, Catia hunched over the neck of her white stallion. She felt beaten down by the deluge. An entire day of ceaseless storm, with no hint that it would break, and now an endless dark swam ahead of her among the trees. However much she squinted, she couldn't pierce it. All she could do was trust her horse to find its way.

With the Lord of the Greenwood keeping pace at her side, they'd chased the dawn east as swiftly as they could. But as they moved across the wind-blasted rocky spine of that land, the furious storm had swept in, and they'd headed down into the wooded valleys in search of shelter. Away from the eastern track, their pace slowed. With Myrrdin lost, they had little knowledge of their destination, only vague rumours Aelius had heard among the forest folk. Hope was all she had that the path to the cauldron could be located. Desperation drove her on.

With his helmet on, her brother seemed like a different person. His conversation became short and intermittent, and he stalked through the undergrowth like a beast, almost as if he'd been possessed by the spirit of Cernunnos' acolyte upon the earth. Or perhaps this was simply how he survived when he was on the road. He'd lived in the Wilds away from all human contact, surrounded by constant danger. That would change any man. Never would she have thought the boy she grew up with in

Vercovicium could have this skill, this strength, but he'd surprised them all.

It was as Lucanus had always said: a man didn't know who he could be until he'd been tested. And a woman too. But she still worried about those changes, and felt the brother she once knew slipping away from her.

'Aelius?' she called out. Only a peal of thunder rolled back.

She'd lost sight of him in the gloom beneath the trees a while back. From time to time, he scouted away from her, searching for any threat in the dangerous terrain, whether packs of hungry wolves or roaming bands of brigands ready to rob and murder lone travellers.

On she rode, hearing only the steady splash of hooves in spreading pools and the gurgling of sucking mud. For a while she felt as though she were floating in that ocean of dark. But then, through the oak and ash ahead, she glimpsed a faint spark.

Catia stiffened. It was a campfire. By all rights, she should keep her distance, she knew, but she was wet and cold and filled with worry about Weylyn. That fire was drawing her on like a moth.

She guided her mount towards it, cocking her head to listen for any voices. The orange glow swelled until she could see that the fire had been lit under a makeshift shelter to protect it from the downpour.

Three men and a boy squatted in the swirling smoke. Their glum stares were levelled at the campfire. Every now and then one of them would toss a branch on the fire. They couldn't see her in the gloom, but Catia studied them. Worn tunics and clothes, matted hair, heavy features, bows but no swords that she could see. Men from one of the nearby villages, she thought, no doubt out hunting and caught in the storm. She could see no game. They must be feeling miserable.

Once she'd weighed her choices, she slipped down from her horse and led it towards the fire. The men jerked, eyes narrowing with suspicion. When they saw it was a woman, they eased back, but the suspicious looks didn't vanish.

Catia pulled back the hood of her cloak. 'May I warm myself by your fire?'

She felt their eyes move across her, but she sensed no lechery, no threat. That was good, but she still gripped the knife hidden in the folds of her skirt.

'A woman, travelling alone? Are you a mad 'un?' one of them asked.

Another furrowed his brow as he looked over her fine woollen cloak embroidered with gold, and the white stallion and the bow across her back, and the quiver, and the way she raised her chin as she looked down at him. She waited for his sluggish thoughts to finish his calculation.

'You're her,' he said. 'The queen. Catia from the western fortress.'

She nodded.

Eyes flickered. Glances flashed. Two of the men opened their mouths, but no words came out.

'Why are you here?' the boy gasped. He looked to be about Weylyn's age.

Catia dropped to her haunches so she could look the lad in the eye. She smiled. 'Do you think I'm so frail that I must shelter in my throne room? You remind me of my son.'

'The king?' His eyes widened.

'What's your name?'

'Anghus,' he stuttered.

Catia eyed the three men. They shifted, and she could sense their reticence, but after a moment one of them beckoned for her to sit. She eased under the shelter and rubbed her hands in front of the fire. The warmth crept into her bones and she breathed a sigh of contentment.

She felt eyes still upon her and looked round. 'What troubles you?'

'Never heard of a queen travelling alone,' one man said. His eyes were slits.

'What takes you east?' the second man asked.

Catia nodded to the skin resting in the lap of the third man. 'Would you let me wet my lips?'

The hunter pushed the skin towards her. Catia raised it to her mouth and tasted sour, cheap wine.

'Some say you're not a queen at all,' the third man said.

There it was.

'Some say that boy of yours isn't a king.'

'Who says?' she asked.

'A queen wouldn't be riding alone.'

'Who says?' she repeated.

The hunter shrugged, trying to play down his accusation in the face of her cold stare. 'Folk. Lots of folk. Talk everywhere. In the market. From travellers passing through.'

'Talk of a true king,' the first man added. 'His soldiers pass through from time to time. Good men. Hand out food for the hungry. For all of us.'

'That is how they twist your minds, with bribes. I know the Dumnonii. You have more wisdom than that.'

The three men looked away.

'My son Weylyn is the True King. This usurper wants nothing more than power. And when he seizes it, his men won't be handing out loaves, they'll be taking everything from you.'

The men grunted. They wouldn't be convinced, Catia knew. Here was the threat made real. If even those living so close to Tintagel were turning from her, soon she'd lose all authority. And then the fall would not be far away.

She waved the skin at the third man with practised regal disdain. 'What have you heard of a man who calls himself the Fisher King?'

The three hunters shook their heads and stared into the flames.

'A king only in his own mind, I'd wager,' Catia pressed, remembering what Myrrdin had told her before his death. 'Yet it's said he holds a great treasure.'

'Heard nothing,' the first man said.

'If he's got a treasure, everybody'd be after it,' the second man said.

'It's well guarded, so I'm told, in a dangerous land . . .'

'Heard nothing.'

'The Fisher King! You *have* heard that story! Everyone knows it!'

Catia turned to Anghus, who was holding out one imploring hand. 'Tell me,' she said gently.

'The Fisher King lives on an island at the heart of a poisonous marsh. Five paths go in, each marked by one of the old way-stones carved with the head of the Green Man. But only one is the true path. The other four lead to certain death.'

'Still your tongue, boy,' the third hunter snapped.

Catia smiled and made an encouraging gesture. Anghus was in full flow.

'They say those who quest for the treasure are really searching for the truth, the great truth of God, and only those with the purest heart will ever find it,' the lad said quickly, clearly repeating some story he'd heard before.

'I said quiet.' The third hunter lashed the back of his hand across the boy's face.

Catia bristled, her hand flying to her hidden knife. 'Leave him be.'

'My boy. I do what I will with him,' the father snarled back.

Anghus rubbed his cheek. His eyes brimmed with tears but his face was flushed with defiance. 'The High Forest in the east. That's where you need to be.'

The third hunter whipped his hand again, but this time the boy rolled out of his reach with ease.

'Be gone,' the first man said to Catia, his voice wintry. 'We've given you enough comfort. And if you're wise, you'll return to where you've come from.'

Catia flashed a look of thanks to Anghus and returned to her stallion. She could feel eyes stabbing at her back.

When she glanced behind her, the hunters hadn't moved. She smelled threat in the air, and only felt the knot in her stomach ease once she was trotting a winding path east through the trees. The wind howled and the rain crashed down still; harder, if anything, than before she'd taken shelter.

Yet her heart began to pound with elation. The boy Anghus had revealed a truth that the older men had tried to keep hidden. This Fisher King was real, not some fantastical story of Myrrdin's as she'd feared. And now she knew where to go. The High Forest lay to the north of the great moor where the druids had been slaughtered. Myrrdin had called it Witch Country, another of the haunted parts of that western land, filled with sacred groves and standing stones erected in honour of the old gods. Or perhaps, she thought, that was just a tale woven to keep strangers away from the treasure.

Only those with the purest heart will ever find it. She shuddered as the boy's words came back to her. Pure of heart? That was not how she saw herself. She'd made too many compromises, seen too many deaths, on the long road to find safety for those she held dear.

Was she riding to her doom?

As if in answer to her question, a mournful blast from a horn rolled out at her back, caught up in the whine of the gale.

Catia stiffened. No hunter would be abroad in that storm.

Guiding her horse around a lightning-split oak, she crossed a stream threatening to burst its banks. Behind her, the horn blasted again. This time another answered, and another.

Catia glanced back. Even though her eyes had adjusted to the dark, she couldn't see far. She urged her stallion on, but the going was hard and slow. She couldn't risk her mount's breaking a leg.

Into a hollow, the leaf mould at the bottom little more than slurry. Around a rocky outcropping where the ground had fallen away in a previous flood. Lightning flashed, shafts of white punching through the canopy. In the afterburn in her eyes, she thought she could see faces. Her own senses were now betraying her.

Was that a cry? A thump of hooves? She cocked her head, trying to capture any sound in the lulls when the wind dropped and the thunder faded.

The horns again, closer this time.

Catia gritted her teeth, turning her horse and bringing it to a halt. No more running. If she were to die, it would be facing her enemy. She pulled her bow from her back and nocked an arrow.

Her ears prickled at the sound of her pursuers. They were close. She peered down the length of her arrow, easing it from side to side, ready to loose it at the first sign of a pale face in the gloom.

A cry rang out, cut short. Movement to her right.

She spun towards it, only just holding back her arrow at the last. A body careered down an incline into a jumble near by. In a lightning flash, she saw the fallen man's gut was ripped open. Not one of the hunters. A stranger.

Shouts now. Alarm.

Catia closed her eyes, judging their position from the sound of the approaching pursuers. When she was ready, she loosed the shaft. Another cry, this time of agony. She nocked another arrow as two black shapes coalesced in the gloom. Men on horseback.

One of the riders was listing, no doubt from her arrow. She loosed the second, and the shaft slammed into the silhouette dead centre. The man crashed back off his mount.

The third rider was bearing down on her through the dark. Flickers of sheet lightning sparked off a raised sword and a helm. But in that flash she also glimpsed another figure moving fast alongside her attacker.

The gloom fell again across sudden activity and another cry. From the sounds, her mind's eye conjured a vision of the rider being dragged from his mount. She winced at the familiar sound of a blade hacking into flesh. When it stopped, nothing moved around her. Her heart pounding, she squinted into the night, one arrow still nocked.

Finally she heard feet splashing through the pools towards her. A figure loomed up at her side.

The Lord of the Greenwood.

'I was returning from scouting ahead when I heard the horns,' he said. 'It was fortunate that I chose to come back at that moment. These men are seasoned warriors. They would not have let you live.'

Sheathing his sword, Aelius reached out his good hand. Catia took it, slipping off her mount on to the sodden ground. They knelt by one of the bodies. When the lightning flashed again, Catia saw that her brother was correct. This was a seasoned fighting man. His sword was nicked in many places, his helm clean but dented.

'No cut-throat waiting to rob unwary travellers,' Aelius said. 'Horses. Armour. Why would they be hunting you?'

Catia stood up, her thoughts racing. 'I met three hunters and questioned them about the Fisher King. Against their will, a boy there answered, and they showed anger almost immediately. This, it seemed, was a secret never to be revealed.'

Aelius pushed himself up and tapped his foot against the body. 'This cauldron must be valuable indeed if they're prepared to go to these lengths to protect it.'

Catia stepped over to the man she had killed and plucked out her arrows, slipping them back into her quiver. 'An attack, here, so far from our destination. What will we face when we draw close to the Fisher King's land?'

The storm crashed around the fortress. The waves were high, slamming against the granite cliffs with a force that made the very stones of the palace shake. The roaring of the ocean and the howling of the wind and the booming of the thunder swelled into every corner. There was no quiet to be found anywhere.

Amarina liked silence. She enjoyed empty rooms and shadowy niches, refuges where she could still thoughts as turbulent as the sea. And places where she could watch the mill of life grind others down small. Long ago she'd learned that watching and listening while others prattled was the best way to gain an advantage. And long ago she'd learned that she'd need every advantage she could lay claim to if she were to survive.

She felt disoriented in this din. She knew the fortress was a safe place. Well guarded at the only entrance gate and perched high above those unclimbable cliffs. Yet still her stomach knotted with unease.

With Catia long gone, Myrrdin dead and the Grim Wolves away, the only other occupant of the royal quarters was Weylyn, and she had tucked him in his bed many hours ago. Even so, she found herself prowling through the empty chambers, checking doors, peering through windows. Trusting no one and never feeling at peace was how she had lived so long, though death had come calling for her many a time.

On her third round, with every door sealed tight, she frowned. Her nostrils flared at the merest hint of an unfamiliar odour.

Loam.

The smallest trace, but she felt her heart beat faster.

Amarina pulled out her knife and hid it behind her back. Then her feet were flying across the flagstones as she followed the scent.

Within the throne room, darkness swelled. Pausing on the threshold, she breathed in, trying to taste the musk of a stranger. All was still inside that dark space.

But as she half turned away, a quiet voice rustled: 'Am-a-ree-na.' Every syllable carefully formed.

'Who's there?' she snapped.

No reply.

'Then I'm calling the guards.' Even as she spoke, she felt a surge of anger. She'd never run before, or called on any man to protect her. Turning to snatch a torch from the wall, she chased the dark away from the room.

From the corner of her eye, in the orange glow, she glimpsed someone sitting on the throne. Once only Lucanus sat there, then Catia, now . . . ?

Amarina whirled.

The witch-child Morgen sat cross-legged on the great wooden chair. Naked, as always, her body crusted with ashes and charcoal and the loam Amarina could smell, her hair tangled with leaves, so that it seemed a part of the forest had moved into the home of men.

'Am-a-ree-na,' she repeated. Her lips curled into a cold smile and her eyes were icier still.

'How did you get in here?' Amarina said. 'What do you want?'

'Daughter wants what is rightfully hers.'

Amarina spun again at the voice. The three sisters stood in the doorway, blocking her exit. The youngest pushed forward. Amarina narrowed her eyes, trying to remember her as the woman she had been before she had accepted her role in the Hecatae.

'What do you mean?'

'Come now, sister. You of all know the weft and weave of this world. Are you the one who measures and cuts the thread? Or are you the thread?' Her smile was not unfriendly.

'You live in your own world, sisters. Why would you want a part of this one?'

'Rome is fading, sister. Their soldiers are abandoning Britannia, fort by fort, ship by ship. Soon they will be gone for good. Then a new age will come. An old age made new again. And we who have been murdered and tortured and driven from our homes will have a voice once more, if only we would speak up.'

The mother slipped through the door. 'We reached a bargain long ago, sister. Surely you have not forgotten it.'

'I've told you all that I know of the palace.'

'True. You told us when the queen abandoned her throne, and her circle of defenders left too,' the younger one continued. 'And now we need more from you.'

Amarina felt her stomach knot. Every day she regretted the deal she'd made with the wyrd sisters. She'd tried to placate them with snippets of information. But she should have known a final accounting would be coming.

'What do you ask of me?'

The maiden and the mother parted and the crone eased a small figure forward. Amarina raised the torch and Weylyn emerged from the gloom. He rubbed his bleary eyes, then saw Morgen on the throne and with a whoop ran to her. They pressed their heads together, giggling and whispering.

'We will have a say in how this new world unfolds, sister, and you will help us.' The mother waved a filthy finger at her.

'You want me to betray these people?'

'You have no allegiances, sister. You know that is true. For all your days, you have taken the path that leads to your survival, regardless of any other. We ask no more of you.'

Amarina eyed the huddling boy and girl, and thought she could already see what the Hecatae desired. 'You want influence here, in the palace. And over the boy.'

'We are of the moon and the night,' the youngest of the three sisters said. 'We listen to the voices of the old gods, who live under hill and beneath lake, and we act on their behalf. Now Rome's time is done the old ways cannot be ignored any longer.'

'Swords are not our way. We have no need of armies,' the mother continued. 'We are a shadow behind the shoulder. A breath in the ear. That is the way we will bring the season round to our own once again. And you will aid us, sister. You will let us shape this boy, and through that our daughter will shape the age to come.'

'How long has this been your intention?'

'These threads have been drawn since before your mother's mother's mother's time, sister. Men think they follow their own will, but they follow ours unbeknownst. Would Lucanus have become king if we had not planted the seed? Would you, and this boy, be standing here now if we had not shown you the safe way to this fortress?'

The youngest of the three witches crouched and levelled a finger at Amarina.

'We have an agreement, sister. This boy is ours now. And you will see that our will is done.'

CHAPTER NINETEEN

The Spiral Path

'THREE DEAD. TWO SLAIN BY A BLADE.'
Bellicus splashed through the pool of rainwater from body to body in the thin grey light. He paused at the third fallen man and looked to Lucanus. 'Arrows ended this one's days.'

Lucanus nodded. Catia, it had to be. They'd been following her trail since they'd left Tintagel.

Wiping the rain from his face, he looked into the shadows clustering among the trees. Though the sun would be at its height, a bank of slate-coloured clouds had already turned the day to twilight. The ceaseless rain still sheeted down.

Mato crouched to examine the wounds on the corpse at the bottom of the incline. 'A short sword, by the looks of it. Whoever is accompanying Catia knows how to handle himself in a fight.'

'Who could it be?' Apullius mused. 'No one else left the fortress with her.'

Lucanus felt the eyes of the Grim Wolves swivel towards him as if he somehow held the answer. 'If he keeps her safe, it doesn't matter who it is.'

He tightened his jaw to hide a wince. His stump was aching. At times he felt pain as if his arm was still there, lines of fire scorching down to imaginary fingertips. The mushrooms the Attacotti had fed him had kept that agony at bay. Supplies of the sacred fungi remained in Myrrdin's quarters, but he had resisted

140

Mato's attempts to numb him. He needed a clear head if he was to aid his wife.

'These don't look like your usual rogues,' Solinus snarled. He rubbed the scar on his face as if that was aching too. Perhaps it was this miserable weather. 'Why would seasoned fighting men be trying to hunt Catia down?'

'A woman, on her own,' Comitinus suggested, as if that was answer enough. Perhaps it was.

'Move on,' Lucanus commanded. 'Catia's half a day away, at best. We can't afford to waste valuable time here.' He squelched through the mud away from the others, up the incline, towards the east.

'Look here,' Apullius called. He was pointing to a track through long grass.

Bellicus loomed over him. 'Others are pursuing her.'

'Bollocks,' Solinus said. 'Looks like . . . five? They're ahead of us. We need to pick up the pace. Someone seems determined to stop Catia getting to that treasure.'

The rain eased a little and the trail led out of the densely wooded valleys and back to the windswept spine of the west. The Grim Wolves marched through a countryside of twisted trees, clipped grass and bracken that reminded them of their homeland in the north. But this was still a haunted land, dotted here and there with standing stones where offerings were left to the old gods, and cairns, black against the wide skyline, and the graves of forgotten kings.

As he loped across the ridge, Lucanus glanced back from time to time. The Attacotti were out there somewhere, he knew, a cold shadow at his heels. He could never see them, but these days he felt them in his head, voices whispering in an unfamiliar tongue. A constant reminder of his ultimate fate.

They slowed their pace at a farm, a stone roundhouse with a turf roof surrounded by several smaller ones that were home to animals and stores of grain. While Apullius and Comitinus hauled fresh water from the well, Bellicus haggled for bread, eventually parting with a few coins. Lucanus saw suspicion in the eyes of the farmer and his wife, perhaps even contempt.

'We were such plain folk, once, with the same simple desires.' Mato pulled a stray strand of hair from his face.

'Before we were dragged into these games of power.'

'In the end, does it serve any of the plotters well? The wood-priests, the witches, the emperors of Rome, Corvus and his mother. They spend precious hours of their lives to buy a little advantage, and the moment they have their hands upon the prize someone else comes along to fight them for it.'

'And men like us are forced to give up our own lives to keep that endless circle going.' Lucanus flinched as a vision of the dragon eating its own tail burned into his mind.

'You can always walk away, my brother.'

Mato had delivered his words calmly, but Lucanus felt as if he'd been slapped. 'Walk away?' This idea was so strange to him he could barely understand it.

'When the witches stole Catia's son and took him into the land of the barbarians, you could have walked away. When you first encountered the Attacotti, you could have walked away. When you led us south, when the crown of the Pendragon was placed upon your head, when you took charge of an army and defended all Britannia against the invaders, when you fled to Tintagel and accepted the wood-priests' plan for the King Who Will Not Die, you could have walked away.'

Lucanus shook his head. 'How could I?'

Mato chuckled. 'And that is why you were chosen. You are not like other men.'

'Not true.'

'You can't see. Men who serve others, who sacrifice and suffer, never can. Your honour is your curse, and everyone else's hope.'

'You could have walked away too.'

Mato only laughed at that. 'You suffer, we all suffer, but we are blessed far more than those poor souls,' he said after a moment, nodding towards the farmer and his wife as they disappeared into their roundhouse. 'This lies at the heart of the teachings of the wood-priests. The Spiral Path.'

'You've been listening to Myrrdin too much.'

'I've been heeding him a great deal. For all his faults, and they were many, he had great wisdom. It's good that what little I've learned will not be lost now he's gone.'

'What is this Spiral Path?' the Wolf asked.

'Life is a labyrinth, my friend, and those who walk it stand a chance of being turned from lead into gold. To have the candle lit in their heads. This is the message of all the religions, yes? The promise of Mithras, of the Christ. It's a journey as old as time. Some turn away when called, some are forced to walk the path through the maze, and some choose.'

'A labyrinth?' Lucanus felt a coldness grip him. His thoughts flew back to that time on the island of the Attacotti when he had walked the labyrinth in his dreams to find the monster at the end.

'The Spiral Path curls round and round. Some turns are blocked, and the one who walks it must double back to find a way through. This is the life of the seeker. Obstacles everywhere. But learn to overcome them, and keep on that mysterious road, and wisdom is gained. The journey is the lesson and at the end is enlightenment.'

'Or a monster.'

'Perhaps the monster is enlightenment.'

Lucanus grunted and looked up to watch a kite wheel across the grey sky. He was a simple man. He had no time for this talk.

'The druids believe that those who walk the Spiral Path to the end, without being deflected by the obstacles they find on the way, are raised up,' his friend continued. 'Made great. Beacons in the dark night.'

Lucanus snorted. 'You'll be hammering out statues to us all soon.'

Mato laughed. 'We'll talk again at the end of this road, brother. Then we'll see what truths we each have learned.'

Bellicus was striding over, glowering from the depths of his wild mane of hair and beard. 'We've waited here long enough,' he said when he reached them.

'The farmer and his wife?'

'Have seen no sign of Catia. Say they know nothing of this Fisher King and his great treasure.'

'What did their eyes say?' Mato asked.

'Truth on the first, lying on the second. Solinus wants to persuade them to tell us what they know.'

Lucanus shook his head. 'No threats.'

'It would also be unwise,' Mato added. 'If they already favour the false king, how will we be seen if we start threatening the Dumnonii? Word will spread, as it always does, and we will be confirmed as the enemy.'

'And we would be the enemy,' Lucanus said. 'Come. We'll reach Catia soon enough.'

Lucanus breathed blood on the wind long before he saw the torches glaring through the trees. Dusk had come down hard, and the gale howled, whipping the roaring flames.

'What do you think?' Apullius whispered. 'The band hunting Catia?'

Bellicus sniffed the air. 'More men than five, I'd say.'

Lucanus raised his good arm and flexed his hand. The Grim Wolves dropped down and crept from oak to ash. As they neared, Lucanus heard the billowing of tents. A camp. He smelled smoke, sweat, and more blood.

Crouching behind a towering holly bush, he glimpsed a shimmer of armour and a familiar standard. Soldiers, about sixty of them, camped beside a stream. Some of the men were standing in the glow of the fire. He could see blood-smeared faces and tunics, others with tightly bound wounds.

The Wolf waved his hand downwards, signalling to his men to stay out of sight. When all were hidden, he called a greeting and walked towards the camp. Cries of alarm rang out as he stepped into the light from the fire, and men rushed towards him. Blades whipped to his throat.

'Who are you?' one of the soldiers snarled.

Before Lucanus could answer, rough hands gripped him and he was dragged to a large tent. Inside, he was thrown to his knees. He could feel the prick of blades at his back.

A centurion was pouring himself a cup of wine. He was swarthy-skinned, his hair jet black. A fresh cut raked across his cheek.

'Found him skulking outside the camp,' one of the men said.

'Are you a scout?' the centurion asked as he looked Lucanus over. He turned up his nose when he saw his captive had only one arm.

'I am,' Lucanus replied. The blades bit deeper into his back. 'Once I took the coin of Rome, like you,' he continued. 'I am *arcani*. I scouted out of Vercovicium, beyond the great wall, among the barbarian tribes.'

The centurion studied him for a moment, then nodded to his men. 'Leave us,' he said. 'Return to the watch.' Lucanus heard the sound of swords being sheathed, and pushed himself up. The centurion poured another cup of wine and held it out. The Wolf took it, nodding his thanks. When the drink touched his lips, he felt his head swim with memories.

'*Arcani*,' the centurion said. 'The hidden ones. I've heard tell of the work you did in the north. They said you were disbanded after the barbarians invaded.'

'We are our own masters now. But we served the emperor well in our day.'

The centurion smiled, sensing a kindred spirit. 'My name is Herminus.'

'Lucanus, the Wolf. My band were the Grim Wolves. We're still together. Most of the other *arcani* are long since gone.'

'What brings you to this forsaken place? No civilization here to tell of. No book has ever crossed the Tamar, I would wager.'

'We fled here when the horde invaded.' Lucanus sipped his wine. 'It's peaceful enough. After the years we've had, that's not to be sneered at.'

'Peaceful!' Herminus scowled. 'I've lost thirty good men today, and as many wounded.'

Lucanus frowned. 'The Dumnonii? They're farmers and merchants.'

'A war-band of barbarians. Picts, some Scoti by the look of them.' Herminus swilled back his wine, barely containing his anger.

'Here? Theodosius the Elder drove the horde out of Britannia.'

'So we thought. But they're back, and that doesn't bode well.

145

We never thought to be attacked, not here. We were returning to the south, to board a ship back to Rome. The barbarians came from nowhere and descended on us. We hadn't expected . . . we weren't ready.' Herminus poured himself another cup and for a moment stared into its depths, no doubt reliving the shock he had felt earlier in the day. 'They were like wild beasts. They couldn't contain their blood-lust. Driven near mad by the desire for vengeance, some of them, demanding death in payment for how they'd been treated during Theodosius' campaign.'

'We've seen no sign of barbarians here. This is the land of the Dumnonii—' Lucanus caught himself. If Gaia and her bastard offspring were looking to build their army, what better way than to buy mercenaries from the tribes? The Picts and the Scoti would still be smarting from their defeat, which had come tantalizingly close to an overwhelming victory, when they had had almost all of Britannia in their grasp. They would seize any chance to strike back at the architects of their rout, especially if they were well paid.

'I'll be filled with joy to see the last of this land. Too much rain, too cold.' Herminus shook his head. 'Though truth be told, Gaul is little better.'

'Why have you been summoned away?'

'No one will say it, but Britannia will be abandoned soon enough. It may be within fifty years.' He shrugged. 'The truth is, Rome has had its fill of this island. Trouble is spreading everywhere, like a dose of the pox from a whore. Better to concentrate our force on protecting the areas that are most valuable, eh?' He sipped his wine again, his face darkening. 'Some say the empire is fading. But who would believe that?' He forced a cheery grin. 'Mere stories told by hungry men who haven't been paid for a long time.'

'What trouble?'

'What news do you get here?'

'A little.'

'Trouble never ends for our emperor Valentinian, it seems. The Moors rebelled in north Africa. They blamed us for failing to protect them from the desert nomads. Sent Theodosius in to quell the troubles. Took him two years. Two years! Along the

Danube, the Quadi have started attacking, like the Alemanni before them. Didn't help that Marcellianus murdered their king at a banquet arranged for negotiations. Two legions were routed by the Sarmatians. Another band of Sarmatians invaded Moesia. Theodosius the Younger drove them back.'

Lucanus thought back to when he had met the general in Londinium, shortly before the army repelled the barbarian horde. 'He's a hard man.'

'Aye, and driven half mad by his love of the Christ. His father is grooming him for big things. Mithras—' Herminus caught himself and forced a smile. 'God help us.' He raised his goblet. 'Time to leave this miserable land, friend. Think on that. Go to Rome. There'll be work for a man with your skills. And the sun on your face, and good wine and food for your belly.'

'I have a family here now,' Lucanus said. 'That's why I'm on the road. My wife was riding east . . .'

'Alone?' The centurion furrowed his brow, but didn't give voice to whatever doubts he had.

'I need to find her, and soon. There are too many dangers, as you know. Have you seen any sign of a woman on a white stallion?'

Herminus shook his head. 'Be sure we will give her good protection if we come across her on the road. Until then, I wish you well with your search. You're welcome to stay here for the night if you wish.'

'My thanks, but my men are waiting for me.'

Lucanus handed back the cup and, with a nod, left Herminus to his dreams of a better life. As he made his way back among the tents, he watched the men tending to their wounds and felt his mood darken. Danger was drawing closer faster than he had imagined. Back in Tintagel, he had presumed there would be time to rally the Dumnonii to the house of Pendragon, and build their army, and construct a strategy that would drive the false king away from Britannia. But if the enemy had already drawn in the remnants of the barbarian horde, if they were already sending their war-bands deep into the west, he had no time left at all.

The Grim Wolves were invisible in the dark beyond the lights from the camp. Lucanus whistled through his teeth, and one by one his men separated from the shadows, dropping from the branches of an ash tree or unfurling from the tangled roots of an oak, or easing out from behind a bank of blackthorn.

'What happened to them?' Bellicus asked.

'Picts and Scoti.'

'Here?'

His brothers stiffened. Lucanus could see they were all leaping to the same conclusions he had.

'The quicker we get on the road, the better it will be,' Solinus grunted. 'For us, and for Catia.'

'If she knew there were war-bands roaming so close to home, she would never have ventured out alone,' Mato added. 'And if she's unaware that they're there, she could easily ride into the middle of them.'

Apullius clenched his fists, his face drawn. 'We know what they're capable of. We've seen the misery they inflict on good people. We'll find Catia soon enough, and if we have to drain the blood of a few barbarians on the way, all the better.'

Lucanus clapped a hand on the young man's shoulder. How could he not understand Apullius' hatred? The barbarians had made him an orphan and destroyed the life he once knew.

Without another word, the Wolf turned and pushed into a loping run. He heard the pad of feet start up behind him. Skirting the camp, he whipped his hand and his men fanned out among the trees, disappearing once again into the dark. Less likely to draw unwanted attention that way.

The lights of the camp were still twinkling when an owl-hoot cut through the whine of the wind. A warning, from Solinus.

The Grim Wolf was hunched over a dark shape. As Lucanus neared, his nostrils flared at the reek of blood again and he saw a dead soldier lying on the edge of a sea of bracken. The slash across his throat was fresh. A guard.

'Bollocks,' Solinus said.

Barely had the word left his lips when the night seethed with life. War-cries boomed. Shapes crashed through the undergrowth on all sides, emerging from where they had been hiding ready for the attack.

Lucanus snatched Caledfwlch from its sheath.

The moon must have broken through the clouds for a grey light suffused the woods. Amid the din and the frantic activity, a towering figure lurched in front of him: a Pict, his head shaven, his face twisted by black, spiral tattoos. He snarled something in his guttural tongue and swung up his short sword.

Lucanus jerked his own blade up. How long had it been since he'd had to fight? His arm felt like lead and his reactions were dull, his muscles creaking.

The Pict hacked down. Though he could not have told how, Lucanus clashed Caledfwlch against his enemy's blade. Sparks arced in the dark.

He felt his heart pounding, his head throbbing with blood. Dread. The sudden knowledge that he was no longer the man he had been. Too feeble, too depleted by time and pain. He could die here, cut down like the rawest soldier, and Catia would be left with no one to protect her.

Silver light flashed in his head and the mind of a man was dashed away. In its place roared the wolf, the beast he had killed the night he had become a true member of the *arcani*.

Lucanus flung himself forward, ducking under the cleaving sword. He sensed his enemy's shock, and then he rammed into the Pict and they crashed to the sodden ground, the wolf wrestling, tearing with its claws, bones clashing, the stink of meat and sweat in its nostrils, gouging, heaving, bucking.

Survival. Survival.

And then his teeth snapping and rending and the feel of hot blood gushing into his mouth. His mind crept back and he realized the Pict was still beneath him. A hand grabbed him and he jerked back, trying to throw it off. Bellicus' face loomed into his frame of vision.

Lucanus swallowed, allowing himself to be helped to his feet. The Grim Wolves clustered in a circle round him, their swords waving from side to side, while the barbarian war-band thundered towards the camp. They heard the cries of alarm ring out, and the clash of steel, and the maddening din of battle.

If the Fates had been kind, they might have stayed hidden there in the shadows with the torrent rushing by, but no. Warrior after warrior all but crashed into them, and his brothers hurled themselves into furious battle. A wild-haired barbarian with a broken nose thrust his sword towards him. This time he was quicker. He swung back on the balls of his feet and the tip of the blade swept a fingerwidth from his chest. Before the enemy could recover, he rammed Caledfwlch into his gut.

As he wrenched his weapon free, the warrior fell away. Another took his place. Lucanus stared into his foe's eyes and felt a pang of shock. A mane of wild black hair, eyes like the deepest well. A familiar face: Erca, leader of the Scoti war-band, who had once seized Catia as his captive. During the time he held her prisoner, the barbarian had learned to desire her. And, Lucanus feared, Catia in return had found something to admire in him.

'The Pendragon,' Erca growled. 'We have unfinished business.'

Lucanus staggered back, his single arm throwing him off balance. In that instant, he could see his death.

The Scoti leader swung his sword in an arc.

CHAPTER TWENTY

The Road of Trials

'LEAVE HIM!'

Apullius threw himself between Lucanus and Erca. Lucanus cried out, too late. The blade raked across the younger man's chest. He spun back and the Wolf caught him, crashing down on one knee.

'Half a man,' Erca spat. 'Too weak to fight your own battles. You need a boy to protect you now?' The Scoti leader yanked his arm back, ready for a killing thrust.

Lucanus fumbled with Caledfwlch, but Apullius pinned him down. He felt hot blood soak him.

Before he could thrust, Erca's eyes darted to the side. Lucanus followed that look and saw pale shapes flitting towards them. He shuddered, his despair at Apullius' sacrifice shading into confusion at the flicker of fear he had glimpsed in the barbarian's face.

A Pict racing by crashed down in front of them, blood spurting from a wound to his neck that had appeared so fast it was little more than a blur. Another barbarian clutched at his tumbling intestines, eyes wide with surprise that he was suddenly dying. And then those pale shapes coalesced as they burst from the shadows and the Attacotti danced forward, still silent, feet barely whispering as they swept through the woods.

His saviours; his captors. If he were to die it would be by their hands alone.

More barbarians fell as the white hunters rushed forward, their blades whisking this way and that. The war-band knew who their former allies were, knew and feared them more than any other. In an instant cries of warning were ringing out. The flood of barbarians drained away.

Lucanus jerked back from the mesmerizing approach of the Attacotti. A hulking shadow was disappearing into the trees. Erca was gone.

The Attacotti ghosted by him, not even offering a glance in his direction. The prize was still theirs. Beyond that, he was not worthy of their attention.

The Wolf flipped Apullius on to his back and pressed his hand on the chest wound. Blood bubbled up between his fingers. In the gloom, the Grim Wolf's face was as chalk white as those of the Attacotti, his eyes flickering half closed.

'Do not worry. My life means nothing compared to yours,' the younger man croaked.

'A lie,' Lucanus snapped.

'It's true. And every man here knows it.'

Lucanus felt acid burn his mouth. He was no more worthy than any of them. 'Mato!' he called. 'Bellicus!'

A moment later he heard feet pounding towards him and Mato dropped down at his side. 'Let me,' his friend said, easing his hand away from the wound.

The Wolf flopped back on to the sodden ground, drained. Apullius tried to force himself up, but Mato pushed him back down, dipping into the pouch at his hip. Lucanus wrinkled his nose at the reek of a foul-smelling paste which Mato smeared on the wound before binding it with cloth.

'More of Myrrdin's potions?'

'The druids are . . . were . . . wise men. Healers as well as teachers.' Mato's voice was barely audible beneath the distant din of clashing swords and battle-cries as he worked to seal the wound. 'If this knowledge is not passed on, much will be lost.'

'Will it work?' Lucanus murmured, trying not to let Apullius hear.

Mato didn't answer.

Apullius' eyelids fluttered shut, but Lucanus could see he was still breathing.

'That's all I can do, for now.' Mato stood and tugged Lucanus to one side. 'We have a hard choice now, brother. If we go on to find Catia, Apullius will probably die. We need to get him to a leech before the rot grips him. If we go back with Apullius . . .'

He let the words hang. Lucanus knew what his friend could not say. Any retreat might mean Catia would die. He felt his throat narrow at the unbearable decision. How could he choose?

'This is talk for later,' he said. 'For now, we need to find safety.'

He blasted a short, sharp whistle and the rest of the Grim Wolves pounded out of the night. Circling him, they stared down at Apullius. All they needed to know they could read from that wound, and Mato's grim face.

'We must be away from here,' Lucanus said, his voice hoarse. 'The barbarians care little about us, for now. They want their vengeance on Rome. But soon enough they'll be back.' He remembered the look in Erca's eyes, the look of a man who was not used to being denied.

The Grim Wolves hooked their arms under Apullius and lifted him as gently as they could. He moaned from the pain, but his eyes remained shut. Through the trees they ran, until the thunder of battle was lost beneath the howling of the wind. Finally, they rested in the lee of a valley beneath a natural shelter of outcropping granite.

While Comitinus moistened Apullius' lips from a water skin, Lucanus trudged away. He felt the weight of the younger man's sacrifice crushing him down. Perching on a lichen-crusted rock, he bowed his head and let his thoughts sweep back, across the fields, hills and moors and through the years, to Vercovicium and the simpler life he had led there. With the coin he took from the army for his work with the *arcani*, he had followed what had seemed a preordained path. Until the druids and the witches had interfered, steering his life off course.

He sucked in a deep, juddering draught of the damp air, feeling the steady beat of droplets on his wolf-pelt from the branches above. And yet there was always Catia. If life had remained the same in Vercovicium, the love they had always felt for each other would never have come to fruition. Her days would have been miserable in the orbit of her brute of a husband. He would never have had a son.

Is this what the gods did? Give joy with one hand, and steal it back with the other?

Hauling himself to his feet, he squelched back through the sea of mud to the overhanging rock. The grey shapes beneath it looked like a sheltering wolf pack. At their heart lay Apullius. His eyes were open again, black pebbles in a frozen pool.

'Leave us,' Lucanus grunted. The other Grim Wolves drifted away as he dropped to his haunches beside the dying youth. 'You saved my life. I'll never forget that.'

'Any man here would have done the same.' His voice sounded like autumn leaves.

'But it's wrong. I'm just a filthy ditch-crawler like the rest of you.'

Apullius tried to laugh, but it rolled into a hacking cough. 'You're not like us, Lucanus. Why can't you see that? Could Solinus command such respect from an army that they would follow him to certain death? Would Bellicus, for all his long years, have the wisdom to be a king who faces questions, new demands, every day? No.'

'I don't want to be raised up.'

'You have no say in it.' Lucanus recoiled at the snap in the voice. There was fire in Apullius' eyes. 'This is the story that's been written for you.'

Lucanus stiffened. 'I choose my own path.'

Apullius shook his head. 'You must embrace who you're supposed to be, for the sake of all who follow you into what is to come. All depends on you, Lucanus. You are the key. You are the Pendragon.'

'My wishes don't matter?'

'Your life ended a long time ago. Embrace that freedom.'

Lucanus looked deep into the face of the other man. There were already lines there. That should not be the case in one so young, but suffering made men of all boys.

Apullius forced a wan smile. 'You don't see yourself as others do. The Grim Wolves . . . they'll follow you anywhere. Do you think a woman like Catia would have chosen a lesser man? Your soldiers, who gave up their families and their work and everything they knew, men who had never lifted a sword before, all of them marching towards a monstrous enemy? You're a good man, with a good heart. That's what everyone sees. In the end, that's all that counts. They don't need a hero of old. Just a good heart.' His voice trailed away into another series of coughs.

Lucanus felt overwhelmed. For a moment, he bowed his head, listening to the steady beat of falling droplets in the dark.

'You're a good man too, Apullius,' he said slowly. 'You brought a light into this dark age in which we've found ourselves. The first time I met you I could see it, that night in the woods, where you waited with the other children, and the old and the sick, comforting Morirex, never thinking of yourself. Though your mother and father were stolen from you that night, you shouldered your burden like a man. You thought only of others. And in the hard days that followed, you grew stronger. All of the other Grim Wolves saw it. That was why you were asked to join us, and mark my words, that is not an honour given lightly. And you met that challenge. You defeated the wolf one on one. You earned your place among us, and we stand shoulder to shoulder. Equals. You've proved yourself time and again. There is no finer man, no one I'd rather fight alongside. You have honour and courage.' Lucanus swallowed. His mouth was dry. 'You're like a son to me, Apullius. My heart swells with pride whenever I look upon you. And that's why I've decided to send you back with the others, to gain the healing you need. I'll go on alone. I'll brook no dissent.'

The Wolf raised his head, waiting for the argument. Apullius would never agree to it. What lay ahead was too much for one man, especially a one-armed shadow of his former self. But he had decided, and he wouldn't back down.

The wind whined in the branches and the raindrops beat upon the mud, and still there was no objection. And then he looked down at the lad and saw the utter stillness that could never lie across a living thing. And he felt himself swallowed by a torrent of grief so deep and black that he thought he would never see light again.

There was no dry wood to build a pyre and they had no tools to dig a grave, so for the rest of that long night they searched through the areas where fingers of granite thrust out from the banks and valley sides to find enough rock to build a cairn.

Solinus would not show any of them his face, but he chose a spot in a clearing that would receive the sun by day and moonlight by night, and vowed to fight anyone who would deny him his choice.

It was a peaceful location, but a sad one, so far from any life, where no one would come to mourn, or in years to come to sit and reflect on what great hero was buried there. But it was fitting too. The Grim Wolves had always lived their days in loneliness, away from human habitation, under the stars, on the windswept moors and in the deep forests, with only the song of the hawk and the hoot of the owl for company.

As the dawn broke, Lucanus stood at the head of the cairn while Mato summoned up some words. The Wolf could see that they touched the hearts of his brothers gathered round that small pile of stone, but he heard none of them. All he remembered later was the steady tidal wash of the blood in his head.

When they were done, the others drifted away to be alone with their thoughts. Mato strode over to him, a sad smile on his lips. Still trying to find some brightness even in the darkest moment. Lucanus knew he would always feel kindly towards his friend for that.

'There are no words that will bring comfort, I know,' Mato said. 'We must keep Apullius in our hearts, that's all. And we will need that light in days to come.'

Lucanus nodded. 'The barbarians will be roaming far and wide, ready to spill blood and plunder. We can expect no help from the Dumnonii. Every step of the way now is fraught with danger.' He tried not to think of Catia and what she might encounter in a land now filled with cut-throats and rogues.

'This is a road of trials.' Mato leaned on his staff, his sodden hair plastered to his head. 'Myrrdin spoke of this. It's said that whosoever searches for the cauldron of the Dagda will be tested time and again. The gods will not allow those who are not worthy to reach that prize.' He squeezed Lucanus' shoulder, a touch of comfort. 'The wood-priest said everyone who quests for the cauldron must at some point defeat themselves. What that might mean, you know as well as I. Myrrdin loved speaking in riddles. But he was adamant about one thing: deep truths must be learned.'

Lucanus shrugged. 'We do what the Grim Wolves have always done. When we know hard times lie ahead, we don't turn away. We do the work we've been charged with. If we win, it's because of what lies in our heart. If we don't have that fire in our heart, we don't win.'

Mato nodded and walked away to find the others. For a long moment, Lucanus stared at that lonely cairn, seeing in it more than just a shelter for the remains of a man he valued. He was not ready for this road of trials.

But who ever was?

CHAPTER TWENTY-ONE

Fang and Claw

THE LAMP OF THE MOON BURNED WHITE THROUGH THE branches. Stark shadows carved across the pools of light leading them on as they raced through the trees.

'Thank the gods it's not a dark night. We'd be dead by now,' Solinus croaked. He was scowling, sweat running along the lines of the scar that quartered his face. Though he looked as vinegar-sour as always, Bellicus could sense the fear washing off him. And who could blame him?

Behind them, howls tore through the night, whipping up into a frenzy.

Bellicus felt his stomach knot. That chilling sound, so familiar from their long nights in the Wilds. The wolf pack sensed their prey was almost in their grasp. They were exhorting their brothers to run faster, driving their meal on to exhaustion. The music of that baying, soaring up then clashing, would wring terror from even the bravest heart, and in that dread mistakes would be made. Wrong paths would be taken. The prey would stumble, or dash wildly into a place from which there could be no escape.

They mustn't make that mistake.

Bellicus threw himself on, leading the way along the narrow trail through the forest. Feet pounded behind him. The others were still keeping pace. That was good. There was no room for even the slightest error, because he knew too well that the wolves were faster, their stamina greater. They would never simply give up the hunt.

His nostrils wrinkled and he smelled brine on the breeze. Had they been driven so far off course that they were near the southern coast? His legs burned. He felt as though he'd been running for ever. Hours now since the wolves had first picked up their scent and decided they would make a good feast.

But they were brothers. That's what he couldn't understand. And he knew all the other Grim Wolves were thinking the same. Never had any wolf threatened them before. Not since the night of their ritual, when they had stalked and killed an old wolf, the king of a pack, and earned their place as *arcani*.

'The gods have abandoned us,' Comitinus moaned at his back. 'There can be no other explanation.'

'You know what would solve this problem?' Solinus snarled. 'If I punched you in your face and threw you back there. We four could get away while they feasted on you. What say you?'

'Silence, both of you,' Bellicus roared.

'I wouldn't be surprised if they can smell Comitinus' fear,' Solinus grunted, demanding the last word as always.

Bellicus thundered to a halt, snatching at a branch to prevent himself from plunging over the edge into an abyss. He sucked a mouthful of air into his searing lungs and peered down. As his eyes searched the dark, which was punctured here and there by silver moonbeams, he sensed the lie of the land. A valley side, so steep at the top it was almost sheer. The earth had fallen away in places and the trees punched up in a jumble of angles, some half slipped, their roots straining. A treacherous route. But they had no choice.

'I'll go first,' he said. He felt a hand grasp his arm and looked round into the face of Lucanus.

'Take care. One wrong foot and you'll break your neck.'

'No great loss,' Solinus muttered. 'Just don't break anything valuable.'

Bellicus glanced back through that black-and-white world. He couldn't see the pack yet – and thank the gods for that; if he could the end would be near – but those yowls were ringing out even louder now. To the left, to the right, directly ahead. Already preparing to circle. Under the baying, he heard a whisper and realized it was Mato muttering a prayer.

'Why do you do that? The gods have abandoned us!' Comitinus said.

Bellicus cuffed Comitinus round the ear. It felt good. A small reward after the hours of running. He spun on his heel and threw himself over the edge.

For a moment, he felt as if he was floating in a great black ocean, and then his feet struck loose soil. Down he skidded, his arms flailing to keep his balance.

Faster and faster he slid as the ground rushed away under him, building up speed until he felt his legs begin to run in his desperate search for equilibrium. An instant later, he was careering madly, each step carrying him yards. He felt weightless. Silhouettes blurred by. Leaves lashed his face. Branches ripped his skin. His shoulder slammed into a listing tree and he bounced to one side. And then he was spinning, even more out of control. His feet swept up from the earth, and up, and he was turning over.

He crashed on to his back, the force so great he bounced and turned again, and he remembered Lucanus' warning about breaking his neck, but it was in the lap of the gods now. And that was all his wits allowed him before he was spinning and crashing and rolling, smashing into trunks, rattling away. Lances of pain seared through him. His temple cracked against a rock and he was done.

Blinking, Bellicus swam up from the dark to feel the damp turf under his back and his head ringing. He heaved himself upright. Fire burned in every joint, in every bone. But he was alive.

For now.

Lucanus, Solinus and Comitinus were picking themselves out of the bracken and the long grass. Mato was leaning against an elm, binding a cloth around a gash on his arm.

'Where are those pale-skinned Attacotti bastards when you actually need them?' Solinus spat.

'Wolves are too great a threat even for them,' Comitinus said, offering a hand to haul his friend to his feet.

Peering up the valley side, Bellicus glimpsed movement along the ridge. The wolves were ranging back and forth. For a moment, the world seemed to hang. Then over the top they bounded.

'Run!' he roared.

He watched his brothers jerk into life at his bellow, and then they were all racing along the valley floor. The trees there were not so tightly clustered. Ahead, brilliant shafts of moonlight punched through the canopy, shimmering beacons drawing them on through a sea of waving fronds. Bellicus thought he could hear the crashing of waves.

'Why are they hunting us? Why?' Comitinus choked back a sob. 'They can't be ravenous this time of year. There's easier prey.'

Their life-candle was close to guttering. Bellicus sensed movement along the valley side to his left. From the corner of his eye, he glimpsed sinuous shadows loping through the moonbeams, amber eyes gleaming and fur glowing silver. The pack was silent now, as they always were when the hunt's end was near. Though he didn't dare look back, he imagined the rest of the wolves pounding closer behind him, another set breaking off to sweep round to their right.

And then they'd come together as one, and the rending and tearing would begin.

Out of the trees they crashed. Bellicus blinked, almost blinded by the broad moonlit vista after the claustrophobic dark of the forest. They were racing across a windswept headland, the grass silver under the full moon hanging amid a river of stars in the sable sky. A white road ran across the black surface of the heaving ocean. Bellicus could hear the booming of the waves breaking on the rocks somewhere below.

'Bollocks,' Solinus said.

Bellicus felt the other man's dismay. The headland was a spur pushing out into the sea from the treeline and they were trapped on it, with no way to escape to the left or the right. The oaks and elms edged dizzying cliffs.

His thoughts whirled back to the island of the Attacotti, and for a moment he hoped the gods would present them with some hidden tunnel once again so they could crawl to safety. It was a futile thought, he knew. There was only the grass and the dizzy-ing drop.

He glanced back and watched the wolves emerge from the trees. They slowed as they came into the open, lowering their heads, cautious even then, for there was nothing more dangerous than cornered prey. But he'd seen the great packs hunt before, in the far north, and he knew even swords would only delay the inevitable for a short while.

But they would fight to the last. That was what it meant to be a Grim Wolf.

Solinus snatched out his sword as if the same thoughts were burning in his head, and then they were running together to the last of the grass.

'Stay.'

Nearing the edge, Bellicus jerked at Lucanus' barked order. 'We can't—'

'Stay.' Softer this time. He felt a hand on his shoulder, turning him back to face his brothers. Then Lucanus was fumbling at his wolf-pelt.

'What is it?'

'Blood.' Lucanus yanked up the pelt to show the brown stain to the others. He scraped his finger on the patch and examined the smear on his skin. 'Still wet.'

And then the other Grim Wolves were dragging up their own pelts as the pack prowled closer. All of them were marked with blood along the lower edge. It had leaked down on their leggings.

'This is why the pack was hunting us,' Comitinus exclaimed.

'Who could have done this?' Bellicus snapped. He was looking past his huddling brothers to where the hunters were circling, slow and steady.

'Someone who wanted to prevent us reaching our prize,' Lucanus said.

'But who didn't want to face our swords,' Mato added. 'While we slept.'

And they'd slept the sleep of the dead after the exhaustion of their trek and the misery of Apullius' death, Bellicus thought.

'Might have been good to find that out a few hours ago,' Solinus said.

But they would never have seen those stains in the dark of the forest. 'I should have smelled it,' Bellicus said.

Lucanus clapped a hand on his arm. A tight smile that told him not to berate himself.

The Grim Wolves turned to face their fate.

Lucanus held the eyes of the leader of the pack. It was huge, far bigger than those that came to a halt around it, and a streak of silver ran along its back. The amber eyes stared, and Lucanus stared back, and Bellicus thought that some silent communication was flashing between them.

Then the majestic creature stepped forward, drawing itself on to its haunches, ready to leap. It was as if a dam had broken. The rest of the pack surged.

'Jump,' Lucanus ordered, thrusting Bellicus towards the edge.

'Are you mad?'

'Jump, and put your faith in the gods!'

A curse rang out from Solinus and then he was running towards the edge. Bellicus watched the others race past him before he too threw himself forward, hearing the thunder of the pack at his back. Torn apart by fangs, dashed to bits on the rocks or drowned? What kind of choice was that for a man?

One by one his friends vanished over the edge. He sensed the great wolf-king snapping at his heels and for a moment he feared he was going to fall to it. But then the ground disappeared beneath his feet, and he was plunging down, the salty air ripping at his hair and beard, the roaring of the waves engulfing him.

Death rushed up to greet him.

CHAPTER TWENTY-TWO

Hunger

G ULLS SCREECHED. WAVES CRASHED. WET SAND GRITTY UNDER his cheek. Pushing himself up, Lucanus blinked into the thin light of a new day.

He felt a wave of euphoria rush through him. He lived, though he had no idea how. His thoughts flew back to the last moment he remembered, hitting that icy water so hard he may as well have fallen on to the jagged teeth of rocks at the foot of the cliff. By rights he should have drowned. He couldn't swim well enough with one arm, not in the high tide. The gods must still have work for him to do. That could be the only explanation.

A vision flashed across his mind. A murder of crows swirling so tightly it was as if they were forming a body, a body made out of black wings and beaks, and from their depths a pair of red eyes burning. The Morrigan had come to him in his dreams while his wits had been dashed.

The gods still had work for him. Of course they did. Would they ever let him go?

A convulsion racked him, and he bucked, vomiting up a stream of brine. After it was done, he shook from the cold seeping out of his sodden clothes, but he felt better. With that came a rush of thoughts, driving him towards panic. Catia. His friends. Lurching to his feet, he spun around. The beach was wide, running up a slight incline to a line of trees in a horseshoe cove.

Of his fellow Grim Wolves there was no sign.

His heart fell and he felt queasy with despair. But then a cry rang out. On a long finger of brown rock, a bedraggled Mato was waving.

'You are well,' his friend said, grinning with relief once he had trudged across the wet sand. 'Solinus and Comitinus are making a fire to dry us out.'

Lucanus could hear the sound of bickering in the distance. 'Bellicus?'

Mato's face tightened and he shook his head. 'Not yet. But if we four have survived there's a good chance for him too.'

Clambering over the rock, Lucanus shielded his eyes against the rising sun. A trail of smoke drifted up from a shelter at the far end of the beach. As they walked over in silence, Lucanus tried to push aside the cold stone of grief he felt for Apullius. He couldn't bear to lose Bellicus too.

Comitinus was carrying armfuls of kindling from the trees and Solinus was on his knees, fanning the flames. He looked up. 'Thought you'd still be alive. Even being half eaten doesn't slow you down.'

Lucanus held out his hand to the fire. 'Once we've warmed through, we'll search the shoreline for Bellicus. If the currents brought us here, then the same will have happened to him.'

'We put our faith in the gods,' Mato said. 'Perhaps that was the lesson of that trial.'

'Or perhaps not,' Solinus said, his voice dripping with acid. 'Perhaps the lesson was not to be such a band of jolt-heads that we all sleep without setting a watch that would stop an enemy splattering us with blood.'

Comitinus pushed his chin in the air. 'I prefer the lesson of the gods.'

'I bet you do. Save you having to do anything, you lazy fuck-pig. Ooh, let the gods sort this out. *I'll just lie back and pray.*'

Mato wrung out his soaking wolf-pelt and studied it. 'Whoever marked us with blood must have come like ghosts in the night. I sleep with one eye open and nothing disturbed me.'

'There are those who will defend that cauldron at any cost. We know that now,' Lucanus said.

Comitinus paced around the fire, kicking up whorls of sand. 'I miss civilization. Bath-houses and taverns that sell good wine, and good food, and wise men discussing the great arts, and books—'

Solinus snorted. Comitinus glared at him.

'This western land is filled with superstition. Witches and druids and charms and magic treasure, and those who are prepared to kill for it,' he continued. 'If this was what the world used to be like before the army came, give me Rome any day.'

For a while, they sat there until the steam rose off their cloaks and pelts and tunics in the heat of the sun and the fire. Then Lucanus pushed himself to his feet.

'First, we search for Bellicus,' he said. 'After that ... We've been thrown off course, which is what those who planted the blood wanted. Catia's trail has been lost. Our only hope now is to find a path to the home of the Fisher King.'

Solinus looked up at the gulls wheeling across the sky. 'No Attacotti to pull our fat out of the fire now. On the bright side, you'll probably be able to hold on to a few more fingers for a while.'

Comitinus and Mato chuckled. Lucanus only forced a tight smile. Let them have their light moment at his expense. The gods knew they needed it. But as he strode away across the beach, he could still feel the Attacotti following relentlessly in his footsteps, even if they were miles away. They would never let him go.

A line of deep footprints ran up from the surf to a track on the far side of the cove. They belonged to Bellicus, Lucanus was sure of that, and he felt a wave of relief that his friend must have survived. But those impressions in the sand were not alone. On either side, the beach had been churned up by other feet.

'Somebody pulled him out of the water.' Mato knelt, trailing his fingertips across the confusion of other prints. 'Three rescuers. Perhaps four.'

'Must have had a lungful of water if he didn't come looking for us first,' Comitinus said. He looked up to the track which ran through the elm trees.

'Wasn't much of a swimmer, though, was he?' Solinus grunted.

'I'm surprised he didn't go straight to the bottom like a rock, big bastard like that.'

Lucanus trudged up the beach along the line of footprints. His relief was already shading to worry for Catia. They'd lost so much time, and after what had happened to Apullius he couldn't help but fear that the Fates were conspiring against him. Whether this was the road of trials that Mato had talked about, the curse of the treasure, or merely the way of the world, he didn't care. The result was the same.

Solinus strode ahead along the track, studying the deep ruts. 'Well used,' he muttered. 'Probably haul a vessel down here to fish. Bellicus is probably sick of garum already.'

Beyond the trees, the track plunged across grassland gently rising to a ridge. Mato pointed to well-tended fields and a collection of stone roundhouses peeping out from behind a copse. He sniffed the breeze. 'Smoke. No food cooking. No garum.'

Sweating in the morning sun, they trekked up the track. All was still, with only the wind rustling across the grassland.

'No beasts as far as I can see,' Solinus said.

When they reached the circular stone-and-turf buildings, Lucanus called a greeting. A moment later a woman lurched out of the largest roundhouse, clawing her fingers through her matted hair to present herself to the strangers. Her dress was filthy and didn't seem to have been mended in a long time. But the Wolf felt drawn to her hollow eyes and gaunt cheeks, little more than a skull. She raised a hand to wave to them, and he saw that her arm was so thin he could get his thumb and forefinger around it.

'Poor as dirt,' Comitinus muttered. 'Out here, away from the trade routes and the markets, they probably claw their way from one harvest to the next.'

'No beasts,' Solinus repeated, almost to himself, as he looked around the farm.

Lucanus strode up to the woman. Several of her teeth were missing. 'We're scouts, from Tintagel. You've heard of it?'

'Aye. The fortress in the west. Who hasn't?' She looked past him to the others. 'Have you food with you? Bread?' Her eyes gleamed with hope.

The Wolf shook his head, sorry to disappoint her. 'Not a crumb has passed our lips in two days. We're searching for a friend of ours. Big man, like a bear, snowy hair and beard.'

The woman nodded. 'My husband and Arden and Pert, from the farms over there, found him, half drowned. A shipwreck, they thought. But he said he'd jumped in.' Her stare suggested Bellicus had lost his wits.

'That's him.'

'He begged for bread, but we had none to give. So he set off up there . . .' She turned and pointed to the track continuing up to the top of the ridge. 'Said he'd find some game. And . . . and . . .' – her voice swelled with enthusiasm – 'said he'd bring some back to us. If you find some, you could do the same? In thanks for aiding your friend?'

Lucanus nodded, smiled. She blinked away a tear and scrubbed her bony hands together, pathetically grateful at his assent. The hunger had a grip on her. He wondered how long it had been since her belly was last full.

The Wolf turned to go back to the others and saw only Mato and Comitinus standing there. Solinus was prowling round the smaller houses.

The woman clawed her fingers and screamed, 'Away from there! Don't you try and rob us! I'll fetch my husband! He'll gut you!'

'Solinus,' Lucanus called, annoyed.

The Grim Wolf was like a dog on the scent, not even looking back. He moved from one roundhouse to the next. Screeching, the woman ran towards him. Uncaring, Solinus plunged into the smallest store. A moment later, he thrust his head out and yelled, 'Here! Here, now!'

The woman threw herself at him, clawing and spitting like a wild beast. Solinus caught her wrists with ease and held her, writhing, while he silently urged the Grim Wolves on. The farmer's wife barely had the strength to stand. Solinus hurled her away like a sack of turnips and she rolled in the dust and lay there, sobbing.

Lucanus barged into the roundhouse behind Solinus. A shaft

of sunlight cut through the gloom and in it lay Bellicus, his hands bound behind his back, his ankles tied too, and a filthy rag pulled around his mouth. His wide eyes urged them to free him.

'I'm a fool,' he gasped when Solinus yanked the rag away. 'My guard was down and they got the better of me.'

Behind him, Lucanus heard Mato and Comitinus draw their swords to guard the door. 'If they wanted to rob you, why did they leave you alive?'

'They wanted to eat me!' Bellicus' voice broke and in his wide eyes the Wolf could see the horror of all his imaginings during the time he had been tied up there in the dark.

'Bastards,' Solinus snarled. He wrenched out his own blade and stalked towards the door. Lucanus thrust himself in front of him before he could exact his vengeance on the farmer's wife.

The woman was on her feet by the narrow entrance to the roundhouse. As she shouted for help, three men lurched out from where they'd been hiding. She clutched at the arm of one of them, no doubt her husband, and pointed at the interlopers.

Lucanus watched the husband snatch up a sickle and move towards him. The silver blade glinted in the sunlight. The farmer was little more than a skeleton clothed in filthy rags, but his eyes burned with a passion far brighter than any Lucanus had seen in even the fiercest enemy.

The Wolf pulled Caledfwlch from its sheath and looked along the length of the blade into the face of the farmer and the two men who lurched behind him; one grasped an axe, the other a cudgel. Behind him he heard Solinus' sword sing as it too was levelled.

The woman's husband looked around the crescent of scouts, and then a strange thing happened. Fat tears rolled down his hollow cheeks, and his thin lips trembled. He began to shake as if he had a terrible fever. The sickle slipped from his fingers and he dropped to his knees in the mud of the track. The two men behind him looked at each other, then at the Grim Wolves' blades, and tossed their own weapons away. The farmer's wife ran forward and grasped him, trying to drag him to her feet, but she was too weak to do so and fell to her knees beside him.

They had nothing, Lucanus thought. Not even the merest hint of courage or strength.

· Solinus stepped forward, jabbing his sword towards the pathetic quartet. Lucanus reached out his arm to hold him back.

'Speak,' he told them, 'or I'll let Solinus do what he will with you.'

'Please,' the woman begged, pressing her palms together. 'We have nothing left.'

'Raiders came and stole all our food and belongings,' her husband whimpered. 'There's no trade here now, not since the army abandoned their forts in the east and stopped protecting the routes.'

'So you thought you'd fill your bellies with my friend,' Solinus barked. 'What kind of devils are you that you'd eat human flesh?'

'What choice did we have?' the woman wailed. 'Hungry . . . so hungry . . .'

'You always have a choice.' Solinus pushed forward, but Lucanus pressed him back.

'You could hunt,' the Wolf said.

'We're farmers, not hunters,' the husband cried. 'We tried, but we couldn't catch enough before we grew too weak. We couldn't even fish. The raiders burned our boat. They wanted to see us suffer. We didn't want to hurt your friend, but we were driven near mad by hunger.'

Solinus spat at them.

'They slaughtered their beasts, and the dogs too,' Comitinus called as he appeared from behind the roundhouses. 'There's a pile of bones back there.'

'What now?' Lucanus eyed the pitiable farmers, then sheathed Caledfwlch.

'Leave them to their fate,' Solinus growled. 'These aren't barbarians, like the Attacotti. These are civilized folk. But they were still ready to eat a man.' He spat again, disgusted. 'They'd have choked on that tough meat. Like chewing leather, I'd wager. That would teach them.'

'Starvation is not a good way to die,' Mato said.

'As if there's any,' Comitinus added.

The Wolf eyed Bellicus, giving him the chance to judge. He only rubbed the blood back into his wrists and shook his head.

Lucanus looked down at the woman and the three men grovelling in the dirt and could see why his friend hadn't demanded vengeance. Their faces were twisted with despair, and they clawed at their hair and their hollow cheeks and wailed – with shame, he thought. They knew the path they'd chosen and they loathed themselves for it.

'Hunger destroys a man,' he said in a quiet voice. 'Who's to say we wouldn't be like those poor wretches if we were starving?'

'Never,' Solinus said.

Lucanus stepped in front of the farmers and their howling rose in a frenzy. They expected the worst. 'Silence,' he commanded. His voice seemed to strike them, and the yowling stopped and they hung their heads.

'What you were about to do was a crime against all that we hold dear. You know that. But you're victims of the madness that has gripped Britannia in this dark age. We'll hunt some game for you, enough to fill your bellies for a few days. Then you'll be strong enough to hunt yourselves, or at least to set a few traps. We'll show you how.'

The starving men and woman flung themselves at his feet as if they were supplicants at a temple, crying with joy, but Bellicus caught his arm. 'Have you forgotten Catia?' he whispered. 'We can't afford to waste a day here hunting.'

Lucanus' heart ached. Every moment of delay was one which might cost Catia her life, he knew. But how could he abandon these wretches? And he also knew that Catia herself would never forgive him if he put her needs above such suffering.

'Let's bring them some venison,' he said, 'and the time lost will only put more fire in my heart to find Catia more quickly.'

Or, he thought, to exact bloody vengeance if a hair on her head has been harmed.

CHAPTER TWENTY-THREE

Lost

LUCANUS JERKED FROM A DREAM OF CROWS. HANGING OVER HIS face was a death mask, the eyes the blackest he'd ever seen. Crying out in shock, he fumbled for Caledfwlch, but by the time his fingers closed on the hilt the ghastly face had retreated into the night.

The vision burned into his mind. One of the Attacotti had been sitting by him, watching him sleep.

Bellicus, Mato and Solinus scrambled up, ruddy in the embers' glow from the dying fire. Comitinus hurried from the dark beyond the circle of light.

'The Attacotti have found us again,' Lucanus said. His heart was pounding, and he sucked in a deep breath to steady himself.

'You thick-headed oaf,' Solinus snapped, rounding on Comitinus. 'You were supposed to be keeping watch.'

'I was! I didn't sleep. My eyes were wide open. I was listening for any sound.'

'Then you're as useless as a holed barrel.'

'Don't blame him,' Lucanus said. 'The Attacotti are like ghosts, you know that. Any of us could have done the same.'

'What did they want?' Bellicus asked. His sword was in his hand, and his eyes darted as he tried to search the deep dark.

Lucanus shook his head. What *did* they want? None of them could know the minds of those devils. His stomach knotted at the haunting image of the warrior watching him sleep: somehow

172

a fanatical worshipper devoted to a prone god-king, and at the same time a gaoler who would never let his prisoner slip through his fingers.

Though it was still the deep of the night, Lucanus felt certain sleep would not return. He hunched over the ashes, prodding the embers with a stick while listening to the moan of the wind. Voices lay within it, he was sure, but whether it was the Attacotti calling to each other in their alien tongue or the gods themselves, he had no way of knowing.

For two days, they'd crept east, keeping close to the coast and away from the tracks. When they delivered the venison to the starving farmers, they let them gorge themselves before questioning them. The three men and the woman had heard something of a treasure, though they couldn't remember exactly what they'd been told. Mostly, Lucanus thought, it sounded like rumours and half-truths whispered by passing merchants in days long gone. A blighted land, five paths to the fortress at its heart, but only one that didn't end in death. It lay somewhere in the east, they said, the way marked by the face of Cernunnos carved in stone.

The farmers had pointed them in the direction they thought correct, and after a while the Grim Wolves chanced upon others who hadn't fallen on such hard times. These knew more, Lucanus had seen it in their eyes, but their lips remained sealed . . . until Solinus jabbed his sword under their jaws and threatened to drain them of their life-blood. This time Lucanus hadn't restrained him. They were desperate now, and he more than any of them.

He couldn't bring himself to think of Catia. No one they encountered had seen hair or hide of her, or her mysterious companion. Sometimes a vision of her dead in a ditch flashed across his mind, and he pushed the ball of his hand into his eye socket to drive it away. His heart ached for all those lost years when he'd been a captive on the island home of the Attacotti. He prayed he could at least grab one sunlit day with Catia before the bargain with the Attacotti ended and he was dragged away to his inevitable fate.

One day. That was all he asked. One day to light him to his

end, to remind him of the joy they once had, and what might have been. That thin hope drove him on.

Black smoke billowed up. At its heart, scarlet glowed like the eye of a great beast waking. Screams from the burning settlement could be heard, but the roars of the jubilant barbarians soon drowned them out.

The ground throbbed with the pounding of hooves and a farmer darted out of the thick cloud of smoke, eyes wide with terror. A moment later, a laughing Pict on horseback crashed out of the fug behind him and eased his mount to one side then the other, forcing the farmer to flee this way and that before ending up back where he'd been a moment before. Toying with him like a mill-dog with a rat until, tiring of the game, he pulled his sword from its scabbard and held it aloft.

As the weaving peasant stumbled, the Pict leaned to one side and swept his blade down in a smooth, easy stroke. The farmer howled and fell. The barbarian urged his horse back into the smoke for more sport, not even caring to look back to see if his unarmed prey lived or died.

Lucanus ground his teeth. These days of slaughter should have been long behind them. They thought they'd won this battle, and now it seemed they'd have to fight it all over again.

He pressed a hand against his mouth as the wind lashed the smoke up to the standing stone behind which he was hiding. When it cleared, he looked again for any sign of the track that a merchant had promised them would lead to the blighted land.

Instead, he saw a barbarian war-band tracking towards him. They were laughing, singing, drunk on victory. Some dragged screaming women by their hair. Others lumbered awkwardly, arms filled with booty. Most wore leather armour and furs despite the heat, their round wooden shields splintered, the paint faded. Their horsemen flanked the column, the riders' eyes darting as they searched for any opposition. There would be none, they knew. These were country folk. They owned no swords, had never lifted a weapon in their lives.

Above the lead rider, on a pole rising from a leather pouch, fluttered the banner of the false king, the red dragon. It stood for cruelty, that was all. Lucanus scowled. What a mockery it made of his own gold dragon banner.

The Wolf flinched as he looked back to the war-band. One of the warriors was pointing in his direction. Fearing they had seen some sign of him, he slid backwards on his belly into a hollow. Barely had he pushed himself to his feet before he heard hoof-beats pounding.

Dashing into a copse, he glanced back and saw the barbarian riders hurtling over the high ground. Briefly, they reined in their mounts to look down on where he had been hiding. Whatever they saw seemed to satisfy them and they threw their stallions down into the hollow with renewed urgency.

Lucanus raced through the birch trees. The land beyond was flat, wide and open, with nowhere to hide.

One slim hope was all he could see: a network of ditches to drain the surrounding farmland, all of them swollen with run-off from the recent rains. Racing to the nearest he threw himself into the filthy water. Brown rats scurried away from him along the banks.

Tracking the sound of the hoofbeats, he bent double and waded along the ditch away from them. He dropped down until his chin rested on the water's surface, half swimming, half kicking him-self along the bottom.

At first, he heard the riders thunder away until the hoofbeats were almost gone. But the barbarians would never give up, he knew. And soon enough the pounding began to grow louder again, until it rumbled all around him. If the Picts thought to fol-low the line of the ditch, they'd see him easily.

Gulping in a mouthful of air, Lucanus rolled on to his back and ducked beneath the surface. The water was too dirty to see clearly. There were no reeds through which to breathe. All he could do was raise his lips to the surface intermittently, suck in air and pray.

His lungs seared. Darkness closed in around his vision. Chok-ing, his instincts swamped him and he thrust his head up and gasped air. To his relief, no tattooed Pict was peering down at him. Instead, he could hear shouting back along the ditch in the direction he'd travelled.

Easing himself up, the Wolf peered over the open ground. The riders were riding hard towards a lone figure, which was waving and shouting to draw their attention. Lucanus squinted; it was Comitinus.

'Come with me.'

He looked up at an outstretched hand, and then into Mato's face.

Once his friend had hauled him out of the ditch and they were racing away from the horsemen, Lucanus gasped, 'You shouldn't have come for me. We had an agreement.'

'As if any of us would care about that.'

'You lied to me.'

'It's the only way to keep you in line, my friend.'

At the woods, Lucanus glanced back. The riders thundered back and forth, but there was no sign of Comitinus. He would have had his route of escape well planned. The Wolf turned back to Mato.

'Things are worse than we feared,' he said.

'They're worse than you fear.'

'What do you mean?'

Mato beckoned and Lucanus weaved through the elms behind him. For a long while they hurried on until the trees ended suddenly at the lip of a ridge. Ahead, the wide land swept out under blue skies, blasted by the ocean winds. Before the Wolf had a moment to drink in the view, Mato grasped a low branch and swung himself up, clawing his way into the treetops. Lucanus shook off a spray of ditch-water and followed, awkward though it was with only one arm.

The tree swayed and bent under their weight, but Mato slithered out along a branch as far as he could go. Somehow Lucanus crawled out on a neighbouring branch, and when Mato pointed, moving his finger in a wide arc, Lucanus saw instantly what had gripped him.

The barbarian war-bands roamed everywhere, some on foot like packs of prowling beasts in their furs and leather, many on horseback. Clouds of dust rolled across the sunlit landscape behind them.

This was as bad as it had ever been in the days before Theodosius the Elder's forces drove the tribes out of Britannia.

Lucanus tracked the bands. Some were descending on individual houses, others were congregating on the east–west road, the main trade route. He felt his heart sink. There seemed to be no path through them. And if Catia had come this way, what chance could she have had of escaping them?

'It looks bad, brother, I can't deny it,' Mato said. 'And if we were a hundred strong, we would have no hope of slipping by them without war. But we are *arcani*. We've picked our way through greater mazes than this without disturbing a blade of grass.'

As always, Mato was trying to offer hope. But it was thin, Lucanus could see that. 'Gaia should have known better than to bring the barbarians in,' he said. 'They can't be controlled. After the invasion they had the taste for Britannia, and for power, and they were still smarting after the legions drove them out. They'll do as they please now. Plunder, rape, destroy.'

'It doesn't bode well for the Dumnonii who befriended them, and allowed them to venture so deeply into their land.' Mato sighed. 'Now that the Picts and the Scoti have given up any pretence of alliance it makes our own task easier. But that's little comfort for the folk here in the west, who are now facing untold miseries.'

'When I was the King in the West, the Dumnonii looked to me for protection.' Lucanus could feel Mato's eyes on him, and he could almost smell the other man's concern. After all he had endured, after Apullius, and Catia, his brothers were fearing he would crumble. A leader made of nothing but dust. Was that true?

Watching the plumes of smoke sweep up across the landscape, he went on, 'At this rate, there may well be no one left to protect – or to join our army – should we even gain that treasure of the gods.'

'Then we shouldn't wait here any longer. We must pick up the pace.'

The case was desperate, and they both knew it. The barbarian horde was creeping closer to Tintagel with each passing day, and no one remained to lead Lucanus' army in a defence.

'I thought we could hide away in the west and all would be well,' he said, watching those rolling clouds of dust. 'But it's clear now that there'll be no peace until this is ended once and for all.'

Bellicus, Solinus and Comitinus crouched beside the ford where Mato had arranged to meet them. Sunlight shafted through the tall elms and glimmered off the stream that tinkled over the stones. All seemed peaceful, apart from the flickering urgency in the Grim Wolves' eyes.

They jumped to their feet when they saw Lucanus and Mato running up.

'You're alive,' Comitinus gasped. 'Thank the gods.'

'No time for idle talk,' Bellicus grunted. 'Those barbarians won't give up looking for us.'

Solinus grinned. 'It's not all bad news. Look what we found.'

He crunched away through the undergrowth. Lucanus found him kneeling beside a fan of yellowing grass. Solinus peeled the stalks apart to reveal a way-stone carved with the face of Cernunnos, eyes and mouth emerging from a tangle of leaf and ivy.

'The wood-priests make it hard for anyone to find the trail, but it's always there,' he said. 'You just need a good nose to sniff it out.'

Lucanus crouched beside his brother and looked ahead. He could just about make out a path through the woods, which, to any other eye, would have seemed little more than a route used by foxes.

'They've built their labyrinth well,' he agreed. 'Only the worthy will find a way through.'

The Grim Wolves pushed their heads down, running at a steady pace through the fern into deep, shaded valleys thick with vegetation, where barely a foot ever fell.

At least it took them away from the barbarian war-bands.

As the day drew on, Lucanus raised his arm and they dropped beside a still pool beneath branches so thick they offered the coolness of a temple. In the shadows, the surface was as black as a mirror reflecting the night sky.

Mato cupped his palms and scooped a handful of the water to his dry lips. 'The wood-priests are cunning, we know that,' he said. 'I've been thinking long about this—'

'Don't think too hard.' Solinus thrust his head into the lake and then shook it like a wet dog.

'—only the worthy will find a way through, Myrrdin said. The path is a maze, that's certain, designed to lead the unwary off by their nose. But it's clear, too, they have set guardians along the way.'

'Whoever Catia encountered,' Comitinus interjected.

'And whoever crept in like ghosts to smear blood upon our pelts,' Mato continued. 'The first were warriors, the second . . .' He shrugged. 'The forest folk? They've lived too long away from civilization. They sheltered the druids during the long, lonely years after Rome came to Britannia and tried to wipe them out. And only they would have the woodland skills to creep into our camp without disturbing us.'

Bellicus looked around. The woods were so shadowed it was impossible to see far, and the silence was profound. But Lucanus knew that was no guide. The forest folk were invisible in their world.

'We should take care,' he said with a nod. 'Even here . . . especially here . . . we shouldn't let our guard down. Treat these old ways as we would if we were trekking across an open plain while the barbarians roamed near by.'

Once they were rested, Lucanus heaved himself up and jogged on. Dusk drifted down, but they couldn't afford to slow their pace. Nor could they light a torch for fear they would be seen.

Their voices rolled back and forth, keeping them sharp and their night-eyes focused, as they had all learned to do in those long treks north of the wall.

'We're adrift here in the west,' Mato said. 'Cut off from news of what is happening across Britannia, throughout the empire.'

'That's a good thing, if you ask me,' Solinus grunted. 'All that news is likely to be bad. Who wants to hear that?'

'What if Rome really is abandoning Britannia, as the centurion told Lucanus?' Comitinus said, his voice low. 'Without the legions, without the coin, the trade, the repairs to the roads, the protection offered to citizens . . . Why, I can foresee a dark age sweeping in faster than a spring tide, and then we'll be taken back to the days of constant tribal wars, endless power-hungry conquerors, sacrifices, starvation . . .'

'You're a seer now?' Solinus snorted. 'And a miserable one at that. You think the towns will just fall apart when the legions aren't here to protect us? You think the trade will stop once Rome pulls back its borders? What keeps us going is men and women, their wits, their hunger.'

'What do you say, Bellicus? Do you think we're staring into the long night of a dark age?' Comitinus asked.

'Keep running,' the big Grim Wolf grunted. 'All I'm thinking about is getting to the end of this road in front of me without losing my life.'

Moonbeams cut through the gloom here and there, transforming the trees into grey phantoms. At least it gave them some light to see by. Lucanus found his thoughts drifting off to the Attacotti, his cold shadows, and he wondered how close they were. Close enough to reach out and—

A howl jolted him from his thoughts and he dug in his heels. Comitinus slammed into his back and he heard Bellicus and Mato cursing behind him.

'Solinus?' he shouted.

Solinus had taken the lead for that section of the journey. Lucanus squinted, but he could no longer see the Grim Wolf's silhouette. There was no movement ahead at all.

'Solinus?' he said, his voice lower.

'Stop talking and help me!'

Lucanus edged forward until he felt a hand grip his arm and Comitinus' breath warmed his ear. 'Not another step. Look down.'

A ragged circle darker than the surrounding gloom had opened up in the path. One pale hand clutched at a shattered branch, the rest of Solinus lost in the swimming blackness of the hole.

The Grim Wolves scrambled around the edge of the pit. Bellicus leaned over, grabbed Solinus' wrist and hauled him up. 'You have the luck of the gods,' the big man grunted.

Once Solinus was massaging his wrist in the long grass beside the track, Mato struck his flint, lit a handful of dry leaf mould and dropped it into the hole. In the brief sizzle, Lucanus saw that the pit was about two heads deeper than Bellicus' height. The bottom was covered with sharpened branches.

'Gave way under my feet,' Solinus muttered.

'If you hadn't acted quickly you'd be dead for sure,' Comitinus said.

Lucanus peered into the dark ahead. 'We knew this road would be dangerous, but it seems now we can't even trust the ground beneath our feet.'

'We could step off the path. Follow alongside,' Comitinus ventured.

'Knowing those bastard druids, that's exactly what they'd think we'd do.' Bellicus cracked his knuckles. 'The next trap may well be there.'

Mato snatched up a broken branch, snapped off the end so that it was the right length, and edged along the path, jabbing the ground in front of him.

'At that rate I'll be a broken-backed old man before we reach that bastard cauldron.' Solinus jumped to his feet. 'That's probably what they want. Win the prize, but your life gets sapped away on the journey. In the end, it's not a prize worth having.'

'And the next trap might not be a pit of stakes,' Comitinus said. 'It could be an axe swinging from a branch. Take the top of your head off.'

'Why are you wasting your breath talking?' Bellicus rumbled. 'There are only two choices. Go on, go back.'

Lucanus walked up behind Mato on the path. 'Then we don't have a choice at all.'

On they pressed into the night. With each step, Lucanus felt his chest tightening. More wasted moments that could cost Catia her life. Yet they'd barely trudged a thousand paces when Mato called out for them to stop. He knelt, examining a way-stone.

Another stood nearby. And another. In the grey light, Lucanus could just make out a crossroads in their trail, the original path plunging on ahead with another crossing it.

'Which way?' Mato asked.

'A maze,' Comitinus muttered. 'Of course it is.'

'Keep on this track,' Lucanus commanded.

For another thousand paces, they marched. But then Lucanus heard Mato's feet begin to squelch and the track came to an end at a vast bog.

'No way through,' Mato said with a deep sigh.

Lucanus bowed his head, then ordered his men to retrace their steps.

At the crossroads, they turned on to the trail to their right. In no time at all they came to another crossroads. Another path chosen at random. Another crossroads, and then another. A second dead end. A third. More crossroads.

Mato stumbled to a halt. 'Though it pains me to say it, I can't tell which way we've been and which way we haven't yet tried,' he said in a weary voice.

'Which way is up and which way is down?' Solinus said, spitting. 'Bollocks. We're lost.'

CHAPTER TWENTY-FOUR

The Bridge

THE GRIM WOLVES BOUNDED THROUGH THE TREES, GREY PELTS flying behind them. Baying. Hunting.

Ahead of them, the two raggedy men scrambled on. Brambles tore at their raw ankles. Branches lashed their faces. Arms flailed, both of them in the grip of terror.

And who could blame them? When the Grim Wolves had come across them, one had been digging up bulbs of wild garlic with his bare hands, the other checking traps for game birds. What must they have thought when they heard that yowling and saw the wolf-men crashing towards them through the sunlit woods?

Now Solinus and Comitinus swept off to the left flank, Mato and Lucanus to the right, circling, drawing in for the kill. Bellicus lowered his head and hurled himself down an incline, driving his prey to claw their way up a muddy bank. Two crows flapping and fighting over carrion, that's what they looked like, he thought, with their mud-streaked woollen cloaks and torn leggings. Skin almost black from the filth of life in the forest, white eyes staring out of smeared faces.

They reached the top of the bank and Bellicus roared, causing birds to take flight from the high branches in a thunder of wings. The two hunters wrenched their heads round, faces twisted with dread. When they looked ahead once more, the rest of the Grim Wolves formed a line in front of them.

One of the men flung himself face down, whimpering. The

other snatched out a short-bladed knife and swung it back and forth. Eyes glittering, he bared his teeth like a cornered beast.

Solinus swatted the knife hand away and punched the man squarely in the face. He went down like a felled tree, dead to the world.

Bellicus hunched over the cowering man and snarled a hand in the back of his cloak. When he'd been hauled to his feet, the captive continued to whine, flapping his hands as if he was wafting away a fly.

'Still your tongue,' Bellicus snarled, 'or my friend here will do to you what he did to that one.' He tapped the unconscious hunter with his foot.

'Then we're going to slit both your throats, cook you over a fire and feed on your flesh,' Solinus spat. 'Because that's what we do to woodland rats.'

The man stopped his whining and hung his head, but he was trembling so much Bellicus thought he might fall to the ground in a daze.

'You hear what we say?' Solinus tapped the tip of his knife against the man's throat.

'Aye-uh.' He stuttered something in the thick, barely comprehensible dialect spoken by these forest-dwellers. Bellicus turned over the words and decided he'd said, 'Don't hurt me. I'm a hunter, nothing more. I only want to be left alone.'

The Grim Wolf thrust him beside his unconscious companion. 'Sit there. Stay silent.'

'Find some wood for the fire,' Lucanus commanded. 'My belly's empty and I want to taste how rich their meat is.'

Smirking, Comitinus and Mato made a play of collecting fallen branches. Their conscious captive didn't see, though. His head was bowed, his shoulders heaving.

Bellicus leaned in to Lucanus and whispered, 'Is this what we've been brought to – pretending to dine on human flesh like those dogs the Attacotti?'

'It rightly fills all with revulsion,' the Wolf whispered back. 'So what better way to make the point that we are not men to be easily dismissed?'

Bellicus wasn't sure about that, as he increasingly wasn't sure about this old friend who had returned from the other side of death. Lucanus had changed, no one could doubt that, but it was a change that had begun long before the Attacotti had stolen him away, when he'd ordered the slaughter of the druids on the high moor. Was this what it meant to be a king? If that were so, Bellicus would never covet a crown.

Behind him he heard a sudden scuffling and then the pounding of footsteps disappearing into the woods. The pagan was already vanishing among the trees, leaving his unconscious comrade behind.

'As easy as getting a dog to dig up a bone,' Bellicus said.

'What if they don't come?' Comitinus asked.

'They'll come,' Solinus said.

Bellicus wasn't so sure. 'Will they risk a fight to save one lone hunter?'

'That depends how honourable they are,' the Wolf replied.

The decision had come to him when they'd collapsed, exhausted, in that maze of paths the night before. 'We don't let the druids write our story for us,' he had said then. 'The wood-priests' intention is clear. Follow this labyrinth until it dooms us. No, there has to be another way.'

And there was, or so he hoped. Break the labyrinth. Make their own road.

'If his friend has the ear of an honest leader, they'll come to save their fellow,' he went on. 'These forest folk are bound close, a tribe in many ways, albeit one that shuns the life of the town and of civilization. But our actions won't easily be forgiven.'

'What's done is done.' Bellicus searched the dense forest. 'We've prodded the sleeping dog. We'd best keep our wits about us and our swords close to hand.'

The rest of the day passed, and the night too. Taking it in turns to keep watch, they peered into the dark beyond the fire, ears cocked for the faintest footstep. Their captive was bound to a tree, and gagged. All of them could feel his cold gaze as they moved about the camp. When dawn broke, they jumped up from their slumber, swilled down some water from the skins, and were ready.

Mato's curlew call rang out in the middle of the morning. Swords flew to hands and the Grim Wolves stepped into line facing the direction of the alarm. Mato raced back a moment later.

Lucanus pressed a finger to his lips as he searched the woods. No sound reached his ears beyond birdsong. But now he could see movement, a shadow here and there among the dense vegetation.

The Wolf frowned. Was that a bear stalking towards them? He tracked the hulking shape moving through the holly and the elder. A glimpse here – a massive head; a peep there – what looked like claws long and sharp enough to rake out a man's throat with one swipe.

Then the bestial figure rounded a holly bush, and Lucanus saw it was only a man. But what a man. A giant, he was, standing several hands taller even than Bellicus, the skull sitting low on hunched shoulders. A mane of brown hair and a beard thick and long, wild and tangled with leaves and ivy. Burning grey eyes set deep in shadowed hollows and a black slash of a mouth filled with brown and broken teeth almost lost in the matted fur.

Life in the wilderness had stripped any fat from him and crafted a body like granite, Lucanus could see. A mottled grey shift flapped down to his knees. Those claw-hands were so big they could have crushed a man's skull. His filthy bare feet were long and skeletal and hairy, the toes clutching at the soil.

Other figures loomed behind him, but none so imposing. All of them looked more beast than man, with unkempt hair and blackened skin. Ditches were their beds, branches their roofs, and if they did build homes they would no doubt be little more than burrows. These people had long ago fled Rome's rule. Perhaps it was true, as some said, that their ancestors had escaped the first invasion and the destruction of the old ways and the slaughter of the druids at Ynys Môn.

For the briefest moment, Lucanus felt he was not looking at the reflection of the distant past, but peering into days yet to come. Was this what waited for them all when Britannia was finally abandoned, when the trade routes failed, and the towns collapsed and weeds covered the roads? Was this the dark age that the druids had sought to prevent when they created their story of the saviour, the King Who Will Not Die?

He shuddered, despite himself.

The giant came to a halt, those huge hands falling to his sides. No fear there, Lucanus could see. The monster turned his head slowly, eyes burrowing deep into each of them in turn. When he was done, he nodded. He'd seen nothing that troubled him.

'They're all mad,' Bellicus breathed. 'The madness of the Wilds.'

Lucanus saw it in their eyes too. All the *arcani* knew of that insanity which settled on a man too long away from the company of others and the comforts of civilization. The whisper of the woods lured them back to the state of beasts.

'Men of towns,' the giant growled, 'you have called us from the trees by your actions.' The dialect was thick, the words slow and rolling. Lucanus heard 'Yow 'ave cold us . . .'

'We will gut you as we do a deer, and let the stream take your blood away,' the tall man continued.

'You have wronged us,' the Wolf replied.

'How so?'

'We've been stalked since we first set foot on this trail. Wolves set upon us. Others who have come this way have been attacked—'

'That is the way it has always been. Any who choose to walk the druids' road must know their lives are at risk. They are to be tested. That is the way.'

'That's your way. The wood-priests' way.' Lucanus shook Caledfwlch. 'This is the sword of the gods and with it I can cut through the ropes that bind us to the old way. And if that means cutting through you, and everyone who stands with you, so be it.'

The giant shook with silent laughter. 'You men of towns, you think you're wise and so strong, but you know nothing. Wisdom only comes from hearing the whispers of the gods in the branches. Strength comes from surviving the knives of winter. Come at us, if you will.' He held up one hand and waggled his fingers and thumb. 'This is all you are. We have the numbers of the blades of grass in the field, and we do not stop when we are threatened. We come like the tide.'

'Try it, then,' Bellicus snarled, levelling his blade. 'This is my scythe for your blades of grass. You may well swamp us, but how many are you prepared to lose to win this fight?'

Silence fell on the crowd of forest men.

Lucanus held the giant's eyes. 'You are their king, yes? And so am I. Then here is my bargain, from one king to another. You and I will fight. No other lives need to be lost here.' He nodded towards the captive tied to the tree. 'And he will be set free now, to show that you can trust us.'

The giant looked Lucanus up and down. His gaze settled on the stump of the missing arm, and he laughed again, like the rumble of distant thunder. 'You would fight me? Men of towns, so great in your ways! And to the winner . . . ?'

'When I defeat you, you'll show us the road to the Fisher King and then you'll let us be.'

The giant laughed again. 'I'll fight you, half-man. And I accept your terms. Word will come when the time is right.'

Lucanus nodded and Comitinus cut the captive free. Without another word, the forest men turned and vanished into the trees.

'Are you mad?' Bellicus blared.

'Why didn't you let Bellicus fight?' Solinus added. 'Look at him, he's like an oak. And you . . .'

'This is my responsibility,' Lucanus said. 'And if I can't win a fight against a man who barely walks on two legs, then I'm not worthy to be king.'

He walked away before any of them could say more. Yet he could feel their eyes on him: worrying if he had gone mad, if he wished for his own death. And he worried about both those things himself.

Sunlight shimmered off the broad, slow-moving river. Lucanus shielded his eyes against the glare as he stepped out of the gloom among the trees. He recognized this watercourse from their desperate journey west while Theodosius' army was routing the barbarian invaders.

The Tamar ran from north to south, all but carving the western lands off from the rest of Britannia. High banks, almost cliffs in many places, bordered by thick woods, too deep to easily forge. There was only one crossing of note. The legions had barely pushed into the lands of the Dumnonii. That was why this place was so haunted, by ghosts and witches, druids, magic and old gods. Cut off from civilization, the old ways had been left to send down deep roots.

'I thought we'd never be crossing this river again,' Bellicus muttered.

'You still might be right.' Lucanus eyed the black smudge along the far bank. A near-army of forest folk watched in silence. So many of them, hidden deep in the Wilds for so long, few knowing they were there.

The Wolf let his thoughts sweep back across the untamed land and three days in time. As the light had waned on that day, the Forest King's emissary had drifted out of the trees. He was a rat-faced man with hollow eyes and few teeth. Beckoning instead of speaking, he'd led them on a winding trek through the densest part of the forest and along gloomy valleys, over windswept high land where jagged fingers of granite jabbed towards the sky. Black smoke from burning homes blackened the clouds here and there, but their silent guide skirted any areas where the barbarian war-bands still roamed. For three days they'd moved relentlessly to the north and east, grabbing sleep wherever they could, until they'd heard the sound of the river booming through the trees.

Their guide vanished in the instant of emerging into the sunlight, leaving them standing there on the western bank, unsure what to do next.

Mato edged next to him. 'There's still time to back down.'

'My mind is made up.'

Lucanus stepped out of the band of shadow to the edge of the steep bank. As he looked down at the grey water, he saw a narrow wooden bridge spanning the divide. Merely a series of silvery, cracked planks supported by poles that had been rammed into the river bed, it was barely wide enough for one man to edge across. A misstep here or there and anyone risking that crossing would be into the current and dragged away.

At the far side of the bridge, a huge shape loomed up. The Forest King stepped on to the first plank.

'He means to fight you out there, over the water?' Comitinus breathed.

At his side, the giant gripped a gnarled cudgel, the length of it almost hanging to his feet. That monstrous weapon wielded by such a man had the power to stave in a skull. In a fair fight, with space to strike and retreat, it would be little match for a sword. But on that narrow bridge?

'Tell me you're not still thinking about meeting him halfway?' Solinus said. 'It'd be hard enough to keep your balance in a fight out there with two arms.'

'That's why he's chosen this place.' Lucanus tried to imagine what it would be like to battle on that narrow plank. 'We need to cross the Tamar if we're to find our way to the cauldron.' *And Catia*, he thought; he prayed. 'And if we're to do that we have to go through him. There's no other way.'

He squinted, but he couldn't make out his opponent's expression in that mass of filthy hair. Yet from the way the Forest King's head bobbed, and that swaying walk along the plank, he sensed confidence.

'Don't do it, you jolt-head,' Bellicus insisted. 'We can find another way, given time—'

Lucanus silenced his friend by drawing Caledfwlch and striding on a dusty path down the bank to the bridge. He glanced once at that long line of forest folk on the far bank, all of them silent, unmoving, and placed his foot on the wood.

The aged timber was cracked by the elements and bleached by the sun. The Wolf winced as it creaked under his weight. Patches where the wood had rotted away stretched out ahead of him. Would it even last the day? He couldn't be sure.

Swaying with each step, he edged forward.

Once again he found himself deep in that labyrinth he'd imagined in his hovel on the island of the Attacotti. The monster still waited for him at the end, the one he could never truly defeat. In that moment, he conjured up Myrrdin's face and heard the wood-priest's lilting voice telling him that this was the ultimate test on his road of trials. If he could not crush those dark, weak parts of himself, he would never be able to progress to the reward of which he dreamed.

And he would never be able to save Catia.

Out over the water, he rolled from side to side as he fought the buffeting breeze to keep his foothold. The Forest King's laughter boomed as the giant marched along the bridge, the planks bouncing so wildly under his thooming step that Lucanus wondered whether he might be thrown off and into those lethal waters before the fight even began.

'Fight or flee,' the Forest King bellowed.

The Wolf levelled his sword. It was all the answer that was needed.

Whirling the cudgel above his head, the Forest King thundered along the timber as if he was running on solid ground. Lucanus bounced into the air, one foot skidding off the edge as he came down. Down on one knee he crashed, spinning to one side. He felt himself sliding over the edge and managed to claw himself back, but now he was half sprawled on the plank and defenceless.

The giant loped towards him.

Lucanus thrust his head up, making himself an easy target. The Forest King slowed as he neared, swinging that monstrous cudgel.

Hold your nerve, the Wolf told himself. From the corner of his eye, he watched the weapon blur towards him.

At the last, Lucanus threw himself flat. He felt the cudgel whistle past the top of his head. For the first time, the giant lumbered off-balance. Rolling on to his stump, the Wolf thrust out with Caledfwlch. It was a feeble strike – Solinus would have mocked him relentlessly – but he watched as the edge of the blade sheared across the Forest King's mud-smeared calf.

The giant howled. Yet even through the pain, he swung from the edge and leapt a few paces back, his balance perfect, not even looking to see where his feet landed.

More beast than man.

It bought Lucanus a sliver of time, though; enough to push himself to his feet and steady himself.

The Forest King's head dropped, his eyes narrowing. 'First blood to you,' he growled. 'Man of Towns, you think you know the way the wind blows. But those thick walls have weakened you. Dulled your senses. No more can you hear the whisper of the gods in the branches. The beat of the heart deep in the soil. You know no truth. Only the lies you tell each other.'

Lucanus grinned. 'I lived my life in the Wilds, Man of Forests. The song of the old ways still rings in my ears.'

The Forest King cocked his head, intrigued. Lucanus felt a new-found attention as the giant looked him up and down. 'You are a brother to wolves.'

'And a brother to dragons.'

The giant nodded. 'Then there is some hope for you. Men of towns could never find their way to the cauldron of the Dagda. You and those you stand with must thank the Fates for guiding you here. Some hope, aye.' He grinned, tapping the cudgel in the palm of his left hand. 'But first you must defeat me.'

He lunged, faster than Lucanus could have imagined for a man of that size. The hunk of wood swept towards his face and he wrenched away at the last moment. Rolling on the balls of his feet, he danced back a step. He felt his vision close in around his hulking opponent, his balance on that narrow path becoming instinct. Dimly, he could hear his brothers on the bank shouting encouragement, but even that faded away.

The cudgel swung. Lucanus danced away again. Under his feet, the timber flexed and groaned.

The Wolf stabbed and thrust. The giant's reach was greater and Lucanus felt a notion settle on him that however well he kept his balance, however skilled he was with the blade, he would never land a killing blow upon this enemy. The Forest King would wear him down until that cudgel shattered his skull.

Lucanus felt his arm beginning to burn. The giant, though, barely faltered. Back and forth the cudgel swung as if it were an axe hacking down an oak, and he could see no way past it to thrust Caledfwlch home.

The Wolf stabbed, nicked a forearm. Rubies glimmered in the sunlight.

He bounced back, fighting to keep his focus, fighting to keep a hair's breadth beyond that gnarled chunk of wood. Under his feet, the timber cracked as loudly as a stone thrown into a frozen lake. The bridge held, just.

Somewhere, crows were cawing. The Morrigan was with him, the Phantom Queen of war and death, as she always was whenever he fought. The sound sliced through the wool of his thoughts and he realized the giant was squinting. The sun had passed the high point and was now shining into his opponent's eyes.

As the cudgel swept by, Lucanus threw himself forward. Shock flared in the giant's face, and he bounded back. The timber cracked again at the same point. Lucanus grinned. There was space between them now, enough to try his plan.

He hacked down with Caledfwlch at the point where the join in the timbers had been patched, where the loud cracking resonated.

Once.

Twice.

And with the third strike the plank shattered and the bridge collapsed.

Lucanus felt himself falling. But the giant was too, in a rain of wooden shards. The cudgel flew from his hand.

The Wolf gripped his blade as tight as he could and pushed off from the last of the bridge as it crumbled under him.

The Forest King slammed down on to his back on the water. For an instant, Lucanus watched his enemy's bewildered expression, and his own shadow swallowing it, and then he crashed on to the sinking figure. He drove his sword ahead of him, and felt it bite deep into flesh and bone.

As they both went under, Lucanus wrenched Caledfwlch free. Strong currents tore him away from the other man. Fumbling, he pushed the sword into its sheath, and then he was kicking and trying to swim with his one arm. But the force of the river was as powerful as if the Morrigan had grabbed him and whisked him up into the heart of a thunder cloud.

Water flooded his nose and mouth for the second time on the journey, and he was aware of one final thought flashing through his head: if he died here it would be a good death. His brothers would finish the quest.

Sunlight flickered into his eyes. He thought he was on the beach again. But no, he could hear the wind in the branches and the birdsong and he wondered if the gods had taken him to their bosom.

A face swam above his own, lost to the glinting sun. Was he in the Summerlands? The face shifted, blocking the light, and the features fell into view. He realized he probably was in that land of endless joy.

It was Catia.

CHAPTER TWENTY-FIVE

The Spirit of the Greenwood

'**Y**OU'RE . . . ALIVE?'
Catia heard her own words as if from the bottom of a deep well. She felt her heart swell so greatly she thought it might burst. In her head a cacophony of voices tumbled into confusion, bewilderment, euphoria, despair at the years that had been denied them – anger that he had abandoned her.

But in the end the rush of emotion swamped her, and she swept this drowned rat up into her arms and buried her head in his neck, laughing and sobbing at the same time.

'You're . . . alive!' she heard him echo.

The only man she had ever truly loved. The only man she would ever love.

For a long moment she sank into his musk and the memories it conjured. When she'd seen the fight on the bridge in the distance, she hadn't allowed herself to believe it was him, and the single arm had given some support to that view. But then she'd seen the two fighting men plunge into the swift current at the centre of the broad river, and the one-armed man struggling to stay afloat while the giant was lost beneath the grey surface.

As she'd scrambled through the trees clustering along the eastern bank, she'd lost sight of him. But then she'd rounded an oak overhanging the water, and there he was, drifting in the shallows. Splashing in, she'd dragged him back, and by then there could be no doubt.

Catia felt her husband straining to break her embrace and she pulled back.

'Not a day has gone by when I didn't think of you and whisper your name.' His eyes roved across her face as if he were making up for years of lost time by drinking in every detail.

'Why did you leave me?' She heard her voice break.

'To . . . to save you.' He coughed up a mouthful of river-water. 'Myrrdin had made a deal with the Attacotti – that I would be sacrificed to them. If I hadn't gone, they would have come for everyone in Tintagel in my place.'

She blinked away hot tears. The confirmation of what the wood-priest had told her did no good. 'Then I'm glad he's dead.' She cradled him again, drawing up every last drop of love that she'd battened down since he'd vanished from her life.

'What was it like for you, there with the Attacotti?' She almost didn't want to hear his answer, but the thought of what he must have endured among the Eaters of the Dead had haunted her.

Lucanus forced a smile, but she could see the truth behind it and she almost wept. 'The days and nights were hard, and harder without you. The Attacotti saw me as a king, though, and treated me well—'

'But your arm . . .' she interrupted.

'I'm alive, and with you now, and that's all that counts.'

Catia felt a wave of pride at his courage. 'Yes. All that matters is that we're together again,' she said, but the words died on her lips when she saw a flicker of despair darken his features. 'What's wrong? Tell me now.'

The Wolf took in a steadying breath. 'The deal with the Atta-cotti still stands.'

'But you're here . . .'

'Thanks to the Grim Wolves. They brought me home. But the Attacotti have only consented to my return for a short time, to aid you in the battle against the false king. Once that's done, I must return with them or risk their wrath descending on you, and Weylyn, and our friends—'

'No!' Catia gripped his shoulders as if she could pin him there for ever.

'I'm sorry. It isn't what I want, you know that. But I must . . . I must keep you and Weylyn safe. That's all that matters to me.'

'I won't allow it.'

'There's no choice,' he breathed.

'I won't accept that. We must find a way . . .'

Lucanus hugged her tight to him. Her head swam with the revelation and she silently raged against it. Gradually, though, the fury ebbed away and then she thought her heart would break in two at the injustice. To be reunited after so long only to know that their time together must be limited.

'We must find a way,' she murmured, burying her head in his shoulder. '*You* must find a way.'

He remained silent, and she couldn't tell if it was because he was searching for a solution or resigned to his fate.

How long she held him there she wasn't aware. All she could think of was the certain knowledge that their parting would be even more painful the second time, and she didn't know if she could bear it.

'We have to make this time together count,' he said, kissing her on the forehead. 'No more thinking of what lies ahead.'

She nodded.

'First, the giant . . .'

Catia pointed to a half-submerged body tangled in the exposed roots of a slanting oak.

'Then we've bought a chance to find our way to the cauldron,' he continued. 'The forest folk will give us free passage from now on. That was the agreement.' He splashed out into the water and looked along the river to the north where the Grim Wolves gathered on the western edge of the break in the bridge. 'Let's get them to us and then we can be on our way,' he muttered, almost to himself.

Catia stiffened. She heard some quality in his voice – she wasn't sure what it was, a detachment perhaps, but it didn't sound like the Lucanus she knew. Something in him had changed. She felt the faintest pang of fear that she'd lost her husband after all. But she swallowed the thought and beckoned to him.

Together they scrambled through the thick scrub along the

edge of the river until it opened out on to a grassy bank where a long line of forest folk stood. Catia winced when she saw the sorrow etched in their faces. They had lost someone who meant something to them today, that was clear. But she saw no anger there, no desire for vengeance.

As Lucanus passed among them, many bowed their heads, almost in deference, as if they recognized something regal in him. Her husband had always worn the crown of the Pendragon lightly, but now it seemed as if some quality of that gold circlet, or what it represented, had seeped into the very fibre of his being.

Lucanus plunged deeper into the crowd and stepped back out trailing a length of filthy rope. With a smile, he took her hand, and she was surprised how good that simple act felt, as if she had been starving for a long time and had been given a meal on the brink of death.

She edged behind him along the narrow bridge. Her face warmed in the sun and she breathed in the scents of the river. After so much darkness and struggle, this was a moment to be savoured. As they neared the line of Grim Wolves on the other side of the break in the bridge, cheers rang out when they saw her. With the help of the rope Lucanus had found, the band pulled their way across the chasm.

Back on the eastern bank, the forest folk had melted into the woods as if they'd never been there. The Grim Wolves clustered around, babbling questions. Relief glowed in their faces. All of them must have secretly believed she was dead. And who could blame them? The days and nights had been nothing but a flight one step ahead of people who had wanted to take her life. The flood of barbarians into the western lands had only made it worse.

'Who's been travelling with you?' Lucanus enquired. 'We saw the signs.'

'You'll see soon enough.' Catia smiled at the baffled looks on their faces. But as she glanced around them, she frowned. 'Where's Apullius?'

Bright features darkened. 'He walks in the Summerlands,' Bellicus replied.

Catia swallowed her sadness and nodded. 'We will talk of him more when we are away from here.'

She beckoned to them to follow her up a steep track which wound back and forth along the soaring bank. At the top, in a cool glade, was her camp, surrounded on three sides by the dizzying drop, a granite outcropping and a fallen oak, so she couldn't be taken by surprise by any of the guardians of the road to the cauldron.

The Lord of the Greenwood stepped out into the sunlight as if he appeared by magic. It helped, she thought, that the lichen which smeared his tunic and helmet allowed him to merge in with the forest greenery. But it was more than that. Whatever had happened to her brother when he'd accepted the role thrust upon him by Myrrdin, had changed him in ways she still couldn't understand. He had the stealth of a wildcat these days, and the strength and skill of a seasoned warrior.

She glanced around at the Grim Wolves. Bellicus was gaping as if he'd seen a ghost, and for a moment she thought he might fall to his knees.

'We thought you were dead,' Lucanus said. 'Though you look smaller, somehow.'

'The Lord of the Greenwood never dies.' Aelius' voice was sardonic. 'There will always be a servant of Cernunnos behind this helmet.' He lifted the protection from his head.

Now all the Grim Wolves were gaping, though Bellicus sagged with seeming relief.

'We thought *you* were dead,' Comitinus gasped.

Aelius grinned, and held out his good arm. 'The Fates chose a different path for me, one that I never imagined travelling. But like all well-read men with a taste for life's finer things, I couldn't turn my back on new experience.'

Catia stared into her brother's face, through the grin which was as much a mask as that green helmet. He was making light of it, but she knew this was an honour that had helped shape him into something new. Somehow Myrrdin had seen something in the drunken youth with the withered arm, as he had seen something in Lucanus. For all his flaws, the wood-priest had had a wisdom that continually surprised her.

Solinus grunted. 'A one-armed leader and a withered-armed warrior. Put you together and we might get close to something that's useful on the battlefield.'

Mato stepped forward and hugged Aelius with some warmth as Catia watched. Her brother looked astonished, but he allowed that moment of connection. But then he stepped away and slid the helmet back on his head. Instantly she saw him transform, his body growing more upright, his shoulders pushing back. Grace and power seemed to flood into his limbs.

'By all accounts, the journey is short now we're across the Tamar.' Even his voice had changed; it was deeper, and more resonant.

Lucanus shivered in his wet clothes and tried to wring out the hem of his wolf-pelt. 'If the forest folk are true to their word, we will, at least, not have to watch our backs once we've found the path.'

Catia stiffened. She didn't wish to dampen the mood of their reunion. 'We've learned many things about this road from the folk we've met along the way,' she said. 'What lies ahead, I'm sure, is far worse than anything any of us have encountered so far.'

CHAPTER TWENTY-SIX

The Druid's Path

MYRRDIN FELT HIS FLESH PRICKLE IN THE CRISP BREEZE blowing through the window. Though a sunbeam slanted on to the dusty flagstones, the wind blasted down from the snow-capped mountain. He always felt cold in that fortress. Shivering, he turned to the boy hunched on the stool. At that moment his pale face was eerily still, his black hair making the skin seem even chalkier.

But he was a good student, the wood-priest couldn't deny that. Receptive to every idea laid out in front of him. That sharp intellect would serve him well in the days and years yet to come. Myrrdin paced around the chamber, his hands folded behind his back. Perhaps the lad could even transcend his incestuous parentage, and the madness that had inflicted both his father and his mother.

When he looked round, he watched the boy's face twist again. All morning the lad had been wrestling with something. Now, obviously steeling himself, Arthur leaned forward, ready to ask what had been consuming him. Finally, Myrrdin thought. At least he wouldn't have to watch these agonies for the rest of the day.

'I . . . I have a question,' the lad began.

'Speak.'

'What if I am the false king?' he blurted.

The lad was clever, he had to give him that. Certainly cleverer than Gaia. She was little more than a sack of cunning. And yet there was a hint of that slyness in the lad's eyes. As charming as his father Corvus, and perhaps as dangerous.

'I've listened to what Mother has said since I was a boy, and what you have told me, about who I am and what the gods intend for me . . . about my destiny. And . . . and about this other pretender. So-called. But who is to say I am the chosen heir?'

He ought to have told the boy not to say this when his mother was around. But he quite liked the idea of Gaia flying into a storm of rage, smashing pots and sobbing into the night. One had to find one's sport where one could. But still, was the boy trying to lure him into a trap? To make him reveal something that could be reported back to his mother?

'I'm happy you mentioned that,' he began. 'There's a lesson here.'

Arthur climbed off the stool and sat cross-legged in front of him, looking up with wide eyes.

'We've spoken of how the followers of the Christ took the story of Mithras and made it their own. Mithras, the great Sol Invictus, who once commanded men across the entirety of the empire, yes? Now little more than a dwindling cult of desperate old soldiers dreaming of their days of glory. Yet the cult of the Christ is spreading across the world. You recall this lesson?'

Arthur nodded, rapt.

'Who then is the true king and who is the false king? Both? Either? Neither?'

'I don't understand.'

'Stories are twisted over time. What was can easily become what was not, and vice versa. In the end, there is no truth, only what the teller has chosen to tell.'

'But how does that answer my question?'

Myrrdin leaned forward and rapped the boy on the head. 'Wits. Wits.' He sighed. 'How are you going to tell your tale? The one of the true king or the one of the false king?'

'But surely the pretender will be doing the same.'

'And the one who is strongest chooses the tale that will be told for the rest of days. We make this world anew every day, in our deeds and in our words. Nothing is fixed. Everything is fluid.

This is the greatest of all the lessons I have taught you, and if you are wise, and you seize it with both hands, you'll bend all that you see to your will.'

The boy stared at him, sunlight gleaming in those black eyes. 'You taught the other king.'

'I did.'

'Did you tell him the same?'

'Why would I tell him anything different?'

'Then why are you here, guiding me? Surely with you at his shoulder, his story could be greater than mine.' The boy's lips licked into a sly smile. There was that glimmer of his father. Myrrdin felt a chill. Hidden depths, that's what he could see, and he would have to plumb them.

'Why do you think?'

'Because neither of us truly matters. It's your story, not ours. Yours, and all of the wood-priests', a story that has been crafted for generation after generation. And perhaps you required someone more pliant to play the king's role in your tale.' The lad looked his teacher in the eye. 'I will not be pliant.'

'I can see that.'

Arthur stood and folded his hands behind his back, mirroring his tutor. In that moment Myrrdin thought he appeared far older than his years.

'You spin words,' the lad said. 'I've seen you twist my mother this way and that. And Severus too, though he spends most of his time plotting how to avoid being strung up from the ramparts. I watch you.' He wagged his finger. 'Nothing you do is without reason. Nothing is left to chance. My mother says she captured you and put you under threat until you acceded to her demands, but I don't believe it. If you are here, teaching me, then it is because you choose to be. And if you choose it, then it must be part of a grand web that you are weaving.'

Myrrdin stiffened. He would have to take more care. 'Well, you have placed me high up on a pedestal indeed. I am merely a man who has spent his days wandering through groves and shivering under the stars—'

Arthur snorted. 'You're wasting your breath. I'll be watching you even more closely from now on. And once I've divined your true intentions, then we'll see what judgement needs to be passed.'

Myrrdin nodded. 'Very well. I have nothing to hide. For now, can we continue with our lesson?'

Arthur slipped back on to his stool. 'Honour. Yes, I know what honour means.' He fixed his eye on Myrrdin once again. 'As Sophocles said, "I would prefer even to fail with honour than win by cheating."'

The horses whinnied and stamped their hooves in the courtyard. The newly returned war-band milled around them, stretching the kinks out of their muscles.

Myrrdin eyed the dust-streaked warriors as he crossed to the gate. Scoti, all of them. Did Gaia not realize she was playing with fire by bringing these men into her army? They would take her coin, yes, but these so-called barbarians were moved by deeper currents. They could damage her cause or turn on her in an instant if they felt it served their purpose.

The wood-priest glanced over to the steps leading up to the royal residence where Gaia watched the proceedings. She was wrapped in a thick cloak lined with fur, the hood pulled over her head, as if it were the middle of winter. The Hanged Man hovered beside her, an insect in his black robes, his head always twisted at an inquisitive angle.

Myrrdin imagined the Ouroboros branded into Gaia's shoulder, the dragon eating its own tail. When she'd been chosen to bear the bloodline of the Saviour King, no one could have realized how power-hungry she would become, what chaos she would cause, she and her mad offspring Corvus.

There was still a chance to right that wrong, to ensure the Great Plan unfolded as it had been foreseen in generations past. He felt that weight upon his shoulders. The survival of everything he believed in was now down to him, one of the last druids.

The wood-priest turned back to the milling war-band. One of them, a bear of a man with a mane of black hair, was striding towards him with intent. It was Erca, the leader of the Scoti, who had taken a liking to Catia when he'd held her captive during the barbarian horde's invasion, or so she had said when her guard was down one night in Tintagel.

Erca jabbed a finger at him. 'You. Wood-priest.'

Myrrdin crooked an eyebrow.

The Scoti warrior looked him up and down. 'You're the one who betrayed his side.'

'I have no side.'

'So say traitors everywhere. Well, traitor, I would know about the strength of the false king's army.'

'I've told the queen here everything I know.'

The barbarian looked around, a little slyly, Myrrdin thought. 'The other queen . . . Catia. She still lives in the western fortress, with the false king?'

'She does.'

Erca nodded. 'As we pushed into the western lands to gain our vengeance on the retreating Roman bastards, I came across a familiar face. The Pendragon.'

Myrrdin flinched, and Erca must have seen it, for he smiled. 'Still alive. Though with only one arm. Weakened, barely able to fight. He was heading east with his wolf-pack. My question for you, wood-priest, is how he yet lives when everyone, including you, said he was dead? Are they true, those stories they tell in the land of the Dumnonii, that he could return from the Summerlands in the hour of greatest need?'

'I know nothing of this.' Myrrdin forced a confused expression, but inside he could feel the furnace-heat growing. That fool Lucanus! Had he broken the agreement with the Attacotti? If he had, they would come for him, they would come for Catia, and Weylyn. They might even come for Arthur. They were a strange breed. Few could understand the byways of their minds. But they held their beliefs strongly, and where agreements were bound into those beliefs, they would demand blood if they were betrayed.

'I've returned with my men to pass this information on to the queen,' Erca was saying. 'Why has the Pendragon left his fortress, and his wife and child, undefended? What is he planning?' His eyes narrowed. 'And if the fortress is undefended, is this a good time to attack?'

'I will advise the queen accordingly,' Myrrdin said, and walked away before the Scoti leader could question him further. But now his stomach was knotting tighter than ever. His calculations would have to change. Chaos was being loosed upon the land, and all his attempts to find a path through it might come to naught.

And if the Saviour King was not willed into being as the druids intended, the coming dark age might continue for ever.

CHAPTER TWENTY-SEVEN

The Blighted Land

FIVE PATHS LAY AHEAD OF THEM. LUCANUS CROUCHED BY THE fire, watching the orange light wash over one of the way-stone markers. In the shifting shadows, Cernunnos' face seemed to be twisting, roaring at him that he was a fool, that only his death lay ahead.

A heavy hand fell on his shoulder and he jolted from his reverie. He looked up into Bellicus' face. In the glow, the lines in his friend's features had vanished. He looked younger, the Wolf thought, more at peace than he had seemed in many a year. Being out here in the Wilds, under the stars, was an echo of simpler times, and it had worked its magic on him.

'Now's the moment of choice,' Bellicus said.

'And no choice could ever be greater. Life or death. One path leads to the Fisher King. Four will end our days, so the stories tell. I don't like those odds.'

'Nor me.' Bellicus tossed more wood on the fire and a fountain of sparks rushed up. 'You've done well in recent days, cutting your own way through the rules that have been set out for us. This time, though . . .' He shrugged. 'I can't see another way.'

Lucanus stared into the dark. He couldn't disagree. Once they'd left the Tamar behind, Mato had soon found the old way, with a little help. The forest folk were true to their word. The journey had been hard, the days hot, the trail almost hidden through tangled forests and lonely valleys where it seemed barely a human foot had fallen in many a year. But they'd kept on trek-king, to the north and east, towards the High Forest, where Catia had been told the cauldron was hidden.

Yet for all the effort, his own feet had felt light, as had his heart. Emotions he'd feared he'd never experience again had bubbled up from deep inside him. To have Catia at his side, that was a joy beyond all others. And whenever they could they'd bowed their heads together, whispering, remembering, reaffirming the bonds that had always bound them.

The joy he felt at their reunion. The unbearable pain, worse than anything the Attacotti had inflicted on his body, of know-ing they'd be torn apart again. How could he bear that for a second time? There had to be a way to avert that ending. He kept telling himself that he was the Pendragon, who'd led his men to victory in many a battle. He'd never given up before. He wouldn't now, right to the very last.

Bellicus sat beside him. He'd been keeping watch while the others slept, but now Comitinus had taken over. 'And will you choose?'

Lucanus shook his head. 'I'm hoping that the Fates will show me a way.'

'Why don't you ask the Morrigan, or Cernunnos himself? They're your friends now,' Bellicus said in a wry tone.

'That may be all we have left.'

They could smell the blighted land long before they reached it that afternoon, a reek of rot and bitterness caught on the breeze. When they came to the way-stones marking the five paths, it was as if an unearthly silence was trapped over the place.

Ahead of them, steaming in the hot sun, black pools shim-mered. Rainbows shone in their oily surfaces. Clusters of sedge and sickly silver birch squatted in the treacherous bogs surround-ing the greasy water. Fat flies droned across the water, but no birds flew anywhere near by. The land was poisoned, that much was clear, but whether it was by the hand of men or an act of the gods, none of them could be sure.

Solinus had walked to the beginning of each trail leading across the waste, and concluded, 'No way to tell them apart.'

Bellicus prodded the fire, sending up another gush of sparks. 'As it was the wood-priests who sent us here, who can be sure of anything about the place? The story itself might be enough to keep people away. For all we know, every path gives safe passage to the treasure.'

'Would you risk it?'

'If it is true,' Bellicus grunted, 'we can't even tell how death will come. Poison? Most likely. Sucked down into one of the bogs? Aye, I wouldn't be surprised. Perhaps the bastards have littered the paths with traps like the ones we encountered on the way here.'

From somewhere across the blighted land, a mournful howl rolled across the sickly waters. It didn't sound like any beast that Lucanus knew. He glanced at Bellicus, but his friend gave no sign that he'd heard it.

No, not a beast. It sounded like a man trapped in agony.

A rosy line edged the eastern horizon. Mato splashed some water on his face and strode into the trees to relieve himself. When he returned to the camp, Catia was flexing her bow and examining her shafts.

'The stench hasn't diminished,' she said, wrinkling her nose.

The foul odour burned the back of his throat and made the acid rise. He scanned the vile swamp, tracing the five paths meandering into the hazy distance. 'Where are the others?'

'Hunting. There'll be little to fill our bellies once we're in there.'

'That might be the least of our worries.' Mato closed his eyes and raised his face to the sun, his morning ritual. He whispered a brief prayer to his long-lost sister. When the last of the words faded, he felt his neck prickle and he looked down. Catia was staring at him, biting her lip.

'What is it?' he asked.

'Lucanus told me that the deal with the Attacotti was not done.'

Mato nodded, growing serious. 'I feel your pain. We all do.'

'You've found no way out?'

'The Attacotti watch him every day. There's no hope of escape. You know the Eaters of the Dead. If Lucanus should try to flee, they'll track him down sooner or later, and the punishment for the rest of you will be great indeed.'

When Catia looked up, her eyes were blazing. 'I wish it was me who'd taken the wood-priest's life.' He felt his blood chill at the hardness in her voice. 'So much misery has been inflicted, all because of this scheme the druids concocted so long ago. Folk's lives mattered nothing to him – to any of them. Only the Great Plan. Sometimes I think an age of darkness stretching out to the end of time would be preferable.'

Soon after, the others returned with a bird they'd trapped. It wasn't much, but it would serve them until they reached their destination. Mato watched Catia greet them, all smiles, showing no sign of whatever she was feeling. The Lord of the Greenwood was nowhere to be seen.

Comitinus plucked the bird and cut out the liver to save for later on their journey, and then he cooked the carcass over the fire. Mato was pleased to relieve the rumbling in his belly, but all of them were distracted by those five paths and the choice they would soon have to make.

After he'd wiped the grease from his mouth, Solinus stepped in front of the centre path. 'We could each choose a path and the one who survives could return to collect Catia and Aelius before continuing on the way.'

'You'd sacrifice four of us . . . perhaps even yourself?' Comitinus said, incredulous.

'I'm just saying it so you think I'm a better man than I am. I'm not setting a foot on any of those paths until we're certain which is the right one.'

'I can tell you which path is true.'

Mato looked round. The Lord of the Greenwood stood on the edge of the camp, looking out across the blighted land.

'How do you know?' Solinus blurted. 'Or did Cernunnos give you some magic along with that helm?'

Mato glimpsed movement at Aelius' side. His good hand was clamped around the neck of a wriggling rat.

'I need you to light a fire,' the green warrior said with a wry tone, 'for as you can see, I am preoccupied with my new friend.'

Under the Lord of the Greenwood's direction, and with much cursing and questioning, they dragged branches and kindling and dry grass in an arc from the head of the first path to the head of the last. Once they were inside that crescent, Bellicus struck his flint and flames raced around the line they'd built.

Mato eyed his friends. Solinus stood with his hands on his hips, his nose turned up in scorn. Comitinus gaped, baffled. But the others watched intently as Aelius crouched and dropped the rat to the turf by the first path.

The rodent scurried past the entrance to the first path, keeping well away from the fire, and the second, and the third. At the head of the fourth trail, it spun and darted along it, past the black pools until it was lost in the distance.

'If there's one thing you can count on with rats,' the Lord of the Greenwood said, 'it's that they always know how to save themselves.'

'I always thought it was that one,' Solinus said.

'So we're putting our faith in a rat now?' Bellicus grunted. 'Of all the jolt-headed things we've done in our time, this must be the most witless.'

Catia was smiling at her brother with pride. All of them had cunning and fire and strength, but Aelius had always had wisdom, from all those books he used to pass his time with in Vercovicium. Catia hugged him, quickly, so as not to embarrass him, and then turned to the others.

'Now. Who goes first?'

CHAPTER TWENTY-EIGHT

The Fisher King

LUCANUS STEPPED ON TO THE PATH FIRST. IT WAS HIS RESPONSI-bility and he was not afraid of death, not after he had lived so closely with it. If it claimed him first, it might at least give the others time to flee back.

On he walked.

After a while, the Wolf glanced back along the line trailing after him under the baking sun. Catia smiled at him, a little sadly, he thought. Comitinus had his head down, muttering a prayer, and Solinus was looking round with a grim expression. Bellicus was unreadable as always. But Mato and Aelius were laughing together at the rear, as if they were ambling out on a summer's day.

Sweat trickled down his back. He'd pulled the snout of his wolf-pelt down low to shade his eyes against the brilliant light, and tied a rag across his mouth against the stomach-churning sulphurous reek. The vile odour was only growing stronger the further they trekked into the blighted land.

The wasteland was a flat pan in the middle of the vast forest which covered the high moor. Black pools gleamed like dark mirrors under the sun on every side. Bubbles burst on the surfaces, releasing a noxious gas. He couldn't see any living creature. The only movement was the swaying of the sickly silver birch that jabbed up from the few patches of dry land alongside the path like the finger bones of a man who had died pleading for mercy.

The trail meandered, and the trees hid the view of whatever

lay ahead. Lucanus imagined a vast fortress, swarming with warriors, bigger even than Tintagel. If that were true, they would
deal with it when they got there. For now, all of them were
preoccupied with not slipping off the narrow path into that vile
stew.

Somewhere, not too far away, lay the ocean. Every now and
then Lucanus breathed a blast of fresh, salty air. The relief was
scant. How anyone could think of living out their days in that
sickening place was beyond him.

'The cauldron has been here for an age, or so we were told on
our journey,' Catia said. 'It always has a guardian. And when one
of them dies, another is chosen.'

'And how many have died trying to find their way to it?'
Lucanus asked. 'The promise of magical powers contained in an
earthly object, something that lifts men up out of the mud of
their existence . . . that calls to all.'

'You don't believe the wood-priest's tale?'

The Wolf tapped the hilt of Caledfwlch. 'This sword—'

'And yet you have never been defeated.'

He glanced up. His wife was smiling at him.

'This is true.' His hand came to a rest on the hilt. 'I wouldn't
tempt the Fates. How much else did you learn about this place . . .
the Fisher King . . . on your travels?'

'The stories were confused. Some said one thing, some another.
The Fisher King comes from the Otherworld and is the gods'
agent upon this world. He is a man who has sacrificed his own
existence to guard an object of power. Only one person can survive the trials to reach it, and then only if they have the purest
heart . . .' She hesitated. 'In truth, they all said that.'

He stared ahead, letting the silence settle on him for a while.

'I miss Weylyn,' Catia said, almost as if the quiet was too much
for her. 'And I fear for him.'

'Amarina will protect our child.'

'You trust her? She always follows her own path, one that bene-
fits her, or allows for her survival.'

'She seems much changed to me.'

This time it was Catia who fell silent.

'Look! Ahead!' Comitinus had broken off from his prayers and was thrusting a pointing finger past Catia.

Through the wall of white, near-leafless trees, Lucanus could just make out a wall of wooden stakes and beyond it the roof of a long hall covered in dead, yellowing turf.

'No fortress, then,' he muttered.

His band fell silent. There was something sour about the place, Lucanus thought, almost as if a suffocating cloud of misery hung over it.

I'm frightening myself like some child by the hearth in winter, listening to the ghosts in the eaves.

As they stood there where no birds sang, that low mournful howl rose up once more, as chilling as when Lucanus had heard it the previous night. It was coming from the hall.

'What is that?' Solinus breathed.

'I'll go no further.' The Lord of the Greenwood had come to a decision.

'Afraid?' Solinus taunted him.

Aelius shook his head. 'I've no part to play in what lies ahead. This is your test, and make no mistake, a test it is. This treasure can't be easily gained. It must be earned. That was always the wood-priests' intention when they secured it here. To hold it in your hands . . . that's proof enough that you are worthy.' He shifted the helmet slightly, and Lucanus caught a glint from the eyes deep in its shade. They seemed moist. 'I'll see you again, sister,' he said, 'on this side of the Summerlands or the other.' And then he turned on his heel and walked away along the trail. He didn't look back.

Catia bowed her head, but only for a moment. She looked up at their destination, her face hardening.

The trail cut through a copse, and when it emerged on the other side it ran straight to a gate in the timber wall. The hall sat on a small, flat island. Nothing moved. More stakes lined the path, and Lucanus looked up at the human remains hanging from them. Some were little more than yellowing bones: a skull, a spine, a ribcage with the stake thrust through it. Others were still rotting.

'The poor souls who never made it to the great prize.' Mato's voice floated up from the rear. 'And a warning to those who do. Death still waits ahead. The quest is not done until the cauldron is in your hands.'

Lucanus drew Caledfwlch. Other blades sang behind him. He dropped his head as he marched past those symbols of mortality, partly out of respect, but also because they pulled up visions of the Attacotti's charnel house.

At the gate, he paused in the shadow of the soaring wall, and then hammered on the wood with the hilt of his blade. After a moment, he heard movement on the other side. The wolf-band stepped back, levelling their blades.

The gate rumbled open.

Through the widening gap, Lucanus glimpsed a dusty yard, dotted here and there with tufts of weed. Figures appeared, standing so still that for a moment he thought they were statues. When the gate was fully open, he counted about twenty, all warriors by the look of them. They wore leather armour and grey woollen leggings, but they had no helms on their heads and all their blades were sheathed.

One of them stepped forward. He was older than the others, with streaks of silver in his hair. He stared a little too long, Lucanus thought, and his eyes seemed glassy.

'Welcome, travellers. Your quest has been true. You have shown your courage and your worthiness by overcoming the trials that have been laid before you. No others have reached this place in my memory, or my father's, or my father's father's. You may sheathe your weapons. You are now guests of the Fisher King.'

'I'll keep mine out, if you don't mind,' Solinus said.

Lucanus gripped Caledfwlch tighter too as he stepped across the threshold. The Grim Wolves and Catia stepped in closer, all eyes searching the guards.

'How do they live here surrounded by the reek and death?' Comitinus whispered.

'They've got the look of zealots about them,' Solinus murmured. 'Those pig-fuckers can put up with anything.'

Behind them, the gate rattled shut. A shadow fell across them. The bar thoomed into place.

'Let's get our hands on this cauldron and get away from here,' Bellicus said.

The Wolf stepped out of the knot and said to the one who seemed to be the captain of the guard, 'Take us to the Fisher King.'

The man nodded and walked away. After a moment, Lucanus stepped after him and the others followed, eyes darting from side to side. The rest of the guard remained as if made of stone, only their gaze following the new arrivals.

The long hall stood in the centre of the compound with what appeared to be barracks beside it. Other, smaller buildings – a place to prepare meals, no doubt, and stores – were dotted here and there.

The leader of the guards led them into the hall. Inside, it was dark and dusty. Lucanus breathed in the suffocating heat from the sun beating on the roof. A feasting table ran along the centre and a large hearth at one end was filled with a mound of cold ash. Behind a wooden throne, a partition wall sealed off a third of the hall, where, Lucanus thought, the king's living quarters must lie.

The Wolf flinched as that awful lowing rose from somewhere behind the wall. The grim sound rolled up into the rafters.

'Is that a man?' Comitinus whispered.

The guard strode through a door in the partition and they heard two voices, the words and the tone unclear. After a moment the guard emerged, saying, 'The king is coming,' and then he marched out.

'This is not the kind of place where I would have expected a treasure of the gods to be hidden away,' Comitinus said.

'It's a place out of time.' Catia's voice echoed. She looked up into the gloom among the roof beams. 'Cut off from the world for an age.'

A shuffling whispered from behind the partition, drawing closer. A moment later a figure stepped out from the dark of the door. The king reeled from side to side as if on the deck of a ship, and eventually stumbled into the half-light.

At first, Lucanus thought he was watching an enormous spider creeping from the dark. There were too many legs. But as the shadows fell away, two of the legs became sticks on which the monarch supported himself. His spine was twisted, and his own withered legs appeared too weak to support his weight.

Comitinus sighed. Just a man after all.

Lucanus looked the king up and down. His skin was almost grey, his greasy silver hair wispy from a bald pate. Cheeks and eyes were hollow and his features were twisted in a permanent scowl, as if he was in constant pain.

The king lurched to a halt in front of them and slowly looked round at their faces. 'I expected more, somehow.'

'So did we,' Solinus muttered from the back.

'My name is Lucanus, the Wolf. I am the Pendragon.'

The Fisher King almost reeled backwards at that. 'The Pendragon, you say? The Pendragon? Where is the crown? Show it to me!'

'The crown is lost. But if you ever leave this hall, you only have to ask any folk you meet,' Lucanus said. 'Britannia was invaded by a conspiracy of barbarians and I was called. Do you not know?'

'I never leave my home.'

'Lucanus was crowned by a wood-priest and led the battle against the invaders,' Bellicus said. 'He is now the King in the West.'

The Fisher King gaped. His stare crept to the space where Lucanus' arm should have been. 'And you bear the wound.'

'He's lost his wits, living here,' Solinus murmured. 'It's that vile stink, I tell you. Drive any man mad breathing that in all day.'

'The wound!' the king pressed. 'Whom the gods choose to be their servant upon this world, they wound. It is the price paid for glory.' He glanced down. 'My legs, you see, my legs . . . and my back—' He choked down his words.

Mato swung out both hands. 'Yes, Lucanus has the wound. He has been chosen by the gods. You mustn't anger them. Give up the cauldron of the Dagda now and we can be on our way.'

'But you are the first to find your way to my home,' he said in his creaking voice. 'This fortress . . . Corbenic, the fortress of the

blessed cauldron. There must be celebration to mark your success. To mark your worthiness!'

'No—'

'I insist. Besides, dark will soon be falling and you do not want
to be on the path through the blighted land at night. You will not
survive to reach the other side. You must trust me on this.'

Lucanus turned over his answer. More than anything he
wanted to be away from that place, to return to Tintagel, and
Weylyn, and prepare for the battle to come. But they'd barely
eaten in days and it would be good to fill their bellies for the long
journey back. He nodded.

'Bollocks,' Solinus said, a little too loud.

'Good, good,' the Fisher King said. 'Come with me. My men
will find you beds in the barracks. You may rest while the feast is
prepared.'

Now he was moving as fast on those sticks as if they were a part
of him, Lucanus noted.

'My name is Pellam,' he said, without glancing back.

Outside, in the choking heat, he scurried towards the captain
of the guard. The other men still stood around like statues.

'The warriors of the cauldron are chosen from the local folk. It
is a great honour to serve here,' the king said. He whispered to the
captain for a moment and then indicated that Lucanus and the
others should follow the man.

'You have shown your true worthiness and I bow before you,'
he said. 'Soon, all that you desire will be yours.'

CHAPTER TWENTY-NINE

The Wound

NO BIRDS SANG AT SUNSET. THE BLIGHTED LAND DUSTED PINK, then red, among the oily pools. Finally it was as if a bolt of black silk was unfurled across all, and afterwards there was only the choking silence, punctuated by the intermittent moan of the wind.

Lucanus was leaning against the frame of the open gate, looking out into the wilderness, when the Keeper of the Flame raised his brand to light the torches around the inner walls. As their glow washed across the dismal courtyard, the Wolf turned to see Bellicus coming out of the barracks. Though he'd slept long and deep, his face was still drawn with exhaustion. The others had dozed fitfully, muttering and calling out from the depths. He'd closed his own eyes, but sleep hadn't come for him, as it rarely did these days.

'The sooner we're away from here the better,' Bellicus said when he came over. 'We were promised wonders, but it's a haunted place in a haunted land.'

'Did you expect any less from somewhere dreamed up by wood-priests?'

'We've paid a high price to get here. Let's hope this treasure does the job intended. If not . . .'

'Let's not think on the "if not"s,' Lucanus said.

A tolling bell echoed from deep within the hall. The captain of the guard flung open the door and a rectangle of golden light fell across the ground. 'The feast!' he boomed.

Together, Catia and the Grim Wolves filed into the hall. Lucanus looked around. With the torches lit, and a fire blazing in the hearth, it felt more welcoming. A tall, pale-faced man in a floppy cap strummed on a cithara in one corner, the lilting music unfamiliar but soothing.

Lucanus eased on to the benches along the feasting table, and Catia slid beside him. As their friends sat, servants rushed in to fill their cups with wine. Solinus held his goblet to his lips, his nose wrinkling. But when he sipped he cocked an eyebrow and nodded. 'Good. As good as what we have back in Tintagel.'

Lucanus watched his brothers grin and swill their own wine before wiping their mouths and cheering. He was pleased to see them at ease; it was the first time in an age. They'd followed him into dangerous waters without question, as always. They deserved their reward.

Catia squeezed his hand under the table and smiled. She didn't need to say anything.

The Wolf looked up when the door in the partition wall creaked open and the Fisher King hobbled out on his sticks. He was beaming too as he looked around the table. Lucanus felt a surprising wave of pity for the man. How lonely he must be. No visitors, nothing but the eternal waiting for the worthy to find their way to him, surrounded by a poisoned land, breathing in noxious air. He deserved his feast too.

Leaning against the head of the table, he raised his own cup and said, 'To the men . . . and woman . . . of purest heart. The gods have bestowed their favours upon you.'

The Grim Wolves threw back more wine and cheered again.

Lucanus had half expected a meagre feast in such an isolated place, barely a feast at all, in fact, but the servants swept in from the kitchens with venison and fish stew, cheese and olives and bread and a never-ending flood of wine. The Grim Wolves gorged themselves as if they'd never eaten before.

Pellam drank with caution, the perfect host, Lucanus noted, more interested in hearing the voices of strangers than in holding forth himself. He sat, near bedazzled, as the Wolf spoke of the barbarian invasion and their flight from the cold north, the battle of Londinium, and then their journey west, to Tintagel, as the army routed the invaders.

'You hear no news?' he asked when his tale was done.

The Fisher King fluttered a hand. 'A little, here and there. My men bring back garbled stories when they travel away from Corbenic to collect our provisions. But they are always only half remembered, and recounted so flatly they are barely worth the telling.'

'When was the last time you left this place?' Catia asked.

'From time to time I venture out a little. But rarely far. I've not travelled a distance from Corbenic since I first arrived and took on the honour of being king, and then I was far younger than all of you here.'

'You were chosen?' Lucanus said.

'There is no royal bloodline here in Corbenic. To guard the great treasure is an honour bestowed on those deemed worthy.' He smiled and looked down.

Humility, Lucanus thought. A good sign.

'The wood-priests keep their traditions well,' he said.

Pellam nodded. 'They see themselves as the golden chain that binds days long gone to the now and the days yet to come. Without them there is only chaos, or so I was told when the crown was first laid upon my head.' When he saw them looking, he raised his eyes and added, 'Oh, I never wear it these days. How pathetic a sight, an old man shuffling around his home with a crown on his head. And your crown? Lost, you said?'

'In the war.'

'I wore it once, you know.'

Lucanus frowned.

'I was the last bearer of the crown of the Pendragon, but there were no battles to be won in those days. Another pathetic sight! The great war-leader with no war to fight.'

'You were chosen by the wood-priests?' Catia leaned forward as the servants placed steaming bowls of stew in front of all the guests.

'I was. I kept the peace here in the west, which they always considered their home after Rome drove them out of Ynys Môn.'

'And this was your reward?' Lucanus swept an arm out to indicate the hall and the surrounding compound.

Pellam's grin tightened. 'There are many who say the crown of the Pendragon is no honour, but a curse inflicted on those foolish enough to accept it. How do you feel about that, Wolf?'

Lucanus stiffened. He couldn't deny that the same thought had crossed his mind, but he said nothing.

Comitinus looked up and said through a mouth full of stew, 'Why do they call you the Fisher King?'

'With this twisted spine and these withered legs, that is all I am good for.' Pellam's voice dripped with acid. He sipped more wine, but ate nothing.

'You were born that way?' Solinus asked. 'I've known fathers who dump their babes in the river when they come out like that.' The Wolf saw Catia and the other Grim Wolves wince at their brother's bluntness, but Pellam only shrugged.

'My wound was received in a battle I did fight, in honour of the gods.' He held up his cup for more wine. 'From time to time, I am allowed to fish from a boat in the sea not far from here. In those moments I can remember the man I used to be.'

'Allowed?' Lucanus said.

Ignoring the question, the Fisher King clapped his hands. Two of his guards carried out a chest, so aged the wood was almost black. The box was carved with spirals and knots, and a face stared out on the lid: burning eyes, long hair and a beard that flowed into those spirals. From the brow, antlers burst.

The Dagda, Lucanus thought. He had seen a carving like this before, on a cup that Myrrdin used in his rituals.

'Let your hearts swell. Here is the receptacle of the Good God.' Pellam reached out his hand. 'Inside is the cauldron of the Dagda. But you must never open the chest. Never. The cauldron is filled with too great a power for men to bear.'

'Seems a waste to me,' Solinus grunted.

'The cauldron has the power of life or death,' the king said. 'The very power of the gods themselves, for that pot once contained the blood of the Dagda. It will raise up the dead, a fallen friend, or a loved one, but they will be changed; changed, for all who spend time in the Summerlands can never again walk well in this world. They will not be able to speak.'

Lucanus watched the guards place the chest on the end of the feasting table.

'Sometimes,' Pellam said, looking down at his venison, his voice falling to a croak, 'sometimes, if you rest your head upon the chest, you can hear the cauldron whispering to you. The things it says . . .'

The Wolf looked back at their host and flinched. Pellam was shuddering, his face like a winter field.

'That should do the job,' Solinus said loudly, rubbing his hands. 'Now, let's be done with this chatter and finish filling our bellies.'

Lucanus lifted his bowl to his lips. The rich aroma of mushrooms flooded his nose, and the delicately spiced stew warmed him as it rushed down his throat.

Catia pushed her bowl aside. 'I've had my fill,' she said.

'Are you well?' Lucanus whispered. She had barely touched her wine either.

'I'm not in the mood for feasting,' she breathed into his ear. 'All I can think of is Weylyn. We must be away at first light.'

The Wolf nodded. Catia rested a hand on his shoulder and stood. She flashed a glance of pity at Pellam and then floated away and out into the night, returning to the barracks, no doubt.

When he looked back along the feasting table, Pellam seemed further away, floating in a golden glow. 'The quest for the cauldron is the quest for truth. This is how the wood-priests always foresaw it,' he was saying as he looked around the Grim Wolves. 'What truth have you discovered about yourselves on this long trek?'

Mato stared at one of the torches on the wall, entranced by the dancing flames. 'I have learned that my sister will never leave me. The day she died changed me for ever, and I can never go back to the man I was, only find a new path. She is here now.'

Lucanus looked round, following his friend's gaze. Mato stared, a faint smile on his lips as if he were welcoming his long-dead sibling. Bellicus had his head hung over his bowl. He was mumbling, 'I will make amends.' Solinus slurped the rest of his stew and tossed the bowl aside. Beside him, Comitinus was listing on his bench as if he were drunk.

Lucanus stared down into his own bowl. Pellam's words thrummed in his head, matching the beat of his blood. Half-memories bubbled up unbidden from the depths of his mind. He gripped the edge of the feasting table and looked across the miles-long distance to where the Fisher King hovered.

'You've poisoned us,' he croaked.

Pellam pushed himself up on his sticks and took a step back from his seat. If he was smiling, Lucanus couldn't see it – the king's face was a blur. But he could sense movement all around. The guards slipping back into the hall.

The Wolf levered himself up with his hands on the table, but his legs buckled under him and he crashed back down on to the bench. 'Why have you killed us?' he said.

Pellam loomed over him. 'You will live, all of you. The poison will seep from your limbs in a day.'

Lucanus fumbled for Caledfwlch, but his fingers slipped off the hilt.

The Fisher King leaned down until his face was only a hand's width away. 'I thought, when I heard you were the new Pendragon, you had come to take my place. That is the only way I can be relieved of my duties. But no. You planned to take this treasure and I would be forced to remain here, for Corbenic must always be occupied by a Pendragon. That is the ruling of the wood-priests.'

Lucanus fought to control his reeling thoughts, dragging the words up from deep within him. 'You can leave at any time,' he croaked. 'And once we recover from your betrayal, we will walk away from here, and hunt you down.'

Pellam's eyes blazed. 'You can't leave. You won't be allowed. The forest folk out there who dogged your every step? They are not there merely to protect the cauldron. They are to keep me captive, to force me to do my duty.'

The Wolf slumped back, sliding off the bench and crashing on to the timbers. He stared straight up, into the shadows among the rafters. He felt ice seeping into his arms and legs, his limbs turning to stone.

From somewhere near by, he could hear the steady crack of the

Fisher King's sticks upon the wooden boards, slowly moving away. 'Enjoy the rest of your days a captive here in Corbenic, Pendragon,' the voice floated back to him. 'Here is your true legacy – a man who has had everything he was stolen from him by the wood-priests and their plans.'

Catia watched a shooting star arc across the vault of the heavens. A portent of something or other, Myrrdin would have said, but of what she wasn't sure. Since her conversation with Mato, she'd felt her thoughts turn inwards too often. Though she forced smiles aplenty, her heart was aching at the prospect of losing Lucanus so soon after she'd found him again. Her husband was a good man, the best she had ever encountered. Sacrifice was in his nature; his own needs, even his own life, put second to those of others. Had Myrrdin seen those good qualities as weaknesses to be exploited?

A door slammed and she jerked from her reverie. When she looked back, she saw a knot of men marching from the hall, and at the heart of them the unmistakable spider-crawl of the Fisher King.

Blood thumped in her head, and as the band moved to the gate, where a laden cart was already waiting, Catia raced back to the hall. Her hand flew to her mouth to stifle a shriek when she saw the Grim Wolves sprawled around the feasting table. When she fell beside Lucanus and felt the pulse in his neck, her fear coalesced into burning anger.

Though his eyes stared blankly and she didn't know if he could hear her, she said, 'I vow that this will be avenged.'

And then she whirled away into the night.

The gate hung open and she could hear the creak of wheels disappearing into the dark. The trail through the blighted land was barely wide enough for that cart. The going would have to be slow.

Pausing briefly at a barrel beside the gate, she darted away from the island hall. The moon was out and the birches glowed like ghosts in the eerily silent landscape. Squinting, she could make out the silhouettes lumbering along the path. By the looks of it, Pellam was perched on the bales in the cart, which two of his men were hauling.

Catia bounded along the track, nocking an arrow to her bow. When she was close enough to the departing band, she shouted, 'Turn round.'

The guards whirled, drawing their swords.

'I'll put this shaft through the heart of the first man who moves towards me,' she said.

The guard at the rear of the line ground to a halt, his blade lowering.

'And I can nock my arrows faster than you can come at me. If you doubt me, try it.'

None of the guards moved. She'd expected to have to down at least one before they understood. Perhaps the cold determination in her voice was enough.

Pellam craned his neck round. When he saw her, he laughed, a reedy sound that rolled out across the oily pools. 'The woman! Kill her, you fools. She is nothing. A soft woman!'

'Turn back,' she said. 'I will not say it again.'

'Never!' the Fisher King shrieked. 'Another day in Corbenic? I would rather die.'

'Very well.'

'But you are a woman,' the Fisher King sneered. 'A soft woman.'

'I am a queen, and a warrior.' Catia slackened her bowstring and in one fluid movement snatched out her flint and struck it. 'This world has turned us all to stone. There is no room for softness.'

The tip of the shaft burst into flame where it had been dipped in the barrel of pitch at the gate. She nocked the arrow once more and let fly.

The shaft thumped into Pellam's back. He screamed and screamed. The fire rushed up his cloak, his hair, his beard. In an instant, his shrieks blurred into the roaring of the blaze. The column of flames grew taller, the black figure writhing at its core. The orange glow washed out across the wasteland and a constellation of sparks glittered in the night of the pools.

One of the guards lunged away from the fire and pitched into the foul bog beside the track. His cry snapped off in a gurgle as he slipped beneath the surface and was gone.

The other men milled around, shouting but impotent, torn

between fleeing and rescuing their master. But anyone could see it was too late for that.

'Run!' Catia bellowed, cutting through their confusion. 'Run!'

And then she was alone with the Fisher King's pyre and the furnace in her heart.

Lucanus felt the warmth seep back into his limbs. He remembered the sensation well, from the night he had been the victim of the witches in the Wilds beyond the wall. The same potion, then. After a moment, as expected, he found he could move his eyes from side to side.

Catia was there, perched on the bench, her chin on her knee. She was smiling at him.

'You're alive. I feared—' He choked down the words. Relief flooded him. He found the strength to lift his head, and then he levered himself on to his elbows.

'Pellam has fled,' he began, his voice like creaking leather. 'We must—'

Catia pressed a finger to her lips to hush him. Lucanus frowned. His wife pointed the same finger at his face, then swept it towards the end of the hall. The Wolf followed her direction, his nostrils now wrinkling at the foul, greasy reek of burning.

Pellam was sitting on his great wooden throne. His body was a blackened chunk of charcoal, the limbs twisted in the final agonies of whatever blaze had consumed him. His jaw gaped in an endless, soundless scream. And from empty sockets where his eyes had melted, he stared down at those he had tried to damn.

Lucanus felt his conscience prick. Here was the resourcefulness of his wife. Here was her refusal to give in to whatever fate was presented to them. She had fought to save him. Surely he could fight to save himself from the Attacotti.

Before they left the compound with their precious burden, Lucanus and Catia slipped back into the feasting hall to look up at Pellam on his wooden throne.

'The Fisher King will remain in Corbenic,' Catia breathed. 'There is no need for another Pendragon to take his place.'

CHAPTER THIRTY

Sister of Dragons

THE TORCHES ROARED IN THE DRAUGHTY CHAMBER. IN THE
wavering glow, shadows shivered over the roughcast walls,
leaping and falling. Caked in clay and charcoal the naked witches
whirled around the boy and girl sitting cross-legged on the floor.
Their chant swirled up, entwining around the heartbeat of the
waves throoming through the stones of Tintagel.

The girl had been painted with the same black spirals as the
Hecatae. She reached out and caressed the forearms of the boy.
His head dropped back, his eyes rolling up so that only the whites
were visible.

Outside the chamber, Amarina closed her eyes and felt the
ocean throb deep in her bones. But all she could really hear was
the strange, lilting song of the witches. The words meant nothing
to her . . . some long-lost language out of the mists of time . . .
but what it signalled, that she knew.

Another ritual.

Another binding spell. More potions and midnight magicks,
all of it designed to twist the mind of Weylyn to their desires.

Pressing her back against the honey stone, she felt her stomach
knot. Sickness seeped into the very heart of her, a self-loathing
born of the fact that this innocent boy had been her charge and
she'd failed him. Out of weakness, out of cowardice. She'd vowed
she'd never hate herself again, but here she was. The poison
burned her as much as it always had.

The song swirled up one final time and drifted away like smoke, and then there was only the tinkling of laughter.

Night after night she'd heard it, as the witches crept into the fortress, how she did not know. But it was always undefended at this time of night, the soldiers – the few who had not deserted since the Grim Wolves' departure – dozing or drunk in their barracks, the guards on the walls barely worthy of the name.

And Weylyn, the heir to the royal bloodline, had almost slipped through her fingers. He'd been seduced by the spells of the witches and by the friendship of the young Morgen too. A friend who was not a friend. Amarina had watched them huddled together, Weylyn entranced by the girl's whispers.

Soon he'd be lost to her; lost to Lucanus, and Catia.

And it would be her fault.

The power would have shifted, and the Hecatae would have complete control of it as they'd always planned. But what could she do? Only three of them crept here, but there was a multitude across Britannia, and right up to the walls of Rome. And these three alone could pluck out her heart, make her blood boil, strip the life from her by degrees. She'd long since seen what the Hecatae were capable of when they were opposed.

And yet, and yet . . .

Amarina clasped her hands together and ground her eyes more tightly shut to hold back the hot tears. She looked after herself, and her alone. That was her code after the terrible things she'd endured in her life. If she wanted to continue living, her path here was clear.

As the laughter chimed around the drone of whatever Morgen was murmuring to Weylyn, Amarina hurried away. In her own chamber, she leaned on the window jamb and looked out into the night. The sea breeze stirred the trees along the valley running inland from the fortress. Here and there, lights glimmered: lanterns in the scattered homes of the Dumnonii. How lonely it looked. She imagined the land rolling out to the east, the wide forests, the bleak moorlands, the deep, untouched valleys.

No friends, no hope.

Folding her fingers around the hilt of the knife hidden in the folds of her dress, she slipped back out. The laughter, the murmuring, were gone now. She snatched up a leather pouch, and after some searching filled it with bread, cold mutton and cheese. Then she crept back to Weylyn's room.

The lad was still sitting cross-legged on the flagstones. He didn't look up when she crept in, and when she neared she saw that his eyes had the hazy look of someone who had woken from a deep sleep.

'Come,' she murmured, holding out a hand.

After a moment, the boy took it. 'Where are we going?' His words were slurred.

'Out.'

'Is Morgen coming?'

'We'll meet her on the way. If you make haste.'

Amarina felt the clamminess of her hand as she pulled the boy through the empty corridors and out into the cool night. She could smell the first crispness of autumn on the breeze. Tugging the hood of her emerald cloak low over her face, she nodded to the guard slumped against the parapet above the fortress entrance, and as the gate creaked open she eased out through the gap and hurried down the steep path to the valley, Weylyn stumbling behind.

Her heart was pounding, her eyes darting all around for the Hecatae. By rights, they should now be on their way to whatever burrow they called home.

Don't be afraid, she told herself. *You have been chosen as one of Lucanus' circle. Not Solinus, not Comitinus. You.* Myrrdin had been adamant about that. The blood of dragons flowed through Weylyn, and she had been chosen to be his sister-protector. She would not shirk that task.

As they plunged into the wood in the valley, she pushed aside all thoughts of the supernatural powers the witches could conjure up, of their claim that they were agents of the gods, perhaps even the earthly vessels of the Fates themselves, as they often asserted.

Clambering up the steep valley bottom as it rose to the high ground, she hauled Weylyn after her. He stumbled over roots, tripping and knocking his knees. When he cursed, she hushed him more harshly than she intended.

'Where are you taking me?' he snapped, his words clearer. The potion the Hecatae had given him must be wearing off.

'We must find your mother and father.'

'I don't want to leave the fortress. Or Morgen.'

'I told you – you'll see her soon enough. Now, still your tongue, or you'll attract the rogues who hide in these woods and they'll cut off your head and leave your body for the wolves.'

Weylyn stopped talking, but she could sense his sullen resistance. Whatever spell the Hecatae had been working on him had already pulled him into their orbit.

On she hurried, keeping away from the track through the trees that all but glowed in the light of the full moon. All she'd thought was to get out of Tintagel and away from the influence of the witches. Now her thoughts burned as she tried to formulate a plan. Where could she hide? What safe space was there for her in a land now filled with the war-bands of the false king?

As she scrabbled past the trees, her thoughts flew back to the last time she'd snatched a child of the royal bloodline, Catia's son Marcus. It had set in motion a chain of events that had resulted in the boy's death. That still haunted her to this day, even though it had been the boy's father who had taken his life. She vowed she would not let such a tragedy happen again.

'Hark.' Weylyn's voice rustled out, dreamy.

'Shh.'

'Can't you hear it?'

She leaned against rough bark and cocked her head . . . and felt her blood run cold.

Distant but unmistakable, a chanting echoed through the branches.

The Hecatae were coming.

Amarina dragged the lad on. The witches were not scouts. They wouldn't be able to follow her trail through the trees, she told herself. Yet for all her common sense, she couldn't push aside that deep part of her that said the witches saw all, heard all. They knew where she was. They knew what she'd done.

And they were coming.

Branches clawed at her face as she pushed deeper into the

woods away from the moonlight. But though the dark cloaked her, she also had no choice but to slow her pace. She tripped, fell, picked herself up, and hurled herself on.

The chanting drew closer, drifting among the trees. Where was its source? Behind her, to the left, the right?

'You can't escape them, you know.'

Amarina shivered at the boy's calm voice.

On she hurried, feeling as if her heart would burst. The chanting in that unfamiliar language whisked around her, clear now, like a tolling bell.

She quickly looked behind her, could see nothing in the shadows. A branch hooked her hood back, fingers of wood catching in her auburn hair. Wrenching free, she hauled Weylyn to the brink of a steep incline into a hollow.

Now he was leaning back, trying to slow her. His head craned as if he could hear someone calling his name.

'I'll say this only once,' she hissed. 'If you try to slow me, I'll cuff you till you see stars and throw you over my shoulder.'

'But Morgen—'

'Come!' She yanked his arm and they careered down the bank into the bracken swaying across the bottom of the hollow.

The chanting echoed all around, and up to the high branches.

Thrusting a path through the sea of fronds, she glanced back once more. Movement shivered among the trees. Whenever a stray moonbeam struck them, the white of the dried clay on their bodies glowed.

The Hecatae swept towards her with unimaginable speed. In her mind's eye she pictured their feet floating a hand's width above the ground, a storm at their backs and the wind thrashing and the lightning clashing. Then the vision moved to what the witches would do once they fell upon her, their claws tearing and their fangs gnashing, and she knocked it aside.

As she ran, she snatched out her knife. Cold iron could harm a witch, so the old stories said. If she was to die, she'd do it on her feet.

At the top of the far side of the hollow, she sucked in a deep breath and turned. She couldn't outrun them, she could see that now, and she wouldn't be hunted down like a hart before wolves. Blood thundered in her head. When her sight cleared, she could see them moving through the trees, afire with that white glow.

Life had been hard, but she'd never weakened, and so it had been good. If this was the end, then so be it, but she still had a duty to discharge.

'If you know what's good for you, young man, you'll forget Morgen, forget the witches and keep running,' she snapped. 'Run until you find your mother and father.'

Only then did she look down and see that the boy was staring past her, his eyes wide.

Amarina jerked her head round. Away in the trees, she could see the glow of what seemed a thousand fireflies. As they bobbed and weaved, she realized they were torches.

She spun on her heel and ran, yanking the boy so hard that both his feet left the ground. His howls of protest drowned out that eerie chanting for a moment. In that instant, she felt ready to throw herself on the mercy of the false king's war-bands rather than face those three terrors at her back.

Holly ripped her skin, but she felt nothing. The torches tantalized her. She raced on, imagining bony hands grasping for her, no longer daring to look behind. And then she skidded down a muddy bank and the lights were dancing all around. She fell to her knees, sensing figures swarming up to her.

'Amarina?'

She looked up into the faces of Lucanus and Catia. The Grim Wolves were there, and more: an army swelled out through those dark woods.

Amarina pushed aside her fear and smiled. 'I brought your son to meet you.'

PART THREE

The Beacon

Hope is the pillar that holds up the world.
Hope is the dream of a waking man.

Gaius Plinius Secundus

CHAPTER THIRTY-ONE

Long March into Night

LUCANUS DREW CALEDFWLCH AND PEERED INTO THE DARK. Amarina stepped in shoulder to shoulder with him, holding her knife out.

'Enemies?' he said.

'We've never been ones for too many friends.'

Squinting, the Wolf thought he could make out movement away among the trees. Pale shapes ranged back and forth like hunting beasts that had been kept at bay.

'The Hecatae,' Amarina said, 'have plans for your son. They've already stuck their hooks into him with their potions and spells.'

'You were supposed to protect him,' Catia snapped. Weylyn craned his neck back to see where the pursuers roamed.

'He has all his arms, legs and eyes, does he not?'

Lucanus waved his blade to curb the bickering. 'What would they want with Weylyn?'

'The same as any other,' Bellicus growled as he ruffled the lad's hair. Weylyn squirmed away. 'Who controls the royal breed controls the power. And the Hecatae have played these games as long as the wood-priests.'

The Wolf weighed his response, then said, 'I'll have words with them.'

'Are you mad?' Bellicus said. 'You'll be a toad before dawn.'

'Heed Bellicus,' his wife said. 'They're too unpredictable.'

Lucanus watched the figures prowling in the dark. 'The wyrd

sisters won't leave us alone if they want something. Best to let them have their say.'

'Take care,' Amarina cautioned.

Lucanus eyed her. She was not a woman to offer easy comfort. 'Whenever we've met, they've never harmed me.'

'There's always a first time.' Tugging her cloak around her, Amarina stepped back into the ranks of men.

The Wolf turned to Bellicus. 'Lead the army back to Tintagel and make sure the defences are secure. I'll return when I can.'

Catia kissed him on the cheek. 'Don't you dare leave me again, now I have only just found you,' she whispered. She didn't want him to go; he could see it in her eyes. But she trusted him.

With a nod, he sheathed Caledfwlch and marched into the hollow. At his back, Bellicus barked an order and he heard the tramp of many feet as the army set off once more.

He could scarcely believe how many had joined them on the journey back from Corbenic. But word had spread quickly that they now carried the cauldron of the Dagda, and at every crossroads on the trail back to Tintagel men waited, young and old, armed with cudgels, or rusty swords that looked age-old, no doubt handed down from father to son, perhaps even from the days before Rome came to Britannia. They were still only a pale shadow compared to the force that the false king had amassed, but now that the gods were on their side they would fight even harder than the enemy.

The Hecatae were still ranging through the trees at the top of the bank ahead of him. Each time he glimpsed one she was gone in a blink. But when he breathed in he could smell the familiar scent of loam and the strange herbs they used in their spells.

Once he'd climbed the bank, he said, 'I am Lucanus Pendragon. You know me. I would hear what you have to say, sisters.'

The soughing of the wind rolled back. As it died away, he heard faint laughter and stepped forward into the trees, catching sight of a shape rising up from the ground at the corner of his vision. A fleeting glimpse, a face in black and white, a hand rising to cracked lips. A puff, as if a kiss were being blown.

A cloud of dust blasted into his face, into his mouth, up his nose.

★

Eyelids fluttered. Lucanus felt cold earth against his back and once again he breathed in the odour of a grave. He'd been here before. Pushing himself up on his elbow, he looked around.

A shaft of moonlight knifed down, forming a circle around a hearth filled with cold ashes. He was in one of the Hecatae's underground burrows, like the one in which he had been held captive in the far north. The walls were packed mud, broken here and there by twisting tree roots.

Letting his eyes adjust to the gloom, the Wolf looked round and realized he was not alone. Three figures hunched against the wall on the far side of the cave, watching him. For a long moment, they stared, unblinking, until the youngest crawled forward to the edge of that circle of moonlight.

'Pendragon,' she said, 'we hear tell you have been to the land of the dead and returned to speak of it.'

'So the stories say.' Perhaps it was the last effects of the powder, but he felt himself swimming in her eyes.

'Stories are power, you know that well. *Tell a man he will be king, and a king he may well be.*' Her laughter tinkled.

'What do you want with my son?'

The crone crawled out of the dark. 'You know what we want.'

'I won't let you take him.'

'You think you can oppose us?' The younger one's eyes flashed. 'You know what we can do.'

Lucanus paused. He did know the things of which they were capable. 'There is always another way.'

'We have something to show you, Pendragon.'

Without turning the lamps of her eyes away from him, the younger one raised a hand and flicked it forward. The third witch, the mother, crept out, and now he could see she wasn't alone. A fourth figure, much smaller, hovered behind her.

'Your daughter,' the mother said.

The girl stepped into the moonlight. She was naked like her sisters, her body smeared with white clay and charcoal, ivy trailing from her hair. Her eyes, too, were wide and unblinking.

'See how she has grown.'

Lucanus felt his stomach knot at the sight. How could he forget that time in their company in the north, when their potions had turned his limbs to stone and dashed his wits away? He had learned later that they'd stolen his seed that night. And this was the result.

'Her name is Morgen,' the mother said. 'She hears the whispers of the lords who live under hill and beneath lake. Their powers course through her blood. Your blood, Pendragon. She will unite the world of men and the world of the gods, and she will rule over Britannia in the age to come.'

'And Weylyn?'

'He will sit at her feet.'

Morgen crouched like a cat, balancing on the tips of her fingers. She looked Lucanus up and down. The Wolf held out his arm. The girl furrowed her brow, and then crawled forward. Lucanus wrapped his arm about her in a tight embrace.

'Daughter,' he whispered. How could he treat as enemy the flesh of his flesh, the blood of his blood? He remembered the ache of emptiness after his father disappeared into the Wilds. Would he inflict that upon this child?

When he looked back at the youngest witch, he saw her head was on one side as she studied him: surprised, it seemed.

'I wouldn't wish any harm on my daughter, or on you,' he said. 'This lust for power has brought misery to so many.'

'Power is all.'

He shook his head. 'There's more.'

'There will be a king, and there will be our breath in his ear.'

'But which king?'

The three witches stared. Lucanus pulled his arm back and Morgen crept to be among her sisters.

'You must have seen the barbarian war-bands roaming everywhere. They are the fighting men of a false king, who would lay claim to the royal bloodline. And if he does, there'll be no room for Morgen, or you.'

'This false king—'

'Arthur. The son of Gaia. You know her.'

The youngest of the Hecatae pulled her lips back from her teeth in a silent snarl. Gaia's son Corvus had slaughtered her original sisters and stolen her from her home, Lucanus knew, and Gaia had been responsible for her ongoing misery in captivity.

'We've built an army, but it's small compared to Gaia's force,' he continued. 'Anyone with coin to wager would not bet against them. And when Arthur is on the throne, and Gaia is whispering in his ear, what then for your plans? Do you think if she ever learns of Morgen she'll let her live? Do you think she'll let you live? Gaia will hunt you down, across all Britannia if need be, and all your vaunted powers will mean nothing compared to the swords and axes she'll set upon you.'

The crone pointed a bony finger. 'You have grown into the king we always promised you would be. What do you say?'

'That there's nothing to gain if we fight each other. We'll both be defeated. Gaia will win. And all that you've planned across the vast sweep of ages will amount to naught. There's no choice for either of us now. We must stand together.'

'Together?'

'Here are my terms. I give you my word that Morgen will sit alongside Weylyn once victory has been assured. Equals. The sun and the moon. The dark and the light. My circle will ensure the balance of power is maintained. You will not rule, but you'll still have the chance to guide Britannia through this new dark age, and into the light.'

Silence settled on the burrow. Lucanus looked around those staring eyes, and for a moment he felt sure the witches were about to fall upon him and tear him limb from limb. But then some silent communication seemed to crackle among them and the youngest said, 'That road will not be an easy one.'

'Are any roads?'

'And you call for our aid in your battle against this false king?'

'As allies, yes. Cast your spells. Bring down storms. Gather the ravens, and summon the Morrigan. I walk with her every day, and I will gladly walk alongside her into this final battle.'

Silence fell again. He couldn't even hear the whisper of their breath.

After an unbearable moment, the first of the Hecatae said, 'Agreed.'

'Agreed,' the second said.

'Agreed,' said the third.

Lucanus pushed himself to his feet. His limbs ached, and he felt a cold deep in his chest. These deals rarely went well, he knew that. But he had made his calculations and he would stand by them, as any king would.

'We'll meet again when the seasons turn once more,' he said, turning to the line of roots in the wall that formed a ladder up to the hole above his head.

'You reek of death, Pendragon.' He glanced back and saw that the youngest of the Hecatae was flaring her nostrils. 'You are not long for this world, it seems.'

'Death comes for all of us,' he said. 'It's what we do with life that counts.'

Lucanus hauled himself up the roots and out into the woods. It was still night, the full moon hanging high overhead. Ghostly figures stood motionless all around.

'Come, my brothers,' he said to the Attacotti. 'There's nothing for you here.'

He stepped away towards Tintagel, hearing the soft pad of feet at his back.

The rosy light of dawn broke through the windows of the fortress. The Wolf walked along the corridors towards the drone of voices. His circle had talked endlessly for a full day, trying to find a way ahead. All paths seemed hopeless, but still they debated. What else could they do?

Catia, Amarina, Mato and Bellicus looked to him when he walked into the throne room. He missed Myrrdin and his ability to cut through the talk to the heart of the matter, and, he suspected, however much they loathed the wood-priest, they felt the same.

Bellicus turned back to the window. 'Unless our new witch allies can whisk us up on broomsticks to fly over the heads of our enemies, there's no choice but to fight every step of the way, even from the very gates of Tintagel.'

'You men with your swords,' Amarina said. 'You think cutting through bone is the only way to an answer.'

'What, then?' Catia snapped. 'We have an army, but it isn't large enough to fight our way through war-band after war-band of blood-crazed barbarians across the length of the western lands, and then north and into Cambria. Every man who marches under our banner will be dead long before we reach the Tamar.'

Catia was right, of course. After they'd captured a barbarian on the road back to Tintagel, and learned from him the location of the false king's fortress, all of them could see how impossible it was for them to reach it.

Mato was smiling at him. His friend had seen subtle signs, as always. 'Speak,' the Grim Wolf said. 'You have a solution. I can see it in your face.'

'Where have you been, anyway?' Catia enquired. 'When you walked away, I thought you'd had your fill of talk.'

'News has come back from the messengers I sent out from the men who joined us after we left Corbenic.'

'You wouldn't tell us their purpose,' Bellicus said. 'Keeping your secrets close, as ever.'

'I didn't want to give you false hope.'

'And now?'

Lucanus turned on his heel and flexed his fingers. He heard them follow him into the quiet morning and then through the gate.

'There,' he said, pointing.

A ship bobbed on the swell in the bay, and beyond it the sails of five more glowed red in the light of the rising sun. A rowboat was making its way ashore from the nearest.

Ignoring the babble of questions, Lucanus strode down the steep path to the narrow beach. There, he watched the rowboat sweep towards him while the others stood together at his back. They'd fallen silent when they recognized the tall figure standing in the prow.

Once the sailors had jumped into the surf to haul the boat up the pebbles, the Wolf walked forward to greet the new arrival.

Niall of the Nine Hostages shook his hand. 'So, Pendragon,' he said in his lilting accent, 'it is time to seal the arrangement we made before your departure.'

CHAPTER THIRTY-TWO

Into Cambria

THE OCEAN HEAVED AND THE SHIP PLUNGED INTO THE GREY bank of mist. Staring ahead, only ahead, Lucanus felt the spray sting his face.

'A clever move, but I'd expect no less from the Pendragon.' Niall of the Nine Hostages stepped beside him, rolling with the heaving of the deck.

Lucanus shrugged. 'All we ever needed were ships to transport our army from the western lands across the channel to Cambria. You're the saviour here.'

The pirate-king threw back his head and laughed. 'Saviours act out of the kindness of their hearts. You've bought my services, and at a good price.'

Lucanus glanced back over the heads of the Grim Wolves to where two of Niall's men sat with swords in hand, guarding the chest that contained the cauldron of the Dagda.

'You must want to defeat this false king badly if you're prepared to give up something of such great value,' Niall said.

'It's served its purpose. The Dumnonii have gathered under our banner. By the time they learn we no longer have the treasure in our possession, the dirty work will be done.'

'Sly dog!'

'The treasure will serve you well?'

Niall's lips curled into a ghost of a smile as he too stared ahead.

'The cauldron of the Dagda is beyond value to any man who would be king of Hibernia.'

The mist parted and the Cambrian coastline hove into view. Lucanus studied a vast stretch of beach beneath a row of cliffs, separated from a horseshoe-shaped bay by a protruding headland. Smoke trailed up into the clouds along the high land. The pirate-king's ships had been sailing back and forth for days now, bringing the Wolf's army across the water, while he and his circle finalized their plans in Tintagel for the coming battle. This was the last of the ferries. Now there was no going back.

'How long, do you think, before Queen Gaia realizes what you've done and that most of her army of barbarian mercenaries is floundering to no purpose, trying to contain an enemy who is no longer there?' Niall asked.

'A small element of surprise is all we can hope for. That may be enough. If the gods are with us, there won't be time for those barbarian war-bands to ride back to confront us.'

'Then it is good that I can tell you of all I discovered about the army that awaits you in Dinas Ffaraon Dandde and about the defences.'

Lucanus watched Niall's lips curl into a sly grin. He had been right to forge an alliance with this pirate-king.

'Dinas Ffaraon Dandde is on the road to the mountains. It is a fortress that has lasted an age, because it is impregnable. If you attack it, you and your army will die in the ditches before you even get to the gates. Draw your enemy out, if you can. Or sit tight and starve them.'

'Before the barbarian war-bands ride back?'

Niall nodded. 'Then all I can say is, may the gods smile on you.'

Lucanus' men leapt to their feet and cheered as he walked into the sprawling camp. The Wolf felt his heart swell, but then Solinus leaned in and whispered, 'Don't let it go to your head. They're cheering the cauldron of the Dagda.'

'You keep my feet on the ground, brother.'

Yet when he looked around, he could see the glow of hope in the faces of these men who had left their wives and children and work to follow him. Whatever Solinus said, they'd placed their trust in the Pendragon. He felt a wave of concern for all of them. How many would survive to make their way back to their homes? Would they all die for the sake of a story dreamed up by long-dead wood-priests?

Mato looked up at the clouds lowering overhead. 'We'll be on the edge of winter by the time we reach Dinas Ffaraon Dandde. That's not a good time to begin a campaign.'

'What choice do we have?' Bellicus growled. 'No point giving it any more thought. It is what it is, and we'll deal with it.'

Lucanus turned and looked out to sea. The ship of the Attacotti heaved at anchor on the edge of that grey bank of mist. Whatever happened in the coming days, his ultimate destination awaited him across the ocean on the Island of the Dead.

'Tell me your thoughts?'

The Wolf turned to see Catia watching him. She was a warrior now, her courtly dresses set aside in favour of woollen leggings and leather armour, her bow thrown across her back. How proud he felt to see her like that. Surely no man could have asked for a better wife.

'The wind comes from the south. If it stays that way, we should make good progress on the march.'

Catia nodded, but she didn't believe him, he could see.

'Weylyn?' he asked, changing the subject.

His wife nodded to the edge of the tents where Amarina watched over their son. 'He's recovering from the potions of the Hecatae. He rarely mentions Morgen these days. He'll want to fight, you know? When we reach Dinas Ffaraon Dandde. He has his father's sense of honour.'

'And that's why Amarina is here. To keep him well away from the front.' Truth be told, he couldn't have kept Amarina away. That surprised him. She seemed much changed, though he wasn't sure why.

'He'll hate you for that.'

'With luck, he'll live to hate me.'

'And I will pray to the gods that we'll be together, all of us, a family again.'

Lucanus looked to the north, where the mountains lay. 'If the gods are with us.'

CHAPTER THIRTY-THREE

Empire's End

T HE AMBER ROOFS OF THE FORT GLOWED UNDER THE THIN
autumn sun. Around it, the settlement throbbed with life,
the shouts of merchants and the thunder of hammers ringing all
the way down to the sparkling river.

Lucanus raised one hand and the column of men behind him
ground to a halt. He studied the busy vicus and the square of
army buildings. Nothing troubling there.

His thoughts drifted back to his last conversation with Niall of
the Nine Hostages. The red-headed man had advised him to bring
the army east to here, Isca Augusta, to replenish their supplies
before the march to the mountains. Niall always seemed to know
more than he was saying, but his guidance was usually good.

In times past, this was the headquarters of the legion II
Augusta, although they'd long since been called away, leaving
only a skeleton force to guard the main roads through this occa-
sionally rebellious area.

Bellicus stepped beside him. 'I've sent Mato, Solinus and
Comitinus on ahead. The last thing these folks need to see is an
army bearing down on them unannounced, with all the barbarian war-bands roaming from the mountains.'

'They'll thank us in the end. And they'll be more than happy
with the coin that buys us food and wine for the journey ahead.'

When Mato and the others returned from their errand, they
marched the army up to the edge of the settlement. The men

threw up their tents, eager for rest. Some played with the curious children who darted out of the vicus, or flirted with the young women come to investigate this abundance of strangers.

Lucanus, Bellicus and Mato left Solinus and Comitinus to barter with the merchants for supplies and strode up to the fort.

'Who are you?' a bored guard shouted from the wall above the gate. He yawned, not seeming to care what the answer was.

'*Arcani*,' Lucanus called back, 'from Vercovicium in the north.'

'By all accounts that's a cold shit-hole,' the guard exclaimed. 'Just don't expect this to be any better.'

The gate trundled open. Inside, the fort was all but deserted. Two soldiers with distant, drawn faces sat on stools, scraping whetstones along the edges of their blades. A boy tugged a horse towards the stables next to the barracks.

The fort was larger than most they'd seen. Mato looked round at several grand buildings – the legate's residence, the headquarters, the tribunes' houses, the workshops and granaries – and then pointed to a large bath-house and a crumbling amphitheatre. 'What a place this must have been when it was filled with life.'

'It'll be empty soon enough, once the emperor has called all the men back.' Bellicus sniffed. 'Then the local folk will be keeping cattle in that amphitheatre and pigs in the bath-house.'

Lucanus strode up to the two soldiers. 'Where's your commander?'

'In the meeting,' one of the men replied, not looking up from his sharpening.

'What meeting?'

'The secret meeting,' the other soldier said.

'What secret meeting?' Mato asked.

'How should I know? It's a secret.' The men continued to scrape. The steel sang.

The Grim Wolves looked at each other and then Lucanus marched over to the headquarters. The moment he stepped inside he could hear voices. The Wolf followed the sound of debate until he came to a large chamber overlooking a courtyard equipped with a stone bench, a pool, and a willow hanging over the water.

A man with thinning sandy hair, bulging eyes and a face like a granite cliff was leaning on a trestle, holding forth to twelve other soldiers of senior rank who were sitting or standing around. He looked over to the three new arrivals at the door and Lucanus jolted with recognition. Theodosius the Younger was once a friend of Gaia's son, Corvus, until the Roman general had recognized the deep seam of madness and treachery in his long-standing acquaintance. The Wolf's thoughts drifted back to the last time he had seen him, in the fort in Londinium, shortly before his father Theodosius the Elder had led the attack that had routed the barbarians.

Theodosius frowned, no doubt recognizing Lucanus too. 'We've been talking long,' the general said to the room. 'Let's rest for a while and return here at noon.'

As the soldiers filed out, Bellicus grabbed Lucanus' arm and whispered, 'I remember him.' He nodded to a tall general with short black hair and a hook nose. 'Met him in Londinium when the army was readying to ride out to attack the barbarians. He was one of Count Theodosius' junior officers. His nephew, I think.' He paused, dragging the name up from the depths of his memory. 'Magnus Maximus. What's he doing here? Everyone said he was moving on to greater things back across the water.'

'What's Theodosius doing here, too?' Lucanus muttered back.

Once the men had left, Theodosius flexed his fingers to beckon the Grim Wolves in. He slopped wine into three goblets on the trestle and nodded to them to each take a cup.

'The Pendragon. I remember you,' he said, folding his hands behind his back and looking down the length of his nose. 'Once a loyal *arcani*.'

'All of us were,' Lucanus replied. 'Out of Vercovicium.'

Theodosius grunted. 'Can't even arrange a secret meeting on the edge of the empire without old acquaintances rolling in.' He sniffed. 'If I recall, you were a pagan. Have you found your way to the Christ yet?'

'We've made our home in the land of the Dumnonii,' the Wolf replied. 'The followers of the Christ have not yet reached there.'

'You must find your way to the light of the True Lord. It is the only way to save your soul.'

Lucanus nodded. He'd forgotten the general's zealotry. 'We're here seeking supplies for my army. We're going to battle north of here, in the mountains. With the mother of your old friend Corvus.'

'Don't speak his name.' Theodosius' sudden wintry expression made his features even harder. 'He's a coward and a traitor. And a heathen worshipper of Mithras, who lied to me daily about his faith. Where is he now?'

'Dead.'

'Good. And his mother?'

'She seeks to take hold of Britannia once Rome leaves.'

'If she's anything like her son, she's a rabid dog who needs to be put down. But fear not, Rome will never abandon Britannia.'

'The Emperor Valentinian has been recalling the army—'

'The Emperor Valentinian will not always be around.' Theodosius stared deep into Lucanus' eyes, a look that crackled with ambition. 'Once Rome has a new emperor, perhaps one who truly proclaims the faith of the Christ and doesn't simply pay it lip service like our present emperor, then perhaps everything will be different.'

Instantly, Lucanus knew the meaning of this secret meeting here on the edge of the empire, away from the eyes of those loyal to Valentinian. Plots took time to find their feet. Alliances had to be formed. He wondered what Theodosius had promised Magnus Maximus in return for his support. Perhaps Britannia itself?

'And where is Valentinian now? In Rome?' he asked.

'He stays at his winter quarters in Savaria, recovering from his campaign against the Quadi. He crossed the Danube at Aquincum after summer's end and pillaged their lands. Met no resistance. Few would call it a campaign.' He turned up his nose, struggling to hide his true feelings. 'How is your wine?'

'Good,' Lucanus said, sipping from his goblet.

'You fought well in the war against the barbarians. There will always be good wine for a man like you. I would hope I can count on you to keep my confidence. I have many enemies, treacherous dogs who would pretend a loyal general like myself might be engaging in foul plots during his visit to this once great fort.' He looked around the chamber. 'I wished to remind myself how great Britannia was and how much it meant to the empire.'

Did he think these former *arcani* were deceived by his lies? Most likely, Lucanus thought. 'We'll keep your confidence, have no doubt of that,' he said aloud. 'We're honoured that so great a general looks fondly on our home.'

'Then we have an agreement,' Theodosius said, 'and know that I will never forget your loyalty.' He paused, thinking. 'You head to battle, you say? Are your men well armed?'

'They're country folk.' Lucanus swilled back the rest of his wine and set the goblet on the trestle. 'Most have only cudgels.'

'I would not have an ally of mine go into battle with so weak a force. There may come a time when I— when the emperor would need to call on you.' He strode to the window and looked out at the peaceful courtyard. 'The armoury here is still well stocked. Take what you need. Arm your men.'

Lucanus looked to Bellicus and Mato, scarcely able to believe their good fortune. Their eyes widened. 'You have our thanks,' he said.

Theodosius spun back. 'Good. Do not forget my generosity.'

As they strode back towards the gate, Mato laughed and Bellicus clapped his arms round their shoulders. 'A stroke of good fortune,' he boomed. 'Now let that witch Gaia quake in her cold home.'

Lucanus glanced back towards the headquarters. The senior officers were trooping back to their secret meeting. 'Let them carve up the empire,' he said. 'Theodosius may really intend to cling on to Britannia, but a shadow is falling over Rome. Sooner or later the legions will be gone for good. This land is ours now, and so it will remain. And it's our job to ensure that the folk who live here thrive under a good ruler, not suffer under one who will break their backs and bleed them dry. If I can achieve one thing before I die, it will be that.'

CHAPTER THIRTY-FOUR

Bad Seed

THE SNOW LASHED DOWN IN THE MIDDLE OF THE NIGHT. FOR the rest of Britannia, it was still a time of crisp browns and ambers and gold, but there on the edge of the mountains winter had already raked its claws into the land.

In the hour before dawn, Myrrdin stood at the window and watched the blanket of white draw across the rocky land. The wind howled in the eaves of the fortress as if the souls of the dead had come to torment them all.

'Am I not learning my lesson well?'

The wood-priest studied the lad shivering on his stool in the centre of the freezing chamber. Arthur stared back, as intense as ever, hair like a raven's wing flopping over that wintry face. Myrrdin nodded. He couldn't have asked for a better student. The lad never complained; more, he seemed eager to learn every bit of druidic wisdom, every ritual, every piece of strategy and tactics. He could make a good king.

'Pay more attention.'

The boy peered into the blood-spattered silver bowl and studied the thrush's entrails. 'What did you see?'

War, bloodshed, death.

Myrrdin turned back to the window. Death. But for whom, he wasn't yet sure. Many would not escape the coming conflict untouched, of that he was certain.

The door swung open and a messenger pushed his head in,

beckoning with such fury that the order could only have come from Gaia.

'Keep studying,' Myrrdin said as he swept past the lad.

His breath clouded as he tramped behind the messenger, but when he reached the throne room a blast of oven heat hit him. Gaia huddled on her chair, wrapped in furs, her once beautiful features twisted into a mean expression of discomfort.

The wood-priest felt sweat prick his brow as he strode past the sizzling braziers. Erca the Scoti chief was there, glowering, as he always did. Why were the northern barbarians so sour? Severus hovered next to the throne, his hands clasped in front of him, his head twisted like a puppet whose strings had been cut. Two men hovered in one corner, their cloaks and tunics splashed with mud, faces whipped pink by the elements.

Taking all this in in an instant, Myrrdin bowed his head. 'You summoned me.'

'Your lessons begin early, wood-priest,' Gaia said, peering at him from the depths of her fur-lined hood.

'I find it sharpens my charge's mind.'

'There will be scant opportunity for lessons in the days to come. We are under attack, druid.'

'Oh?' Myrrdin frowned.

Gaia waved a hand towards the two mud-flecked men. 'My scouts have returned with news of an army bearing down upon Dinas Ffaraon Dandde. An army led by your former ally, the Pendragon.'

Myrrdin thought he heard a note of suspicion, as if he could have known about this. 'I'm as surprised as you. Do they have the power to challenge your force?'

'Most of my mercenaries are in the western lands, where they were to contain the Pendragon and his bastard son in their fortress home. That was always our strategy. Contain them with the sea at their backs until we could swamp them or starve them. But somehow the Pendragon has found a way past my army. Not a single alarm was raised, not even a whisper that their army was on the move. When I find out how that could possibly have come to pass, heads will roll.'

Gaia craned her neck up to stare at the Hanged Man. He flapped his hands and said, 'It is true our mercenaries will not reach us in time should it come to a battle. However, as you know, the defences here at Dinas Ffaraon Dandde are formidable, and we have more than enough men to crush any attack. We will be able to pick off the Pendragon and his men at our leisure. If they try to storm the fortress, they will die in the ditches. If they try to starve us out, our mercenaries will be back long before we have no bread.'

Gaia bowed her head, simmering for a moment. When she looked up, her eyes were sparkling and she smiled like a playful girl.

Myrrdin shifted. He felt unnerved by these unpredictable switches of mood, as did everyone there, to judge from the flickering eyes.

'I hear the Pendragon has built an army of farmers, as he did before,' she chirped. 'Does he think I am some common barbarian, to be run ragged by men with sticks?'

Erca stared into the dark corners of the hall, his face like granite.

'No,' Gaia continued, 'an army is only as good as the ones who lead it, in this case the Pendragon, his queen, and those filthy *arcani*. Take them away and the resistance will vanish like mist in the sun.' She waved a finger at Erca. 'Everyone here says you are a good leader, perhaps the best of my mercenaries, so I have work for you. Take a small band. Shadow this so-called army. And kill those leaders, one by one if necessary, or all at once if you have the opportunity. Cut off the head of the false king's force . . . indeed, cut off all their heads and bring them to me.' She smirked. 'And I will shower upon you riches of which you could only ever dream.'

Erca nodded. 'I'll take a handful of men and ride this night.'

He turned on his heel and walked away, flashing a glance at Myrrdin that made no attempt to hide his contempt for the woman on the throne.

Gaia clapped her hands. 'This will work in our favour. Why launch a campaign in the western lands when we can slaughter our rival on our doorstep? Yes, I look forward to this now. And once it is done we will have no more worries, and Arthur will be at once and for ever more the Rising Dragon, the bearer of the royal blood, the saviour.' Closing her eyes, she leaned her head back, her breath hissing between her teeth.

When her reverie was done, she looked straight at Myrrdin. 'Arthur is a frail child. He must be protected at all costs. If any of your former allies should find some way to breach our defences, I would expect you to give up your life to protect my son. I can trust you, can I not, wood-priest?'

'I've betrayed those allies. I've taught Arthur to be the king you want. My fate is bound with yours now.'

Gaia nodded, liking what she heard. 'Arthur tells me he likes you. That is good. You've met your side of our agreement, so I don't need to take your head.'

Myrrdin walked along the empty corridor, his heart pounding to the beat of his footsteps. If Gaia had known what he was really doing, she would have had him hacked to pieces there and then. He'd been cautious, of course, but with someone as erratic as the queen a stray glance could have given him away at any time.

Pushing open the door to the chamber set aside for his charge's lessons, the wood-priest jolted to a halt.

'Forgive me,' Arthur said. He was holding out both his hands, but they were stained with blood to his elbows, and more gore was splattered on his tunic.

Myrrdin nodded. 'There's fresh water in the antechamber. Wash yourself.'

Bowing his head, the lad trudged towards the tiny adjoining room, leaving a trail of rubies in his wake.

The signs had been clear from the first. It was in the eyes, mainly, a deep well of darkness that seemed to go on for ever. Just like his father. Just like his mother. He'd prised it open a little with his teachings, here and there, just enough to let small amounts surface.

Arthur was a good student. He understood his destiny, and that nothing should stand in its way. Not even his mother. He was quite sure the lad would push Gaia off the ramparts on to the rocks below if that was what was called for. Yes, he'd taught him well. The Dragon was all. The royal blood. The King Who Will Not Die. A prophecy from the gods. Who could deny that?

Once Arthur had absorbed that story, it was easy to push him by degrees to this point.

Myrrdin walked into the antechamber. His charge was hunched over the pail, now filled with pink water.

Arthur looked up and bit his lips, unsure if he was going to be reprimanded.

The dead dog sprawled in the corner, its entrails torn out. Perhaps the lad had been trying to read his destiny. Myrrdin could have told him what that was.

Would he be capable of wringing the lad's neck when this business was all done? Throwing him out for the ravens to feast on? An innocent, for all his madness? Myrrdin swallowed. Did he have that in him? But he'd already sacrificed so much to ensure that the True King would rise. The plan must unfold, as it always had.

'Forgive me,' the boy murmured again. 'The men in the kitchen loved that dog.'

Myrrdin tousled the lad's hair. 'Fear not,' he said. 'Good boy. Good boy.'

CHAPTER THIRTY-FIVE

The Season Turns

A<small>S THE SUN SLIPPED BELOW THE HORIZON, THE WIND STRIPPED</small> the last of the leaves from the trees and for the first time bent them towards the south. Bellicus heaved himself up from beside the campfire and sniffed the air.

'Fuck,' he muttered.

His nose burned from the cold. A wind like that could bring snow once they were in the foothills of the mountains, even at this time of year. That was the last thing they needed.

Sleep wouldn't be coming for a while now, he knew that. He wandered away from the fire towards the river, hoping he'd find some peace there. He imagined Catulus scampering at his heels, and felt his heart swell.

A long, low creak echoed from the direction of the fort and he turned. The gates were opening. A line of soldiers on horseback was trailing out, cloaks billowing in the cold wind. Keeping their heads down, the men urged their mounts along the road to the east, perhaps to Londinium. Theodosius, no doubt, and Magnus Maximus, and the rest of the plotters. Had they reached agreement, one that would end up written in blood, as such plots usually were?

Bellicus spat. All this misery expended, and for what? A few moments sitting on a grand throne before the next pretender came along? Why couldn't men be left alone with their dogs?

Putting his head down, he trudged along the dusty track. Theodosius and Magnus Maximus might be back at some point, as Theodosius promised, but it wouldn't be for long, that much was clear. Rome was losing its appetite for Britannia. Too distant, too unruly. The dark age was coming, as the prophecies foretold. Perhaps the King Who Will Not Die was needed, as Lucanus believed. Or perhaps they should throw all the plots aside, lop off all those hands grasping for power, and merely let folk live their lives. They'd find a way, he was sure.

Leaning on one of the trees on the river bank, he watched the slow-moving waters of the Usk sparkling in the first glimmer of moonlight, but barely had he let the peace settle on him before he whirled, snatching out his sword. Someone else was near, he was sure. Searching the dark along the bank, he glimpsed a hint of an outline that was not a tree trunk.

'Step out where I can see you.'

Without a hint of hesitation, the figure glided forward until the Lord of the Greenwood moved into the half-light.

Bellicus grunted. 'If I didn't know you were that drunken sour-mouth from Vercovicium, I'd say you'd got the power of the gods in you. How'd you get here from the western lands?'

'You were right. The power of the gods. I flew.'

'Ho, ho.' Bellicus sheathed his sword. 'Can we count on your blade in the battle to come?'

'Here and there.'

'Every little counts.' Bellicus eyed the warrior. Even though he knew the face that lay behind that green helmet, he still felt a tremor of awe. 'The one who came before you in that role . . .'

'Dead, I suppose. Or I wouldn't be here.'

'You know who it was?'

Aelius didn't answer.

'Lucanus' father, that's who. I spent years thinking I'd killed him in the Wilds beyond the wall. My rage . . . it surges through me like wildfire at times. I lost my temper and I hit out at my best friend as if he was my worst enemy. Knocked him over a cliff and into a river.' He tasted acid. 'Couldn't bring myself to tell Lucanus, because I'm a coward. I tried to make amends . . . tried to be the father Lucanus had lost . . . but how could I measure up to a man like that? The guilt ate away at me.'

'Is that why you turned out to be such a miserable bastard?'

'I've never spoken of this before.'

'So why are you telling me?'

Bellicus looked down and saw that his hands were trembling. 'The followers of the Christ confess their sins, so I hear tell. They say it unburdens them.'

'I'm no priest.'

'Who else can I tell?'

Aelius sighed. 'This role is a gift and a curse, a joy and a burden. The Lord of the Greenwood is Cernunnos' agent upon the earth, or so I was told when Myrrdin persuaded me to take the green helm. But let me tell you this: the wood-priests and the witches and the forest folk watch and watch and are never seen. The elder Lucanus would have been chosen long before you struck him, as the younger was chosen for the Pendragon. Good men and women are needed in these dark times. You were chosen too.'

'Me?'

'You think the Wolf would have been left without a shepherd?' Bellicus heard the other man's smirk at his wordplay. 'Lucanus the Elder was taken away to the greenwood because all knew there was a good man to fill his role in shaping Lucanus the Younger. Today you see his honour, his courage, his sacrifice. These things don't emerge unbidden. You shaped Lucanus, *you*, and your work has been magnificent. If the King Who Will Not Die arises as we all hope, then you will have played a vital part.'

Bellicus gaped. 'I am nothing.'

'Of all who know you, you are the only one who thinks that.'

For a long moment, the Grim Wolf watched the river, letting this notion settle on him. 'Lucanus is like a son to me, that's true. And it's like a blade through my heart to see him here and know that those flesh-eating bastards will drag him away to a miserable death once all this is done.'

'And when Lucanus is gone, who will be the shepherd then?' The Lord of the Greenwood stepped back into the edge of the trees, the shadows swallowing all but his hand upon the hilt of his sword.

Bellicus felt his anger surge. He understood the implication of that question. 'Once this battle is done, I want no further part of this.'

'Even if it means misery for all who live in Britannia, now and for generations to come?' Aelius stepped back again, so that only his voice floated in the dark. 'Men of honour do not own their own lives. Good-hearted men must always do what is right or they can no longer live with themselves. The wood-priests knew this when they set their plot in motion. They never needed to threaten or twist arms to achieve their ends. They only needed to show a beacon in the dark, knowing full well that the best of us would march towards it. We are the architects of our own misery, Bellicus, and that is a terrible truth to bear.

'You are cursed to be a good-hearted man, my friend. The battle ahead will be terrible indeed. There isn't a single man or woman who thinks otherwise. What comes after might be even worse. How hard are you prepared to fight? How much are you prepared to sacrifice? These are the questions of our story, and we all must answer them.'

And then he was gone.

CHAPTER THIRTY-SIX

Three Again

A RED KERNEL GLOWED IN THE MOUND OF ASHES. CATIA HELD one hand over it to test the warmth, then glanced around at the footprints in the packed mud, the discarded bone of a game bird with a chunk of gristle hanging at one end, the hole where the tent had been pitched.

The camp had not long been abandoned, and it had been done hurriedly, possibly when they heard her approaching. She nocked an arrow in her bow, but held it loosely as she scanned the shadows among the trees and the looming rocks around the gurgling stream.

She stepped back, shifting her bow from side to side. Perhaps it had been a mistake to come hunting alone, just after dawn. But they'd encountered no resistance since arriving in Cambria, no sign of any war-bands. Most felt their enemies were still focused on the western lands and hadn't realized the battle was being brought to them.

The march north from Isca Augusta had taken them through lush valleys rich with game and along the edge of shadowed forests where rooks shrieked around their high nests. Folk crept out from the scattered farmsteads to puzzle over the army tramping past their doors. They gleaned news from the south, but scrambled back into their homes whenever any questions were asked about the queen of Dinas Ffaraon Dandde. Fear rustled among the dead leaves.

A hand clamped across Catia's mouth.

She thrashed, but another hand on her belly jerked her in tightly and hot breath warmed her ear. 'Silence, or you will summon them. And then I won't be able to protect you.'

She stiffened, then sagged. She knew that voice. She had thought she'd never hear it again. Then the strong hands turned her round, and she allowed it, and was instantly gripped by what she saw in the black eyes staring back at her. How much she had shared with this bear of a man, with his wild hair and beard. First he'd taken her captive and threatened her life. Then he'd shown compassion and saved her life. He was her enemy, but she couldn't hate him.

Erca's hands fell away and his gaze flickered around the trees. Pressing a finger to his lips, he led her away from the campsite to a cleft between two towering rocks where they wouldn't be seen.

'Why are you here? To attack us?' she hissed.

'Aye.'

Catia gaped at the bluntness of his response. 'Then why—'

'Gaia has ordered me to kill the leaders of your straggling army, and that includes you.' Erca folded his arms. 'I choose not to kill you, but the men I brought with me would not understand.'

'*I* don't understand.' Catia held his gaze for a long moment, a silent communication. She did understand. Of course she did, though it was a matter she could not address. 'Why do you serve her?'

'She pays well.'

'We could pay you more.'

'You'd want me at your side?' Erca shrugged, saving her the difficulty of having to find an answer. 'It would not be honourable to change sides, not now I have pledged to her.'

Catia pushed her arrow back in its quiver and threw her bow over her shoulder, averting her gaze from his searching look. 'In the battle that's coming, I'll be there, at the front.'

Erca reached out a hand to her, letting it hang for a moment as he fought to speak. 'I offered you the chance before to come with me. I'll protect you, and your son.'

'I have a husband.' She winced inwardly. *For now.* 'I love him more than life itself. I'll never go with you. If you can't accept that, you should kill me now. Make your queen happy. Collect your gold and buy whatever it is that fills you with joy.'

Erca nodded. 'But you don't hate me. I'm no fool. I can read a heart, be it man's or woman's.'

'Step back!'

Catia jerked round. Lucanus was standing on the path to the cleft in the rocks, Caledfwlch levelled. He must have followed her trail when he found her gone from the tent they shared. Yet when she stared at her husband's stony expression, she felt a sudden pang of panic. How would it look, Erca and she standing there, two supposed enemies, talking quietly, staring at each other, almost close enough to embrace? And how much had Lucanus heard of the conversation? Enough to leap to assumptions?

'Wait,' she began.

But Erca whipped out his own blade and stepped on to the path. 'Perhaps here is a solution,' he said.

Catia reached out to pull the Scoti chief back, and then felt another pang, this time of regret, when she saw the fleeting look of hurt cross her husband's face. But she was scared. However good a warrior Lucanus might once have been, he had lost an arm, and Erca was bigger and stronger.

'You killed my brother Apullius.' Lucanus' voice cracked with grief-driven anger. Catia swallowed, waiting for her husband to look to her, accusing her of betraying Apullius, of betraying him, but he only glowered at his hated enemy.

'This is not personal, Pendragon,' Erca said. 'It's war, and any man who stands up to fight must be prepared to die. Your brother will have known that.'

The Scoti chief lunged, hacking and slashing, trying to crush Lucanus by sheer force of his greater strength. Lucanus leapt back, darting to one side. He thrust Caledfwlch, raking the bigger man's arm. First blood.

Catia's hand flew to her mouth. She knew her husband had been practising hard with Solinus and Comitinus since they'd been reunited, trying to make up for what he'd lost on the Island of the Dead. But she'd never expected this. How fast he was, how athletic, with all the grace and power of the beast whose pelt he wore. Erca's eyes had widened. He too was surprised.

Lucanus ducked, parried, danced this way and that. His blade blurred. Erca gritted his teeth, putting his head down and renewing his attack. He lashed his sword back and forth. The Wolf clashed Caledfwlch against that attack and a shower of sparks flew. Before the Scoti chief could rebalance, Lucanus darted to one side and hammered a foot on the back of his enemy's knee. Down crashed the barbarian with a roar. And then Lucanus was above him, his weapon poised to stab his fallen enemy through the chest.

'Wait!' Catia cried, reaching out one hand. 'Don't kill him.'

Lucanus blade hovered above Erca's chest as he looked to her. Erca looked too. Catia felt a rush of cold. Two pairs of eyes, each of them asking a different question, one despairing, one hopeful.

'Erca saved my life,' she said, 'and risked everything to kill the Pictish king who was trying to slay me.' She swallowed, trying to find words that would convince her husband. 'For that, I owe him. *We* owe him.'

Lucanus' sword wavered. Catia held his eyes, hoping he could see in hers the love she felt, be reassured of her intentions. Perhaps he was, for he pushed himself back and sheathed Caledfwlch.

'Go,' he said to the man at his feet. 'Next time you'll not be so fortunate.'

Erca stood, brushing himself down. He licked his fingertips and wiped them across the scratch on his forearm as if he had all the time in the world. 'We're fighting men, you and I,' he said. 'We stand on different sides, but we understand each other, as any man who has been in war does. The only difference is what you want, and what I want.' The Scoti warrior looked up to the sky, reflecting, and added, 'Who knows? One day we may want the same thing.'

He looked to Catia and nodded his thanks. She thought she saw a hint of regret there too, but then he turned and stalked off into the trees. 'I'll lead my men away from you,' his voice floated back, 'but none of you stray from your army from now on. And make sure you mount a watch every night.'

Once he'd gone, Catia threw her arms round her husband, feeling the thump of his heart against her own. When she pulled back, she said, 'Whatever you might think, he's an honourable man.'

Lucanus raised a hand. 'I don't doubt you. Know that. I have never, ever doubted you.'

Catia felt a wave of emotion well up in her and she fought to hold back tears.

'I can never forgive him for the death of Apullius, in battle or not. But if you see value in him, then that's good enough for me.'

As they made their way back along the trail she had followed from the camp, she said, 'We're near the end now. Time is running away from us.' When he looked away, she could tell he knew what she meant.

'You don't know the Attacotti as I do,' he said. 'Kill one, two, twenty, they'll keep coming. The agreement Myrrdin made with them is sacred. They were offered power, as they see it. The flesh of a king. Royal blood. They believe that by consuming it, that power seeps into all of them.'

Catia shuddered. She felt overwhelmed by the horror of the fate that awaited her husband. A vision flooded her mind of the Attacotti at feast, images too monstrous for anyone to bear, but try as she might she couldn't force them away.

When she stumbled into him, he wrapped his arm around her and held her so tight it was as if he would never let her go. There, with his heart thumping against her, she could almost feel the emotion coursing through him, his agony at being torn away from them, his fear. But most of all she felt his love. She was swallowed by the warmth of it, the bitter cold pushed out, her despair crushed down.

'You know that I, the Grim Wolves, all of us would sacrifice ourselves if we could save you,' she said.

'That's the last thing I want. If any of you suffer harm because of this, then all that I've done has been for nothing.'

Catia brushed away a tear before he could see it. 'They're monsters.'

'They are . . . who they are. As are we.'

'What does that mean?'

Bowing his head, he strode in silence for a moment. 'When I'm gone, you shouldn't be alone. A man, a good man, someone who can care for you, and guide Weylyn—'

'Silence!' Catia grabbed his shoulder and spun him round so she could stare into his eyes. 'I will not let you go, do you hear me?' Her nails dug into his flesh. If she could hold him there for ever, she would. 'If you die, then I die.'

His eyes widened. 'No!'

'Then find a way to save us.'

Lucanus stared into her eyes for a long moment, and then he nodded.

Away from the camp, Lucanus squatted with his back against rough bark and unfurled his hand. On his palm were the last of the sacred mushrooms taken from Myrrdin's chamber before they'd left. He'd half thought about consuming them before the battle, to feel that rush of blood and fire that signalled the berserker rage. But this quieter time felt more apt. He popped them in his mouth.

After a while, he cocked his head to the first whispers of the gods.

The snow among the trees glowed brighter than he had ever seen it, suffusing the lower branches with soft light. Lines of blue fire seemed to be shimmering just beneath the surface.

When he heard – or thought he did – the crunch of feet, he stared deeply into that black-and-white world. The dark swelled and he felt sure he could see figures arriving to observe him: a king and queen, their skin shining golden, and an otherworldly court of strange beings, some short and twisted, more beast than man, others tall and seemingly made from leaf and fur.

Or perhaps it was all in his imagination.

The Seelie Court faded in and out of that white glow, but then he felt himself drawn to another, larger silhouette crashing back and forth through the trees, antlers protruding from its brow. The creature put its head back and roared.

The great god Cernunnos.

A thundering of wings throbbed in his ears. In the shadows,

crows were thrashing in a tight group, red eyes glowing at their core.

The Morrigan, the Phantom Queen of war and death.

They'd come to witness his final hours, these strange companions that had attached themselves to his life since he'd been dragged into the wood-priests' plot.

Gone, all gone. Nothing but empty woods.

Blood thundered through his head. Lucanus closed his eyes.

'A prayer,' he murmured, 'to the gods who watch over me. I am nothing. I will sacrifice all I have . . . my very life . . . to keep Catia and Weylyn safe. Watch over them for me. And if there is any action I can take . . . anything . . . which may benefit them, show me the way. I beg of you.'

His whispers rolled out through the chill air, and Lucanus felt his heart swell with a terrible sadness that by this time on the following night he might have been torn away from the ones he loved, never to see them again.

The labyrinth.

The words rustled, and he couldn't tell if the gods were speaking to him, or if they came from the depths of his own mind.

Remember the labyrinth.

And his thoughts took wing, to the vision that he had had on the Island of the Dead, and then across the great sea to the western lands, to the quest for the cauldron of the Dagda. And he remembered what he had said then, and what had been done.

A spark flickered in the depths of his head, the first glimmer of a beacon that might lead him out of the darkness of what lay ahead.

CHAPTER THIRTY-SEVEN

The Song of the Attacotti

S NOWFLAKES DRIFTED DOWN FROM THE GREY SKY. MATO
looked up, brushing one from his eyelash. Those clouds were
full. This did not bode well.

The trees stood stark against the colourless landscape, rocks
thrusting up from the earth here and there, the wind howling
among them. Bleak. This was no place for men.

Mato pushed on.

The road had started rising a day earlier. On the horizon,
snow-topped mountains loomed. The worst part of the journey
lay just ahead. The plan was to skirt those soaring peaks, following the road to the north-west and the fortress of the false king.

But first he had to die.

Mato rested one hand on the trunk of an elm and sniffed the
air. He nodded. This was the way.

Tugging his wolf-pelt around him for warmth, he bowed his
head into the gusts and walked on. They would know he was
coming. There was no point in hiding it.

The Attacotti squatted around a wide clearing, running whetstones across their blades, cutting wood for the fire, carving meat.
Mato didn't look too closely at that. They were bare-chested and
bare-legged, as if they couldn't feel the knives of the mountain
wind. Snow drifted down on their white-crusted skin. They didn't
brush it away. Mato imagined them still sitting there, lost to white
drifts, frozen to death, not caring. Death was their friend.

He stepped to the edge of the clearing and waited, half expecting them to fall on him like wolves. Three of them looked up, then turned back to their chores. He was no threat.

Steeling himself, he strode into the centre of the circle. 'I would have words with you.'

The wind moaned through the silence that followed. No one there paid him any heed.

Mato sucked on his lip. This wasn't how he'd imagined it. Searching the faces, he tried to see which one was the leader. But the clay and the charcoal made them all look the same. With a sigh, he wagged a finger towards the nearest warrior and squatted to face him.

The man dragged the whetstone along the edge of his blade with slow, deliberate strokes. The steel sang.

'My name is Mato,' the Grim Wolf began.

The Eater of the Dead didn't look up; didn't acknowledge his presence at all.

'We are not so different, you and I,' Mato continued, knowing his words were lost on his companion, but hoping the tone would soothe. 'We are born, and we love, and we dream. We have our gods, and our hopes for a life beyond this one.' He swallowed, lulling himself with the rhythm of his speech. He looked down at the settling snow and found he was talking to himself too. 'I saw your kind on your island. There are some who feel you are little more than beasts. You feast on the flesh of our own, something that fills us with disgust. And yet there's more to you, I'm sure. You care for your children and love your women. You pray to your gods . . . you believe. You make music. Those are not the actions of beasts.'

The whine of the whetstone had ended. Mato raised his head and stared into the eyes of the warrior opposite. Had his calm tone reached the man? As if in answer to his question, the Attacotti warrior began to sing. The notes rose up from the depths of him, at first seemingly random, but then forming an odd melody that rose and fell repeatedly. Mato was reminded of the wind above the trees.

He furrowed his brow. Profound emotions rose unbidden from

the deepest part of him, as if the song was a spell which could conjure up memories and hopes and fears that he'd long hidden away. And as he juddered with that rising tide, the other Attacotti picked up the melody, their voices pushing it higher, harmonizing, until the music rolled around him in waves and he felt transported to another place, where the sun shone on a cool glade, and all was right with the world.

Mato closed his eyes and saw his sister standing there, welcoming him with open arms. She was as he remembered her before the day she was snatched away: locked in time, for ever young, eternally innocent.

Entwined in the melody, he somehow knew that death was no threat to the Attacotti, and the miseries of this world were as nothing. Joy lay at the heart of everything.

As the song ebbed away, his eyes fluttered open. Most of the Attacotti were still hunched over their tasks, but the warrior opposite him was staring. Mato followed that gaze to see blood seeping from a cut on his arm. He'd torn his flesh pushing through a gap between two holly bushes on his way to the camp.

Mato stiffened, unease running through his head. His companion eyed the cut, then raised his hand and called out in his strange tongue. Two other Attacotti rose from their positions and came over to eye the dripping blood. Finally, one of them dipped into a leather pouch at his hip and dropped to his haunches.

Cool fingers folded round Mato's wrist, gentler than he could have expected. Then the new arrival was smearing a thick paste on the cut. The wound stung, but only for a moment, and Mato felt a not unpleasant tingling in that region. He was surprised. The healing paste was a kindness he had never expected.

The time had come.

Plucking up the stick he'd broken off a branch on the way over, he scratched out a drawing in the hard earth: a one-armed man wearing a crown.

'Lucanus. Pendragon,' he said.

The warrior stared at the image, then looked at Mato. He seemed to understand.

Mato dragged out an outline of a second man. He tapped his fingers against his chest. 'Mato.'

The Attacotti seemed to understand this too.

How many times had he imagined this moment, turned over his decision, since he had overheard Lucanus and Catia talking about the fate that awaited the Wolf when the battle was done? He had been hunting in the woods, had heard their voices; had been on the point of hailing them when he had seen Catia fall into Lucanus' embrace. The anguish etched in their faces at that moment, and heavy in their words, had almost been unbearable.

Mato circled the space on the Lucanus figure where the arm should be, then scrubbed out the drawing. On the second figure, he rubbed out the left arm.

'Take me,' he said, tapping his chest once more. 'Not Lucanus. I will go with you in his place.' Scratching out more figures, he continued, 'Lucanus has a wife, a child. I have nothing. Take me.'

He'd jerked from sleep in the middle of the night with the notion burning in his mind. Immediately he had felt it was right. He could take Lucanus' place when the Attacotti decided the time was right. True, he was no king. But he was one of the king's circle, and that, surely, would carry some power. As he lay there, staring into the dark, he'd realized he wasn't afraid. If truth be told, he would find peace walking with his sister again, in the Summerlands. Once death has touched you, it never lets go. Not in a way of misery and shadows. It transformed a man. Since his sister's death, he'd learned to love life even more.

No, he was not afraid to die.

'Take me,' he repeated.

Was that compassion he saw in the Attacotti warrior's eyes? He couldn't be sure. Their thoughts, their ways, seemed impossible to define.

'Lucanus is a good man. Take me,' he said a final time, to himself.

But this time the other man shook his head.

'You understand my words? How long—'

Standing, the warrior took his hand and tugged him towards the edge of the clearing.

There, Mato looked back at the group. 'Take me,' he said, his voice rising. 'Take me.'

His Attacotti companion stared at him, and Mato felt sure he saw pity in those eyes. With that silent communication, he turned away and walked back to his post.

CHAPTER THIRTY-EIGHT

The Mountain's Teeth

T HE WORLD HAD TURNED WHITE. THE WIND HOWLED AND THE
snow blasted and not a man could see more than two sword-
lengths in any direction. The army huddled in the lee of
overhanging rocks, the bitter cold stripping the life from them by
degrees. Snow frosted hair and beards. Hunched inside their
cloaks, the shuddering men pushed themselves as close to the
fires as they could. But though the flames roared up in the gale,
and the smoke billowed around them, the heat died before it
warmed them.

'We can't survive this much longer.' Bellicus shook his head
and a mist of snow flew from his mane.

Lucanus stamped his feet as he paced around the huddled
groups. 'If we try to leave this shelter, we'll die even faster.'

He looked over the bowed heads into the wall of white. They'd
been pushed much further up the mountain than they'd planned.
But it seemed the only way to avoid the war-bands that now
roamed across the landscape. Perhaps Gaia was getting worried
and wanted to destroy them before they drew close to Dinas
Ffaraon Dandde. Or perhaps this had been her plan all along. Send
them up into the harsh region higher in the mountains and let
the elements do the work for her.

Lucanus winced, his face as numb as that witch's heart. They'd
thought they would be able to shelter on high until Gaia's warriors passed, then find a new route to re-join the road in the

north-west. But the storm had come down like a hammer, trapping them on the mountainside, blinded by that endless cloud of white, the cold digging deep into their bones.

And now they were running out of wood for the fires.

Bellicus was right. They couldn't take much more of this punishment. 'We'll give it until the fires start to burn low. Then we'll march down again.'

To his credit, his fellow Grim Wolf didn't point out the terrible flaws in that strategy. He knew as well as any of them that there was no other choice.

Lucanus walked to the edge of the overhanging rock, hoping he might glimpse a break in the weather. But there was no sky, nor any land, only the white. The wind flayed his skin and threatened to throw him off his feet, and he turned back.

Further under the rock, a small cave offered some shelter. He hoped to find Catia, but was not surprised to see she'd given up her place to someone else. Instead of his wife, he found Amarina nestled in a cleft in the rocks in front of a small fire, the hood of her cloak pulled down to hide her face. Weylyn was asleep, his head in her lap.

'Wolf,' she murmured, as he crouched beside the glowing branches and rubbed his hands.

'How are you? How is Weylyn?'

'As hard as any *arcani*. A little cold doesn't bother him.' She put out a hand to stroke his head, then thought better of it. 'He never complains. Me ... I'm wishing I'd stayed behind in Tintagel.'

'You're not alone.'

'You have a plan?'

'Aye. It's not a good one, though.'

Amarina shrugged and a strand of red hair tumbled out of her hood.

Lucanus slumped back against the cold stone. 'We're not going to die here, not after all we've been through.'

'The men think you can't die.'

Lucanus glanced at her, puzzled.

'They believe the story that you were brought back from the

Summerlands in the hour of desperate need. That you are the true King Who Will Not Die. They believe it even when they are told the truth. And why? Because they *want* to believe it.'

The Wolf sucked in a deep breath, the cold burning his throat as it travelled to his lungs. 'Believe in a story hard enough and it will come true. That's what I was once told. But this one . . .' He grinned without humour.

'Your wife and I, we've never seen eye to eye. But on the long journey into the western lands we found some common ground. Surviving, when death is at your shoulder: that forges a bond. And we vowed then that we wouldn't be subject to a story written by others, by the wood-priests. We would write our own tale, and our own ending.'

He sensed her turn her head towards him and felt the weight of her attention.

'Some stories are written by the Fates,' he said, pushing himself to his feet. And yet as he walked away he felt her words settle on him, as they always did. Amarina knew how to worm her way into his mind. For now there was only one tale, and that was of them all freezing to death there on the mountain.

And he could see no other ending.

Bellicus scrabbled together the last few twigs and tossed them on the fire. 'That's the end of it.' He stood, resting his hands on his hips, and looked down at the paltry glow.

Comitinus and Mato sat cross-legged, trying to warm their hands. Solinus squatted near by, hands around his knees as he looked out into the snowstorm. Bellicus had never seen him so quiet, so reflective.

'It's not that far down the mountain,' Comitinus lied. 'We could do it.'

'We could,' Mato said.

Bellicus nodded. He wouldn't put it past them either. He looked round. But the others? Farmers, merchants? They'd never seen hardship, like the *arcani*.

Solinus shook off his reverie and crawled over, his eyebrows white with snow. The scar that quartered his face flexed as he grimaced. 'We could freeze to death here,' he said, looking round at the other Grim Wolves, 'or we could look to the horizon and think what might lie ahead.'

'What good would that do?' Comitinus rocked as he hugged himself.

'Nothing, probably. But hear me out.'

Bellicus eyed the other man, seeing the lines in his face. This was serious talk. 'What's on your mind? A plan made by fools?'

'Aye. No doubt.' Solinus looked down, plucking at his wolf-pelt. 'We could die here. We could die in the battle at Dinas Ffaraon Dandde. But there's going to be death, we know that. We're not coming out of this in one piece.'

'Enough talk of defeat,' Bellicus snarled.

'I'm not. I . . .' Solinus held up a hand as if he could pluck the words out of the air. 'I'm not much of a talker. Never read a book in my life. All I know is the hard land, and the wind in the trees, and the peace of a starlit night. But when you get close to death, you start to think of what's right and what's not.'

Comitinus snapped. 'What's wrong with you? You're talking like a jolt-head.' Bellicus could hear the unease in his voice. It was true – Solinus had never spoken like this before, and it was worrying them all.

'I'm talking about Lucanus.' Solinus' eyes sparked. 'And we should have spoken about this long ago. Who are we, eh? His brothers, that's who. We've followed him for years. He's given up his own food in the Wilds so that we could eat. He's saved our lives time and again. Those Attacotti bastards say they're going to take him and finish their feast. They say he's as good as dead. And what do we do? We roll over like whipped curs.'

Comitinus' gaze fell. No one spoke.

'I say no!'

Solinus' words rang with conviction. Bellicus saw Comitinus look up, his eyes now glowing as brightly as his friend's.

'They don't decide Lucanus' fate, not without a fight. We're brothers. We've got the wolf-blood coursing through our veins, and the wolf-spirit burning in our hearts. And Lucanus is as much a part of us as our right arms. We owe him everything.' His voice crackled with passion. 'We should all give our lives for him.'

'We fight the Attacotti for Lucanus,' Bellicus said. 'That's what you're saying.'

'There're more of them than there are of us,' Comitinus noted. 'Then we die.'

'And if we win they'll keep coming back, time and again, until they get their way.'

'Then we die the next time, or the time after that. Somebody's going to die, today, or tomorrow, or the next. One of us, maybe all of us. Let's go out as we've lived. Together.'

Bellicus looked round and saw that Mato was smiling. Anybody else would have thought he'd lost his wits, smiling at the prospect of death. But Bellicus knew. They all did.

'We go out together,' Bellicus repeated. 'It's agreed.'

The red glow in the ashes faded. In the cave, Lucanus' voice echoed, rousing the men to their feet. Filling their hearts with hope for what was probably a march to their deaths. Aye, he was a good leader. A good man.

As he turned to help the Wolf direct the army, Bellicus squinted into the blizzard beyond the overhanging rock. Something had caught his attention in that swirling curtain of white. As he stared, shapes began to appear, darkening, taking on weight and form. The Attacotti emerged from the storm with measured steps.

'What are they doing here?' Solinus grumbled.

On they came, looking from side to side. *Searching for someone,* Bellicus thought. The Eaters of the Dead passed through the uneasy, watchful army like ghosts. Finally, one in the centre of the group stepped to the front. Both arms were outstretched, and on them rested a staff, the wood intricately carved with spirals.

The man came to a halt in front of Mato and waited. Mato hesitated, then took the staff, examining it, bemused.

'What's that all about?' Solinus muttered. 'When did Mato become their friend?'

Leaning on his new staff, Mato nodded his thanks. The Attacotti warrior showed no emotion.

With all eyes on them, the Eaters of the Dead turned and

walked away. But on the edge of the blizzard, the one who had presented the staff turned back. Raising one arm, he flexed his hand, beckoning for everyone there to follow.

'What do we do?' Comitinus asked.

Bellicus looked over to Lucanus, who had emerged from among the men. Their eyes met for an instant, and then the Wolf nodded.

'We follow them,' Bellicus said.

Into the swirling storm they trekked. The knives of the wind carved their flesh. Bellicus heaved his way to the front to walk beside Lucanus. Ahead, the hunched forms of the Attacotti faded in and out of the blizzard. Scarcely could he believe he was doing this, following the Eaters of the Dead as if they were saviours sent by the gods. Still ghosts, their white-caked flesh making them almost a part of the elements. He half believed that this was some final judgement and the Attacotti might simply evaporate, leaving the rest of them to die there.

'We're putting our trust in these bastards now?' he grunted.

The Wolf said nothing. Perhaps, Bellicus thought, they'd cast a spell over him long ago.

Bowed into the howling gale, the army trudged down the slope. Just when Bellicus thought the snow would swallow them all, the Attacotti spun away to one side, clambering between boulders twice the height of a man. Squeezing between a cleft in their wake, Bellicus took two more steps and then looked around in amazement.

The snow was gone, the wind too.

Above them, overhanging rock between two cliffs formed a near roof with only narrow gaps between the two sides. A few flakes drifted down. Ahead, the trail ran down steeply, almost a tunnel between the soaring cliffs. His feet crunched over gravel. He imagined the spring floods rushing down here from the high land.

Out of the storm, Bellicus felt the blood start to thump through him. His fingers tingled; his cheeks did too. Still couldn't feel his feet, though. He glanced at Lucanus. The Wolf cocked an eyebrow, said nothing.

They hurried down the slope. Behind them, Bellicus could hear rustles of surprise turning into waves of jubilation. The sound of hope.

After a long trek with the dark growing around them, Bellicus stepped out to see the ghosts of stark trees reaching out into the twilight. Firewood. Shelter. Game, as well. The storm still crashed above them, but here the wind was low and the drifting snow bearable.

Squinting, he looked ahead. Nothing moved. The Attacotti had already vanished into the dusk.

Comitinus loomed up at his elbow. 'They saved us,' he whispered, baffled. 'The Eaters of the Dead saved us.'

'They're just trying to make it harder for us to kill them,' Solinus grumbled, but Bellicus could already hear the doubt in the other man's voice.

'Saviours come in many forms,' he said.

CHAPTER THIRTY-NINE

The Pool of the Dragons

'*I*F YOU WISH TO WALK INTO THE REALM OF THE GODS, FIRST CONSUME *the flesh of the sacred mushroom.*'

Myrrdin closed his eyes. The creaking words of his aged tutor flew back to him from the day when his mother and father offered him up to the College of the Druids to begin his new life. It was the first lesson, the one from which all the other wisdom sprang.

In later studies, he would learn that this was the path taken by all who wanted to walk with the gods. Yes, even back to those time-lost days when man took his first steps upon the world. In the hot sands of Aegypt, in the shadow of the great pyramids, when Osiris had been summoned. In Greece, when the wanderers had searched for Olympus. In the rituals of Mithras. Even among the new religion chosen by the followers of the Christ. All of them chewed upon the sacred flesh to hear the words of those who shaped this world.

'*The gods have given this gift to us. It is the sacrament, to allow them into your heart. To use it for any other reason invites the madness that only the gods can bring.*'

The wood-priest snapped his eyes open and peered into the still surface of the black pool. There, in the womb of Dinas Ffaraon Dandde, his ears throbbed from the heartbeat of the earth. He felt the first whispers of the Otherworld lick around his mind.

'What do you see?' Arthur's voice echoed around the walls in the dark.

'If you would learn, keep your tongue still and watch.'

Myrrdin stared deep into the depths until he felt as if he were looking into a black mirror. There was his face, and the boy's hanging opposite. The more he stared the more he felt he was looking through those faces, deep into the heads of both of them.

Movement stirred far below.

Sinuous, swimming back and forth, slowly surfacing.

'We have nothing to fear, surely,' the boy babbled. 'Mother is confident. "We shall lure the false king in," she says, "and we will destroy him here, at our fortress, so there can be no doubt of his survival. And word will go out to the four corners of Britannia that there is now only one king, one royal bloodline. The Dragon will have risen." That's what she says.'

'Silence.'

Myrrdin felt himself swimming with those serpents, enveloped by their coils in the dark depths. He could feel the crackle of blue fire sizzling off them into his flesh, into his heart, into his mind. Becoming one with them.

If truth be told, worry was eating away at him day and night. He rarely slept, and when he did his dreams were terrible, of gods and witches tearing him apart, and the Fates cutting strand after strand with their shears.

One serpent flashed near the surface. He jolted, more visions tumbling. He saw lines of blue fire stretching out across the land, from the heartstones to the other great circles that his kind had guarded since those who had originally thrown those sacred places up had vanished from the face of the earth. The land healing, after this time of war and destruction.

One dragon. Only one could usher in this coming golden age.

The wood-priests who came before him had planned this. They knew all the tales from the other great religions, going back to the earliest days. A saviour was needed. One figure who could gather the people around them and lead them out of the dark. A saviour chosen by the gods, and imbued with the powers of the heavens, for then who could ever doubt them? A leader who could defeat death itself, who would always return in the hour of greatest need.

And what of those who guided this great king? Would they not have the greatest power of all?

Myrrdin drifted back across the years, remembering the discussions in the great council, and the words of the most learned. How the story was shaped. And so their spies went out from the deep forest where they were forced to hide after the Roman bastards had invaded. The search for the right candidate over those long years.

How had they ever thought Gaia would be the mother of that royal bloodline? He choked back acid as he watched the water roil.

But in the end he had found Lucanus, and he had persuaded the other wood-priests that this might be the way to save their Great Plan. And he had not been wrong. Lucanus, of everyone he had encountered, had the heart of a king blessed by the gods.

'What do you see?' Arthur breathed again. 'Please . . . tell me.'

'Two dragons fighting for supremacy. Only one can live. Only one.'

The time was coming fast.

Gaia's scouts had told her their enemies were marching closer, and with each report her bravado had grown. But Myrrdin had seen her eyes. It was her terror that was really growing, the fear that she might lose her grip on the thing that she'd yearned for all her life.

And that was when she was at her most dangerous.

This plan that had been generations in the making all turned on the coming days. He alone could decide the outcome.

Raising his eyes, he peered across the dragon pool.

'Only one dragon can live,' he murmured to himself.

Arthur would have to die.

CHAPTER FORTY

Samhain

O UT OF THE WALL OF WHITE THE DARK FIGURES TRUDGED.
Heads down, furs crusted with snow, they hunched into the
blizzard. Some Scoti, about twenty of them, bearlike with their
unkempt hair and beards; a handful of Picts, shaven heads, tattoos blackening their features. Swords swung loosely in their
hands as they hunted. Eyes roamed. On the flanks, four riders
eased their mounts among the sparse trees.

A single line of footprints ran ahead of them through the waves
of snow. Their enemy's scout would be dead before he reached
his lines. They were all thinking that. Any man could see it.

Too confident. Too confident by far.

The arrow whined out of the gale and thumped into the eye
socket of the front rider. Red rain splashed across the white.

Before the dead barbarian had crashed down into a drift, battle-
cries drowned out the howls of the wind. Soldiers thundered
from every side, swinging the swords they'd trained with every
day since Isca Augusta.

Lucanus felt his heart swell with pride as he watched those
farmers and merchants risk their lives for this good fight.

'Now!' he yelled, dashing forward. He could feel the Grim
Wolves racing at his back.

All his friends had tried to persuade him not to be in the first
line of battle. Solinus had taunted him mercilessly about his single

arm. He was having none of it. He wouldn't ask such sacrifice of any man if he wasn't prepared to do it himself.

The barbarians whirled, bewildered. This was the last thing they expected. But the Grim Wolves had long since learned how to use the elements to mask their passage and their men in turn had learned that lesson well. Creeping through the trees under cover of the blizzard, hiding their tracks, smearing their clothes with snow so that they didn't stand out against the white background.

A Scoti warrior spun towards him, whipping up his blade. His snarl turned to a mocking grin when he saw what he was up against.

Lucanus ducked under his lumbering strike and rammed his sword into the man's guts. He held the blade there as he peered into his dying enemy's shocked eyes. 'Half a man is twice the man you are,' he said, before wrenching Caledfwlch back in a shower of entrails.

This was the end of a long game. It was not a time for weakness.

The Wolf hacked into the side of the next barbarian, still rooted in shock at the attack. His third opponent was ready, though, balancing on the balls of his feet, both hands wrapped around the hilt of his sword, hunched, arm muscles flexing to swing.

From the corners of his eyes, Lucanus glimpsed Bellicus cut down a Pict. On his other side, Solinus thrust his sword through a red-headed Scoti.

As his enemy's blade whisked in an arc, Lucanus swung up Caledfwlch. Sparks glittered. He felt his arm joints burn from the clash, but he narrowed his eyes. Focused. This was his time. He danced through the gusting flakes, the two swords whirling, high, low, the whine of blade on blade.

When his foe's foot skidded on crushed snow, the Wolf lunged, ready for the opening. The gush of hot blood steamed in the bitter cold. As he wrenched his blade back, he looked around. Bodies littered the pink snow. The victory had gone as smoothly as he had wished. Two of his men nursed deep gashes, that was all. Mato and the leech bound the wounds. Bellicus looked from the wounded to him and nodded, pleased with the outcome.

The snow whipped down on vast, buffeting gusts that raced straight from the mountaintop. Soon enough there'd be no trace of this encounter.

'Strip them of their furs,' Lucanus commanded. 'Make it quick. We don't want our enemies to know how close we are.'

'Don't let those horses wander off, you lead-footed oafs,' Bellicus bellowed.

Soldiers threw down their weapons and raced off to bring in the riderless mounts roaming among the trees.

The Grim Wolves strode up, rubbing their burning arms and flexing their shoulders.

'Lured them out easy enough,' Solinus said. 'Not a bowlful of brains among them.'

'It won't always be this easy,' Lucanus said.

Comitinus was still frowning, as he had been since Lucanus had planned this attack. 'I don't understand. We could have skirted them easily enough. Why risk a battle?'

'Trust Lucanus,' Solinus snapped. 'He knows what he's doing. If any of us thought you knew what you were doing, you'd be leader.'

Comitinus grumbled, kicking up whorls of snow as he marched away.

'Don't be too hard on him,' the Wolf said. 'This will look less like madness soon enough. And by then we'll have a different kind of madness.'

The army trailed out among the trees. Lucanus peered through the blizzard to the east. The going would have been easier on the road, but they couldn't risk encountering any more of Gaia's warbands. Surprise was key.

'Too cold for this time of year. The gods have it in for us.' Solinus brushed the frost off the snout of his wolf-pelt as they trudged.

'It's Samhain. By rights we should be huddled around the hearth, keeping ourselves safe from the dead walking the land,' Comitinus grumbled.

'When the doors to the Otherworld swing open, you never know, you might find a few allies dancing through.' Amarina strode beside them, her cloak billowing behind her. Lucanus eyed her. Never a complaint. Never a moment of weakness. She was as strong as any Wilds-hardened *arcani*.

'Or they'll drag us back under hill or beneath lake and a hundred years will pass here in the passage of one night there, and all our loved ones will be gone,' Comitinus said.

'Stop whining,' Solinus snapped. 'You haven't got any loved ones.'

As dusk fell, the army pushed down into a valley where their fires would not be so easily seen. Once the tents were pitched, Lucanus stood looking out at the specks of light flickering in the sea of night. The Grim Wolves huddled round their own fire, the orange light washing across the snow. Solinus waved a knob of dry bread in front of his eyes. 'Tonight we should be drinking. Living life to its full. And what have we got? Only fit for pigs, this.'

Bellicus just grunted, for once. The flames danced in his eyes.

Mato leaned on his staff on the other side of the fire, peering away into the dark among the trees. How like Myrrdin he seemed in that moment, Lucanus thought.

'What are you looking for?' Comitinus asked.

'The Attacotti. Will they help us in the battle? Or simply watch and wait? Will they turn on us in the final hour?'

'Well, you'll be all right, you bastard,' Solinus said, stuffing the bread into his mouth. 'You got a new staff out of them. They're your best friends now, though I've no idea why. Unless they've decided you look like a tasty morsel for the pot.'

Mato forced a smile, but Lucanus could see his eyes were troubled. 'Still, we should keep an eye on them none the less, wouldn't you say?'

The others nodded. The Wolf sensed some kind of silent communication among them, though what it was he couldn't tell. As they drifted into reminiscences about Vercovicium, he stepped away. In the dark, he glanced back at the faces glowing in the firelight, setting the vision of his friends in his mind.

Trudging through the snow, he found his tent and slipped inside. Catia and Weylyn huddled together under the furs.

'Preparations for tomorrow have been made?' his wife asked.

'As much as can be.' Lucanus pushed his way in between the two of them, sinking into the warmth of his family.

'You know I'm going to fight tomorrow,' Weylyn muttered. His voice was heavy with sleep.

'I expect no less. And I have work for you – to protect Amarina. She will need your sword-arm more than any other.'

Weylyn nodded and let his head fall against his father's chest. 'I'm proud of you, my son,' Lucanus whispered. The boy nuzzled against him and the Wolf felt a wave of love. He looked to Catia and her eyes gleamed. She leaned in and kissed him on the cheek, her lips pressed there so long he thought she was never going to pull away.

'We are together,' she murmured. At that moment, it seemed the greatest prize of all.

Lucanus settled against her. This might well be his last night among the living, one way or another. He couldn't imagine a better way to spend it.

The Wolf felt the skin of his face flayed raw by the wind as he bowed into the blizzard. The snowstorm had barely eased since they'd set off at dawn. Behind him, his army crunched through the deepening snow in silence. It could have been the bleakest midwinter in the Wilds, with not a soul around for miles.

In the quiet, he could sense their apprehension. These were not fighting men, but they were prepared to lay down their lives; for the gods, for a dream that the wood-priests had conjured up out of nothing.

He felt a pang of bitterness. But the dream was real now, and they were all caught up in it. The result would be the same if the prophecy and everything the druids had imagined were true.

'So serious.' A hand fumbled for his, fingers folding into him. Catia had stepped beside him. 'Your thoughts are on the battle?'

Lucanus nodded. And more, but whatever was forming was like a ghost appearing out of the dark, and he didn't dare give voice to it in case it vanished completely.

'I won't let the Attacotti take you away from me,' she said, her voice now as hard as the cold earth under their feet. Before he could respond, she slowed her step, letting the Grim Wolves and some of the other men pass her by.

A whistle cut through the howl of the gale and he jolted, all thoughts of what Catia had said falling away. The sound of feet crunching through snow echoed nearer, and then he looked up at the advance scout appearing on the ridge ahead. He was beckoning furiously.

Lucanus threw himself into a run.

When he reached the ridge, the scout said breathlessly, 'There,' and pointed.

Suddenly, it was as if the gods had drawn back a curtain. The blizzard fell away, the wind dropped, and there were only fat white flakes drifting down and a terrible quiet.

A rocky hill rose up out of the white landscape. A series of steep banks and ditches ran around the slopes, and on the top of the hill towered the thick stone walls of Dinas Ffaraon Dandde. The only way in was a steep track on the western side of the hill.

Slowly, he raised his eyes to the flag with the red dragon, fluttering above that impregnable fortress.

Here was the place of death.

CHAPTER FORTY-ONE

The Last Battle

BLOOD SEEPED INTO THE THICK SNOW. A BODY SPRAWLED in the dark pool of slush, an arrow protruding from an eye socket. Two ravens stabbed their beaks into the fallen man's face.

As four men scrambled up the track to the fortress gate to claim the remains, arrows whined down from the walls. The soldiers threw themselves to one side and the shafts rattled off the rocks. In the lull that followed, they darted out again, grabbed the tunic of their fallen comrade and dragged him back down the slope. A trail of crimson flowed in his wake.

Lucanus watched his men pull the body back into the trees. It was a fisherman from the south coast of the western lands, who knew the weather well and always had a helping hand for those around him.

Fourteen, they'd lost so far. Fourteen struck down by Gaia's archers as they'd failed on three attempts to claw their way up that steep track to the gates. After the third, all could see there was little hope of success with a frontal assault. Their enemy held an unassailable position, able to rain hell down on anyone who tried to reach the walls. The army of barbarians might be far from full strength with the majority of the force sent to the western lands, but even a handful could keep that stronghold.

Lucanus prowled along the lines of his men, waiting just beyond the range of the archers. They were showing brave faces.

That was good. Eyes flickered towards him as he passed, all of them waiting for his next command.

When he reached the end of the line, Mato was leaning on his staff, peering towards the southern horizon.

'Look,' the Grim Wolf said, pointing.

In the far distance, a beacon blazed on the top of a hill. Lucanus felt his heart sink. 'I'd hoped for more time,' he said.

'We knew Gaia's reinforcements would be riding hard at our backs,' Mato said. 'At least this warning buys us space to make the hard choices.'

The Wolf nodded. And hard choices they would be. No chance now to try to starve the enemy out. No chance to pick off odd bands of reinforcements making their way back. That beacon spoke of a major force coming their way. He looked back up the slope to the fortress, those towering stone walls, that steep hillside, those ditches and that single, narrow way to the gate. There would be death, on a huge scale. They couldn't avoid it now.

'Get them ready,' he commanded.

Mato nodded and hurried away.

Lucanus bowed his head, brooding, until he heard the stamp of hooves and the snort of breath from the horses they'd captured from the war-band. He turned to see Mato leading three barbarians towards him in front of their mounts. Their heads were lowered above the filthy furs of the Scoti, the cracked leather armour, those familiar short swords that the warriors from the north preferred.

When they neared they raised their heads and he looked into the eyes of Bellicus, Solinus and Comitinus.

'I'm just warning you, I might die if I breathe in the reek from these furs,' Solinus grumbled.

'Are you ready for this?' Lucanus asked.

'We were ready when you asked us,' Bellicus replied.

'There are others—'

'We're the best ones for the job and you know it,' Bellicus grunted. 'Now are we going to stand here talking or are we going to fight?' The big Grim Wolf strode to the largest stallion and heaved himself on to its back.

'You look like a cunt,' Solinus said, looking Comitinus up and down.

'You look like a bigger cunt, you scar-faced bastard.' Comitinus held the other man's gaze for a moment and then hauled himself on to his own mount.

Lucanus felt a pang of regret. He could see through their bravado. 'I feel as though I'm sending them to the slaughter,' he muttered.

'They look the part. Any man would think they were Scoti.' Mato paused. 'They know what they're doing.'

Even if his plan worked, what chance did his friends have? He bit down on his tongue. No good would come from showing doubts.

'There's no other way to get inside that fortress in what little time we have left, and you know it,' Mato continued, as if he could read the mind of his leader. 'This is the only hope we have.'

'I should be—'

'You should be here, commanding the rest of your army. You owe them that.'

Lucanus nodded. He couldn't argue. 'Ready the army.'

When Mato had gone to spread the plan among the ranks, the Wolf turned on his heel and plunged into the trees. It was time for his biggest gamble. The moment when his prayers would be answered or his final hopes dashed.

Large snowflakes began to drift down from the colourless sky. The wind picked up. More bad weather was sweeping in. He hoped it was not an omen.

He heard the familiar *whick-whick-whick* of small knives being sharpened. There they crouched, almost invisible against the sweeping drifts. All heads turned as he stepped towards them.

Lucanus swept his arm towards his constant companions and said, 'I would have words.'

The day boomed with the roar of battle-cries and the thunder of swords beaten against shields. The din drowned out even the howl of the wind. Step by step, the army advanced into the blizzard, the ground slowly rising ahead of them. Still beyond reach of the archers, still safe. But that would soon change.

Lucanus squinted through the whirling snow. He could just make out the grey walls of the fortress. What were their enemies thinking, hearing that blood-curdling clamour? Were they confident? Were they filled with terror? What was on Gaia's mind? For both pretenders to the royal bloodline, everything turned on what was about to unfold.

And if the enemy didn't fall for this ploy, all would be lost.

Finally, he glimpsed movement along the foot of the walls, and nodded. 'The weather has helped us,' he said.

No one had seen the Attacotti creep up there past the crags and the ditches on the near-impossible-to-climb southern slope. The enemy wouldn't expect anyone to come from that direction, and they would have been distracted by the tumult his army was making.

The Eaters of the Dead were crouching at the foot of the walls, all but invisible. Waiting.

'Offer up a prayer, my friend,' he said to Mato. 'We need the gods on our side.'

Mato bowed his head, resting his forehead against the carved staff.

Lucanus stepped away to the back of the advancing lines and roared. The advance ebbed. The battle-cries died, and the beating of the shields stilled. The whine of the wind rushed in.

'Let your hearts fill with fire!' he shouted into the howling blizzard. 'Victory will be ours! For never has there been a more courageous army. The gods are watching over you. They see that you fight in their name. They see that you fight for the good of all in Britannia, for the True King. The King Who Will Not Die!'

'Pendragon!' the men boomed as one. 'Pendragon! Pendragon! Pendragon!'

The Wolf steeled himself. Lies did not trip easily off his tongue – he was not a wood-priest – but these good men deserved to have the fear banished from their hearts.

'I have passed days in the Summerlands,' he said, his voice soaring over their heads. 'But death could not hold me. I have returned to you, to Britannia, in this darkest hour. And know

now that only glory awaits you, in this world or the next. Seize this day, brothers! Seize this victory! Forward!'

A full-throated battle-roar rumbled out like the earth cracking, and his army heaved as one. Lucanus threw himself into their midst. Despite the bitter cold, the packed bodies sweltered around him and he breathed in the bitter tang of their sweat. His fingers clasped tight around the hilt of Caledfwlch. For a fleeting moment he believed his own legend. This was a sword of the gods. With it in his hand, he could never be defeated. He had slipped loose from the shackles of death and returned to the world of the living. He was a saviour now, chosen by the gods.

But then the clamour crashed in, and his thoughts rushed back to the heaving mass of fighting men forcing its way up the track to the fortress. The path was choked, the way steep. Snowflakes stung his eyes as he tried to see the way to those solid wooden gates, past the waving swords and his fluttering banner. Thick timber bound by iron braces with two heavy bars on the other side, no doubt. Breaking them down would be impossible.

And then he glimpsed Catia, in the crush just ahead, braided blonde hair dancing behind her, face as cold and determined as any man's there. He felt his heart leap with apprehension. He'd pleaded with her to stay behind in the camp, with Amarina, for Weylyn's sake. She would have none of it. And despite the terror that rushed through him that she might die, he also felt a burning pride. His Warrior Queen.

But then a cry rang out and Catia was lost to view in that churning mass. Men were pointing. Lucanus followed the direction. Silhouetted against the white sky, a row of figures now ranged along the battlements.

'Shields!' he roared.

Wherever they could, his soldiers wrenched their shields up high. But for many the crush was too tight and they were left defenceless as the arrows whined.

Lucanus heaved his own shield up. The shadow fell over him. Bracing his legs, he felt as if the gods were raining stones down upon them. The tip of a shaft cracked through the wood a hand's width from his face. Screams echoed, and as he eased his shield aside, he saw a man reel back, an arrow jammed into his fore-head. Others dropped on every side. His nostrils wrinkled at the stink of shit and piss and blood.

'Onward!' he yelled. How many more would they lose before they reached those walls?

But as his men lurched forward, stumbling over the bodies of those who had fallen, he caught sight of a smaller figure clamber-ing out of the throng on to a large boulder at the side of the track.

Catia again.

He felt the urge to scream out to her to get back, keep her head down, hide, not make herself an easy target for Gaia's archers. But she knew what she was doing, as always. His wife pushed her-self up tall, braced her legs and nocked an arrow to her bow. When an archer on the wall bobbed back up once more, ready to launch an assault, she let fly.

Catia was the best archer among them by far. Her shaft flew true, slamming into the enemy's face. He spun back, trailing a stream of black blood. A cry of alarm rang out and all the other heads that had been emerging along the wall instantly ducked down.

With cool, measured movements, Catia nocked another arrow and waited. She'd bought them some time, at the risk of her own life.

'Onward!' he bellowed, waving Caledfwlch over his head to exhort the soldiers to push on harder.

The second arrow flew from Catia's bow. Another cry. But no more arrows rained down from the archers on the walls, not for now at least. Soon her shafts would be exhausted, though, and the enemy would find what little morsel of courage they had left.

His feet squelched through the pink slush underfoot, sliding as he tried to push on. Whoever had built that fortress understood how to make it impregnable. A view over the surrounding coun-tryside, so any approaching enemy could be easily seen. Those steep, inhospitable slopes, littered with rocks and rotting tree stumps, ditches and walls of earth. And this track as the only way in, not too steep for carts but hard enough for any army to claw its way up, twisting this way and that around the contours of the hillside.

As they rounded a curve in the path, Catia shouted a warning and he threw his shield up again just in time. More arrows rained down. They crunched through wood, cracked through bone, tore through flesh. The Wolf gritted his teeth at the cries of agony that thrummed in his ears.

Looking through the row of heads, he could see some men at the front giving in to the terror of the death falling from on high and scrambling ahead over the frozen ruts to try to reach the cover of the base of the walls.

'Stay back,' Lucanus shouted. But if they heard him they gave no sign. The fear had smashed their wits away. His heart pounding, he yelled again, but the men threw themselves on, up to the gates, arms flailing, and feet slipping and sliding on the ice.

He sensed a dark shape looming above the walls, a barrel being heaved. A stream of boiling pitch flooded down on to the scrambling men. Lucanus pushed his head down, trying to block out the terrible screams. When he looked up again, though, the gates were just ahead, their prize almost close enough to grasp but still seemingly a thousand leagues away.

And then a horn blasted, low and mournful, somewhere at his back.

Bellicus felt his blood thunder at the wail of that horn. Among the trees, Mato was playing his part.

'You don't know how to live until you smell death!' he roared. He dug his heels into the stallion's flanks and it jolted forward. Behind him, Solinus and Comitinus drove their own mounts on.

The pound of hoofbeats drowned out the wind's whine, and his fear too. He was not a fighting man, not really – he loved nothing more than the peace of a night in the Wilds – but he was ready to give his own life here if it should be called for. The cold blast flayed his face as he guided his mount out of the woods towards the track up to the fortress. Rivulets of blood trickled down through the churned snow, but far less than he'd expected. That was good. Perhaps the gods really were on their side. But then he looked up at the multitude of bodies jammed into the way and his heart sank at the monumental task that lay ahead.

On he thundered. He couldn't afford to slow his pace for an instant, not if this ploy was to succeed. The horn moaned again.

His stallion galloped up the steep incline until he saw the rear of the army. 'Make way. Make way,' he breathed, almost a prayer. But he didn't dare call out.

And the army was well prepared. The moment the lowing of Mato's horn rolled out, they'd started to throw themselves aside from the centre of the track. With the second blast, they were pushing to each side with force, hauling themselves out on to the rocks and banks of earth.

Though he'd feared crushing his own men under the stallion's hooves, a narrow path opened up and his mount crashed through it. Behind him he could hear the grunts and snarls of Solinus and Comitinus as they followed.

In the midst of the throng, he yanked out his sword and waved it one way and the other, making a play of hacking out at the soldiers surrounding him. A few stabbed their own blades towards him in return, while others cried out and feigned injury. Bellicus prayed that it was enough for anyone watching from the walls.

His stallion forced its way up through the mass. Looking down, he saw Lucanus raise his head and nod his support. For an instant, their eyes locked in a silent communication, a hope that they would see each other again on this side of the Summerlands. And then he was through the heaving mass of bodies and pounding up the final stretch to the fortress.

The gates loomed up ahead. This was the moment on which everything turned.

Bellicus whirled his sword in the air and stabbed it towards the gates. From under his brows, he glimpsed Gaia's men hanging over the battlements watching his progress. They would understand what he wanted. Lucanus' army was far enough away to mitigate any fear of being overwhelmed before the gates crashed shut again. Now he only had to pray that they had some loyalty to their own side.

The gates stayed shut.

On his horse thundered. He muttered another prayer, but with each hoof-fall that sped by beneath him his heart fell further. Despair pushed acid into his mouth.

'Open the gates!'

The bellowed command came from behind the walls. Bellicus felt his spirits soar as he heard that cry. It rang out again. This time his neck prickled at something familiar, but he had no time to wonder what it was as he urged his mount on, bending low over its neck so that his face wouldn't be seen as he neared the walls.

Ahead of him he glimpsed a sliver of grey light as the gates cranked open. The space grew wider, wider. Snow whipped past him. He dropped his sword to his side, tightening his grip on the hilt.

The roar of the army throbbed like the sound of waves crashing on a beach, and the hooves of the three horses thundered as one with the blood pounding in his head.

Head still lowered, he stared at that wide gap. And then he felt a jolt of shock as he saw the figure standing in the courtyard in front of him.

Myrrdin, the wood-priest, was alive and beckoning him into hell.

CHAPTER FORTY-TWO

Into the Fortress

BELLICUS HAULED THE STALLION TO A STOP JUST OVER THE threshold, blocking the path of the closing gates. Picts and Scoti threw their arms in the air, roaring at the new arrivals to move.

The courtyard was heaving with barbarian mercenaries. Others swarmed up the stone steps to bolster those defending the walls. Roughly twenty breaths, that was about as long as he'd survive, he calculated. The wood-priest had already vanished, if he hadn't imagined him.

Bellicus glanced at Solinus and Comitinus. A silent agreement, a signal, and he swung up his sword and bellowed.

The Scoti warriors gaped, eyes wide. Then he hammered his blade down into the neck of the man nearest him.

The moment hung across the courtyard, breaths held tight in chests. And then every man there erupted in fury at the realization that they'd been tricked. The sea of bodies rose up and washed towards the gates.

Fighting to keep their mounts under control, Bellicus, Solinus and Comitinus slashed their blades down at anyone who ventured near.

Fifteen breaths, Bellicus thought. *Gods, let me buy enough time for Lucanus.*

Through the haze of blood, shadows shimmered on the edge

of his vision. Bellicus glanced round to see white figures dancing through the open gates.

Swords raised, the Attacotti swept into the fortress. Silent as death, they didn't slow their step, those blades sweeping with elegant grace. Picts and Scoti fell as one, clutching at throats and guts. On went the Eaters of the Dead, as relentless as the incoming tide.

Bellicus saw terror etched into the face of every barbarian within range as they realized what they'd allowed into their midst. Many had fought alongside the Attacotti during the invasion. They knew what these strange creatures were capable of. Some of the Scoti fled. Others backed off, levelling their blades, none of them risking getting too close.

'Now we have a fight on!' Bellicus roared.

He kicked his heels into his horse's flanks again and urged it into the melee. A barbarian sprawled under the hooves, his howl cut off as his skull was crushed. The Grim Wolf turned towards the men trying to heave the gates shut and lashed his blade down, once, twice, three times, and then Solinus and Comitinus were at his side, stabbing and thrusting.

The gates had barely budged. As the blood of the guards washed into the snow, Bellicus heard another roar and Lucanus' army flooded through the opening. He felt his heart soar. He'd done what was asked of him. Perhaps he'd even paid Lucanus back for the years of silence about his father.

'Not dead yet,' he shouted, unable to stop his triumphant grin from spreading.

'Still time if you don't move,' Solinus yelled back.

Bellicus slipped down off his horse – he could see the danger of being pinned against the gates by the attacking barbarians. Solinus and Comitinus jumped down too, and back to back they raised their swords.

The Scoti and the Picts were ebbing away as the army swept in. The Attacotti had carved a swathe through the barbarians, and now, as Bellicus looked across the courtyard, he could see only heaving bodies and flashing blades as the forces of the Pendragon clashed with the false king's men. Contained within these walls, this last battle would be a slaughter one way or another.

'Over there,' Solinus shouted.

Bellicus spun and saw Lucanus beckoning furiously to them. He thrust his way through the flow of men still streaming into the courtyard, and came to where the Wolf huddled with the wood-priest behind a cart piled high with straw.

'How did you survive?' Solinus shouted above the din.

'Have you betrayed us, that's the question?' Bellicus snarled his fist in the druid's robes.

Myrrdin knocked his hand away. 'Would I have commanded the gates be opened if that were the case? They would never have done so if I hadn't called out. And now you'd be dead outside with all the rest and a river of blood would be flowing down from the walls. You owe your lives to me.' Brushing down his robes, the wood-priest eyed Lucanus. 'Only you could have dreamed up such a terrible plan.'

'This is no time for talk,' the Wolf snapped, stabbing Caledfwlch towards the cart. 'Burn this.'

Bellicus understood what he wanted. Striking his flint, he lit the straw, and within no time, flames were licking up. 'With me,' he commanded, grabbing one arm of the yoke. Solinus grasped the other, and together they heaved the wagon forward. The wheels ground on the frozen yard, picking up speed as the two men pushed harder. As soon as the straw crackled and blazed up, Bellicus and Solinus shoved it with force one final time and it rolled away.

As a path opened up between the warring men, Lucanus leapt into the space and ran behind the trundling cart. 'Now, take us to Gaia and her bastard,' he shouted to Myrrdin. 'This must be ended once and for all.'

Catia raced through the ringing chambers of the stone buildings on the other side of the courtyard. Not a single barbarian had challenged her as she rammed her way through the horde. Perhaps they thought she was no threat.

The gloomy chambers were deserted. Every soldier was fighting to defend the poisonous queen, her mother.

'Where are you, Gaia?' she muttered.

The throne room sweltered in the sickening heat of ten hissing braziers, but the carved wooden chair stood empty. The council chamber, the feasting hall, the bedroom . . . only her footsteps broke the silence.

As she stepped back out into the corridor, she cocked her head. The distant tones of a woman's voice echoed through the shadows. Catia crept forward, following the sound.

At the end of the corridor, a dark doorway loomed. She lifted a torch from the wall and held it in front of her as she ventured to the top of a set of stone steps winding down to . . . what? Cells, catacombs, a tomb?

The dancing light washed over the slick wall as she descended. She breathed in dank air.

'Do not abandon me now,' the woman was imploring. It could only be her mother. 'Victory is within my grasp . . . within our grasp.'

Catia stepped into a long, low-ceilinged room. Echoes of her footsteps bounced back and forth; there was water here.

'You.' An accusation.

Catia held the torch high and the dark swept away, past a pool in the centre of the chamber and her mother standing beyond it. The rear of the chamber was still swallowed by inky shadows, but Catia felt her mother had been talking to herself, or the gods, or both.

'Victory is not in your grasp,' Catia said, walking towards the other woman. 'You've lost.'

'I should have strangled the life from you the night I birthed my son,' Gaia hissed. 'Or when you were a babe. The gods know I tried hard enough.'

'I don't regret not killing you when I had the chance, though you've caused endless misery since that night.'

'Then you are weak. Even if you were, by some chance, to win this day, I would never end my fight to claim what is rightfully mine. One day I would seize the life from you, and your son.'

Catia shivered, perhaps from the chill air. How could this be her mother, someone filled with so much poison that she would murder her own blood without a second thought?

302

She stepped to the pool and held her torch over it. The fire glowed in the black surface.

'I would have won by now if not for you.' Those flames danced in her mother's eyes too.

'What is this place?' Catia stared into the depths of the water. The hairs on her neck prickled. She felt as if it was summoning her.

'Two dragons swim in this bottomless pool . . . swim between here and the Otherworld, where the gods live. They bring power. Our power. The endless source of our destiny that courses through our blood.'

Catia couldn't believe her mother's words, and yet she couldn't forget the brand on her shoulder, and her mother's, of the Ouroboros, the dragon eating its own tail. The wood-priest's symbol of all that the druids had invested in their dream of the King Who Will Not Die. Despite herself, she lowered the torch and leaned down to search those depths.

Movement whisked across the oily surface. Catia recoiled, realizing at the last that it was only a reflection.

Gaia's hands clamped around her throat and she crashed back, her head bouncing off the flagstones. For an instant, she felt her wits jolted free of their moorings. When her vision cleared, she was staring up into a face twisted with fury, the lips pulled from the teeth, eyes wide and staring.

'First you, then your son,' Gaia hissed.

Catia choked, clawing at the iron fingers digging into her neck.

'All that has gone wrong is your fault,' her mother snarled. 'Since you were born, you were a curse upon me.'

How could her mother move so fast, be so inhumanly strong? Darkness swam at the edges of her vision. However much she flailed, Gaia pressed down on her with all her weight.

'I will kill you and throw you in this pool for the dragons to feed upon. No one will ever know what happened to you. Not your husband, not your—'

Gaia's head snapped down and Catia felt hot blood shower over her face.

Her mother reeled away, hands flapping at the air. Her eyes rolled and she wrenched herself round.

A boy stood behind her, a bloody rock clutched in his right hand.

Catia sucked in a juddering gasp of chill air and heaved herself up on her elbows. Her thoughts still spinning, she blinked until the lad's pale face fell into focus.

'Arthur?' Gaia reached out one wavering hand, the other trying to stem the blood from the wound on the side of her head. Her features were red with it.

'Myrrdin said you had a black heart.' Catia felt chilled at the calmness in the boy's voice after the violence he had committed. And that face, as still as the pool in which it was reflected. 'Myrrdin said you would try to kill others, and then try to kill me.'

'No, my darling boy. No.' Gaia's mouth worked against the blood dribbling into it. 'I love you.'

Catia gasped. Her mother's words somehow seemed to whip Arthur into a fury. Snarling, he grabbed Gaia's sticky hair and thrust her head down, and down, until it splashed beneath the surface of the water. Gaia flailed, but her son was too strong.

'Don't!' Catia cried.

Arthur didn't seem to hear. He yanked Gaia's head up. She choked and gasped, spewing water, snot bubbling from her nose. 'Can you see them, Mother?' he raged. 'Can you see the dragons swimming? They will eat your face off, Mother.'

He thrust her head down again.

Lucanus choked as he raced through the smoke billowing along the hall from the blazing cart just outside the door. His footsteps cracked on the flagstones, puncturing the clamour of the battle echoing through the walls.

'Where's Gaia, and the boy?' he shouted. 'This slaughter won't end until we have her.'

'I know where she'll be.' Myrrdin hurried ahead, his robe swirling around him. Bellicus, Solinus and Comitinus pounded behind.

The five men thundered down winding stone steps. At the foot, Lucanus skidded to a halt, taking in the scene in an instant: Catia, sprawled on the floor beside a flickering torch, a boy – no doubt

Arthur – plunging Gaia's head into a dark pool. The queen's feeble thrashes didn't deter him. The lad scowled, as cold as anyone the Wolf had ever seen. He glanced at Myrrdin's face, just as cold, and knew what part the wood-priest had played in this.

'Wait!' Lucanus cried.

Arthur looked up at him, huge eyes staring.

'If you kill your mother here, you will be damned for all time. The memory of this will eat away at you like a worm in an apple, until there's nothing left but rot. You'll never be a good king. You'll never meet the promise of the prophecy. You'll be a part of this dark age that's coming.'

'She is damning me!' Arthur's voice cracked with such emotion that Lucanus took a step back. The lad looked to Myrrdin, almost pleadingly, the Wolf thought. 'She has twisted my life, soured everything that she touched. And she would sour me too if I ever became king.'

Here was the poison Myrrdin had been pouring into the lad's ear. But he was still just a boy, false king or not.

'She cares nothing about me!' Arthur continued. 'Only the power I can give her.'

'Leave her,' Lucanus said, as gently as he could. 'Spare yourself. I will deal with her.'

The boy sagged back as if all the emotion had been sucked out of him. Gaia wrenched up from the pool, gasping, water streaming from her.

Lucanus strode across the chamber and held out a hand to pull Catia to her feet. He wrapped his arms around her, just for an instant, as she glanced at Gaia, her expression caught somewhere between disgust and pity.

'Leave,' he whispered to her, 'and take the boy with you.' When she started to protest, he shook his head once. He watched acceptance light her face, and then a curt nod. Everyone there knew there was only one way now to prevent this battle from raging for ever.

Catia grasped Arthur's hand and tugged him towards the steps. The boy's gaze never left Myrrdin, Lucanus saw. Gaia cowered on the flagstones, surrounded by a growing puddle. She looked around the faces of the Grim Wolves. 'Please,' she begged. 'I am a mere woman. Would you harm someone so frail?'

Lucanus felt a hand on his arm. Solinus was easing him to one side. 'This isn't a job for you,' his brother said. 'I'll do it.'

'No. There is something I need to say—'

Feet clattered down the stone steps. Thinking it was Catia returning, Lucanus spun round, but it was only Mato. His face was lined with worry.

'Quickly,' he said. 'The Attacotti are coming.'

Lucanus frowned as the Grim Wolves snatched out their swords and formed a line in front of him. 'What are you doing?'

'We're not going to let those Eaters of the Dead take you,' Comitinus replied.

Lucanus felt his heart swell. Four Grim Wolves against that band of Attacotti? They must know they had no chance of victory.

Grey shapes appeared in the gloom by the steps. The Eaters of the Dead had arrived without even a whisper of a footstep. They prowled forward, crusted white forms emerging into the wavering torchlight. The shifting shadows added to the charcoal around their eyes so that Lucanus felt he was looking into empty sockets. As the Grim Wolves levelled their blades, he stepped forward and pushed his way among them.

'We won't let you sacrifice yourself,' Bellicus growled.

'The deal with the Attacotti for my life was made without my knowledge,' the Wolf said, eyeing Myrrdin. 'But I will be the one who decides my story.' Gently, he eased the Grim Wolves aside. 'The Eaters of the Dead are not here for me.'

All eyes flickered towards Myrrdin, but instead the Wolf strode over to where Gaia hunched. Her eyes widened in fear and she tried to push herself back, though there was nowhere to flee. Lucanus wrenched off her cloak and snatched down the strap of her dress. Yanking her round, he showed her bare shoulder blade and the brand of the Ouroboros upon it.

'See the mark of the dragon,' he called, his words reaching past the Grim Wolves to the Eaters of the Dead. 'Here is what I promised you. In exchange for a king, you get a First Mother, the chosen vessel for the royal bloodline, sealed by the brand of power.'

Lucanus unfurled his fingers from Gaia's shoulder and let her fall away. Without a backward glance, he marched past the gaping Grim Wolves, past the motionless Attacotti. His brothers followed him.

As the Grim Wolves climbed the stone steps, the *whick-whick-whick* of small knives echoed behind, and a scream that seemed as if it would never end.

CHAPTER FORTY-THREE

The Curse

T HE PICT CLAWED HIS WAY PAST THE CHARCOAL BONES OF THE wagon, rivulets of blood streaming across the black tattoos on his face from the wound on his head. He levered himself up on shaking arms and then collapsed into the drifting snow. Lucanus watched the light go out in his eyes.

Across the courtyard, the two armies crashed against each other, churning as swords hacked and thrust, shields clashed, and battle cries boomed. The Wolf stood on the steps to the queen's residence and looked around the carnage. Bodies washed in a lake of blood. The cries of the dying and the wounded soared up into the howling wind whipping the snow into a wall of white.

'The queen is dead,' he roared, but his words were snatched away by the gale. Before he could utter another word, movement flashed on the edge of his vision and he slammed down to the frozen stone. He stared along a length of steel into the glowering face of Erca. The tip of the sword bit into his throat and he winced.

'One move and he's dead,' the Scoti chief bellowed. His eyes flickered towards the Grim Wolves.

'Gaia is gone,' Lucanus said. 'You're relieved of your duty to fight for her standard.'

For a long moment, Erca's eyes locked on to his, and in their black depths Lucanus thought he could read exactly what the other man was thinking. One thrust of that blade would end the life of his rival for Catia. An easy thing to do in the midst of a battle. What point living a life alone, raising a son, when there was another who would stand at her side?

The Scoti warrior wanted to do it with all his will, Lucanus could see that, but then he yanked his sword away and said, 'The battle is over.' He was an honourable man.

Lucanus levered himself up and ran out into the courtyard, barking, 'The queen is dead. The battle is over.' Erca's voice echoed his, repeating his words to his own men. Swords slipped down, heads turned, the clamour stilled. And then there was only the moaning of the wind and the cries of those still clinging on to life.

As the two armies broke apart and tended to their wounded, Lucanus tramped over to Catia, who was huddling in the shelter of a grain-store doorway.

'The Attacotti . . .' she began.

'Will be leaving without me.' The Wolf held her searching gaze for a moment, and then she fell into his arms. A single sob of relief juddered against his chest.

'They took your mother instead,' he told her. 'That was the agreement I made with them before the battle. Hate me if you will—'

'How can I hate you?' she said, pulling back. 'Gaia didn't deserve that fate . . . no one does. But if it means you're safe . . . if it means . . .' Closing her eyes, Catia leaned her head back and breathed in a steadying draught.

'We'll be together again,' he said, 'you, me, and Weylyn . . .' His words died on his tongue when his wife opened her eyes. Tears shone in them. 'What's wrong? It's over.'

'It will never be over. The crown of the Pendragon is a curse. Today we have victory, but tomorrow another enemy will rise, or the day after that, or in the coming year, because the royal blood-line means power, and that's a prize too great not to be seized by those who hunger for it. They will come for you, again and again and again. And then they will come for Weylyn, until his dying day. This will never end.'

Catia closed her eyes again and one hot tear slid out beneath her lashes.

Lucanus opened his mouth, but no words came. What could he say? His wife was right.

'Why are we here, Myrrdin?' Arthur shuddered in the bitter cold of the blizzard blasting across the battlements. He was not dressed for this weather. But what did it matter?

'So you can look out across your kingdom.' *One last time.* The wood-priest felt his chest tighten as he looked down at the boy who had been his student for so long.

This was the moment. One shove over those battlements was all it would take. One shove to break the lad's body on the rocks below.

'Look,' he said, resting his left hand on the boy's shoulder and pointing with his right into the curtain of snowflakes.

'What? I can't see anything.'

'Lean forward.'

One shove and it would all be over. With Arthur gone, there would be no other rival. Weylyn would be free to claim the mantle of the royal bloodline and usher in the age of the King Who Will Not Die. Weylyn, who was sane, who did not have a bloodthirsting heart.

'Where?'

'There, in the distance. Lean forward.'

Myrrdin stepped behind the boy and rested both hands on his shoulders. Arthur clutched the snowy battlements and pulled himself right to the edge.

The wood-priest braced himself and readied to shove.

Except he couldn't.

His arms trembled as he fought against himself for a long moment. But though the slightest effort would have tipped Arthur to his death, the will was not there. The druid pulled back, covering his eyes.

'What's wrong?' Arthur asked. 'Have I disappointed you?'

Myrrdin felt small arms wrap around his waist and he shook with emotion. 'Run now,' he said. 'Down to the courtyard.'

'Have I?'

'No. You are a good boy.'

When he heard the footsteps patter away, he rubbed his burning eyes. Through the blur, he saw another figure striding towards him, a man this time. Lucanus stepped up to him, his cloak billowing in the gale.

'I couldn't kill the boy,' Myrrdin blurted. 'I wanted to . . . It was the only way to clear a path into the new age, for Weylyn. But I couldn't . . . I couldn't do it.'

'Then there is a heart beating in that cold shell after all.'

Myrrdin pulled himself up, finding his composure. 'You'll regret my weakness.'

'No I won't. The death of an innocent boy is not a price I'm prepared to pay.'

'Innocent!' The wood-priest choked a bitter laugh. 'If only you knew what lurks inside him. He is as mad and bloody as his father.'

Lucanus' stare was so piercing he flinched. 'I know you well enough, wood-priest. You and your kind have twisted lives with your plot. You've helped make this boy what he is. Now he's your responsibility, to repair the damage that you have wrought in him, and to keep him on the side of all that is good. Make sure he doesn't follow the path of his father and mother. Fan the flames of the humanity that must lie in his heart still.'

'I don't know if there's any hope of saving him.'

'We're not bound by the stories others force on us. Dream up a better one for him.'

He turned on his heel and walked away. Myrrdin breathed in a blast of the bitter air, but still he was shaking. He felt as cold and desolate as the storm that swirled around him.

CHAPTER FORTY-FOUR

The Last Kiss

THE SUN GLISTENED OFF THE WAVES CRASHING ON THE BEACH. Out on the swell, the ships heaved at anchor, the sailors on deck basking in the last of the autumnal warmth. The bitter cold and snow now seemed a distant memory, but the battle stayed with them, in the wounded limping down to be helped into the rowboats, and the ghosts of those no longer there.

'You survived, Pendragon, and what's more you won a battle that by rights you should have lost,' Niall of the Nine Hostages boomed. 'Perhaps you are deserving of the title the druids have given you after all.'

Lucanus watched the oarsmen pulling another rowboat towards the ships in the bay. Most of the army were on board now, ready for the last stage of the journey back to the western lands. His heart ached for those farmers and merchants. They'd survived, but they wouldn't be able to return to the lives they once knew. War changed men.

'And what for you, pirate?' he asked. 'More plundering along our coast? You know we'll make your life hell if you try.'

The red-headed Hibernian grinned. 'I have my own crown to earn. And with the gods on my side, I'll wager it will be in my hands sooner than any think.' He looked around at the few still waiting on the windswept beach. 'Don't tarry here too long. I would be away soon and catch the currents.'

He strode off to inspect the soldiers splashing through the surf to their transport. He had a brightness to him, however dark things got. Lucanus liked him.

The Wolf sensed a presence behind him and he turned to see Amarina there. The hood of her cloak was pulled high, but he could just glimpse that familiar enigmatic smile in the shadows within.

'Remember when we stood on the wall at Vercovicium looking out into the Wilds and we spoke of daemons and two worlds existing side by side?' she said. 'We've walked with daemons since then. And invited them into our hearts.'

'We're changed,' Lucanus said with a nod. 'None of us can deny that. And yet much remains from the days we remember so fondly. They were hard too, in their own way. But we have a habit of surviving.'

Amarina kept looking out to sea, but he sensed she was still smiling.

'We've been friends for a long time,' he continued. 'I remember you rolling into Vercovicium with your girls, face like stone and a knife ready to wield on any man who said a wrong word. Truth be told, I was scared of you.'

'Very wise.'

'But now I'm proud of the woman you've become. You've earned our trust.'

'No kind words, Wolf. It makes my stomach turn.'

Lucanus grinned. The same old Amarina. 'I'll need your wisdom more than ever now, with Arthur in Tintagel, and the wyrd sisters wanting their share of power with Morgen.' He eyed Arthur and Weylyn kicking up sand further along the beach, for all the world like two young boys without a care. 'You'll need to walk between those two worlds, the worlds of men and daemons. Only you can do it. Only you know both.'

'I can do it. Rest assured.'

The Wolf looked up at the seagulls arcing across the blue sky for a moment, and then said, 'You never told me how you learned the ways of the Hecatae.'

'And you will never know, so think on other things.' She turned to him, and for a moment he thought she was going to hug him.

But that was not Amarina. 'Take care, Wolf. You trusted me with your plans. Now's the time to realize them. And yes . . . you can trust me still.'

And then she was gone, sweeping across the golden sand towards the surf and the next rowboat.

For a while, he eased his head back, enjoying the warmth of the sun on his face. When he was ready, he strode to where Myrrdin sat on a rock in the shade, watching the two boys at play.

'It's time,' Lucanus said.

The wood-priest pushed himself up. 'I ask you one more time – turn away from this path you've chosen.'

'Your days of twisting my life are over.' Lucanus strode away, knowing the druid had no choice but to follow him.

At the far end of the beach, the small band of Scoti sat around the remnants of a fire, all glowering looks and hunched suspicion. The Grim Wolves squatted near by, hands never far from their swords, eyes darting. It had been the same ever since he'd asked Erca and his closest advisers to journey with them from Dinas Ffaraon Dandde.

Bellicus caught his arm as he passed. 'I know you well enough. You've been planning something ever since we set off for home. Isn't it time you spoke up?'

'It is,' the Wolf replied. 'Come, all of you. You must hear what I have to say.'

Erca stood to meet him.

'You're ready?' Lucanus asked.

'This still sounds like some kind of trick,' the Scoti chief replied.

'No trick. Nor should you see it as a prize. It's a duty.'

'Why do you think I'd want that? My duty is to my men, my tribe, my village.'

Lucanus held his gaze. 'You're a strong man, and that's what's needed for hard times. And an honourable one, and that's needed too, more than ever. You'll not be short of gold in Tintagel. The western lands are rich with promise and we trade with all the empire. You can do good things for your men there, and for your tribe and your village.'

Erca weighed the words and then nodded.

'What are you saying?' Bellicus asked, his voice thick with suspicion. Lucanus turned and looked around at the Grim Wolves. All of them had read the truth in what he'd said, but only Mato put it into words.

'You're leaving,' he said.

Lucanus watched the horror dawn in their faces. 'This has not been an easy decision. My friends . . . my brothers . . . the bonds that bind us are unbreakable, forged through good times and hardship. By rights I should now be sailing back to the Island of the Dead, torn from Catia and Weylyn and all of you, my life and all I dreamed of stolen to advance a plot designed by others.' He eyed Myrrdin, but this was not a time for recriminations. It was a time for hope. 'I've earned a second chance to live, with my wife, and my son.'

'You deserve it,' Mato said, before any of the others could speak. 'No man has given more.'

'Where will you go?' Bellicus asked, crestfallen.

'Somewhere beyond the reach of wood-priests and witches. Beyond talk of destiny, and royal blood and magic swords.'

'Will we see you again?' Comitinus stuttered.

Lucanus grinned. 'I'll return when you need me most, in your darkest hour.'

Myrrdin dipped into his robe and pulled out a circlet that glittered in the morning sun. Lucanus furrowed his brow as he studied the golden dragon design.

'The Pendragon crown was lost on the high moor,' he said. 'Corvus took it with him when he fled.'

The wood-priest smiled. 'And yet here it is.'

The Wolf eyed the shiny, newly worked gold, devoid of any of the scratches and tarnish that had marred the original crown. Myrrdin, still twisting truth and making lies real to further the story his kind had been dreaming up for so long now.

The druid reached up and placed the crown on Erca's head. 'The new Pendragon.'

The barbarians roared, stabbing their swords towards the sky.

'Why him?' Solinus said, aghast.

'I wouldn't wish this burden on any of you,' Lucanus said. 'You'll find he makes a good leader. And a wise one, if he listens to your counsel.' He paused. 'Catia speaks highly of him.'

Erca eyed him, then looked away.

'You must choose a new name now, for your new role,' Myrrdin said to Erca, 'one that befits you now that you are no longer a barbarian Scoti, but the great Pendragon, leader of the Britons. Do not take too long in your selection. You are about to be reborn. Transmuted from lead into gold. Let your name be a sign of your enlightenment.'

Lucanus felt oddly pleased to see that Erca seemed genuinely humbled by the honour.

'I'll serve well,' the Scoti chief said. 'Have no doubt of that.'

Lucanus unsheathed Caledfwlch and offered it to the barbarian. 'This is yours now.' Erca took it, turning it over in the sunlight and watching the runes glimmer along the blade.

'And Weylyn goes with you?' Bellicus said, frowning. He was struggling to keep up.

'Weylyn will be free. Arthur will sit on the throne now, and lead Britannia out of this coming dark age, along with his half-sister Morgen.' The sun and the moon, under the guidance of Myrrdin and the witches. Power shared. That seemed a good arrangement. Power in one hand alone eventually destroyed the one who wielded it.

Lucanus clapped Erca on the arm, though in congratulation or pity he wasn't quite sure, and then he walked away. The Grim Wolves stalked behind him, like birds behind a plough.

'We should come with you,' Bellicus said. 'You need someone to watch your back.'

'Aye, look what happens when we're not there to keep an eye on you,' Solinus jibed. 'You lose an arm. Soon there'll be nothing left of you.'

'Don't go, Lucanus. You're our leader,' Comitinus said.

'Stop whining. You sound like a babe.' Solinus kicked out and his friend danced away.

Mato waved his staff at the others to silence them, then said, 'We'll miss you, brother, of course we will. But we all know in our hearts that you deserve this peace, and your time with Catia and Weylyn.'

'You have important work still,' Lucanus said. 'You'll be Arthur's circle now. You'll need to keep an eye on him, teach him how to fight, how to scout.'

'True. We can't leave it all up to the wood-priest,' Solinus said. 'The poor bastard wouldn't stand a chance if that happened.'

'And Erca too,' Lucanus added, glancing at the knot of barbarians. 'He'll need guidance, to learn our ways. But he's an honourable man.'

'If you say so.' Bellicus narrowed his eyes at the Scoti. 'But if he steps out of line, I'll knock him on his arse.'

'I'd expect no less.'

For a while they laughed, as they had done in those long days in the Wilds, and they remembered how things had once been. And when they felt the ache in their hearts growing unbearable, they clapped each other on the arms and said their goodbyes.

The Wolf watched the last rowboat, laden with his old friends, with Myrrdin and Arthur, haul out on to the swell, and then he turned from the past.

Catia waited with her arm round Weylyn's shoulder. Lucanus thought how bright her face seemed lit by that smile, the one he remembered so clearly from the days when they ran through the fields of Vercovicium, a smile he had not seen for long years.

He pulled his wife into his arms and pressed his lips against hers. 'This is our last kiss as king and queen,' he said when he pulled back. And then he brushed her lips again. 'And this is the first kiss of our new life.'

Together they watched sails billow and Niall's ships pull away towards the horizon. Then they turned to face their new life together, a story as yet unwritten.

What you leave behind is not what is engraved in stone monuments, but what is woven into the lives of others.

Pericles

ABOUT THE AUTHOR

James Wilde is a Man of Mercia. Brought up surrounded by books, he studied economic history at university before travelling the world in search of adventure. It was while visiting the haunted fenlands of eastern England, the ancestral home of Hereward the Wake, that he decided that this legendary English rebel should be the subject of his debut novel. The first in an acclaimed six-book sequence, *Hereward* was a bestseller. His novels, *Pendragon*, *Dark Age* and now *The Bear King*, explore the origins of what would become the myth of King Arthur.

James Wilde divides his time between London and his family home in Derbyshire.

To find out more, visit www.manofmercia.co.uk